REVERSIBLE ERROR

Robert K. Tanenbaum

A SIGNET BOOK

SIGNET
Published by the Penguin Group
Penguin Books USA Inc., 375 Hudson Street,
New York, New York 10014, U.S.A.
Penguin Books Ltd, 27 Wrights Lane,
London W8 5TZ, England
Penguin Books Australia Ltd, Ringwood,
Victoria, Australia
Penguin Books Canada Ltd, 10 Alcorn Avenue,
Toronto, Ontario, Canada M4V 3B2
Penguin Books (N.Z.) Ltd, 182–190 Wairau Road,
Auckland 10, New Zealand

Penguin Books Ltd, Registered Offices:
Harmondsworth, Middlesex, England

Published by Signet, an imprint of New American Library,
a division of Penguin Books USA Inc. Previously published in
a Dutton edition.

First Signet Printing, June, 1993
10 9 8 7 6 5 4 3 2 1

REGISTERED TRADEMARK—MARCA REGISTRADA

PRINTED IN THE UNITED STATES OF AMERICA

PUBLISHER'S NOTE
This is a work of fiction. Names, characters, places, and incidents either
are the product of the author's imagination or are used fictitiously, and
any resemblance to actual persons, living or dead, events, or locales is
entirely coincidental.

ACKNOWLEDGMENTS

Special and profound thanks to Michael Gruber, my partner, collaborator, and confidante whose brilliance, expertise, and devotion helped make this manuscript what it is.

And a special tribute to Cliff Fenton, my dear friend and mentor.

ONE

The dope dealer Larue Clarry was in the bedroom of his apartment with one of the fourteen-year-old white girls he fancied, and Booth, his old buddy, was in the living room watching Carson on the big TV and growing bored. Booth glanced at his imitation gold Rolex and adjusted his feet on the coffee table, a thick red marble thing four feet on a side. The couch was red too.

A compact, broad-shouldered man just past thirty, Booth was dressed for the summer as a semiprosperous Harlem player of the mid-seventies: peach cuffed slacks, a loose alpaca V-neck sweater in lemon yellow over bare brown skin, the showing V of skin adorned with three gold chains, from one of which depended a gold goat's head and a tiny gold spoon. His feet were shod in two-tone (green and red) bulbous-toed shoes with three-inch leather heels.

He fingered his little spoon and considered the bowl on the coffee table. It was a lidded crystal sphere containing approximately half a pound of the purest Bolivian flake cocaine in

New York City. Always, when he waited for Clarry like this, he considered lifting the lid and taking a monster snort, and as always he declined. Larue knew it too, that Booth was reliable, that he wouldn't lift a man's blow when the man wasn't looking. A guy who would take a little snort without being asked would start bringing vials into the house, and then jam jars. Booth was not that kind of guy, which was why from time to time his buddy Larue would lay a baggie on him, holding a casual scoop of flake, maybe fifty grams, and so pure that Booth could step on it three times and move it to a couple of kids he knew for up to five large.

Booth himself was not a dope merchant, nor even much of a user. He did what he had to to survive, which was generally acting as a reliable assistant at various illegal activities; he was a street watcher, a follower of people somebody wanted followed, a deliverer of packages, a driver. From time to time he took people like Larue around town in their big cars. It was a living. He had been arrested fourteen times, convicted twice, and imprisoned once, a four-year stretch in Elmira for assisting at an armed robbery.

He heard the door to the bedroom open. The girl who emerged was a redhead with a skin so pale it shone blue in the bright track lighting. She was in her stroll duds, the little tap pants that showed plump crescents of buttock, the laced vest open down the front, the tall high-heeled boots. She looked at Booth, at the bowl on the table. She gave him a trial look; he could have anything she had for a pinch of that, said the look. He shook his head slightly and flicked his hand toward the door. She seemed about to say something, but detected an element in Booth's demeanor that stifled dalliance. Shrugging, she hoisted her fake leather bag to her shoulder and trudged out of the apartment.

Booth heard the shower start and stop, and ten minutes later a cloud of sharp and manly cologne heralded the entrance of his host. Clarry was dressed to kill in a suit of sea green over a white spread-collared shirt open to the breastbone. He had six gold chains. As he entered the living room, he smiled broadly at Booth, but his eyes flicked briefly over the crystal bowl.

Booth caught the look and said, "You took your time."

"Yeah, I did. That little girl won't be able to *say* fuck for a week. We about ready to cruise, my friend, after we fix our heads. You want to snort some?"

"No, I'm cool."

Larue shrugged and sat down on the red couch. He pulled the bowl to him and inserted the little finger of his left hand, the nail of which had been allowed to grow out half an inch beyond the fingertip. He scooped up a mound of cocaine, dumped it on the marble surface, chopped and raked it with a gold-plated razor that hung from one of his chains, and constructed two fat lines, which he proceeded to suck up, one to a nostril, through a gold tube that also hung conveniently about his neck.

He leaned his head back and sighed, and paused while the coke flooded his brain. Then he popped to his feet with the flying jitters, tossed Booth a set of car keys, and hurtled out the door, off to the hot spots, to see and be seen and to ply his trade.

Larue Clarry was a scuffler from 136th Street who had started dealing heroin at fifteen and had been one of the first Harlem dope peddlers to switch from selling heroin to poor black junkies and whores to selling cocaine to rich white executives and whores. By now, by the late 1970's, it had made him wealthy, and more than wealthy—sought after and jollied up by people whose faces appeared on TV and whose names appeared in newspapers. He had a cachet throughout tony Manhattan undreamed of by previous generations of pushers, undreamed of by the Mafia itself. For the first time since the Prohibition twenties, people of Clarry's moral provenance were welcome among café society. He could get in anywhere, any club, Studio 54, you name it. The candy man.

And it was, he believed, just the beginning. There seemed no limit to the demand, no limit to the amount of disposable income available for fine blow. He was still amazed at his good fortune. He could have ended like the other dudes he had come up with: dead, or bums, junkies, jailbirds, or square, working for chump change at dead-end jobs—bus drivers.

Or like Tecumseh here, a cheap rip-off artist, a gofer. As he considered his companion, a wave of cheerful generosity swept over him. He touched Booth's arm.

"Hey, Booth—I been meaning to ask you— what say you start running some stuff for me?"

They were just leaving the paneled lobby of the building, and Booth paused and looked at Clarry with an irritated frown.

"Ain't you got enough mules?"

Clarry shook his head. "What, did I say mule? I ain't talkin carryin, I'm talkin sellin, man. I'm talkin a territory, man. You gettin on, boy, you oughta think about gettin yourself a little something outta your hustle, you know?"

Booth's expression turned suspicious. "What you talkin about, man? How come you want to give me somethin?"

Clarry chuckled and clapped Booth on the shoulder. "I don't need no reason. I like you, man. I wanna see you smile. You too serious. Besides, I got to take care of my homeboy. We a long way from hangin out on Thirty-six, now, hey? They ain't no catch, man—I mean it. So, smile!"

Booth managed to comply with a thin one as they left the building and approached the glittering dark blue Mercedes 600 sedan parked illegally in front. It was a mild spring midnight. For the moment, at this latitude, Park Avenue was as deserted as the streets of a small town. Booth opened the rear door for Clarry and walked around to the driver's side. He got in, settled himself, and started the car.

The engine rumbled to life. From the back, Clarry said, "So what you think, man? We in business?"

Before Booth could answer, the man who had been crouched in the foot well of the passenger's side uncoiled his body, reached over the front seat, and shot Larue Clarry in the face with a small-caliber revolver. Clarry fell back and his left foot kicked out spasmodically. Booth felt it kick the back of his seat twice. The shooter fired another two rounds into Clarry's head.

Booth rolled down his window and headed the car north on Park Avenue. The stink of gunpowder and death mixed unappealingly with the remnants of Larue Clarry's ultimate cologning. The shooter fired his last three rounds into Clarry and then turned around in the seat. He carefully buckled his safety belt.

"You think he dead yet?" Booth asked.

The other man reached into his jacket pocket and took out a thick brown envelope, which he handed to Booth. "Just drive, Tecumseh," the man said. "I don't need any wise-assery tonight."

Booth put the envelope in his belt under his sweater.

"And what the fuck took you so long?" the man asked. "I almost got a hernia scrooched up like that."

"Man had to get his last fuck in, blow some coke. I figure there's no rush. He was feeling pretty good anyway. He ask me if I want a job."

"Yeah? You take it?"

"I was thinking about it. This where you want to go?"

The man looked out the window. "Yeah, pull over here. OK, take this load of shit down under the highway, like we said. Make it look like somebody roughed him off. Take the watch and the chains. And don't fuckin let me see *you* with any of that shit on you, understand?"

"Shit. What you think, I'm a fool?" answered Booth, insulted.

"And this." The shooter held out the empty revolver. He had wrapped it in a piece of rag. "In the river. Ditch the car where we said. Take the subway after. Anybody know you was with him?"

"Just the ho."

"She don't count," said the shooter.

Booth nodded and put the gun next to him on the seat. The shooter slid out of the car without another word and walked a few yards to where a tan Plymouth waited at the curb, its engine running. The shooter got in and the car took off.

Obediently Booth drove east on 96th Street, then north on First to 120th Street, where he turned right and drove until he was under the humming FDR Drive. These truncated streets, which lie in perpetual shadow and endure the stench and noise of a major elevated highway, constitute a sort of grease trap, catching the lumps of urban detritus no longer wanted in the lighted zones. In the especially dark area in which Booth chose now to stash the great automobile, there were, for example, a burned sofa, two cars stripped of everything merchantable, their hoods and trunks gaping like starving seagulls, a coil of rusted mesh fencing, a wooden cable spool, half a dozen fifty-five-gallon drums, windows of corrugated cardboard and paper trash, and any number of dead dogs, cats, pigeons, and rats, slowly decomposing into gritty city humus. All this lay on a surface of crushed glass glittering in the scant light.

Booth now began the distasteful task of stripping Larue Clarry's corpse of its valuables. Wallet from the inside jacket pocket, vial of traveling coke from the side jacket pocket, gold watch, four finger rings. The neck chains were embedded in a thick mass of congealed blood, and rather than fumble with the catches and get all messy, Booth cut them off with the efficient pliers supplied by the Mercedes-Benz Corporation. After pocketing the cocaine and the money from the wallet, Booth tied the rest of the swag in Clarry's handkerchief.

He was just about to back out of the car's rear compartment when he heard the unmistakable sound of a man clearing his throat. The weird acoustics of the underfreeway made it seem to come from directly behind him, as if a passing stranger were about to ask him directions or politely offer help; it froze his blood and brought his head up sharply, cracking it against the door frame. Stunned, he fell back, landing on the filthy pavement, with his feet still in the car.

He stifled a curse and rose shakily to stand, glancing about wildly, vainly attempting to read the darkness. Under the traffic sounds, silence. He waited a long minute. Another.

Then he realized that he was still holding in his hand the things he had taken off Clarry. He looked dumbly at the bundle as if for the first time, a lumpy white package slowly turning pink. Street instinct kicked in and he began to run, south and east toward a little park under the highway, toward the river.

It was only after he had flung the heavy package as far toward the lights of Randall's Island as he could manage that he realized that he had forgotten the little pistol. It was still wrapped in its rag on the front seat of the car.

As Booth walked out of the park toward the subway, he tried to figure if he was in any real trouble over this. Going back was out—no way was he going to get anywhere near that car this night. For all he knew, somebody had spotted him and called the cops. If the cops found the gun, he would be in trouble, but the shooter would be in worse trouble and would probably leave him alone for the foreseeable future, which in Booth's case amounted to about four days.

But the likelier outcome was that a big expensive car abandoned in that neighborhood would be stripped that night, the gun scarfed up by some street kid. It might as well be in the river. He walked on, relieved. He had nearly a thousand dollars and two grams of prime cocaine. Time to party.

The face that peered in through the window of the Mercedes was a junkie's face; yellow and thin, with a twisted scar over one eye and an expression of deep pain and profound fatigue. A heroin addict of long standing, the man couldn't recognize the bullet-riddled face of the man in the back seat, but he knew the car. Making the logical jump that he was looking at its late owner was easy.

The man's name was Enrico Laxton, known as Po'boy. Like many aging junkies, he made a modest living as a snitch, trading bits of information to the police for small sums, or better yet, bags of smack.

He saw Larue Clarry's end as Tecumseh Booth had seen it—as a business opportunity. Laxton was debilitated and shaky, but there was nothing wrong with his eyes. In his yellow sweater and pale slacks Booth had shone like neon and Laxton had got a good look at his face as he ran by the pile of cardboard and rags on which Laxton had nodded out, as invisible as city grime.

TWO

Three months out of law school, Peter Schick sat in the outer office of the Criminal Courts Bureau, of the New York District Attorney's Office, watching the action and waiting to be called into his third job interview of the day. He crossed his legs and glanced at his watch and then at the round clock on the wall. His watch was running but the clock had stopped. At the two Wall Street firms where he had interviewed that morning, the clocks worked, the secretaries were cool and competent, and the furniture was polished wood and real leather, not painted metal and cracked vinyl. The office staff here looked toughened and tired, and drawn from the less prestigious minorities of the city.

He discovered he had been picking nervously at a crack in the covering of the tan couch and stopped. There were no magazines to read. He went back to staring at the woman sitting on the edge of a desk across a narrow aisle. She was making call after call on the desk phone. She kept the receiver crooked against her shoulder and made an occasional note on a yellow pad, afterward shoving the pencil into the thick mass of lustrous black hair that, from Schick's location, concealed her face from view. She was wearing a black skirt of some rustling material; it was slit and rode entrancingly up her thigh when she crossed her legs. The legs were marvelous, tapering without fragility, wrapped in shimmering mist-colored stockings. She wore a black kid glove on her left hand, like a gunfighter.

Schick adjusted his position slightly, so as to improve his view of inner thigh for the next leg cross. But something must have lit up the invisible radar that is the secret possession of the girls; she snapped her head around and gave him the stare.

He felt his jaw drop and a blush rising up his jaw. The woman was a classic cover-girl beauty—large black eyes over razor-sharp cheekbones, a wide lush mouth, the skin a delicate pink bisque. Schick took in that there was something wrong with one of her eyes, a crazy light in it, or perhaps it was slightly, but fetchingly, crossed. He felt the blush rising to his cheeks and pointedly looked away from her at the unmoving clock.

Just then, the door to the bureau director's office opened and Schick's interview walked out. Schick was over six feet tall, but the bureau director rose nearly four inches higher than that. He extended a big hand and Schick took it. Schick looked him in the eyes, which were a strange deep gray with little yellow flecks. They slanted slightly above broad cheekbones. Karp's nose was fleshy, his mouth full, his chin bold and knobby, his hair neatly cut, medium length, and ash-brown.

"Mr. Karp?" Schick said.

"Yeah. You're Schick. Let's go in my office."

The big man gestured toward the open door, and as he followed Schick he said something in a low voice to the dark-haired woman perched on the desk. She responded with a hearty guffaw. Karp stopped and said something else. Out of the corner of his eye Schick thought he saw the woman make a casual grab for the rear end of his prospective employer—if true, yet another sign that he was not on Wall Street.

Schick entered the bureau chief's office and looked around. In the center of the room a long scarred oak table was surrounded by a dozen or so miscellaneous chairs. At one end was a massive walnut desk, with a battered brown leather chair behind it and two straight chairs before. The desk was cluttered with a drift of russet case folders, assorted papers and yellow pads. Schick noticed his own résumé floating on top of the pile.

There was a coat stand in the corner, from which hung a navy-blue suit jacket, a set of sweat clothes, a N.Y. Yankees hat, and a first baseman's mitt. On the wall behind the desk hung some framed photographs: one of a softball team (Karp in the third row), one, cut from an old newspaper, of a much younger Karp shooting a basketball through the arms of an opposing player (caption: "Karp Scores 26 Against UCLA"), a photocopy of a news photograph showing some horsemen in white uniforms charging with lances, and what looked like a "wanted" poster printed in a foreign language. Schick was just leaning over the desk to inspect this last more closely when the door swung open and Karp came in.

Karp threw his long, narrow frame down on the chair behind his desk and motioned Schick to sit across from him. He glanced at the résumé for a moment and then looked directly at Schick.

"So. How come you want to work for the D.A.?"

Schick smiled nervously, thought of an idealistic answer, looked at Karp, who was not smiling, rejected the idealistic answer, which was in any case not true, decided to blurt it out, and said, "I want to try cases. I can't afford to set up my own practice, and if I work for a big firm, I won't get to stand up in front of a jury for years. So . . ."

Karp's mouth twitched in what might have been the shadow of a grin. Schick noticed again that his eyes had little yellow flecks in them, and were set in his broad face at an almost angle. Not a companionable face. Schick could not help contrasting Karp with the senior lawyers with whom he had interviewed that morning. They had been smooth, confident men, strong, but with their strength buoyed by the power of a deeply established order, symbolized by polished wood and thick carpets. Karp's strength seemed to be an interior toughness, owing little to the tacky office or whatever status he happened to have at the moment.

Karp said, "OK, so you want to use the D.A.'s office for a little legal practice before you go out and get rich."

"I didn't say that!"

"Yeah, but it's not unusual. We don't get many career people here. In fact, it's a seller's market right now. A lot of the bureaus will take anybody who isn't actually drooling." He looked down again at Schick's résumé. "Good grades. Law review at NYU. Very impressive. You're a friend of Tony Harris, right?"

"Yeah, we grew up together. He's a little older than me, more my brother's friend, but the same crowd and all."

"He recommends you. He says you can hit."

"Excuse me . . . ?"

"Hit. As in baseball. You did play varsity ball at Pitt?"

Schick nodded, confused.

"So I got a hole at third base I could use you in. You look puzzled. Here's the deal. We have a team, the Bullets, in the city rec league. We play law firms, the sanitation guys, the cops; it's a big thing around here. When Mr. Garrahy was the D.A., he used to come to every game. We try to keep it alive, and we win a lot, which is more than you can say for what happens in court. What do you think of that?"

"You hire lawyers because they play ball?"

"Of course. If possible. This is jock country, Schick. If we had a guy in a wheelchair, I'd expect him to want to come out and cheer. I need people who are competitive and aggressive and can keep coming back and playing even if they get beat every day. Which is not unusual, by the way. You get the picture?"

"Yeah. Sounds OK by me."

"OK. Let me tell you something about the job. The Criminal Courts Bureau was set up to deal with minor crimes, and that's still most of the work, but a lot of the crimes we tend to deal with are technically felonies. When Criminal Courts was set up, in the old days, cops had time for a lot more of the petty shit. Now they don't, unless the individual is making a particular pain in the ass of himself. Selling blowjobs in a car at night is one thing; if you try it in the skating rink at Rockefeller Center in broad daylight, they'll bring you in.

"So most of what we do is workaday small crime: purse snatches, pross, pickpocket, larceny, assault, some sex crimes, drunk driving. All the Fun City stuff. Felony Bureau gets the heavy crime, the armed robbery, arson, safe and loft ripoffs, hijacking. About ninety-eight percent of our work is stoking the system. New York County racks up around 130,000 felony and misdemeanor charges every year. Only about one out of a hundred felony charges in New York actually makes it to trial, and it takes an average of fifteen court appearances of one kind or another to clear a single felony case. So what do we do?"

Schick realized that this was not a rhetorical question, that Karp expected a response. He cleared his throat. "I don't know—I guess the cases back up."

"Of course, but only to a point. Speedy trial rulings mean we got to run the cases through at a certain rate whatever, or else some people are going to walk, and you never can tell who. It's never the guy who kicked his landlord in the ass, it's some mutt who killed six people. Big scandal.

"No, what we do is plea-bargain. The defendant's lawyer cops him to a lesser plea. Burglary goes to trespass, attempted homicide goes to simple assault, and so on. The mutt's been sitting in jail a couple of months, he gets out with time served. Case closed. It sucks, but what can you do?"

Karp paused and fixed Schick with a fierce stare. "But there's a right way and a wrong way to run the game. The first rule is to keep respect. You got to have the trial slots, so that if the defense holds out for some outrageous deal, you can spit in their eye and go to trial. Which means you have to prep cases like you *were* going to try them, and then not be afraid of going to court if you have to. And the second rule is: nobody gets away with murder."

"Murder? But I thought you said, um . . ."

"Yeah, minor crimes. Well, it turns out we do a lot of work on murders too. And some rape when there's violence attached. Not the easy ones, either. The reason for that is me." Karp caught the inquiring look and held up his hand. "A long story," he continued, "which somebody will convey to you if you're interested. The main point here is that our current D.A., Mr. Bloom, and I don't particularly agree about how the office should be run. Not to get into details, but Mr. Bloom, he basically doesn't like trials. He's not a trial lawyer himself and he doesn't understand how trial lawyers operate. What he understands are committees and deals.

"He wants the machine to run smoothly— that's his main thing. So we drag these mutts into the building, wave some hands, run them through a courtroom, and cop them out. A murder trial is like sand in the gears. A lot of time, a lot of effort, a lot of publicity, and—you could lose. Bad publicity, questions of competence are raised, people start to remember that the point of a prosecutor's office is to prosecute, so how come Bloom is fucking up? Impossible! Much better to avoid it all and plead the goddamn killer to second-degree manslaughter. A year in the slams and another case closed."

As Karp spoke on this subject, his face darkened with angry blood, his heavy brow bunched, and little sparks seemed to flicker around his strange eyes. Schick unconsciously hunched a little in his seat. His thought was that he never wanted to be on the receiving end of that kind of anger.

Karp seemed to catch himself then. He sat back and grinned and shook his head ruefully. "I'm on my toot again. I was talking about our work. Yeah, we do murder trials. There used to be a Homicide Bureau, but there isn't anymore. What I try to do here is to do what the old Homicide Bureau did really well, which is to train lawyers to try cases, eventually to try homicide cases.

"So if you want to learn that, this is the best place to be. The down side is, if you work for me, you will not have a happy time with the powers upstairs. You will have the shittiest little office, you will have the slowest promotions, and if you ever need an administrative favor, you'll hang by your eyelids before you get it. Sound good?"

"Who could ask for anything more?"

"Good. Any questions about the job?"

"A million, but nothing urgent. Anything else you want to know about me?"

"Yeah," said Karp. His smile melted back into the rock of his face and his jaw set hard. "How come you were staring up my girlfriend's dress out there?"

Schick goggled and felt the red rise up his throat. "I . . . didn't . . . um . . ." he stammered.

"Schick," said Karp in a gentler tone, "if you get red when you lie, you'll never make a trial lawyer. Work on it! Meanwhile . . ."

There was a sharp series of raps on the office

door. Karp looked annoyed at the interruption, but said, "Yeah? Who is it?"

The door opened and a stocky mustached black man in a sharp tan chalk-stripe suit came in. Karp's face lit up. "Clay Fulton! What's happening, baby!"

The man noticed Schick. "Am I interrupting something?"

"No," said Karp, "we're just finishing up. This is Peter Schick, our new third base. Peter, Detective Lieutenant Clay Fulton."

After mutual handshaking, Karp said, "OK, Schick, go out there and see the bureau secretary—Connie Trask, the good-looking black lady on the center desk—and tell her you're hired. Tell her I said she was a good-looking black lady too. She'll give you a pencil and a yellow pad and somewhere to sit. You might even get paid eventually. And go find Tony Harris. He'll give you some stuff to do." Thus dismissed, Schick mumbled good-byes and nice-meeting-yous and left the office. It was only later that he realized that Karp had never considered that the offered job would be refused. In an odd way, Schick took that as a compliment.

When Schick had left, Fulton gestured toward the closing door. "What is he, twelve?"

Karp laughed. "God, it looks that way. But that's a law-school graduate. We're getting old, friend."

"Older but still tough. Speaking of old, I got your invitation."

"You'll come . . . ?"

"Yeah, me'n Martha'll be there. I can't believe it, you and Marlene, the end of an era. I saw her outside just now, still a fox . . . still a dirty mouth. You gonna make her stop cursing that way when you got her legal? Slap her upside the head?"

Karp whooped. "It would be my last act on earth. But let me say this, Clay: if she ever does kill me, I want you to catch the squeal. Might as well keep it in the family."

The two men talked easily for the next few minutes, the man-trivia of sports and politics. They were friends from Karp's earliest time with the D.A.'s office, when he had been the most junior member of the fabled Homicide Bureau, and Fulton, already the owner of a glowing reputation as a detective, had taken him under his wing, taught him police procedure, and provided the evidence and witnesses that enabled Karp to make his own reputation as a prosecutor.

"So," said Karp after a pause, "they still killing people in Harlem?"

Fulton's face grew serious. "Yeah, that's what I need to talk with you about. Somebody aced Larue Clarry last night."

Karp searched his mind for the name and came up empty. Fulton saw the blank look and explained, "The dope dealer. Ran coke for the flashy set. Somebody killed him in his own car and left it under the FDR at 120th. Left the gun he done it with too."

"Any reason why we should especially mourn Mr. Clarry's passing?"

"No, unless you his momma. But look here. The last three months we had five major dope wholesalers knocked off in Harlem. Clarry's number six. Listen to this." He consulted a notebook. "April 2, Jimmie Williams, shot in the back of the head with a large-caliber pistol in a vacant apartment, Harlem. Nobody saw nothing. April 28, Togo McAllister opened the door to his apartment, Morningside Heights, and walked into a shotgun blast. Nobody saw nothing.

"May 12, Sweets Martin, found in an alley, Lower East Side, hands tied, throat cut, puncture wounds all over him, ditto. May 16, Bowman 'Heat' Fletcher, shot in the heart with a large-caliber pistol, also in his apartment, Upper West Side, also ditto. June 3, Ollie Bender, found in a construction site, Eighth and 43rd, with his head bashed in: fucking ditto."

Fulton put his notebook away and looked at Karp. "Anything strike you as odd about that set?"

Karp thought for a moment, then shook his head. "I don't see any pattern, except that there isn't any pattern. It just looks like a bunch of guys in a tough business got taken out in a short period of time. Their number was up. I mean, what's the average life span of a dope dealer? Three, five years? Or do you see something I don't?"

Fulton grimaced, a comical wrinkling of his

heavy brow and broad nose, as if he smelled rottenness, and began pacing to and fro in front of Karp's desk. "I don't know what I see yet. Like you say, it looks like a normal couple of months in the dope scene. Maybe that's what's bothering me: it's *too* normal, too—I don't know—miscellaneous. Like somebody was painting a picture for the cops that's saying, 'Ain't nobody doin nothin special down here, boss!' "

"Like in Sherlock Holmes," Karp put in, "the unusual incident was that the dog didn't bark in the night."

"Yeah, like that! And look here: six different M.O.'s, in four different detective zones, and not a single witness in any of them worth a damn. Like somebody was designing the set so that it wouldn't be seen as a set, somebody who knows how cops think."

"Who benefits?" asked Karp abruptly.

"How do you mean?"

"Well, you say 'somebody,' implying that there's a single agent responsible for all six crimes. Assuming you're right, and that you've got no good leads, why don't you start with whoever you think might want to have all six of these guys killed?"

Fulton shook his head. "Yeah, I thought of that. It could be any of a dozen, twenty people, guys who could move in on the business with the dead dealers out of the way. That's in the city. God knows about out-of-town gangs, Colombians, Cubans, Jamaicans . . . where to start?"

"So you're stumped?"

"Yeah, and I can't stand it. God damn, I hate a mystery! Some slick fucker going around getting off on spitting in my eye. I ain't whipped yet, but I need help. That's why I'm downtown. If I'm not crazy, the only chance we got is on this Clarry hit. It's fresh and the guy made his first mistake."

Karp made an inquiring sound, and Fulton went on. "He left his gun on the seat of the car. It's a cheap piece of shit, a twenty-two, but it's something."

"Prints?"

Fulton snorted. "Not *that* good, but we got a serial number. Something could turn up. I want to squeeze the street hard on this. I'm gonna put the King Cole Trio on it, full-time."

Karp grinned and raised his hands in mock horror. "Uh-oh. Are they gonna be good, or am I gonna have 'police brutality' all over my cases?"

"Come on, Butch, these are changed men. They've seen the light. They're gonna treat every skell in Harlem like their momma. The thing of it is, I need to run everything that anybody finds out on all the investigations of all these killings through me. If there's a pattern, that's the only way to find it."

"That could be a problem."

"No shit! I made the case to the zone commander and he·shined me on to the borough commander and he said he agreed 'in principle' that I should coordinate, but whether he'll do fuck-all about it, I don't know."

"Anything I can do?"

Fulton flashed a bright sudden smile. "Hey, I resent you implying that this wasn't just a social call. But since you ask, yeah. Just keep your ears open to anything that fits in the pattern. I might miss something. Also, I'd like just one ADA on all six cases: somebody good. And if the Chief of D. happens to call you, you might put a word in."

"No problem, Clay," said Karp, although they both knew it was in fact a considerable problem to juggle cases around like that.

But Clay Fulton was one of only a handful of people whom Karp considered to have a blank check on his help, and he did not begrudge the effort, although he personally believed that Fulton was chasing shadows. Karp was not a hunch player. He liked evidence in plastic bags and sworn depositions. He liked witnesses.

Was there a hidden conspiracy to kill drug dealers? Maybe, but thinking about it did Karp no good. At a certain level, he well knew, he found it all too easy to imagine that the whole city was engaged in a conspiracy. Karp's tendency toward paranoia was well-established and familiar to him, fed daily by the hostility of his management, and nurtured by the environment of the criminal justice system, itself a vast lie. He felt for the detective, his friend, but was not about to give him any enthusiastic encouragement.

The business done, some desultory conversation followed and then Fulton looked at his watch and stood up. The two men shook hands warmly. "Take care, man," said Karp.

"Watch your own butt, hear?" answered Clay Fulton.

Fulton went back to his office, the office of the Zone 5 homicide squad, which operated out of the Twenty-eighth Precinct on 135th Street off Lenox Avenue, and was responsible for homicides occurring in the northeastern section of Manhattan Island, a chunk of territory that included most of Harlem. Fulton ran the squad. It was rarely at a loss for work.

There were three detectives waiting for him in the squad room. They were the best men he possessed and as good as any team in the city. They had been famous when he had taken over the squad, and he had left them more or less alone. They were known on the street, for obscure reasons, as the King Cole Trio.

Fulton perched on a desk and looked inquiringly at the most senior of the three, a lean, intense man of about fifty, with skin the color of black coffee, yellowish eyes, and cropped natural hair growing gray on the sides. "What've we got, Art?"

The man, Detective Sergeant Art Dugman, pulled a spiral notebook out of his suit jacket pocket and placed a pair of cheap reading glasses on his nose. When he spoke, it was in a voice dry but vibrant, dressed in the accents of prewar Harlem. "I went down with Mack as soon as we heard the squeal. Got there about, oh, two this morning. The first officer was still on the scene. Couple of D.T.'s from the Two-three showed up; I told them it was ours, orders from downtown. They split."

He peered at Fulton over his glasses. "We do got the case, am I right?"

Fulton nodded and motioned him to continue.

"OK. Man was shot in the face at close range with a twenty-two-caliber revolver, sitting in the back seat of his own car. The shooter probably was in the front seat when he did it. Initial M.E. report says he'd been dead no more than four, five hours when they examined him, which puts the crime around midnight, day before yesterday.

"Crime Scene dusted the car; nothing but Clarry's own prints in the back. The front's been wiped. The gun's wiped too. The RMP cop found it sitting on the seat of the car. It's a little piece-of-shit gun. The lab's checking it out now. The driver's-side door was left open. That's what attracted the RMP to the scene— the door light."

Fulton said, "Looks like the shooter took off in a hurry. Something must have spooked him. Did the RMP see anything?"

"Didn't see shit. Nobody saw shit. We did a canvass the next morning . . ."

"Nobody heard the shots?"

"No. But I don't think he was popped there."

"I thought you said he got it in the car."

"Yeah, yeah, in the car, but not at the place—under the FDR."

"How do you know that?"

"The blood. From his face—it was streaked back along the side of his head, like when it rains against the side windows of a car and the speed of the car drags it backwards. And there was a big mass of clotted blood piled up against where the deck behind the back seat meets the back window. They shot him somewhere else and drove him there and dumped him. Took all his stuff too—wallet, jewelry. Look like a deal gone bad or a ripoff. Tricky fuckers, whoever."

Fulton worried his mustache with his lower teeth. "Yeah, but not tricky enough, this time. What about his place?"

Dugman looked across the room at a stocky white man in a brown nylon jacket, gray work pants, and a blue plaid shirt. The man was in his early thirties and had a lumpy face with a strong jaw. The dark eyes were slightly too close together, but his mouth was wide and humorous. His dirty-blond hair was worn as long as the police department then allowed; the picture was redneck, working stiff, union-card-carrying, not a bright light. It was a picture he cultivated. His name was Lanny Maus, and he had been a detective-third for a little over ten years.

Maus was leaning backward in his chair against the scarred police-station-green walls and had his feet propped up on his desk. He wore the kind of heavy tan leather shoes favored by construction workers. He removed the wooden match on which he had been sucking and consulted his own little book.

"We tossed the place at five-ten P.M. on the night of. Ton of coke, some smack, pills. Could he have been a dope dealer? Man had a gun, a nice nine, didn't take it with him. Glass on the table in the living room, fresh prints, not Clarry's. We're checking that out.

"Moving to the bedroom, we find signs of recent sexual activity. Clarry apparently got one last piece of ass before he checked out. Bed sheets gave us head hair, female, Caucasian, dyed red, pussy hair ditto, not dyed, brown. She wears purple lip gloss, assuming the Kleenex in the wastebasket belongs to her. That's about it, except a lady in a front apartment said she thought she saw two men get into a big black car parked in front of the building and drive off a little past twelve."

Fulton acknowledged the report with a nod and said, "Ok, the girl left, then Clarry left with somebody who drove him someplace and shot him and drove the car with the body in it under the highway, and left on foot." He stood up and started pacing back and forth in front of the three men.

"This is looking good. This is the first time

we got *anything* on these killings. We need that girl."

Maus cleared his throat. "Loo, I'd like to volunteer to go up to every redhead in the city and ask them what color is their snatch. I'd have to verify their answer, of course."

Fulton gave him a look. The fourth man in the room, who had been silent up to now, said in a voice so deep and rumbling that it was like the noise made by a piece of heavy machinery, "Clarry like them young."

They all turned toward him. Detective Third Class Mack Jeffers was a very black and extremely large man, was, in fact, as large as it is possible to be and still be a member of the police force in New York. He was just under the six-foot-seven limit and weighed over 285 pounds. He was the youngest member of the Trio, not yet thirty, and had made detective with record speed because, it was said, they had run out of blue cloth. He was taciturn, patient, and like many big men, friendly and even-tempered.

"He got his girls from Slo Mo," Jeffers continued. "You know Slo Mo, Art?"

"Yeah, he pimps down on the Deuce. Picks the moppets up at the Port Authority. OK, we'll check it out."

Fulton said, "Good, that's a start. Now, on these other dope-dealer hits, we're taking all of them over."

Groans all around. Dugman said, "Loo, what the damn hell! We don't pull enough murders in Harlem? You got to drag in stale fucked-up cases from all round town?"

Fulton set his jaw. "Can it, guys! This is real, and this is big, and I want complete control of it all. I want every one of those case files squeezed until the juice comes out. There's a pattern here, and you're gonna find it. That's all!"

He turned and strode into his private office, slamming the door behind him.

The three detectives looked at one another, their expressions exhibiting mixed feelings of disbelief, annoyance, resignation—the standard cop expressions. But there was also the beginning of something else, a kind of fascination, the first faint scent of prey in the air. The King Cole Trio hated mysteries too.

THREE

"What did he do then?" asked Marlene Ciampi, trying to keep the weariness out of her voice as she moved through yet another rape interview. This victim—she glanced down at the name . . . Paula Rosenfeld—was shut down, reciting the facts of her recent violation as if she were reading off the periodic table. You got them like that; you also got the one who couldn't stop shaking, and the weepers, and the cursers. Those were just the ones who came in. Marlene suspected that the majority of the raped of New York were in another class entirely—the no-shows, the ones who turned off the memory, told no one, denied it happened, took a long bath and tried to get on with life.

Rosenfeld shrugged and said, "He didn't do anything. He got off me, pulled on his pants, and went out."

"He didn't say anything to you?"

The woman thought for a moment. Marlene observed the signs of grief and stress ooze subtly onto her face. It was a pretty little face—short dark hair, small even features, big brown eyes that would have looked better without the dark circles beneath them. A good figure too, small and slim, not unlike Marlene's own, but muffled by a shapeless black sweater and jeans. After a while she cleared her throat and said, "Yes, he did say something. He smiled and waved and said, 'Well, be seeing you.' "

Marlene wrote it down in the appropriate space on her five-by-eight index card, the space for "vocalizations–post" Marlene had designed the card herself and had paid for the two rubber stamps that printed the categories on the front and the back of each card. The card was supposed to help you to set down in an orderly way all the information about a rape: about the victim, about the setting (place, time of day, phase of moon), about the rapist. There was a space marked "signatures." Marlene tapped her pencil on this spot and reread what she had written there.

"About the panty hose—you said he wrapped it around your neck. Did you think he was going to strangle you?"

The woman shook her head. "No, it wasn't like that. He had this big knife, you know? He didn't need anything else. No, he just draped it around my neck and sort of played with it while he . . . you know."

Marlene knew. She nodded, made a note, and looked up brightly. "Well, Ms. Rosenfeld, I'd like to thank you for coming in. We'll get in touch with you if we need you again, when we make an arrest."

The woman looked at her dully. "They're not even going to look for him, are they?"

"Who told you that?"

"Nobody. But I could just tell—the cops who interviewed me after—they thought it was, like, an argument on a date or something. It got out of hand, no big thing. They kept asking me if I was going to press charges."

Marlene sighed, leaned back in her chair, and stuck her pencil in her hair. "OK, look—from the point of view of the law and law enforcement, rape is an unusual crime because almost always the only witness is the victim. We can have evidence of the sex taking place, but whether it's rape or not is a question of belief. The state legislature changed the rape law last year, so you no longer need independent corroboration of the crime, but you do need evidence that force was used and consent not given.

"So the cops look for certain things—was it a stranger, was there breaking and entering, was there beating of the victim? Places—in a back alley is good, a parking garage, a park. Also they look at the social stuff. Cops like big differences in the ages. The eighteen-year-old and the grandmother, or the forty-year-old guy and the twelve-year-old girl.

"And, I'm sorry to say, they also like black on white, although that's a lot rarer than most people believe. In any case, they like a middle-class victim. What they definitely do not like is when it takes place in the woman's bedroom, and she let him in and she knew the guy. Like in your case, a guy she met in a bar."

"You don't believe me either!" the woman said in a small voice, accepting it.

"No!" Marlene nearly shouted, and the woman jumped. "I do believe you. But that's not what matters. What matters is do we have a case." She tapped her stack of five-by-eights. "That's what these cards are for. If he did it to you, he did it or will do it to other people, and probably in the same way. We establish there's a pattern, a serial thing, it gets the cops interested. They put more energy into it. Also, we have a pattern that makes it a lot easier to convict, and to get a decent sentence when we do.

"I know the system sucks, but it's the system. I've got to play in it the best I can. But believe me, I understand what you're going through . . ."

At this, the other woman's face, until then a frozen mask, twisted into a hostile grimace. "You do?" she spat. "Why? Did you get raped too?"

Marlene's stomach churned. She understood why many of the women she interviewed took out their rage on her. She was available, and the rapist wasn't, but it didn't make it feel any better.

She took a slow breath, folded her hands on her desk, looked Paula Rosenfeld straight in the eye, and said, "Actually, Ms. Rosenfeld, I believe I can sympathize with your situation. Not too long ago I was drugged and kidnapped by a bunch of crazed satanists, stripped naked and presented as a toy to a mentally defective child murderer, given the starring role in a variety of depraved rituals, during which I was masturbated upon by a substantial number of men and had various of my personal orifices penetrated by demonic instruments wielded by my charming hostess. So yes, I believe I can sympathize with your situation."

The other woman's eyes had gone wide and her jaw dropped. "Oh, my God! You're that one! It was on TV."

"Yes, dear, I'm that one—my fifteen minutes of fame."

Pause. Marlene waited for what she knew was coming. "You killed that guy."

Marlene nodded. "Yes, I did. He was going to shoot a couple of friends of mine, had shot one of them already, so I killed him."

"I'd like a shot at that bastard too," the woman said bitterly.

"Yes, you would. But it's no fun killing somebody. It doesn't take away the violation." Marlene gestured widely toward the four corners of her tiny office. "This. All of this, the courts, the system, is supposed to do all that for you. It doesn't, but we keep plugging anyway. What else can we do?"

Paula Rosenfeld, rape victim, had no answer to this question, and she wound up the interview and left shortly afterward.

Marlene lit a Marlboro and watched the smoke eddy up to the ceiling high above. The office was an architectural oddity, having been constructed out of a dog-leg end of a hall corridor on the sixth floor of the Criminal Courts Building. Its height was therefore nearly twice its other dimensions, so that Marlene worked in what was effectively the bottom of a narrow shaft.

Office space was scarce in this era of New York's perpetual losing battle against crime. The building at 100 Centre Street had been constructed in the late thirties, a period when the poor knew their place, organized crime exerted a kind of discipline on criminal activity, and the police were able to apply such deterrence and punishment as they thought necessary without having to bother the courts: a golden age and long gone.

Now the system was operating at a level ten times higher than it was designed for and, when this was added to the normal tendency of bureaucracies to bloat with time, it meant that the building was bursting at the seams with the varied servitors of justice.

Given the strictures of civil service, a pleasant office is one of the few real gifts in the hands of an elected official like the D.A.; the D.A. did not incline to shower gifts upon Karp, and thus office space was especially scarce for his minions, among whom Marlene was, naturally, more than prominent, being, as was known, Karp's main squeeze.

Marlene didn't mind the office at all; it had zero status, which obviated the need to protect it from the more ambitious; it was out of the way, so that people had to make a special effort to bother her; and while it had no ventilation, it had plenty of room for cigarette smoke in its upper regions.

The alternative was accepting a cubicle in a big office bay, with only a head-high glass partition separating one from one's neighbor, who was likely to be a health fascist who would cough pointedly whenever one lit up.

Marlene put the card she had just filled out in its alphabetical place in one of her long boxes. Something about this particular case niggled at her mind, some pattern. . . . She rubbed her temples, massaging them to stimulate greater brain power, a trick of hers since schoolgirl days. It had worked for Latin declensions and principal products of distant lands; but no longer. Her brain sat inert. She was sinking into bovine placidity, the old sharpness just a frustrating memory. She was three months gone and the baby was obviously starting to leach vital brain material from her very skull.

No, that couldn't be true! Plenty of women had borne children without any diminution of their mental powers, or sacrifice of career opportunities, or self-respect.

"Name three," said a voice in her head, the prosecuting attorney. It was a real voice and not Marlene's own, which caused her no little wonder; in fact, she admired its tone of affable contempt, and wished that she were able to summon it up herself in court. She was even able to visualize him, as composed partly of the Daumier print of an advocate that had hung in the anteroom of one of her law professors at Yale, jowly and lidded of eye; partly of that law professor himself, the son-of-a-bitch, and partly, just a hint, of her dear intended, Karp.

"Marie Curie," said Marlene out loud, whipping mentally through the pages of her NOW calendar, "umm, Rebecca West, and writers, lots of women writers—Anne Tyler, Margaret Drabble . . ."

"Oh?" said the prosecuting attorney. "And are you intending to become a writer? If so, you'd better hustle and establish your reputation in the next five months, so you can live on your fat royalties and hire a nanny. But you're not a writer, are you, Miss Ciampi? You're an assistant D.A. with $234.12 in your bank account and a fifth-floor walk-up loft in an industrial neighborhood. How do you intend to keep working once the baby comes?"

"I'll think of something," said Marlene, without conviction.

"Will you, now? Like what? Carrying a baby on your back while you run from courtroom to courtroom or out to crime scenes? Not likely! No, your career, such as it is, is over. It's diapers and the soaps on TV, and waiting for him to say, 'Hi, honey, I'm home!' You'll be *dependent*."

This last word seemed to reverberate in the courtroom of Marlene's mind like a cheap echo effect in a horror movie. *Dependent*. The jury in her mind, twelve aged Italian women in black, with cameo pins, rubbed their mustaches and nodded. It served her right, the crazy girl, what scandal . . . *che pazza ragazz'. Che vergogna!*"

This was too much. Marlene jumped to her feet, rapping her knees painfully against the bottom of her desk. The flash of agony cleared the court in her head. She grabbed her bag and an armload of current-case jackets and limped out of her office toward the hall to where the Criminal Courts Bureau had one of its main blocks of cubicles for junior staff.

Tony Harris was in his cubicle, on the phone. He was a gangly and engaging youth in his mid-twenties, with bright blue eyes, bad teeth, and no haircut. Seeing Marlene, he smiled and motioned with a helpless gesture to the only other chair in the tiny space, which was filled to overflowing with case jackets and stacks of green-and-white computer printouts. Marlene did not, in any event, wish to sit. She paced and smoked while Harris managed to convince a reluctant witness to appear in court for the third time.

When he finished, Marlene asked him, without preamble, "Will they do it?"

"What, your rape case correlations? Yeah, Data Processing farted around about it for a while, but I finally got them to admit it was a legit run."

Marlene brightened. "They'll do it? Great! When can I get the results?"

Harris crinkled his face. "That's the problem,

Marlene—the when part. It's got—your job's got—no priority; it comes after the bookkeeping, the trial schedules, the rosters, the clearance stats, everything . . ."

"So, when?" Marlene snapped.

"Months. Maybe three, maybe four . . . and it can get bumped by nearly anything."

"But it's important!" Marlene wailed, and ran a hand through her thick tresses. "We're talking about finding criminal patterns, catching multiple rapists. And they're worried about *bookkeeping*?"

"Yeah, but bookkeeping is what they do, Marlene. Maybe you'd have better luck with the cops."

"Oh, sure! I tried that already. They want money to do the programming. Then maybe they'll think about it, the fuckers! I can't fucking *believe* this! How much time could it take? I thought computers worked like in no time at all."

Harris coughed and waved his hand against the smoke cloud. "Yeah, they do when they run," he explained, "but you got to put a lot of time in up-front to tell them what to run and make it all work. You would have to keypunch all those cards, for starters. Then you'd have to write the program, debug it, make your run, fuck with it some more, and run it again until it was right. Then, if you had any more questions, based on what you learned from the first run, you'd have to write a mod and then go back to the end of the line and wait again."

"That's outrageous," cried Marlene. "I thought the goddamn things were supposed to make life easier!"

Harris grinned. "Your first mistake. But really it's not the machines, it's the people. And let me say that anyway these guys in D.P. are not exactly the cream of the crop when it comes to programming the kind of stuff you want to do. I mean, they can do tweaks on big standardized COBOL programs, and keep the payroll going, but correlations, social-science packages, ANOVA—it's out of their league."

"*You* sound like you know something about it. Could you—?"

Harris shook his head strenuously, held up both hands, palms out, and affected an expression of horror. "No, no way!"

Marlene said, "Tony, what, am I losing my charm? Wait, let me moisten my lips . . ."

"Marlene: N. O. Look, this is a serious piece of work, weeks at least for one guy. And I don't really know it. I mean, I made the stupid mistake of telling Karp that I knew something about computers from school and now he's got me riding herd on the numbers, so we can keep the data weenies honest, but that doesn't mean I could do a program like this right off the bat. I'd have to hit the books again—and then you still have the scheduling problem. Unless . . ."

"Unless what?"

"If your bureau chief went to data's bureau chief and did a deal."

"My bureau . . . you mean Karp? And *Wharton?* Not in a zillion years. God! If Wharton ever thought that Karp was connected with this . . ."

"Yeah, its priority might drop even further, like they'll do it right after they solve Fermat's Last Theorem. Which reminds me, maybe a university would be your best bet."

"How do you mean?"

"It's an intrinsically interesting project; it might make a good dissertation—an analytical method of discovering serial rapists. Get a criminology professor up at John Jay or NYU involved, and you're home-free. Universities got better computers than we do, and the people who can use them."

Marlene nodded without really listening. Tony said something about being sorry he couldn't be of more help, and she thanked him vaguely and left.

It was too much, another thing to think about, to set up, to marshal barely willing people into doing something that was so *obviously* important. Or maybe not . . . who, after all, gave a shit? Women got raped? Hey, baby, might as well relax and enjoy it, right? If somebody was going around town grabbing middle-class white guys and pulling their pants off and fucking them up the ass, *then* there'd be priority. The fucking cops would work on nothing else for a year! Thinking these and similar thoughts, Marlene stomped off to meet her lover, boss, and fiancé, Butch Karp.

Horace Jordan, the pimp, called Slo Mo by his many friends, was not hard to find. Pimps are public figures. They must see and be seen, show their flash on the street, monitor and discipline their whores, and recruit new ones. The King Cole Trio found him at just past eleven that night, on the Deuce, the strip of 42nd Street between Sixth and Eighth avenues that is New York's semiofficial sex, drug, and mugging emporium, standing under a sex-show marquee, talking with a black woman in tiny vinyl shorts and a pink bra.

The conversation must have been gripping, because Slo Mo did not notice Jeffers and Maus until they had grabbed him, each by an elbow, and were carry-dragging him out to the curb, with the tips of his white Guccis just bobbing along the concrete.

Without a word spoken, the two detectives threw him up against their unmarked Plymouth, patted him down, and emptied his pockets. "Hey," Slo Mo said mildly, "what the fuck's happening, man? I got no beef with you guys." Jeffers opened the rear door of the car and tossed Slo Mo in like a bag of laundry.

Art Dugman was sitting in the back seat of the car. Jeffers settled his huge form on the other side of Slo Mo and Maus drove off.

"Hey, wha' you doin', man? Wha' the fuck's

goin' down? Hey . . ." said the pimp, to no response. After a while, he shut down, adjusted his gold chains and his lavender do rag, and waited philosophically for what might happen. Maus drove west on 42nd, south on Eleventh Avenue to West Street, where he pulled into an alley between two deserted warehouses.

Dugman flicked on the dome light. "What do we got?" he asked Maus. Maus said, "A switchblade knife, a vial of a suspicious-looking white powder, keys, a roll of ill-gotten gains, looks like eight, nine hundred. It's enough."

Slo Mo said, "What you talkin' about 'enough'? You ain't got shit on me! Hey, what you doin'?"

Jeffers had opened the door of the car and yanked the pimp out. He threw him against the alley wall. Maus followed them out. "Fuck this shit, man!" shouted Slo Mo. "Po-lice brutality. I wanna see my lawyer!"

Jeffers spread his legs and stood in front of the pimp and hooked his thumbs in his belt, revealing his service revolver where it rested in its holster on his left hip. Slo Mo saw the gun and seemed to register his situation for the first time. His thin tan face turned ashy gray and his knees sagged. "No, man, I ain't no dealer, man. Shit, I just got that stuff for the girls, man. I never . . . I never . . . oh, Jesus, fuckin' shit . . . not me, man."

Jeffers said, "You got a girl for Larue Clarry last night."

Slo Mo looked at him blankly, his teeth set in a grimace of terror. Jeffers could see several gold teeth, one set with a small diamond, glittering in the faint light from the car lamp. He repeated the question. This time Slo Mo seemed overjoyed to answer. "Clarry, yeah, yeah, Haze . . . he like Haze."

"You sent Haze up to him last night."

"Yeah."

"What does she look like?

Slo Mo had recovered some of his initial cool. He straightened himself and said, "What she look like? What you think, man? She look like a damn ho."

"Redhead?"

"Yeah, curly hair, short, little tits, nice ass. Wear that purple lipstick. Got real white skin."

"How old?"

"Fuck I know, man. Old enough to fuck."

"Sixteen? Fifteen?"

"Yo, aroun that. She fresh, whatever."

"Where is she now?"

"What you want with her? You homicides. She ain't killed no one. What, they bust you down to vice now?"

Jeffers reached out and grabbed a handful of the gold chains that looped around the pimp's neck and lifted him a half-inch clear of the ground. "Where she at, scumbag?" he asked softly.

The pimp made a strangled reply, the address of a hotel on Eighth Avenue. Jeffers let go; the pimp staggered and fell against the alley wall. Maus got out of the car, took the switchblade out of his pocket, snapped the blade off and threw it away, crushed the glass vial of cocaine under his heel, dropped the ring of keys, pulled the rubber band off the roll of bills and tossed them into a puddle of greasy water. The two detectives entered their car. Dugman flicked the dome off and they drove off, leaving Slo Mo scrabbling in the alley after his drifting loot.

"That was real cruel, Maus," said Dugman.

"That's our motto, Dr. D.," Maus replied. "Cruel, but fair. Shit, that little mutt was scared, wasn't he, Mack? What the fuck did you say to him?"

Jeffers shrugged. "Didn't say shit. He just started whining that he wasn't no dealer. But you're right, I thought he was gonna wet his drawers."

Maus laughed. "Must have a guilty conscience, I can't figure why. Where to, Mack?"

Jeffers gave them the address. But the wretched little room, when they arrived, was empty. Back in the car, Dugman said, "OK, let's knock off for tonight. We'll pick her up—she ain't gonna go off to college. Circulate the description and get the word out we want her."

They drove north, talking little, listening to the calls on the police radio. In the rear seat, Art Dugman sat thinking about why a tough little pimp like Slo Mo should have been so frightened of two police detectives, and why he should have been so desperate to convince them that he was not a drug dealer.

Karp was not, to Marlene's no great surprise, in his office (his "palatial office," as she always referred to it). He never was, if he could avoid it. To Karp, the office meant paper, and irritating phone calls from upstairs, and the attentions of those few of his staff who still thought that hanging around Karp and flattering him was the way to get ahead in the D.A.'s office. In fact, the opposite was more nearly true.

When Marlene asked Connie Trask where Karp was, she shrugged helplessly and rolled her eyes. Marlene knew that Karp was not in court, because it was already late afternoon, past the time when tradition declared that the judges of the city should be in their sedans on the way to the suburbs.

Marlene did not feel up to chasing Karp through the warrens of the bureau's staff, one of his favorite haunts. Instead, she took the elevator down to the main floor of the Criminal Courts Building, where she knew he would eventually show up. And it was a place where she could probably catch up with some of her own business.

This zone was known to the inhabitants of the criminal justice system as the Streets of Calcutta. Even this late in the day, the corridor was crowded with the human material of justice: the accused, their defendants and prosecutors, the victims, the witnesses, friends and families of all of these, plus wandering cops and the various officers of court. Besides these the long hallway held a changing group of people for whom the courthouse represented a source of free entertainment and a refuge from the street: bag ladies, defectives, zanies, homeless families, retired lawyers, bureaucrats on the coop.

In this medieval atmosphere was accomplished much of the real business of the building, the actual courts being used largely as a form of record-keeping. Since most of the people arrested for criminal offenses in New York are indigent and since the immense majority of such offenses are disposed of without trial, criminal justice in New York County is largely a business of conversations between assistant district attorneys and the men and women of the Legal Aid Society, who act as public defenders in the city's courts.

These people met throughout the day in the corridors and offices of Centre Street, which they made into a continuous legal bazaar. Things were especially bazaarish toward the end of the day, when the overworked representatives of both the accused and the People attempted to dump whatever they could of the next day's business before the resumption of court in the morning, and the new intake of cases from the coming night's criminal escapades.

Marlene bought a cardboard cup of coffee

from the snack bar and opened her stand in the hallway just outside its steamy portal. Word got around; Legal Aids with cases for which she was designated prosecutor found her and made their offers, which Marlene either accepted or rejected. Within broad limits, the rest of the ponderous system would support her in these decisions. The Legal Aids understood that too. Those who played hard-ass for their clients would be brought up short by their own management, who just as much as the ADA's had to stay on the good side of the judges, who insisted above all else on the expeditious clearing of their calendars.

So Marlene flipped through the case files with practiced speed, looking for the decisive detail. Was there serious violence, was this the second or the thirty-second arrest, did the cops seriously want the guy off the street, was the guy in jail, and for how long?

Here was a kid, ripped off a tourist's gold chain in front of Grand Central, arrested, in Rikers Island for six weeks. The tourist was back in Missouri. OK, go for a six-months-sus-pended, the weeks in Rikers were enough. Thus spake Marlene, playing judge and jury with the authority and aplomb of an Ottoman pasha.

After an hour or so, the crowd thinned out. Marlene stepped into the main hallway. One of the advantages of having an enormous boy-friend, Marlene reflected, was that you could spot him at a mile: he was, in fact, standing at the opposite end of the block-long hallway. She waved to him, but he was locked in a Mutt-and-Jeff tableau with a short portly man in a pin-striped suit.

As she approached, she heard Karp say, "In that case, I guess I'll see you in court, Mr. Simoney." The man opened his mouth to say something, thought better of it, nodded curtly, and stalked away.

As Marlene walked up, she was struck once again by the haggardness of Karp's face, like that of a fighter about to lose a fifteen-round decision. There were circles under his eyes that hadn't been there a few years ago, and lines carving down from the high cheekbones. He was looking Lincolnesque, in a Jewish sort of way. The pile of her own crap that she was about to lay on him drifted away, and she put on a happy face.

Karp brightened when he saw her. "Hi, cutie," he said. "Having a nice day?"

"Assistant D.A.'s never have a nice day, as you well know," replied Marlene grumpily. "I see you made Simoney mad again. He ran away without even saying hello, and he's one of my favorite slime molds."

"He's the defense for Lattimore."

"The pusher who shot his partner? Is there a problem? I thought you had a good confession."

"We do," said Karp. "But while he was resisting arrest the cops bopped him a couple on the head. He came to, the cops were there, read him his rights, and he voluntarily confessed. Good procedure for a change. Simoney is now claiming the confession was offered when Lattimore was not in his right mind due to the severe beating he got. He's waving Jackson-Denno at me."

"I thought the decision in Jackson was based on coercion—the guy was in pain, the cops wouldn't give him water—like that."

"Yeah, it's horseshit legally, but I still don't love taking it to a jury. It's too easy for the defense to make the case be about the injuries at the time of arrest and the validity of the confession, not about the murder. Also, I don't have a good witness, the physical evidence is ambiguous, the vic was a scumbag . . . what I have is a confession with a cloud. Another 'he did it, but . . .' "

"So you'll cop him?"

"Maybe. I don't know. I can't think about it right now. Harris told me, by the way, that we just passed eight hundred homicides this year, and it's only June. We're gonna set another record."

"Calls for a celebration."

Karp grinned and rubbed his face. "Yeah, how about a good meal, a hot bath, a back rub, and a terrific piece of ass?"

Marlene twitched her eyebrows. "Sounds great! Why don't you go out and get all that, and I'll meet you back at my place for a hand of rummy."

Karp laughed. "Fuck you, Ciampi."

She twined her arm through his. "Actually," she said, "you took the words right out of my mouth."

FOUR

The bar and dance hall known as Adam's occupied a large brick-built, iron-fronted former warehouse at the foot of West Houston Street off Seventh Avenue. For the first hundred years of its existence it had stored the spices of the gorgeous East; on damp days the wooden floors still gave off a pale redolence of cinnamon and cloves. More recently, with the emergence of the district below Houston Street as a residential and artistic center, it had shifted to commodities that were only figuratively spicy: sex, romance, adventure, driven by flashing lights, the beat of the music of the moment—disco, salsa, punk, metal—and the availability of drugs.

The establishment was one huge high-ceilinged room painted black and equipped with a stage for live acts, a raised platform supplied with chairs and small tables, a long bar and, at the center, a dance floor. Between the bar and the tables was a long narrow zone which, by custom, was occupied by masses of people of both sexes moving slowly to the music, drinks in hand. These announced by their presence in this zone their availability for an approach by a member of the opposite sex. The demographics of New York in this era dictated that most of the people in the meat market of Adam's would be women.

The rapist sat on a bar stool and allowed the parade to circulate slowly beneath his gaze. The image of a hawk sitting on a tree limb, waiting for the rabbits to venture within range was one that had occurred to him, and despite its triteness, it still amused. Choosing his victim in this way filled him with delicious feelings of power and was quite the most amusing part of his whole enterprise. Adam's was not his only haunt. He had been away from it for some time, making the broad circuit of the city's singles bars, and was pleasantly surprised by the richness of the night's pickings.

He had particular standards. No cows, for one thing; no fleshy, smothering, maternal women. He liked small, compact women, women who looked like they could be tossed around by a man of moderate size. And no blonds. Blonds were dumb, he believed, and so many of them were phony. He thought hair dyeing was just that kind of disgusting treachery that was so typical of women in general, and which tended to justify anything he might care to do to them.

So he was looking for small, dark, and lithe—and something else. There had to be a certain look, a high carriage, an aloofness. Anything

that appeared to say "I'm too good for you"—
or what he called privately the my-shit-doesn't-
stink look—was intensely attractive to him. He
realized that it was comparatively rare in the
singles bars he hunted. He often cruised the
campuses of the city's many colleges, and the
theaters and museums, where women of this
type were apt to be found in greater concentra-
tions, feeding his fantasies, exciting himself almost beyond endurance.

Yet he never approached any of these women
in such places. Like a forest predator, he was
uneasy away from his territory, where, sitting
on his bar stool, he was in control. The women
he desired were perhaps uncommon in this
ambit, since what he liked, his true *meat*, was
that sense of social competence, of inviolability
and pride, that would typically lead a woman
to avoid a place like Adam's.

But there were always a few. And he was
patient. A disturbance on the periphery of the
meat market attracted his attention. A woman
was telling off a short, squat man with a monkey face and greasy black hair. The guy was
trying to calm her down, but she was blowing
him away. The rapist couldn't hear the exact
words she was using, but her expression, and
his expression, and her tone of voice attested
adequately to the force of her invective. The
squat man threw up his hands, said something
nasty, and disappeared into the crowd. The
woman turned back to her drink at the bar.

The rapist studied the woman with growing

interest and excitement. She was wearing a sleeveless jersey dress in some silvery shade, which showed off the slenderness of her back and her lean arms. He could see the delicate bones of her cervical vertebrae through the cloth and above it, under her short dark hair.

Her hair was glossy and reflected the strobe lights from the dance floor. There was an empty space at the bar next to her, and he went over and stood in it. He ordered a drink. She pulled a cigarette out of her purse and he snapped a lighter under it. Their eyes met as she puffed, and he smiled his most harmless smile and said, "That was quite a performance. You really scorched that guy."

She snorted. "Yeah, the asshole! My girl-friend talked me into coming here. What a pit!"

"Yeah," he agreed, "I never come here either. I was supposed to meet somebody here, but she never showed. You're right, it's a slime joint. Amazing, in a way—all these supposedly civilized young adults. Get them in a place like this and they turn into cavemen. And women."

"And women, right. I should know. I haven't screamed at anyone like that in years." She looked at him with more interest. She saw an ordinary but not unpleasant face: dark eyes, a good tan, a long bumpy nose, dark hair growing low on the forehead and swept back in an old-fashioned ducktail. He wore a nice silk cable-knit over an open white oxford shirt, tan slacks, and tasseled loafers without socks.

"It looked OK to me," he said. "The slob was probably asking for it."

On the basis of sympathy thus established, the two of them exchanged names and talked congenially for twenty minutes, about how unlike the unhappy people in this bar they both were, about their jobs, their likes (her: Jamaica; him: underwater photography) and dislikes (her: the arrogant; him: the phony), their apartments, how they were both Italian, how rotten the city was to live in.

Much of what she told him was true. She was a naturally frank person and was attracted in a cautious way to this well-built, good-looking young man, who seemed mannerly, open, and pleasant. Nice eyes, she thought. Well-dressed. No gold chains, seems smart.

Everything he had told her about himself was a lie.

She waited for him to make his move, but here she was surprised, and, she had to admit, disappointed. He looked at his watch and gulped the remains of his gin and tonic. "Damn, I've got to go to work."

"This late?"

He stood up and smiled ruefully. "Yeah, like I said, I'm a film editor at ABC. If you want to see film on *Good Morning America* tomorrow, I've got to run."

"Well, it was nice talking to you," she said.

"Yeah . . ." He paused, shuffled his feet shyly. "I was wondering—maybe we could get together sometime. I'll buy you some spaghetti."

She laughed. "Anything but," she said, and gave him her number.

The girl lay curled up on the front seat of the car, a white '68 Pontiac, leaning against the door, her left hand drawn protectively up to her face. Except for the blood and the smell, she might have been sleeping next to Daddy on a long car trip.

"When did you find her?" Art Dugman asked the patrol officer.

"About seven-thirty this morning," the young cop replied. "A trucker spotted the car when he came in to make a delivery and called it in. When we got here, we saw it was the girl in your citywide, and we called you."

The killer had stashed his car on one of the short streets that lead to the Hudson River just south of the Thirtieth Street Terminal. There were truckers all around, standing impatiently beside their rigs, barred from the loading docks by the police vehicles and the portable barriers that had been set up around the crime scene. The crime-scene-unit people were poking through the car, taking photographs, and collecting anything that looked like evidence. Dugman doubted they would find much.

After speaking briefly to the medical examiner at the scene, he walked back to his own car. Maus was in the front seat, talking to someone on the police radio. He hung up the receiver and said, "The car's stolen. Belongs to a Hector Baldwin, lives up on St. Nick. He parked it at six-thirty last night and missed it when he wanted to go to work this morning. What's it look like?"

Dugman leaned against the car and chewed his lip. What did it look like? From one angle, another dead whore down by the docks. Not that unusual. Whores went into cars all the time, worked in cars. There was an extensive trade in quick hose jobs for businessmen on the way home. Sometimes they got unlucky, got picked up by a john whose particular fancy was not on any girl's menu.

"You think it was Slo Mo?" Maus asked.

Dugman looked up. "No. Slo Mo didn't have no cause to kill this girl, and if he did, he wouldn't have stole no car in Harlem to shoot her in."

"So what, then? A perv? Robbery?"

"Possible, but I don't think so. There's something too clean about it. Girl was shot in the head point-blank with a small-caliber weapon. She's fully dressed, or as dressed as she ever got, with no real obvious marks on her besides the shot to the head. It don't sing perv, do it?"

Maus shrugged. "The fuck should I know? I'm not a perv. The robbery angle any better?"

Dugman shook his head. "It sucks too. Her bag's missing, yeah, but I been trying to think of another case where a guy robbed a whore, killed her, and left her in the car. It doesn't figure. Why not dump her and drive away? It also means he needs another car. What's he gonna do, walk back from the river at night? Call a cab?"

Maus considered these questions for a moment. He knew Dugman had already figured it out, was waiting for Maus to catch up. Dugman always did this, would always diddle with him like that. Maus didn't mind playing the straight man. Maus thought Dugman was the best detective in the city, and understood that this was part of his own education. Playing the honky fool was the tuition.

Maus said slowly, "You're saying like maybe it was a . . . a hit—not just any whore, but *this* one, because . . . because we wanted to talk to her on the other thing?"

Dugman's pouchy face broke into a broad smile. "Yeah! That's thinking, Maus!" He poked his head into the back of the car, where Jeffers sat calmly reading the *News.* "You hear that, Mack? I told you we get a white boy on the squad, we start solvin' some *crime!*"

Jeffers looked up from his paper. "He can't dance, though."

"I can too!" said Maus indignantly.

"Shit, you can," responded Jeffers. "It took me six months to teach you to clap on the off beat."

Dugman raised his hands, palms out. "Brothers," he said, his voice assuming orotund tones, "this is not a time to be confusin' our-selves with racial disharmony, discord, and dissensions. Rather, it is a time to rededicate and remotivate our own selves to the cause."

Jeffers said, "Hear him tell it!"

Maus said, "Yes, Lord!"

Dugman climbed into the car and slammed the door. "And what is our cause, brothers?"

"Say it out!" said Jeffers.

"Let us hear it!" said Maus.

"It is to investigate and invigilate. It is to detect and suspect. It is to bring to the bar of justice lowlife motherfuckers of every description, but especially the lowlife motherfucker responsible for the heinous crime which we got before us now."

"That the truth!" said Jeffers.

"Hear his word!" said Maus.

"Because he has not only done fuck' with the citizens; because he has not only done fuck' with the *po*-lice; but he done have the temerity to fuck with the *Trio*, and therefo' he has fuck' with the *wrong dudes*! Mr. Driver, take us to the Deuce!"

"A-men!" said Maus, and cranked the engine to a roar.

"I wasn't going to come in," said the dark young woman to Marlene Ciampi. "I figured, what the hell, I was stupid, I learned my lesson. Looking for Mr. Goodbar, and all that, I figured I was lucky not to be dead. But, like, I couldn't just leave it. I started jumping at shadows, being nervous on the street. My sleep is shot. I can't work.

"So I went to the cops. It turns out, if you don't go right away, you might as well not go at all, because you washed the evidence away and also they figure if you waited days, how bad could it be? But they gave me your name down at the precinct, so I figured it was worth a shot and, so . . ."

Her voiced trailed off. Marlene looked at the card she was filling out. Name: JoAnne Caputo, West Village address, worked at NYU, age twenty-six, date of incident, description of assailant. JoAnne had been explaining, without being asked, why she had delayed a week before reporting the rape. It was a familiar reaction, and one that added an additional burden to the prosecution of such cases.

Marlene said, "OK, Ms. Caputo, what I want you to do now is tell me about the incident in as much detail as you can remember."

Caputo took a deep breath. "The incident . . . OK. I met this guy two weeks ago this coming Saturday, June 10, in a bar called Adam's. It's in SoHo, I don't know the exact address . . ."

"That's OK, I know it."

"He seemed OK—calm, decent; said his name was Bob Graziano. Didn't put any heavy moves on me. I gave him my number.

"He called me a couple of days later, nice conversation, asked me for a date for the next Saturday, the seventeenth, for dinner and a show. I said OK.

"He showed up around eight. I ask him in,

offer him a drink. Right away I notice something different about him—he's more nervous, more agitated. I sat down on my couch, he's still pacing back and forth, rattling ice cubes. So I get up and say something about shouldn't we be going, and he grabs me.

"I thought it was a joke for a second there, like he was parodying a horny guy. But then he started really mauling me, squeezing my breasts, and trying to grab my crotch. I managed to push him away. But when I saw his face was when I really got scared.

"I said to myself, 'JoAnne, you have really done it this time.' I began shouting at him, that he was an asshole, that I wanted him out of there right now, and like that. That's when he pulled out the knife."

"Describe it, please."

"A regular knife, like a kitchen carving knife."

"Not a hunting knife or a switchblade?"

"No, I don't think so. A regular carving knife, about eight or ten inches long, and shiny."

"All right, go ahead. What happened then? And please try to remember his exact words, if you can."

Caputo's voice became lower and more strained. "He told me to take my clothes off. 'Strip, cunt! Now!' is what he said. 'I want to see that precious cunt!' I said, 'Please don't hurt me.' And he said, I forget what, something about don't make me angry, and I'll do anything I want to you—he got real crazy then, so I started taking my clothes off.

"When I was naked, he told me to sit on the couch and keep my mouth shut. He couldn't stand women running off at the mouth, he said. Cunt bullshit, he called it. Then he picked my panty hose up and sort of played with it for a minute, rubbing it on his face. I'm thinking, this is a real fruitcake, all the time I was sitting there frozen, part of my mind was clear as a bell, observing it, looking for a way to make a break.

"Then he came over and wrapped the panty hose around my head, the seat part, and knotted the legs around my neck, tight, but not enough to cut off the air. Just to hold them on. I thought, this is it, he's going to strangle me.

"But he backed away and said, 'Spread your legs and show me your cunt! Wider, wider! So I did. He made me pull my knees way up. Then he must have bent over, because the next thing I felt was the knife poking around down there, between my legs."

"Did he cut you?" Marlene asked as calmly as she could.

"No, he just poked around the . . . area, just hard enough not to break the skin. Look, could I have a drink of water? Talking about this, my throat is clamping up."

Marlene poured a paper cup of water from the carafe on her desk. After the woman had drunk it down, she continued.

"While he was doing this he was insulting

and threatening me, like saying stuff like, 'I should cut it out, bitch,' and 'I ought to fuck you with this, you whore.' He was really working himself up. I was concentrating on not wetting myself, that's how scared I was.

"Then he raped me. It hurt like crazy but at least it was over fast. He lasted about eight seconds. Then he stood up and grabbed my head and rubbed his genitals on the panty hose. That was it. He left."

"He didn't say anything as he left?"

"He might have. I can't remember."

"I don't guess you kept the panty hose."

"No, that was a dumb move, I realize it now. But I wasn't thinking of that at the moment. I buried them in the trash and took a shower for about an hour and a half. And then took a bunch of Valium. Which was another dumb move. I should have just gone down to the emergency room and had them take a sample. Now I know, but I, um . . . but I'd never been raped before."

Caputo sat silently for a moment, taking deep breaths. Tears oozed slowly from her eyes and rolled down her cheeks. Marlene passed her a box of tissues, without comment. She completed her card and resisted the temptation to glance at her watch; she was due in court in a few minutes, but something was nagging at her mind and she didn't want to let it go.

She slid one of her shoeboxes across the desk. What was that woman's name? Feldman?

Rosenberg? She started shuffling through the files, muttering and cursing quietly.

"What are you doing?" asked JoAnne Caputo.

"Oh, sorry. It just occurred to me that your rapist may have done it before—that trick with the panty hose. I had a woman in here a couple of weeks ago with a similar story, but I'm ashamed to say I've forgotten her name. I have them filed by name, and there are over two thousand."

Caputo leaned forward. "You don't have them cross-indexed?"

Marlene shook her head. "No, see, this is strictly amateur hour. It's a shoebox with cards. I've been trying to get some better analysis, but there's all kinds of problems . . ." Now Marlene did look at her watch. Almost out of time.

"Let me see the card," said Caputo.

Marlene passed it across the desk and Caputo read both sides. "I see the problem. A lot of the key information is in text fields—what he said, what he did. You'd have to input the whole field as text and then do a string search subroutine to pull matches out. SPSS could handle it, or you could write a little Fortran program."

"You *know* about this stuff?" Marlene asked hopefully.

"It's what I do. I told you I worked at NYU. I'm in social stat."

"I'm afraid to ask," said Marlene. "Would it be possible . . . ?"

"Would it help to find that bastard?"

"Girl, it's about the only way there is."

"OK, give me the boxes. I'll start right away."

"You can *do* it? Just like that?"

"No," said Caputo, her face tightening. "I'll have to steal and lie and forge my boss's signature and do nothing else for the next week or so, but there's nothing much else I feel like doing anyway. I'll get back to you in a couple of days."

Pepper Soames's club, on the old part of 125th where it curves down to the river, was one of the last of the old-time Harlem jazz clubs. It was a relic of the days, thirty years past, when the audience for real jazz was small, hip, and almost entirely black, before stereo, heroin, integration, or rock and roll.

Art Dugman walked into Pepper's around midnight, took a table in the nearly empty room, ordered a J&B on the rocks, and watched his boss, Detective Lieutenant Clay Fulton, finish his set. Fulton was playing keyboard in a trio: a hotshot kid alto player and an elderly man on bass. Dugman thought they were pretty good, but he didn't know anything about jazz.

After they finished playing, Fulton came over to Dugman's table and sat down. He was holding a glass of what Dugman knew was club soda. Fulton didn't drink anymore.

Fulton said, "Why ain't you home, Dugman? Streets are dangerous this time of night."

"You said report to you. I'm reporting."

"So cop a squat, Jack. What's happening on the dealer murders?"

"Let me spin it out for you, just like we got it. See if you come up with the same bad thoughts I did."

"Bad thoughts?" said Fulton.

"Just listen up, Loo," said Dugman, and quickly recited what he and his team had learned since the night of Larue Clarry's murder: the details of the killing itself, the evidence from Clarry's apartment, their interrogation of Slo Mo, and the murder of what ought to have been their best witness, the prostitute Haze.

"Whores get killed all the time," said Fulton after a thoughtful pause.

"Yeah, but look here, we know who did it," said Dugman. Some of the girls on Haze's stroll saw Haze getting into a car with a black man about one-thirty this morning. The M.E. says she was killed between two and three the same morning. Nobody ever saw her alive again."

"You got a good make on the guy from that?"

"No, we had to shake the place up a little."

Fulton grunted. "Am I gonna have trouble on this?" Fulton understood what happened when the King Cole Trio shook the place up a little. People came flying headfirst out of shooting galleries. People found themselves hanging by their ankles from rooftop parapets. TV sets fell from windows. Normal trade shut down at the public drug markets and the places where stolen goods changed hands. The underworld got sick, heaved its belly, and spewed forth a sacrifice.

"No trouble," said Dugman, "we just hustled the mutts. Anyhow, a junkie name of Laxton shook out. Says he saw the whole thing."

"He saw the whore get it?"

"Shit, no! He saw Clarry get it. The fuck I care about some whore—he saw the guy did *Clarry,* and if you right about this, the guy that did all the dealers. And the whore."

"This Laxton witness the actual killing?"

"No, what he saw was Clarry's car pull up under the highway, and the guy get out, go in the back of the car for a minute, and get out again and walk away. Laxton was nodding off in a pile of trash. He jumped when he saw the guy, made some noise, and the guy spooked and got small real fast. That's probably why he left the piece on the seat of the car."

"So did he see the guy close enough to put him on the mug books?"

Dugman smiled. "No need. He made the guy right there. He knew him from way back."

"Who was it?" asked Fulton, taking a sip of his drink.

"Name's Tecumseh Booth."

Fulton let loose a great snorting laugh, spraying soda from his mouth over the table. When he had stopped coughing, he wiped his face with a cocktail napkin and said, "God damn!

You got to be shittin' me, man. *Tecumseh?* I know Tecumseh Booth. I sent him up for armed robbery a couple of years back. He's a lot of things, but he ain't no hit man."

"Maybe he changed professions," Dugman said carefully.

"Uh-uh. Not likely. Tecumseh will hold your horse while you ace somebody. He might drive you away from the scene. But he never shot nobody in his life. Never even carried heat, that I know of."

"He was there," said Dugman.

"Yeah, could of been. Go ahead and pick him up if you want, but he won't tell you shit."

"He won't?"

"He didn't tell me shit when I picked him up, back when. Three guys shot up a liquor store, and Booth was the wheel on the job. The other mutts got loose and Booth took the fall—eight years, I recall it was. Never said shit. Boy can hold his mud, I'll say that for him."

Dugman pushed back from the table. "We'll see about that."

Fulton frowned. "Art, no roughing. I know it's Harlem, but times has changed, you dig?"

"Yeah," said Dugman, standing up. "They sure has. Teddy Wilson used to play this room. Catch you later, Loo."

Outside, Dugman cursed himself for a short-tempered fool. He knew Fulton was good—a smart and competent detective. Yet Dugman could not help harboring resentment for the other man's success, for his rocketing rise through the ranks. Fulton was the first college-educated black detective lieutenant in the history of the NYPD. If the paddies downtown ever let a brother in as chief of detectives, it would be Fulton.

No, it was not precisely resentment; it was anger at what his own life had been, a grinding rise through the ranks, nearly ten years in a blue bag before they gave him his gold tin. Now he was taking orders from a man ten years his junior.

At some level, he wanted Fulton to acknowledge that, to honor him for it, at least to credit him with some smarts. He didn't deserve a laugh in the face and a nagging about questioning suspects.

He got in his car and drove fast across town. He realized that he had not conveyed to Fulton the three points he had wanted to bring out about the rash of dope-dealer killings. What had puzzled him from the outset was the lack of resistance on the part of the victims. Not one of these people had been shot down in a hail of lead. At least one of them had opened his door to his assailant. The killings had been done almost at the leisure of the murderers, and against a group of men who were typically suspicious to the point of paranoia, well-guarded and well-armed.

The second point was what Slo Mo had said when Mack braced him against the wall in that alley. The pimp knew Mack was a cop. Why had he been so frightened, and why did he so urgently want to make it clear that he didn't sell dope?

The third point was the clincher to Dugman. They had dropped Slo Mo in the alley at a quarter to twelve. They had called in the pickup request on the prostitute Haze about twenty minutes later. Within the next hour somebody had picked her off her stroll, taken her down to the docks, and put a bullet in her head.

It was indeed a bad thought, almost too heavy to hold by himself, and Dugman briefly considered turning his car around, driving back to Pepper's, and laying the burden on his superior. But something made him stop. Would Fulton laugh at him again? He didn't need that! No, the better move was to nail it down, to pick up Tecumseh Booth and make him talk, to make him reveal that the cool and casual murderer they were hunting was a cop.

FIVE

Sugar Hill had fallen some from what it had been thirty years earlier, but it was still a pretty nice neighborhood, for Harlem. The apartment occupied by Tecumseh Booth was located in a still-handsome tan brick building on 149th off St. Nicholas Avenue. The class of the area was demonstrated by the brass mailboxes in the lobby, which had retained their doors, locks, and polish. Detective Jeffers read the name of Tecumseh Booth's girlfriend from one of them, and headed up to the third-floor apartment with Maus.

The two detectives drew their pistols and clipped their police identification to their breast pockets. Jeffers was about to knock on the door, but Maus stopped him and placed his ear against the door. It was the kind of hollow metal fire door that was good at transmitting certain sounds.

"Hear anything?" asked Jeffers.

"Yeah," answered the other. "Music. Earth, Wind, and Fire, I think. And a banging sound. And a kind of squealing. Maybe he's beating a dog to death with a stereo."

Jeffers placed his massive head against the door and listened. He smiled. "I think what you hearing there is Tecumseh on the job."

Maus raised his brows and pressed his ear more tightly to the door. "You think so? Making a lot of noise, ain't he?"

"You think that 'cause you unfamiliar with the sexual habits of my people. Being naturally more attune to the physical propensities of life, we get more juice out of the berry, so to speak, in the way of hump. Therefore the noises of ecstasy which we hearin now."

"Yeah, you keep telling me that, but I got to take your word for it, since I notice you haven't fixed me up with any of your sisters yet."

Jeffers laughed softly. "You not ready for that, boy. I got to bring you along slow, got to pace you."

Maus said, "I appreciate that, Mack, I do, and meanwhile I'm working hard to overcome my objection to miscegenation. Meanwhile, what the fuck are we doing here? I'm getting horny listening to this shit."

"My plan, little man, is to wait until Tecumseh have pop his rocks and then we gonna swoop him up while he lie in the sweet afterglow. Besides, he ain't gonna be getting none of that for a long time where he goin. It's my act of Christian charity for the month."

They waited in the hall until the sounds stopped. Then Jeffers pounded mightily on the door and shouted, "Open up! Police!" He pressed his ear to the door again.

"Are they coming?" asked Maus.

"So to speak? No, I hear escapin noise. I think he's goin out the window."

"You going to take the door down?"

"Don't be funny, son. This a steel door. I go through a door like this, they better have my momma's ass on fire on the other side. No, we just gonna go downstairs again. Tecumseh ain't goin nowhere."

And indeed, when they arrived back on the street, they found Tecumseh Booth facedown on the ground, dressed only in a pair of slacks, with his hands cuffed behind him. Art Dugman had picked him up easily as he dropped from the fire escape.

Jeffers stooped and jerked Booth to his feet with a single yank on the handcuff chain. Booth yelped sharply and said, "Hey, what the fuck you want with me? I ain done nothin!"

Jeffers popped the rear door of the Plymouth open and threw the prisoner in. He got in himself and Dugman went around to the other side. Maus drove the car south toward the Twenty-eighth Precinct.

Booth sat between them calmly with his hands cuffed behind his back, waiting. He had learned, from a lifetime of arrests, the wisdom of the sages, that silence was the ideal state of being. He had also learned that cops made mistakes, and that in some mysterious way these mistakes had the power to cancel guilt, so that you could walk away from a crime that the cops and kids on the street and old ladies knew you had done, and they couldn't do shit to you. This had happened to him a number of times. The main thing was to shut up.

Booth became aware that the two cops on either side of him were staring at him. He looked straight ahead. After a while the older one said, "Turn off here."

The driver swung left, heading toward the blackness of Colonial Park. He stopped the car in the dark of a big tree.

The older cop said, "Look at his head. It's the perfect shape."

"Don't start that again!" the big cop said nervously.

"I'm telling you, it'll work this time," said the older detective. Booth felt the older cop's body shift, and looked to see why. He had drawn out his pistol.

The driver turned around in the front seat. "Damn it, not in the damn car! The last time it took me three hours to clean all the blood and crap off of the upholstery. You want to play games, do it outside!"

Booth felt a cold touch at his right ear. His head jerked away by reflex, only to be stopped by a similar but harder pressure on the other ear. The big cop said, "Boss, I sure hope you know what you doin. You say this really works?"

"I know it," affirmed the older cop. "Now, just get it stuck in there solid, and don't be twitchin like you done last time."

Booth now could not move his head. He understood why. He had the muzzle of a .38-caliber revolver stuck firmly in each ear.

"Hey," he said. "Hey, what . . . ?"

The driver leaned over the front seat and addressed him conversationally. "See, what *he* says, is if you do this just right, the two bullets will meet in the middle and cancel out. The same slug, the same load, same gun, understand. It's like physics. *I* happen to think it's horseshit, myself, but try and tell *him* anything!"

Booth's face twisted in a ghastly smile. "You shittin me, man. They can't do that. They's cops, they can't . . ."

The smile faded and Booth's jaw went slack, as if something more frightening than having a pistol in each ear had just occurred to him. A trickle of sweat fell into his eye. The older cop caught the change in expression.

"Say what? What can't cops do, brother?" Dugman asked.

Booth opened a dry mouth as if to say something, then shut it.

The cop in the front seat began to talk again, in the same tone of calm explanation. "Yeah, see, we know you killed Clarry, and we know there was cops involved. Now, ordinarily we would take you in, book you, and question you. We would figure, maybe we can make a deal—you give us the guy, we put in a good word with the D.A., and so on.

"But the word is, you don't deal. You're a stand-up dude. Fine. The problem is, we really need this guy. So we figured, you're no good to us on that, the best thing we could do is, maybe if we ace you out, your guy will—I dunno—get a hair up his ass. Do something dumb. Maybe he'll think we're in the same business, and he'll come after us. Or whatever. I mean it's pretty thin at this point, but I don't see the percentage in doing anything else, if you catch my drift—"

The older cop broke in, "That's enough. God damn, man, you ain't got to ask his fuckin permission!" He addressed the big cop on the other side of Booth. "OK, we gonna do it now."

"Just a second, lemme shift around here. Is this gonna fuck up my suit?"

"Not if you do it right. You lined up good?"

"Yeah, I guess."

"OK, squeeze off on the count of three," said the older cop.

"Um, hold it . . . you mean, right *on* three, or just after? Like, one-two-*bang*? Or one-two-three-*bang*?"

The older cop sounded exasperated. "Damn! I told you before; take up all the slack, then let go as soon as I say 'three'!"

Booth could hear surprisingly well, considering that his ears were full of gun. He understood the explanation given by the man in the front seat, and even sympathized with it, as much as he could, considering his position. He would have used the same reasoning himself. He heard the count, as from a great distance.

Closer, more intimately, he heard the whisper of the revolver mechanisms as they brought the new bullets around to be fired. He seemed separated from his trembling body, floating above his own head. He heard the cop say "three" and, a pulse-beat later, the tiny *snicks* as the mechanisms released their hammers.

The hammers took a long time to fall. By the time they did, Booth was already far away.

"I don't think he believed us," said Maus, looking down at Booth's flaccid body.

"He ain't dead, is he?" asked Mack. Booth's head was resting on his knee.

Dugman reached out and touched Booth's neck. "Naw, he just fainted. God damn! He let go his business too!" Dugman flung open his door and stepped out onto the sidewalk. In another second, Mack cursed and did the same. They stood on either side of the car hooting and waving their hands past their faces.

"Say, Maus," said Dugman, "why don't you drive on down to the precinct and book the prisoner. Me and Mack got to do some detective work here on the street."

"Yo," said Mack. "We got to stay close to our people."

Maus rolled down his window. "Fuckin guys. I knew I was gonna have to clean the fuckin car again."

Marlene's bed sat on a high sleeping platform at one end of her loft, and from this vantage, at six-thirty on a workday morning, she watched the naked Karp drink water from her sink. He chugged a glass down, then filled another. Karp drank a lot of water, like a horse. It was the only healthy aspect of his diet, which consisted otherwise of junk food from cancer wagons and takeout windows—soggy pizza, elderly gray hot dogs, orange-colored knishes heavy as cinderblock, souvlaki oozing toxic oils, lukewarm eggrolls packed with substances mysterious as the East. Karp ate these in combinations and in quantities that would gag a wolverine, and washed it down with colorful, bubbled sugar-water.

Marlene had vaguely considered a campaign to change his diet into one that would enable him to survive into the coming decade. This was but one of the many such campaigns she had planned for after the Big Day. Karp, though a fountain of many virtues, could stand considerable improvement.

Once they learned about the baby, and Karp began to spend most of his time with Marlene, she had attempted to get her kitchen act together. She was a reasonably proficient cook, but like Karp, was no slave to the four basic food groups. Marlene subsisted largely on chocolate bars and yogurt.

Since she had started eating for two and began an effort to reform, Marlene had cooked a number of what she considered decent meals. Karp responded with enthusiasm, but he would have responded with equal enthusiasm to raw vulture, as long as there was enough of it.

More recently, she had been too exhausted to spend time in the kitchen, and on most evenings it seemed easier to take-out from one of the many grease joints, Italian, Chinese, or Greek, that perfumed the streets of lower Manhattan.

She watched Karp top off his tank and walk to the toilet. The diet hadn't affected his body yet, she thought approvingly. As large as he was, he was graceful and precise in motion, grounded and radiating contained power when at rest. The morning light flooding out through the big east windows of the loft lit up the hanging dust around his body like an aura.

The legs were long and smooth, the arms suspended from wide square shoulders down to those enormous hands, with their bony spatulate fingers. The scars—the Dr. Frankenstein mass of ladders from the knee operations and the smaller ragged ones in the shoulder where he had taken a couple of assassin's bullets—added somehow to the appeal. Scars: a real man!

What a nice butt he has, thought Marlene, scrooching around in the bed to get a better look. And how nice that he's retained that jockish habit of walking around naked all the time. How dull to be married to some lard-ass in a plaid robe. We like each other's asses, she mused; is that a really solid basis for a life relationship? Because although she knew his body nearly as well as she knew her own, her knowledge of what went on within that high and narrow skull remained vague and confused.

The light moved slowly across the floor of Marlene's loft. The big skylight in the center of its patterned tin ceiling was beginning to glow as well, like milk glass. The loft was one huge room, a hundred feet long by thirty-three, divided by portable screens into a living area, a kitchen, a dining area, and then the Limbo, a dusty zone occupied by athletic equipment—Karp's rowing machine, Marlene's body and speed bags—assorted junk, and the huge motors that ran the building's freight lift. Under the west windows, at the far end, Marlene had set up a little office, and about a hundred potted plants, ranging from African violets to giant ficus trees.

The place was entirely Marlene's creation, and waking up in it always gave her a little charge. The summer she had moved in she had taken on the herculean task of cleaning out the remnants of a defunct electroplater, heaving great tangles of wire and scrap down the freight shaft, scraping, sanding, painting, until it was as she wanted it, a great white, calm room, high above the street, flooded with light.

That summer, eight years ago, barely twenty-five people had lived full-time in the old industrial area south of Houston Street. Now they called it SoHo, the hottest property in New York. Recently a thin creature with black clothes and white hair had offered Marlene thirty thousand dollars for the key.

Marlene sighed and got out of bed, wrapped a frazzled pink blanket around her shoulders, and scooted down the ladder from the sleeping platform. She walked across the wide-planked white-painted floor, dropped the blanket, climbed four steps, and plunged into the hot water of the thousand-gallon hard rubber electroplating tank that served her as a bath.

Seated on the floor of this tank, perfumed water to her chin, she could not see over its rim. She heard the toilet flush, a door open, the sound of heavy naked steps toward the far end of the loft.

She stood up and began soaping her body and hair with almond liquid soap. She saw that Karp had pulled an old pair of sweatpants on. Now he sat down on his ancient rowing machine and began to pull at its wooden handles.

She watched the muscles in his back work as he pulled. He would row for exactly fifteen minutes, take a short wash in the tub, and be dressed and ready to leave ten minutes after that, impatiently pacing while he waited for her to complete her more complex preparations for the outside world. Then they would walk down the five splintery flights and the two grim industrial streets to the BMT subway at Prince and Broadway, or, if it were nice out and she felt up to it, they would hoof the distance, a little over a mile, to 100 Centre Street.

A routine. Marlene thought, ambivalently,

about it going on indefinitely, with, eventually, a stop at the day-care to drop off the kid. Or kids, as it might turn out. She looked down at her belly. Only a slight rise as yet; she could still see her mop of pubic curls. If her mother could be believed, she would carry high and small, like all the women in her family. And have an easy labor, to hear her grandmother tell it. According to her grandmother, her Uncle Marco had been born late one night with so little trouble that he barely woke her up.

An easy slide into a stable life. Something tugged in a different direction. Watching Karp work out, the dense muscles rolling under the glowing skin, a familiar feeling spread through her groin. Her fingers began soaping more deeply between her thighs than proper hygiene strictly required.

It's been a while, she thought. She could hide in the bath and then when Karp appeared for his dip, she could spring on him, soapy and hot, and they could spend a delicious morning messing around.

But no, that would require calling in to the office, and a massive rescheduling of appointments and appearances. She could seduce Karp from his duty, but he would be racked with guilt for days afterward, and take it out on her. Besides, the staff, being skilled investigators, would soon figure out what was going on, with both of them out for the morning, and so they would also have to put up with the leers of their coworkers, ace leerers all:

Uncle George and Aunti Mabel
Fainted at the breakfast table
This should serve sufficient warning
Never do it in the morning.

No, on second thought, better later. She rose
from the bath, thinking, I'm getting to be a horny
old lady. Not too surprising, since I was a horny
young lady too. Tonight, then, or earlier—maybe
I can inveigle him into my office. Hard and fast
on the desktop, amid the papers. The thought
warmed her and brought a giggle to her throat as
she reached for the towel.

Dressed and primped, she in black linen suit,
he in his eternal blue pinstripe, they thundered
down the stairs, Karp way in the lead, Marlene
feeling like Winnie-the-Pooh bumping along after
her gigantic Christopher Robin.

Out in the already dieseled air, Karp bought
two newspapers, the *Times* and the *Daily News*.
He stuck the *Times* and the brown accordion
folder he used as a briefcase under his left arm
and flipped through the *News* as he walked along.
He was looking for crimes, and this morning he
didn't have to flip long.

"Ah, shit!" he snarled, half under his breath.

"What's happening?" asked Marlene.

"They got another one. Jason Brown, twenty-
seven. AKA Joker Brown."

"A personal friend?"

Karp gave her a look. "A dope dealer. Or 'drug
lord,' as they now get called in the papers." He
showed her the front page. The photograph was
of the type familiar to *Daily News* readers for five

decades: cops standing around appearing hapless, a shrouded form on the ground, black splotches on the white covering, an arm sticking out, palm up, rivulets of what you knew was blood, looking like shiny tar.

"You're right. 'DRUG LORD SLAIN. THIS MAKES EIGHT,' " read Marlene from the huge black letters of the headline. "The same guys doing it, you think?"

Karp shrugged. "I don't know. Clay thinks so. I'd like to talk to him about it, if he would ever get back to me. What I'm worried about is his excellency the district attorney. This is the kind of crap Bloom lives for. Guaranteed he'll have a fucking press conference this morning and promise to set up a special unit to bring the perps to justice. Bloom loves special units."

"And he'll put you in charge?"

"No, dear, he won't put me in charge. Bloom doesn't put me in charge. He'll put some crony of his in charge and I'll get to do all the work and get axed if something goes wrong."

Marlene assumed a sympathetic expression. "Poor Butch! Maybe when you grow up you can be D.A. and do all the work *and* get all the credit."

Karp snorted and stared away south down the length of Broadway, as if sizing up the run to a pole vault. Marlene caught the look and said firmly, "I'm taking the subway. Momma needs a sit-down."

"C'mon, kid, it's a nice day. And the subway's supposed to be dangerous."

"Walking with *you* is dangerous. You go twenty

miles an hour reading the paper and you think walk signs are for wimps."

"OK, candy ass, suit yourself. I'm walking. Here's the *Times*. I'll see you downtown." He squeezed her shoulder and kissed her lightly on her head, and turned and sped away.

Arriving at the office, Karp found it was as he had feared. Connie Trask lifted her chin skyward as he came into the bureau office. "He wants to see you," she said, holding out a short stack of yellow phone slips.

"The TV guys were going up in the elevator when I came in," she continued. Karp grunted and turned toward his office. "Say, Butch, how come we never get to be on the TV? I'd like to be on the TV once."

"Stick around, Connie," said Karp over his shoulder. "You could be the one who gets to find my dead body."

He slammed into his office, put down what he was carrying, hung up his suit jacket, sat down behind his desk, pulled two toasted bagels (one butter, one cream cheese) and a container of coffee out of a brown bag, and began his day.

First the phone messages. Bloom's office, defendant's lawyer, ditto, ditto, ditto—they all could wait. Nothing from Clay Fulton: a pain in the ass, that. He checked the schedule of appointments Trask had typed up for him. It was clear that a meeting with Bloom was in the offing, and, if precedent held, it would be a nice long one.

Everything was going to have to be shoved around, people were going to have to be marshaled to fill the court dates and appointments he would miss, and of course their own appearances and appointments would have to be shifted around too. Bloom didn't get much affection or respect from his troops, but he was at least able to stir the ants' nest around in this way. Karp suspected it was one of the things he enjoyed most about the job.

He sighed and called Bloom's office, was put on hold for a considerable period to teach him his place, and then his reluctant ear filled with the district attorney's mellow, fruity voice.

"Hello, Butch! How's the guy?"

How's-the-guy was new. Bloom was trying to incorporate a snappier Nelson Rockefeller-type lingo into his front, and this was the latest.

Ignoring it, Karp said flatly, "I heard you wanted to talk to me."

"Yeah, yeah—terrible thing these killings. I was on the *Morning Show* today about it. Did you catch it?"

"No, I didn't," said Karp in the same tone. "Was that it?"

"Was what it?" asked Bloom, puzzled.

"Was that what you wanted to talk to me about? Whether I saw you on TV?"

"What? No, of course not! I told the media I was making these drug-lord killings my top priority." A pause for effect: "You know about the big breakthrough we've had in the case. I announced that too."

Karp felt his face grow warm. "Oh? What breakthrough was that?"

Even over the phone, Karp could hear the tone

of relish with which Bloom informed him that the killer of Larue Clarry had been arrested the evening before last and was now in the custody of the police. "I guess you didn't get the word," Bloom concluded.

"No, I guess I didn't. I should watch more TV, so I'll know what's going on in the D.A.'s office."

This was ignored and Bloom went on: "I'm organizing a task force on these drug-lord murders. Blue ribbon all the way. We're going to use this breakthrough to blow the whole mess open."

"Un-huh. When's the meeting?"

"Call my girl," snapped the man of action, and hung up.

Karp called, and learned that the meeting was scheduled for ten o'clock, less than an hour away. Karp then buzzed Connie Trask and told her to get busy shifting people around, canceling and rescheduling, and also told her to get Roland Hrcany for him as soon as possible.

Ten minutes later, Hrcany appeared at Karp's door, heralded by two glass-rattling knocks. Roland Hrcany was a man of average height, but was so heavily developed in his neck, chest, and shoulders that he appeared squat. He had a face that at first glance seemed unlikely to belong to a lawyer, or even a highschool graduate. It was ruddy, hawk-nosed, heavy around the brows and jaw. The eyes were vivid blue and small. His hair was white-blond and worn swept back and collar-length, in the manner of professional wrestlers. His eyebrows and lashes were similarly pale and nearly invisible, which only added to his disturbing appearance.

"Sit down, Roland," said Karp. "I think I have a treat for you."

"Yeah?" Hrcany grinned, showing long yellowish teeth. "You're gonna let me have a crack at Marlene before you tie the knot?"

"You know, Roland," said Karp mildly, "it's remarks like that make you unpopular around the office. We were going to work on your popularity, remember?"

Hrcany laughed and leaned back in his chair, lacing his hands behind his head and flexing his football-size biceps. "So what's this about?" he asked.

"The dope-pusher killings. Apparently we have an arrest."

"Let me guess. A gentleman of the the Afro-American persuasion with a yellow sheet from here to Canarsie?"

"I don't know, Roland. It could be an Episcopalian minister's wife. Or a Hungarian. I just found out about it ten minutes ago from our maximum leader."

"A Hungarian wouldn't have gotten caught," answered Hrcany. "So what's in it for me?"

Karp said, "Bloom is organizing what he calls a blue-ribbon task force to coordinate the work on the whole set of killings. Needless to say, a crock of shit, but I need somebody I can count on to hold their hands and make sure they don't fuck things up."

Hrcany stood up and straightened the already wrinkleless belt line of his white shirt. Smiling, he said, "Well, Butch, it's been a pleasure, as always, but I got to run—I'm having a thin glass tube inserted in my penis and I don't want to be late."

"Roland, don't give me a hard time," said Karp wearily.

"Hey," said Hrcany, pointing a stiff finger at Karp. "I'm not giving you a hard time. I ask only the same. Butch, this is Roland—I'm not a hand-holder, I'm an ass-kicker. Whyn't you ask V.T. to do it, he's the big-time diplomat."

In a patient voice Karp explained, "Because V.T. is not a homicide prosecutor and you are, and you are the best I got in that line of work, and this is a multiple homicide case. Not only that, but if I recall, the last time V.T. got some exposure I heard all kinds of whining from certain parties about how nobody ever paid any attention to them, and how V.T. got all the goodies—"

"Butch, that's different—"

"*If* I can finish—so when this opportunity came along, to shine in a major case, and to bask in the light of favorable publicity, and to mingle with some of the most powerful folks in the city, natu-rally, *naturally* I thought of you, Roland."

Hrcany held up his hands. "OK, Butch, OK, I give. But if I get cornholed during this operation, I would expect you to apply the Vaseline."

"A deal, Roland. You can count on me, as you know. I knew I could count on you. OK, see you in the throne room at ten. I got to call the elusive Lieutenant Fulton and find out what the fuck is happening before we go up there."

Hrcany laughed loudly and left, slamming the door behind him. Karp pushed the intercom button. "Connie? You know Bill Denton's secretary? Can you make yourself sound like her? Yeah? No, you won't get into trouble, I promise. Yeah, not more than six months in the slam for a first offense. Look, here's what you do: call Clay Fulton and tell whoever answers the phone that the chief of detectives is holding. When Fulton picks up, switch him in here."

Three minutes later, Karp's phone rang. Clay Fulton's voice said, "Chief?"

"No, Clay, it's Butch Karp."

"Sorry. I thought Chief Denton was calling me."

"Yeah, something must be fucked up with the phones. But while I got you, talk to me—I've been trying to get you for days."

"Yeah, well, I've been real busy, Butch. You know . . ."

"So I understand," said Karp as calmly as he could. "You had a big arrest in the Clarry case. I had to find out about it from the ruby lips of the D.A. himself. I had kind of hoped that with that conversation we recently had you would've kept me up-to-date on those cases."

"Well, yeah, Butch, but . . . it's kind of hard to explain right now."

"It sounds like it. Look, Clay—this is Butch. Remember? I understand things might be tentative. I been around. Just tell me who you arrested and what the situation is. We don't have to go to the grand jury this afternoon."

"Oh, that. It's bullshit. Guy named Tecumseh Booth. He's no killer. We're just cooking him on Rikers. We really got nothing on him."

"Wait a minute, Clay. Why'd you arrest him? What's the connection with Clarry?"

"Ah, one of my guys thought he was driving Clarry's car. Some skell spotted him on the night. It's no big deal."

"Sounds at least a solid medium-size deal to me, you got a guy who maybe drove for the shooter. When am I going to get to meet what's-his-name, Pocahontas?"

"Tecumseh. Yeah, well, when I get a chance I'll set something up. Look, Butch, I got to run now. I got another call."

"Fuck your call! What the fuck is going on here?" Karp shouted this into the phone, but he knew that it had already gone dead.

SIX

The district attorney's conference room was not called the throne room during the long administration of Francis P. Garrahy. Karp remembered it as an austere, slightly battered place with a heavy glass-topped oak table and cracked brown leather chairs. The air had been redolent with the odor of the D.A.'s pipe and the cigars of his cronies. There had been a dusty, bad portrait of FDR, in a naval cloak, on the wall.

All this was gone. The walls were decorator gray and there was a vague, pastel semiabstract painting in place of FDR. The furnishings were motel modern and color-coordinated: teak table, teak chairs upholstered in nubbly bluish wool, and, of course, the throne itself, a special chair in which only the D.A. himself was allowed to sit, a chair that, while still harmonious with the decor, was slightly larger, somewhat higher, a bit more luxuriously padded and a bit more richly covered than the other twelve chairs in the room, as befitted the august behind that occupied it.

Karp used to make it a habit to come late for meetings with Bloom, and when he entered, Bloom would always say something designed to be embarrassing and sarcastic. But when Bloom had discovered that Karp didn't care, he took to delaying his own entry until Karp had arrived. This succeeded in making all the other attendees angry with Karp. Karp now arrived precisely on time and left immediately at the time the meeting was scheduled to end, whether someone was talking or not.

At ten o'clock that morning there were four people sitting around the table when Karp and Hrcany entered. Two of them were cops, in plainclothes, but with their police ID clipped to the breast pockets of their jackets. One was a heavyset light-complexioned black man, the other was a thin, smaller, dark-complexioned white man. Both were dressed in similar dark well-cut suits. The white man wore a white-on-white shirt and a red silk tie. The black man wore a blue shirt with a white collar, and a blue silk tie. Karp knew they were narcotics cops, just as he knew they would have $120 Bally loafers on their feet.

Sitting close to the throne was the D.A.'s chief of administration, Conrad Wharton. Wharton was a small pink man with thin blond hair combed straight across, blue eyes, a pink cupid's-bow mouth, and a little round belly.

"Hello, Conrad," said Karp. Wharton looked up from the papers he was studying and looked at Karp as if Karp were a large turd that some stray dog had deposited on the table.

"Hi, Chip!" said Hrcany, imitating the voice that schoolgirls use to call each other to play. Wharton liked to be called Chip, which he considered a more regular-guy name than Conrad. Hrcany never failed to use "Chip" in that tone, in nearly every sentence he directed at Wharton—not exactly what Wharton had in mind when he concocted the nickname. Wharton pursed his lips and studied his papers, while a faint flush rose up his neck.

The fourth man was a sleepy black gentleman in his mid-fifties, with graying hair, dressed in a rust three-piece suit. When Karp and Hrcany came in, he looked up and gave them a bright smile, then went back to thumbing through a well-worn diary and making notes in it with a mechanical pencil.

At five past the hour, the door to Bloom's office opened and the D.A. entered with a well-dressed man of about sixty in tow. Bloom was a man somewhat below the average in height, trim, with large moist eyes, a wide mouth, and a thin prominent nose. His gray-blond hair was razor cut and set like an anchorman's. He sat in his chair, seated the other man to his right, and made introductions. The cops were Narcotics Squad, working out of the Thirty-second Precinct in Harlem—Dick Manning and Sid Amalfi.

The other black man was Dwight Hamilton, there representing Harlem's congressman, Marcus Fane, who was unavoidably detained in Washington. The man with Bloom was Richard Reedy, a Wall Street lawyer. Reedy and Fane were co-chairmen of an organization called Citizens Against Drugs.

Bloom began to speak. Like many men who enjoy the sound of their own voices and have the confidence attendant on a captive audience, he was not succinct. There was a good deal of "this great city" and "this scourge of drugs that is sapping the vital energy" and "citizens working together for the common good." Wharton took, or seemed to take, voluminous notes. Karp doodled idly on the pad placed before him, while his mind drifted.

His eyes lit on Reedy. He knew the man slightly by reputation, as someone who had made a lot of money in the sixties and continued to grow richer in the various ways that lawyers can grow rich in New York. He was on committees. He owned a good deal of property in Harlem and was a close political ally of Marcus Fane.

He looked the part: a square, ruddy Irish face, a big nose, a broad brow, a humorous twist to the mouth, shrewd blue eyes. He looked up and met Karp's stare. There was a moment of sizing up; Karp felt he was being explored by an intelligence both cynical and amused. His eyebrow twitched upward a fraction, his eyes rolled slightly toward Bloom and then up toward the ceiling: the universal facial gesture signaling that one is suffering a bore.

Bloom ran down at last. "And now, I'd like to turn the gavel over to my very dear friend Rich Reedy. Rich has done so much, *so* much for the people of this city. I'm just tickled to death that he's gone ahead and volunteered his valuable time to help us out in this so important undertaking. Rich?"

Reedy cleared his throat and spoke in a pleasant tenor voice. "Thanks, Sandy. I don't have much to say. I'm flattered myself to have been asked to serve. I see our role, mine and Congressman Fane's, mainly as support, getting the word out to the community that something's being done to clean up this mess, to stop these monsters from thinking they can flout the law and kill with impunity on our streets.

"That, and generally overseeing the conduct of these cases, so that citizens can believe that the . . . processes of the law retain their integrity. The police, the courts, and so forth. Right now we're in the early stages. It's a police matter, so let's hear from the police."

He turned and looked across the table at Manning. Manning glanced briefly at his partner and said, "All right, as many of you know, we finally have an arrest in one of these killings. A man named Tecumseh Booth. The police picked him up night before last. He's got a long sheet. He was spotted at the scene of the crime by an informant. Right now we're keeping him on ice; maybe when he sees we're serious about this he'll want to talk.

"On the other seven murders—not much, but we have people working on them. We have other likely victims—major traffickers—under surveillance. Sooner or later somebody's going to make a mistake."

Manning spoke further about the details of the surveillance operation, what resources were being applied to it, and then summarized the circumstances of the eight killings, focusing mainly on the most recent one. "We think we have some real chances with the Joker Brown hit. It's fresh, anyway. We got a witness says he saw Brown talking to a black male shortly before he disappeared."

"That sure narrows it down," said Hrcany, as if to himself. All eyes turned his way.

"Did you have a comment, Roland?" asked the D.A.

"No . . . actually, yes, I did have a comment. I didn't catch the charge on this Booth guy."

"Charge?" asked Manning.

"Yeah. What did you charge him with? Intentional murder? Driving without a license . . . what?"

A barrage of looks was exchanged around the table. Papers were thumbed through. Finally Manning said, "We actually haven't decided yet. It depends."

Karp spoke up. "Another point of clarification, Detective Manning: are you or Detective Amalfi the arresting officer here?"

"No."

"But the arresting officer was in your squad? Or out of your precinct?"

Manning paused for several seconds before replying. "Not exactly. An associated unit."

"An associated unit," Karp repeated. "Does this associated unit have a name?"

Manning slowly pulled out a small loose-leaf pad and paged through it. "Detective Maus was the arresting officer," he said.

"That's interesting," said Karp. "And since Maus doesn't work for you, he works for . . . ?"

Manning paused again, waiting for someone to say something. No one did, so he said, "Ahh . . . Lieutenant Fulton, over at the Two-eight."

"Thank you," said Karp. "That's what was confusing me. I was wondering why Lieutenant Fulton was not present, since I was given to believe that he had been placed in charge of the dope-dealer murders."

Dwight Hamilton now spoke for the first time. He had an elegant voice, quiet but nevertheless commanding attention. "Fulton won't do."

"What does that mean, Mr. Hamilton?" asked Karp.

Hamilton smiled sadly and shook his head and said, "I'm very much afraid you'll have to get that from the police, Mr. Karp."

Karp had turned inquiringly toward Manning, when Bloom said peevishly, "Would you please tell me what's going on here? Why are we getting bogged down in these details? Let's stick with the big picture, people!" He might have said more, had not Wharton leaned over to him and begun whispering rapidly behind his cupped hand, like a Shakespearean villain.

Karp resumed his conversation with Manning. "Detective, can you illuminate us here? Why won't Fulton do?"

Manning shrugged. "Hey, I just go where they send me, boss. Maybe they think Fulton is unreliable. There's a lot of money floating around up there, around drugs. Maybe some of it ended up in the wrong place."

"Who's 'they,' exactly? Is there an active investigation now on Lieutenant Fulton?" Karp snapped back.

"That would be confidential information," said Manning.

"Fine," said Karp "Let's talk about nonconfidential information, then. Our prisoner, Booth. My colleague here asked a question about the legal situation with respect to Booth. What's the charge, and what's the evidence?"

Bloom broke in again. "Butch, could we move on? All these legal games can be dealt with later."

"Oh, legal games? Sorry, I thought legality was the point of this operation. But since you bring up 'games,' I'd like to have a turn. See if anyone remembers this one: in all criminal prosecutions the accused shall have a right to a speedy and public trial by an impartial jury of the state and district wherein the crime shall have been committed, which district shall have been previously ascertained by law; and to be informed of the nature and cause of the accusation; to be confronted with the witnesses against him; to have compulsory process for obtaining witnesses in his favor; and to have the assistance of counsel for his defense. Ring a bell?"

Bloom relieved himself of a small chuckle. Wharton assumed a pitying grin. No one responded, and Karp went on. "What I've heard here is that somebody has been arrested and imprisoned for going on forty-eight hours without a charge, and without, to my knowledge, anybody from the D.A.'s office interviewing him, or even being informed of the arrest—"

"Hold on, Butch," Bloom spluttered. "*I* was informed."

"Right, I forgot. So you've personally interviewed the prisoner and determined that there's sufficient evidence to support a charge under law? No Gosh, that's a shame. Because when I call Tom Pagano over at Legal Aid and tell him that we're holding a prisoner who hasn't even seen a *D.A.*, much a less a defense lawyer, and is being held without

charge, God knows what kind of shit is going
to hit the fan!

"Besides which, we have omitted to invite
either the arresting officer on our big breakthrough, or his superior, and we have hanging
in the air an innuendo against the reputation of
that superior, who happens to be one of the
most decorated members of the NYPD."

"Fulton's dirty," said Manning flatly.

Karp turned on him, eyes narrowing, and
met Manning's defiant gaze. "Is he? Are you
from Internal Affairs?"

Manning smiled. "You know I wouldn't tell
you if I was."

"No, you seem like a pretty tight-lipped
guy," said Karp. He was about to go on, but
something nagged at him—the last conversation he had had with Clay Fulton. Fulton was
certainly not himself. Could it be true? It took
some of the steam out of him. Damn Fulton!
Why hadn't he kept in touch?

Reedy jumped into the tense silence. "What
we have here, it seems to me, is an example of
why we need this task force. There's an accusation in the air, unfounded maybe, but there it
is. There may be others. We're all grown-ups
here. I don't think it implies any disrespect for
the police department to say that corruption
has been a problem, especially in the drug area.
We also see what happens when there isn't co-
ordination. Everybody starts playing their own
game, running their private systems, their private
deals.

"Let's start over. We have a suspect. Obviously, the thing to do is what Mr. Karp has suggested so eloquently—bring him into the compass of the law, but at the same time being conscious of the need for the utmost security. I'm sure the business about who's running the police end can be straightened out by consultations with the NYPD at the highest levels. But above all, let's keep talking to each other! I trust that will suit both Mr. Karp and Detective Manning?"

Karp had to admit it was smoothly done. He met Reedy's eye and saw once again that amused twinkle. What Reedy had said made a certain amount of sense, given the information Karp now possessed. Besides that, he had realized (somewhat to his surprise) that he wanted Reedy to see him as a reasonable man. He nodded and said, "Sure," and so did Manning.

That essentially wound up the meeting, except for some administrative details. Karp left Hrcany to deal with those, and went out to wait for the elevator. As he watched the lights, he felt someone come up behind him. It was Reedy.

"That was quite a performance," Reedy said. "Do you have the whole Constitution by heart, or just the Bill of Rights?"

Karp grinned and replied, "Still working on it. I think you might've been the only guy in that room who got the reference, God help us."

"I'm afraid you're right. Sandy, dear man that he is, is something of a dim bulb in the legal firmament. And he does go on!"

The car arrived and they stepped in. Karp said, "I'm surprised you think so. To hear him talk up there, you're like his closest friend."

Reedy laughed lightly. "Anybody Sandy is with at the moment is his closest friend. He likes to be liked. As for me, I agree with Molière, 'the friend of all the world is not to my taste.' " He paused. "Nor to yours either, I've been told."

"Yeah? Let's just say that the district attorney and I have had some professional differences over the years."

"He's no Phil Garrahy, that's for sure," said Reedy sadly.

"Who is?" Karp replied, recording, as he was meant to, that Reedy was one of the select group who had known that Francis Garrahy liked his friends to call him Phil. The elevator door opened. Karp turned and extended his hand. "This is my floor. Nice meeting you, Mr. Reedy."

Reedy returned the handshake warmly and then placed his finger on the door-hold button. Karp paused in the elevator doorway. Reedy said, "I'll tell you what—Butch, is it?—I'd like to buy you lunch. We can talk about the Constitution and other things of mutual interest. How about tomorrow, noon?"

"OK," said Karp after the briefest pause, intrigued by what had turned out to be an odd twist to the morning's doings. And at least Reedy hadn't said "Call my girl."

"Is the Bankers' Club all right?" asked Reedy. Karp was about to make a smart remark, when someone hailed him from the corridor. It was a small fat man of about forty-five, with a sallow homely face, big ears, thinning black curls, and a mouth of prodigious width from which stuck the stump of one of those dense black cigars known in the city as guinea stinkers. He was wearing a red tie and red suspenders that strained to their limit against the hard gut that protruded over his belt line. Numerous reddish stains specked the white acreage between his tie and his suspenders.

"I'll be there," said Karp to Reedy, who smiled again and released the door. To the fat man he said curtly, "What is it, Guma?"

Guma waggled his hand as if it were loose and hanging by a thread from his wrist. "Ooooh! He's got the rag on today! What happened, another tiff with our glorious leader, the scumbag?"

"You got spaghetti sauce on your shirt, Goom," said Karp. The transition from trading quips with Richard Reedy to kanoodling around with Raymond Guma was proving hard for him to handle. Was he just a hair embarrassed about Guma? Was there something mocking in Reedy's farewell smile?

"It's marinara sauce and I wear it like a badge of honor," replied Guma, lifting his chins proudly. "You're marrying a guinea, you should get used to it. Who was the suit on the elevator?"

"Guy named Reedy. The scumbag, as you call him, has him working on these drug killings, some cockamamie task force. Interesting guy, by the way. He's buying me lunch."

"Yeah? He's gonna eat pizza off the truck?"

"Uh-huh. I'm gonna see if he'll spring for two slices *with* pepperoni. Let him show a little class."

"Ah, these white-shoe types are all dickheads. You know, you shouldn't be seen with guys like that. People might start thinking you're selling out."

Karp looked pointedly at his watch. "Thanks for the advice, Goom. You wanted to see me about something."

"Yeah, speaking about fucking Italians. Petrossi fishtailed on us."

"What! When was this?"

"Hearing this morning. We had it worked out he would plead guilty on the intentional murder charge and we'd drop the felony murder charges for the other two guys who were killed at the scene. Now he says he wants a trial. I guess he got to thinking why take fifteen, twenty in Attica for free. He could be in there a real long time if we convicted him on all three counts, but he could also beat it entirely and walk."

"Not a fucking chance!"

"*We* think so, but there's no law against the

asshole betting on the come. That's what makes Vegas. Meanwhile . . ."

"Yeah, we got a trial we didn't expect. But you should be in good shape—you're prepped and all."

Guma inspected his feet and said hesitantly, "Yeah, that's what I wanted to see you about. I'm really strapped here, Butch. I got the Rubio Valdez trial, the world-famous burglar and amateur lawyer wants his twenty-third trial. I got that abduction thing from Washington Heights, I got to go on the appeal in Bostwitch—"

"Goom, what is this shit?" Karp cut in. "This is a multiple homicide. It's your case. The kids can handle fucking Valdez."

"Um, and also there's the judge in Petrossi. Judge Kamas."

"Who? Oh, yeah, the new one they got to replace Birnbaum. What's wrong with her?"

"Nothing, but . . . ah, there's a conflict, with me. I mean, I know her."

"Yeah, she's a judge, of course you know . . . Oh, you mean outside. She's a friend of yours?"

"Ehhm . . . somewhat more."

Slowly Karp's eyes widened and he placed his hands carefully over his ears. "I don't want to hear this, Guma."

"Butch, it was fate. How the fuck was I supposed to know she was going to be moved into Supreme Court? She was a Family Court judge. We met in a restaurant, for Chrissakes."

"I can't believe this. You're *schtupping* the judge in Petrossi. But now she knows you're her ADA. What'd she say?"

"Well, to tell the truth, she *doesn't* know. That's the point. That's actually why I can't do the trial. Look, it's a long boring story . . ."

Karp casually wrapped a long finger around one of Guma's suspenders and said, "Bore me, Mad Dog, I think I need to hear it."

"Butchie, believe me, someday we'll laugh about this whole business. Anyway, the thing of it is, we met in this restaurant, we fell into this conversation about her kid's teeth—she's divorced, right?—a common interest there, and I was giving her all this advice because of what I went through with *my* kid's teeth. I mean, did you ever see her? Kamas? Forty years old, but a terrific body, you know?

"Anyhow, we were making good progress, a couple, three drinks, and then she says, gosh, you must be an orthodontist, and—so help me, Butch, I didn't think—I pulled out this card I happened to have on me and gave it to her. Yeah, I *am* an orthodontist, ha-ha, et cetera, et cetera. So she thinks I'm him."

"Who, Guma?" asked Karp, fearing he already knew the answer.

"Well, remember when Marlene was nice enough to refer me to her brother John . . . ?"

"Oh, that's a relief!" said Karp, his hands clenching stiffly before him, his voice rising. "There's no problem, then. You're fucking the judge in what is probably the most famous and press-ridden murder case in the last six months, and you told her that you were *my* future brother-in-law. It's perfect. Guma, just tell me one thing: most guys only got one cock to worry about. How come I got to concern myself with yours?"

Guma said, "C'mon, Butch, that's not fair."

"No, you're right. My apologies. I'll calm down in about a fucking week!"

"So I'm off the case?"

"Yeah, Goom, go play with the burglars."

"Who you gonna give it to? Be a shame to blow it at this late date."

Karp gritted his teeth and took a long, slow breath. He patted Guma softly on the shoulder. "Goom," he said, "you're . . . a one of a kind. Don't worry, I'll think of something."

Two hours later, his mood in no way improved, Karp was sitting in front of a gigantic desk in a gigantic office on the fourteenth floor of police headquarters. Across the desk was a smallish man wearing a neat blue suit and hard blue eyes, who looked enough like Karl Malden to use his American Express card. The man's name was William Denton, and he was the chief of detectives of the New York City Police Department.

Karp got right to the point. Denton was not big on pleasantries in any case, and Karp had no stomach for them this afternoon.

"Clay Fulton," said Karp. "I'd like to know what he's doing."

"Why don't you ask him?"

Karp paused and swallowed. He had worked with Denton closely over the years, and trusted him—so far. On the other hand, Denton was a cop, and one of the half-dozen most powerful men in the city's criminal justice system. Karp was, in contrast, a bureau chief in what was but one of the five independent prosecutors' offices operating in New York. There was just the one police department, and although legally the police were supposedly there to serve the district attorney, the reality was more complex.

There was no way he could pressure Denton. He had used up all his chips just getting an immediate appointment with the C. of D. Karp determined now to lay out his problem as squarely as he could, and if Denton wanted to tell him to get lost, that was it.

"Well, Chief," Karp replied, "I have tried that. The problem is that my buddy Clay, who I have worked with on and off for nearly ten years, and who has always impressed me as the straightest shooter around, has apparently traded in his personality on a new model, something out of the KGB stockroom.

"These dope-pusher homicides. He comes in, tells me you're going to let him coordinate them as one big case. Fine. I don't hear from him for a couple of weeks. I call him, I don't get called back. Fine, too. He's busy, it's going slow—I can understand that.

"Then I hear, like by accident, he's arrested

somebody in connection with the Clarry thing. The guy is squirreled away in some pen, no contact with me, no charge even. Not fine, Chief. I go to a meeting this morning with some heavy hitters, the D.A. wants a task force to coordinate the operations on these hits with the cops and the community. There's two cops there, playing hard ball for no reason I can see, and when I ask why Clay isn't there, everybody looks at me like I just farted. Then everybody starts acting like Clay Fulton is in the tank on this, and I'm the only one in town who hasn't got the message. Also not fine.

"So I put it to you, out front, what the hell is going on?"

Denton did not answer immediately. He looked at Karp for a long moment, and then picked up a yellow pencil from his desk and stared at it, held between his two hands, as if it were an oracle, as he rocked gently back and forth in his chair.

At last he spoke. "What if I said you're going to have to trust me on this one?"

"I'd trust you. If I ever thought I couldn't trust you, I'd move to Ramapo, New Jersey, and do divorces and real-estate closings. But that's not the point. *Something's* moving, out of Bloom's office. Maybe it's just typical smoke and mirrors, but I doubt it. The guys in that room—Reedy, Fane's guy—don't show up for a private meeting unless they have a serious interest in an issue. They might be on a platform or cut a ribbon for any kind of bullshit, but when they show up personally in a little room, something is going down.

"If you tell me you're in control on that end—OK. But somehow I doubt it. I'm involved, like it or not, and if I'm not helping you, there's at least a chance that I'll miss something important or actually screw something up.

"Also, there's Clay himself. Now, we both know that the only way to survive in this business, where everybody's fucking one another as hard as they can, is to put together a bunch of people you trust. At least that's what keeps *me* alive. Clay is one of my people that way, and I'm one of his, or at least I thought so. If he's in trouble, I want to know about it. I'm not talking officially here, I'm talking personally."

Karp stopped talking and shrugged helplessly. That's it, he thought, it's my only card, and I played it. He hadn't mentioned that if he was the only one who didn't know what was going on, he couldn't protect himself. Bloom could sucker him into something nasty and destroy him. He knew Denton liked him, but he doubted that such a consideration would be particularly telling to the chief of detectives.

Denton considered Karp's statement for a moment and then seemed to make a decision. He placed the pencil on his desk with a snap and rolled his chair forward, as if ready to issue orders.

"Clay's not in any trouble with the department. Far from it." He paused and gave Karp one of his intense stares. "Let me ask you something. What's the thing the department fears more than anything else?"

"You mean corruption?"

Denton grimaced in distaste and shook his head.

"Corruption! Hell, no! Corruption has been part of police work since the beginning of time. We root it out when we can, but we basically accept it, like flat feet or hemorrhoids. Every so often we drop the ball and something like the Knapp Commission goes into action.

"Look, I've been a cop for thirty-four years this October. There's less corruption in the department now than there ever has been, but people are more worried about it than ever before. If it goes on like this much longer, it's going to wreck the department, and then where will they be!

"But it's not corruption I'm talking about. That's not what scares the bejesus out of me. Look, we've got over twenty-eight thousand men out there, almost all of them with little more than a high-school education, all of them armed to the teeth. A lot of them spend eight hours a day in hell. They see what crime does. They see what junk does. They see the mutts laugh in their faces day after day. They arrest some scumbag and he's out on the street before they are." Denton paused again, and seemed to sigh. He lowered his voice.

"Did you ever think that one or two of them might crack, might decide to, say, abbreviate the judicial process? I'm talking Guatemala. Argentina. El Salvador."

As he grasped what Denton was saying, Karp felt a violent chill run through him, and he gritted his teeth to control it.

"You . . . think it's a rogue cop? Killing these pushers?"

"Yeah. We're pretty sure. Clay's accumulated a lot of evidence. The victims all went with their killers willingly, or let them in without a hassle. We don't have any witnesses who were close enough to make a definite ID, but we do have one person who saw one of the victims get into a car with two men, and his hands were cuffed behind him. At least one of the killers is a black man. That's all we know."

"But couldn't it be an impostor—somebody with fake ID?"

"Very doubtful. The kind of victims we have are wise to that scam. If it was a thug doing it, the word would have spread around. No, it was somebody they knew by sight was a real cop. He came, he arrested them, they went quietly, and he killed them. Or he killed them when they opened the door.

"The other thing that's convincing is the pattern. These guys, the killers, are smart in ways that only a cop is smart. The hits are absolutely clean. They're designed to have no apparent connection with one another, so that we'll think they're the result of a drug war."

Karp marshaled his thoughts against the horrifying scenario that Denton was calmly building for him. "What about this arrest in the Clarry killing? This Booth guy? How do you figure that?"

"I think they've changed their pattern. Makes sense. We're catching on, after all. This was an assassination in the back seat of a car, using a driver that the victim trusted. A Mafia-style hit. Once again, clouding the waters. It was only luck that we nailed Booth. And we got the gun too. Know where it was last seen? A police evidence locker. That was the clincher."

Something still didn't jibe for Karp. "Chief, assuming you're right, why haven't you got five hundred guys on this thing? What is this business about not charging Booth?"

"Think it through for yourself," Denton replied. "You know what kind of hell we go through when a cop kills somebody in self-defense. Can you imagine what would happen if it came out that a bunch of cops were setting themselves up to be judge, jury, and executioner? Butch, the Knapp business left this department lying on it side, gasping for air. If this came out, it would kill it dead. They'll take our guns away. They'll break up the force. It'll be chaos.

"When Fulton came to me with this, it struck me that in one way we were lucky that it was him that discovered it. He's probably the best man on the force for the job. He's a brilliant detective. He's emotionally mature. He's black and he knows Harlem. And one of our main suspects is in his unit.''

''Who?''

''You're familiar with the King Cole Trio? Rough boys. That Dugman is from another age—a head breaker. It could be that they got too rough one day. Maybe they got to like it. Maybe just one of them is involved. We decided on a strategy. You heard the rumors that Fulton is dirty already? That's by design. I want him close to the scumbags up there, in a way that you can't get close unless you're bent. I guarantee you somebody up there knows who's doing these guys, and sooner or later one of them is going to cross paths with Fulton and let it drop.

''The main thing, though, is that it meant that we didn't have to tell anyone else. Fulton's working alone.''

''Completely alone?'' Karp said in astonishment.

''Completely. He came to me with his suspicions and I decided that full knowledge had to be limited to him and me. And now you.''

Karp wrestled with the enormity of this statement. Then he said, ''But, Chief, that means he's got no backup. If some wacko asks him for a meet at three in the morning in a vacant lot, what's he gonna do? Beg off?''

''If he thinks it's worth it, he'll go,'' said

Denton. "There's a hundred undercover cops on the force that take risks just as bad every day."

Karp had ready in his mind the argument that those cops had radios and people watching out for them and people they could at least *talk* to, but his reading of Denton's expression convinced him that the chief of detectives had already written off Fulton's safety as a necessary sacrifice to his plan.

Karp changed tacks. He said, "But it's all going to come out anyway, when it goes to court."

Denton looked at Karp silently, his face a mixture of sadness, anger, and massive determination. Then slowly he shook his head.

Karp felt another chill, and this time his scalp prickled and sweat broke out on his palms and on his forehead. Karp ran a hand across his face and took a deep breath.

"Chief, if you're going to tell me that when Clay finds this guy he's going to kill him, with your . . . blessing, then I don't want to hear it. I can't know it. Maybe I better go now."

"Stay where you are. I'm not at the point where I'm hiring assassins myself. Maybe I should, but I can't. There's a little mental hospital upstate that specializes in caring for the violent offspring of the very rich. Whoever this cop is, he's a sick man, and he has to be taken care of. He'll go there. Quietly, discreetly, and for a very long time. I've already made the arrangements. I've moved police funds into an account that will pay for it when the time comes. Illegally, of course. If this comes out, my own career will be ruined as well, not that it matters much in the scale of things.''

Denton sighed and seemed to survey his office, with its awards and memorabilia, as if he were imagining what it would be like to be hauled out of it, to jail. When he resumed speaking, it was from behind a wan smile.

''You know, I liked what you said about trusting people. I guess I operate the same way. But this thing . . . it's something else. You and I have always gotten along pretty well. You're smart and honest, and you know how to treat cops, which is rare down your street. I understand the kind of problems you have over there. That's by way of saying we have a relationship that means something to me.

''But let me say this. Nobody is to know anything about what we've just discussed. I gave my word to Clay that it was between him and me, and I've broken that word. I think for good reason, but he may not. So you can't reveal your knowledge to him either, ever. And when I say nobody, I mean *nobody*. Not your best friend, not your girlfriend. Is that agreed?''

Karp cleared his throat and said, ''Yes.''

''I'll try to keep you up-to-date on what's happening. I expect the same from you. And, Butch . . .''

"Yes."

"I have to say this. If you tell anybody, I'll find out about it, and if I do, I'd say a career in Jersey doing divorces will look pretty attractive to you."

SEVEN

Karp dragged himself to Marlene's loft that evening like a whipped dog. He had difficulty drawing a full breath, and was nearly winded when he arrived at the fifth-floor landing outside her door. The door was steel, painted glossy black, and he could make out a faint and distorted reflection in it of his own face.

Faint and distorted was indeed how he felt, as if some internal glue had been dissolved and his inner parts were free to travel independently of the structure that had ordered them. Karp was, of course, no stranger to the petty stratagems and evasions that make up much of the life of any participant in an adversarial system of justice. But until the revelations in Denton's office, and his own acquiescence to what the chief intended, he had always maintained a core of integrity, had never gone completely outside the law.

Now he had. He was conspiring in the extra-legal abduction and confinement of a multiple murderer in order to protect the police. He still couldn't quite believe it. A structure of rationalization flew to his aid: he might not have to do anything after all. They might never find the guy. The guy might die. Fulton might die. Denton might die. Karp might die. Now, *that* looked good.

Suddenly he missed Garrahy with a pain that was almost physical. If Garrahy were still alive, this never would have happened. He would have toughed it out. The criminal justice system would never have decayed to the point where an honest cop like Bill Denton would have had to consider something like this. Or maybe that was an illusion too; maybe everything had always been totally corrupt and he, Karp, was the last real sucker in the city.

As from a distance he heard the sound of singing coming through the door, with an accompaniment of rattling noises. Marlene was singing a sad ballad, a sign that she was in a good mood. He pressed his ear to the cold black metal. It was "The Wagoner's Lad":

Oh, sad is the fortune of all womankind,
She's always controlled, she's always confined . . .

She should only know, thought Karp, and pushed open the door. Marlene, dressed in her Japanese kimono and Nikes, was standing in the kitchen area stirring something in a pan. She saw Karp, flashed a smile, and sang, a little louder:

Controlled by her parents, until she's a wife,
A *slave to her husband* the rest of her life.

Karp flung his suit jacket and his folder on a chair and went over to her. The kiss tasted of garlic and sweat.

"You're supposed to shout, 'Hi, honey, I'm home,'" said Marlene.

"Stipulate it," said Karp. "What are you doing?"

"I'm cooking," said Marlene. "You're familiar with the process? See, you buy *raw* food in a *store*. Then you put it in a *pan* on a *stove*." She tapped the gas range with her wooden spoon. "This is a stove."

"I think I'm beginning to understand," said Karp. "It's like a restaurant, except you have to wash the dishes yourself. But also, if you fondle the breasts of the attractive waitress, you don't get into trouble."

At this, Karp slid his hand inside Marlene's kimono and did just that. Her nipple hardened against his thumb, and the miracle spread down his arm and soothed him. He was always amazed at how strongly Marlene's moods affected him. Her cheerful state seemed to pump sunlight into the darkest crevices of his soul. A minute ago, he was nearly suicidal; now he was cracking jokes and feeling both hungry and horny.

Marlene looked back over her shoulder and said, "If you keep that up, you'll never get to eat this terrific dinner. Go sit on the couch. This'll be done in about two minutes."

A final tweak and Karp went. "What is it, by the way?" he asked.

"It's an exotic dish of my people, called, if I may translate, 'lots of different stuff from the

Italian deli, bought at the last minute and smooshed together with olive oil and garlic in a frying pan.' It's a traditional treat for special occasions."

"Is this a special occasion?"

"Yes, in a way. Let me just turn this down and I'll come over."

When she was settled next to Karp on the couch, she said, "Well, first of all, I had a really good day. The calendars went like clockwork all morning, and in the afternoon I put a really nasty strong-arm robber away for a year. I blew them out of the water, one-two-three.

"But the best thing that happened, is this woman I've been working with at NYU called and said she'd finished computerizing all my rape files, and yeah, it looks like we had a serial rapist doing all these panty-hose jobs."

"Come again?"

"I'll tell you the whole story later. But I felt great. Then, at five o'clock sharp, I was waiting at the Leonard Street side for my honey babe to show up, so we could go up to the diamond district to pick out a ring . . ."

Karp groaned and slapped his forehead. "Ah, shit, Marlene!"

"No, wait! OK, I'm standing there, fuming, starting to hate you, getting depressed, thinking, 'That son-of-a-bitch, how could he forget?' and all the rest, when all of a sudden I had, like, this illumination. It was almost a voice in my head, like in those cartoons—you know—there's a little angel on one shoulder and a little devil on the other? Well, this was the angel.

"And it was saying, look, if Karp missed this, he has to be in some serious shit, because you know he's been wanting to buy this ring for a while, and it's *you* who've been calling it off on one excuse or another *because* you're still freaked out about the fact that you don't have any ring finger to put it on, et cetera.

"It made perfect sense to me, and so then I started thinking about you, and what *you* must be going through, whatever it was, and I decided that I wasn't going to have a tantrum or collapse. Instead I was going to buy some wine and nice things, and make dinner for a change, and sit down and talk about it. What do you think of that?"

Karp swallowed hard, and hugged her. He felt something shift within him, like the tumblers of a rusty lock, something opening. Marlene looked him full in the face and said, "That's better. Let's eat."

They did, and Karp ate a portion nearly as large as his head. He had eaten nothing since his two-bagel breakfast. And he drank a glass of wine too, which was not something he usually did, but then, it was not every day that he sold out everything he believed in.

Finally, in a silence, Marlene said, "Well, you seem a little more human now. You looked like death on toast when you walked in here, so I knew I was right that you had a real bad day. What happened?"

"Um," said Karp, "I need to tell you this but I can't. What I mean is, whatever I say, you have to not try to guess the details, all right? You can't know this."

Marlene nodded solemnly and Karp continued. "Basically, I've been asked to suppress the prosecution of a set of major crimes. I respect the people who asked me to, and there are reasons for them to do what they're doing, and they're endangering themselves. I mean, it's not a cheap scam. On the other hand . . . I don't know what the other hand is. I'm kind of, I don't know—morally paralyzed. It's like a musician waking up one day and he's tone deaf."

He laughed bitterly. "It's funny. Today in this fucking meeting Bloom had I gave this big lecture about constitutional protection, and now I'm a party to serious subversion.

"I don't know, maybe I've just been lucky. Maybe corruption comes to everybody in this business, like a rite of passage. Like losing your virginity. No, worse: somebody close to you dying. You think everything's over, your life's finished. But it's not. You go on. But I can't. The thought just popped into my mind while we were eating. If this thing has to go down, I'm out. I'll keep my mouth shut, but I'm finished at the D.A."

"Your good angel," said Marlene.

"You're my good angel," replied Karp.

Marlene drew back and shook her head. "Uh-uh, don't lay *that* on me! Let's try to avoid the merging of our personalities as long as possible. I meant that you'll do what you have to when the time comes. Meanwhile, do you want to see my printouts?"

"Can I get drunk first?"

Marlene ignored this and went to her briefcase

and drew out a sheaf of computer tractor paper and several sealed envelopes.

Sitting next to Karp again, she spread the printout across both their laps. "This is terrific. We have a serial rapist. Nine rapes averaging around two weeks apart. Victim always the same physical type—thin and dark, short brown hair. Each time the victim was accosted in a singles bar. The rapist gets her phone number. In each case, he shows up at her house for a date, pulls a knife, makes her undress, insults her, wraps panty hose around her head, and rapes her."

"Panty hose?"

"Yeah, it's his trademark. The guy's a serious nut."

"Has he hurt anybody yet?"

"No, he just raped them. That doesn't hurt."

"Come on, Marlene, you know what I mean."

"Yeah, were they beaten or cut? No, as a matter of fact. Not yet. You want to give me odds that this bozo is going to stay such a sweetheart?"

Karp thumbed through the printouts. "Good point. Meanwhile, as I'm sure you know, it's hard to get the cops pumped up about date rape."

"This isn't date rape," snapped Marlene.

"No, but the bastard is smart—he knows as well as we do what brings the heat down." Karp pointed to a column on the printout. "What does this mean here? It looks like he had blond hair, then brown, then black. Mustache, beard, clean-shaven . . . you sure it's the same guy?"

"It's got to be. He disguises himself in the singles clubs, but he always does it the same way. Why, don't you believe it's one guy?"

Karp said nothing for a moment or two. He was thinking about Fulton's killer, the cop, and how the drug-lord killings had assumed a pattern that was no pattern, had been designed to attract the minimum attention from the police. Could Marlene's case be the same? Another cop? That was all he needed.

"Yeah, it could be," Karp said at last. "It could be. Look, Marlene, this is really good work. Let me talk to a couple of people over at the cops. Not to get your hopes up, but maybe we can figure out a way to nail this guy."

Marlene whooped and hugged him tightly. "Oh, I knew I would wrench some advantage out of fucking the boss one day!" she exclaimed. "And here it is. You really think it's a good idea? The pattern analysis?"

"Yeah, I really do. The problem is how to use it and how to build cases based on pattern as evidence. But it does get around the only-one-witness problem in taking rape cases to trial, which should help."

Karp leaned over and picked an envelope off the floor. "You dropped this in your ardor." He gestured to the dining and kitchen area. "I'm going to start cleaning this up and then I'm going to bed. I'm whipped."

"God, he cleans, he pulls strings, he fucks women . . . the last good one in New York, and I got him," said Marlene as she opened her letter.

Karp began to clear the table, stacking the dirty dishes neatly by the side of the steel sink. He had just started to run hot water into the basin when Marlene let out a cry of anguish.

"What is it?" asked Karp in alarm.

"*The fuckers!* They're firing me!"

"What!" Karp dried his hands and went to her side. She thrust the letter at him and flung herself down on the couch.

The letter was from the director of the Administrative Bureau, Conrad Wharton. It said:

> It has come to my attention that you are planning to marry a member of the district attorney's staff who currently occupies a supervisory position on that staff. This is to inform you that New York State antinepotism regulations [NYSAC 32-5436(e)] prohibit spousal, or other close familial connections, between persons at different supervisory levels in the same department or office.
>
> Therefore, be advised that your employment with the District Attorney's Office, County of New York, will terminate fourteen (14) days after the date of such marriage, unless, by that time, your spouse shall have left the District Attorney's Office or is no longer in a supervisory position.

"Ain't that some shit?" said Marlene when Karp had done reading.

"Yeah," answered Karp, "especially since we were just planning a little nepotism ourselves."

"You call catching a serial rapist *nepotism!*" cried Marlene.

"No, I'd like to think I'd go out of my way and use up chips with the cops for any ADA who came to me with a good theory and no solid evidence—but try to prove it in an administrative hearing. Look, I'll check the regs to-morrow, but I think they got us, kid. I recall a case when I first got to the office. An ADA—Frank Hobart his name was—married a secre-tary and she had to quit. I never thought about it until now."

"*She* had to quit, huh? They never make the *man* quit. *You're* not getting fired."

"That has nothing to do with it, Marlene. I have seniority. The junior spouse is the one who goes. Christ! Listen to me—he's got us talking like a couple of bureaucrats. OK, look, how bad could it be? You have to leave any-way, for the baby. What's a couple of months?"

Marlene stood up in a combative posture, tense, with her hands clenched at her hips. "It's *not* just a couple of months. It's my career! And what about the rapist? The tracking sys-tem? That's going to go out the window too. And that shithead is going to keep raping women until he checks into the geriatric ward, not to mention any other rapists who are bouncing around doing the same kind of thing."

"But, Marlene," said Karp, "you *said* you wanted to relax and take care of yourself. And the baby. So how come you're generating what could be a major investigation? Hey, roll with it. Wharton's doing you a favor."

This was the wrong thing to say, which Karp discovered when Marlene crumpled up the let-ter and threw it at him, screaming curses, and then followed it with her stack of printouts, a couch pillow, and an ashtray. She then raced out of the living area and up the stairs to the sleeping loft. He could hear her strangled sobs and honking nose-blows continuing as he glumly finished the dishes.

"Roland, I don't understand," said Karp. "You gave me all this shit about doing this task force, and now that I'm getting you off, you're bitching and complaining."

This was the next morning, in Karp's office. Roland Hrcany was pacing back and forth before Karp's desk like an overdeveloped puma. "Yeah, but that was when I thought it was horseshit. I didn't realize Reedy and Fane were in on it. That's heavy muscle and heavy exposure."

"I didn't know you had political ambitions, Roland," said Karp diffidently.

Hrcany flushed. "Yeah, well, I don't intend to cop robbers to larceny fifty times a day for the rest of my life either. There's a world beyond this horseshit, boy. What's the matter, don't tell me *you* never thought about it!"

The words took Karp aback. In fact, he hadn't, but now, for the first time, he began to think of this lack of ambition as a defect rather than as a point of pride. Grubbing for power sucked, but watching assholes who had it fuck over you and your friends (not to mention your one true love) was getting less and less attractive.

Karp shrugged and went on. "The main thing is, I need you on Petrossi. We're going to trial this week."

"Petrossi? That's Guma's."

"Not anymore it isn't. It's our hottest case, speaking of visibility. I figured you'd lap it up."

Hrcany smiled crookedly. "Yeah, if I can learn the case. Fucking Guma keeps it all in his head or on little scraps of paper. By the way, why'd you can him off the case?"

"He was fucking the judge."

Hrcany laughed. "Yeah, right! No, really, why did you?"

"Ah, it's complicated—he wanted to dive into something else, there was a conflict— and, between you and me . . . I'd rather have you in there. It's a major case, and Guma . . ." Karp waggled his hand like a plane in an air pocket.

Hrcany nodded in agreement. "No kidding. OK, I'll see what I can do. Give my love to the big shots."

"Good-bye, Roland," said Karp.

Ten minutes later, Peter Schick was standing in Karp's office saying, "Why me?"

"Because I think you can do it. Because I haven't got anybody else," Karp replied.

Schick laughed. "Is that an insult or a compliment?"

Karp leaned back and considered the younger man for a moment. He seemed to be doing well. According to Harris, who was minding him, he was hardworking and cheerful. Karp felt a vague twinge of guilt.

"A little of both," Karp said. "Mostly it's going to meetings and listening to what the great ones say. You'll be taking notes, writing up memos—crap like that. Also, catching the legal work that's associated with these cases."

"What, the murder cases?" Schick asked nervously.

"Well, obviously, any really big cases, I'll be there personally, or one of the other senior people. But there's a lot of other stuff that a big investigation like this generates, and you'll be catching all of that. Just use your judgment; handle what you can handle, and if you can't, let me know."

What Karp did not say was that the assignment of his most junior attorney to the drug task force was a clear signal that Karp cared little about what went on there. And Karp didn't. Bloom, he knew, was incapable of running a serious investigation. Whatever was going on in the drug task force was important only as politics.

There *was* something deep running underneath the conventional assertions of concern about drugs in Harlem, which was why Reedy and Fane were involved. But Karp now had a direct line into that, outside the machinations of Bloom and Wharton, and he intended to pursue it, starting at lunch, that very day.

*　　*　　*

The Bankers' Club occupied the penthouse floor of a seventy-story tower on Manhattan's southern tip. Through the great windows that stretched from floor to ceiling one could look out on sky and harbor as from the pilothouse of an immense and barely moving vessel. Once, New York's bankers had clubbed together in red leather chairs in paneled rooms, shielded from the un-elect by thick Florentine walls and plush draperies. Now, however, in the mid-seventies, they spent their last years as the world's undisputed financial lords, in such mortgaged aeries, flaunting it proudly to the ants below.

Karp and Reedy sat at one of the select window tables. The waiter stopped by for their drink order and Reedy ordered a Tanqueray martini. Karp ordered a Coke. Reedy raised an eyebrow and the waiter almost did too.

"Don't you drink, Butch?" asked Reedy.

"No," said Karp. "It's my Indian blood. I go crazy and take scalps."

Reedy laughed, perhaps a trifle more than the joke was worth. He had a good laugh, hearty and loud, with lots of air expelled. The laugh reminded Karp of the crusty Irish homicide D.A.'s of Garrahy's generation, the men who had taught him his trade, and of Garrahy himself. They had laughed like that. He found himself being charmed, and not minding it.

The charm continued. Reedy was a splendid raconteur and knew everybody in New York.

He told a funny story about the mayor and one about the cardinal archbishop, and one about how the chairman of a major bank and the heir to a real-estate fortune were both trying to get into the pants of a prominent TV personality.

He also talked about himself, interspersing bits of personal information, between the funny stories. Karp learned he had grown up in Irish Yorkville, one of ten children of a news truck driver, and worked his way through St. John's and Harvard Law School hauling boxes at the Fulton Fish Market.

"And do you know," Reedy said, "from that day to this I've never put a piece of fish in my mouth or allowed it in my house. And on Friday, before they changed the rules, we had salad, omelets—pizza pie, for God's sake! But no fish."

Today Reedy was eating filet mignon for lunch, with a glass of the house red, which today was a '66 Chambertin. Karp was having the same, and also drinking the wine. Marlene had been working on him over the past months, and while she had not yet convinced him that the ability to drink wine was as much an appurtenance of civilized life as the ability to control the bowels, he had gotten to the point where he no longer gagged when the stuff hit his throat.

So he was relaxed, and well-fed and entertained, content to wait for Reedy to deliver whatever punch line he had in mind. It came over the coffee, which was served in little *café filtre* silver pots. Reedy's came with a slice of lemon, something Karp (the big-city provincial) had not seen before. A man of definite tastes, Reedy.

Reedy had gradually steered the conversation toward the subject of Karp himself, pumping him skillfully about his background and his work. Karp went through the whole sad story: the basketball wonder boy, all-state guard, high-school All-American, Berkeley, the accident, the knee, the lost chance at the NBA, law school, working for Garrahy.

"Now, *there* was a man," Reedy said reflectively.

"Yeah, I sure thought so. Did you know him at all?"

"Not as well as I would've liked. We were on committees together, Church and Irish functions and all. But being in different branches of the law . . . and"—a sudden sly grin—"I was always after the money, to be frank, and Phil, well, as you know, he was after something else. It's not often you meet someone of whom you have no trouble saying, 'There's a better man than I am.' " He raised his glass. "To his memory," said Reedy, and they both drank and were silent for a long moment.

Karp was aware of the other man watching him closely. Finally Reedy said, "I daresay he's missed at the office."

"You could say that."

"Especially given the present incumbent."

"Especially," Karp allowed cautiously.

"He has ambitions, you know," Reedy said.

"Bloom? Does he?"

"Yes, he wants to be governor."

"He's got my vote," said Karp sourly. "I might even vote twice."

Reedy laughed. "Yes, I expect you might. He's a plausible candidate. In fact, I will tell you, in the strictest confidence, mind, that he *will* be the candidate."

"Oh? No damned nonsense about the primaries?"

Reedy smiled and shook his head. "Butch, be serious. In an open race like the next one will be, the primary is a bought thing. Sandy is personable, he speaks well on civic issues, he hires the best speech writers and pollsters, and he's already got the smart money lined up. Unless he gets caught with his hand in the till or his dick where it shouldn't be, he's a shoo-in for the nomination.

"Which leaves an interesting opening. Assuming he declares in, say, February of next year, it will leave whoever is appointed to replace him nearly seven months of incumbency before the general election. He'd be hard to beat."

"Yeah, he would," agreed Karp.

"Any ideas on who it might be?"

"I haven't thought about it much. I'm sure Bloom has any number of people he could recommend. The governor's got cronies too. It's a nice plum for somebody."

Reedy's smile became broader. "You don't see it? Look, Butch, these people"—he cast his hand to encompass the room and the towers of Wall Street beyond the glass—"the people who run New York, what worry do you think is uppermost in their minds? Crime!

"There's no damn reason to strive and hustle to accumulate wealth if you can't walk in the street without being hit over the head by some bastard who just walked out of jail. The city's crying for leadership to stop this, to drive the scum back into their holes, and to punish them when they dare to come out.

"Leadership. Now, don't sit there and tell me you've never imagined yourself in that role."

"Me?"

"Yes, you, and don't act so surprised. Who else is there? You've got a solid reputation in the criminal-law community, a splendid record as bureau chief—and you've never lost a murder case. For God's sake, man, you've actually been wounded in the line of duty! You're a natural!"

Karp felt his stomach rolling. "But I've never been involved in politics . . ." he protested lamely.

"Nonsense! Who organized Phil Garrahy's last campaign? And besides, that's all to the good. So you're not a pol! We've had enough of political wheeler-dealing in that office. We need somebody reliable, professional, tough as nails. I'm telling you, as sure as we're sitting here, you can have it if you want it. But you've got to know you want it, Butch." Reedy's sharp blue eyes locked in on Karp as he said, "Do you want it?"

As from a long distance away, Karp heard his own voice say, "I want it."

Tecumseh Booth came easily out of the light sleep favored, of necessity, by the incarcerated, to find a familiar figure in his cell. The cell was in a precinct station in Harlem, and Booth had been there for nearly three days. This was unusual, but then there had been nothing usual about this arrest. He was also alone in his cell, which was even stranger. Precinct pens were ordinarily standing-room-only until they were cleaned out each morning by the zone wagons that circulated around Manahattan, picking up prisoners and bringing them to Centre Street for arraignment.

"About time you showed up," said Booth sulkily. "S'pose to get a goddamn trial before they lock you up for life."

The shooter said, "How about keeping your voice down? Look, I hear you been doing good. I want you to know we appreciate it."

"Yeah? You got a funny way of showing it, man. When the fuck am I getting out of this shithole?"

"Soon. I can't just come in here and sign you out. You're gonna have to go to an arraignment."

Booth stood up and said angrily, "Fuck arraignment, man! That wasn't in the damn deal. I'm s'pose to be covered, and now you tell me my black ass is hanging out of the blanket? What the hell happens if I get bound over, man? I'm looking at six months in Rikers, if they want a trial, even if I beat it. No way, motherfucker! I stood up once, and I'll stand up again, but not on this shit. It don't work that way; you hump for the Man, you don't see no jail."

"Relax, will you!" said the shooter, looking nervously over his shoulder. "The fix is in. You go up to court tomorrow, and you'll be walking by lunchtime. I guarantee. Just keep your cool."

Booth sank down again on his bunk. "I better be walking," he said. "I go up on this, and they gonna put you *under* the jail."

Detectives Lanny Maus of the King Cole Trio and Dick Manning of the new drug lord task force sat near the back of Part 10 waiting for the arraignment of Tecumseh Booth. Maus was there because he was the arresting officer and because Dugman had told him to keep track of what happened to their only suspect. Manning was there because he was handling the cop end for the drug task force.

The two men knew one another slightly, and conversed in a desultory manner while the boredom washed over them from the front of the courtroom. After fifty minutes the door to the pens opened and a gang of a dozen prisoners straggled in, one of whom was Booth.

"We're on," said Manning.

"Tecumseh's looking well," responded Maus.

"I don't care how well he looks as long as we get him nailed down. Hey, who's the kid D.A.?"

The court officer had called, "Two-seven-seven-one, Booth," and Tecumseh had risen together with his Legal Aid attorney and a tall, very young assistant district attorney.

Manning shrugged and shook his head. "I never saw him before. I thought the D.A.'s guy on all these cases was supposed to be what's-his-name—the weight-lifter, Hrcany. This guy looks about fifteen. I hope he knows what the fuck he's doing."

The judge, a beetle-browed red-faced man named Nolan, looked over the case file before him. He appeared unhappy with what he read there.

"Are the People aware that this defendant has been incarcerated for more than seventy-two hours? Mr. Whatever-your-name-is, I'm talking to you."

"Uh . . . Schick, your Honor," said Peter Schick, riffling through the file and trying to make sense of the arrest report. Karp had called him five minutes ago to tell him that one of the drug-lord cases he was supposed to look out for was coming up that morning. The judge repeated the question. Sweating and distraught,

Schick blurted out, "No, your Honor . . . I mean, yes, he has."

"Good, then are the People ready for a preliminary hearing or presentation to the grand jury within twenty-four hours?"

"Ahhh . . ."

In the back, Lanny Maus pounded a fist into his thigh. Between his teeth he whispered, "Schmuck! Say yes! Say yes!" Manning rolled his eyes.

"Mr. Schick, are you familiar with the seventy-two-hour rule?" asked the judge with a tone of menace.

"Ah, I think so, your Honor," said Schick.

"You think so," said Nolan. "So may I assume that since the defendant has been in jail these past seventy-two hours the People have prepared a presentation to the grand jury today?"

"I'm . . . I'm not aware of that, your Honor."

"You're wasting my time," snapped Nolan, and then, addressing the Legal Aid lawyer, asked whether the defendant had community ties.

The Legal Aid, who was as surprised as anyone by this turn of events, said, "He has a mother, your Honor."

"Mother is OK," replied the judge. "Release on recognizance. Barney, give us a new court date. Next case."

"Two-eight-six-six-one, Maldonado," said the court officer.

Maus stood up. "Look at that asshole D.A.!

He's still standing there. He still doesn't know what hit him. ROR for a murder—our fucking only lead! I can't believe it!"

Manning said sympathetically, "Hey it happens. Nolan runs a tight ship and the D.A. had this baby in there. Look, I could use some coffee. Let's sit down and see where we go from here. We should work together on this."

The two cops stomped out. Still stunned, Peter Schick gathered his papers and drifted out into the hall. He went in the twelfth-floor men's room and washed his face and combed his hair. Then he went down to the bureau office and braced himself for one of Karp's infamous reamings.

Which, in the event, he did not receive. Karp listened calmly to his embarrassed narrative and briefly pointed out what he had done wrong, including the admonition that certain questions from judges were always to be answered with the word "yes."

Then he seemed to drift into thought, leaning back in the big chair and rocking gently. Schick listened to the chair squeak for several long minutes.

"It's odd, though," said Karp at last.

"What is?"

"Judge Nolan. Mealy Nolan, as we call him. A well-connected man, a political man, a man not above doing little favors for other well-connected people. But not, until today, widely known as a strong advocate of due process, especially not where black street criminals are concerned. Quite the opposite, in fact."

"So what does it mean?" asked Schick.

"Oh, nothing much," said Karp lightly. "Just another little ripple on the great cesspool of justice."

But, in fact, Karp thought it meant a great deal. Somebody had put the arm on Nolan to walk Tecumseh. Was it the chief of detectives? A possible; the chief wanted the thing handled out of the courts, but would he have gone to a slimeball like Nolan to do the job? Not really, and why would he have had to? He could have quietly slipped Booth out of police jurisdiction anytime in the last three days.

No, there was something else going on. Somebody with enough clout to roll a judge had wanted Tecumseh Booth out walking the streets. Did the rogue cops, whoever they were, therefore have something on Nolan? Another possible.

But now there began to intrude into Karp's mind a third possibility, even more disturbing. Suborning a judge was not exactly the style of a crazed vigilante killer. Maybe Nolan was in it out of conviction. Maybe there were others. People, even quite decent people, could do some strange and nasty things when convinced that they were right. The possibility of a truly massive conspiracy to wipe out the drug trade outside the constraints of the law darted like a giant, filthy cockroach across the surface of his mind. Who was involved? He thought of Denton, of Fulton.

Of Guatemala.

EIGHT

The voice on the phone was pleasant, but only vaguely familiar. "Hi! This is Cliff Elliot. Is this Ellen Wagner?"

Ellen Wagner responded with a hesitant "Yes?"

The voice sounded amused. "You don't remember me? Cliff? From Cheetah's last Saturday night?"

"Oh, Cliff!" she exclaimed after the briefest pause. One met so many men in the bars. Ellen Wagner was a secretary-receptionist in the president's office of a large insurance firm. She had a boyfriend, of sorts, but in that era, the last when a single wage earner could afford to live alone in a Manhattan apartment, and the last when sex with strangers was more like romance than like Russian roulette, Ellen was not ready to, as she put it, "make a commitment."

The boyfriend was all right, for an insurance executive, steady and dependable, but in the night, in the city, the possibilities were infinite. She was good-looking: neck-length dark hair worn in a frizzed style that framed her round face and delicate, even features, and a small but well-proportioned body. She was twenty-six; there was still time for the unexpected. Anyone could walk into one of the bars, on any night, and see her, and whisk her away to the land of dreams.

She tried to bring Cliff's face to mind. Crinkly blond hair, smiling blue eyes. Gold jewelry, she remembered that. Good shoulders—he was wearing . . . ?

"You were wearing the tight white jeans, right?" she asked.

"Yeah, you were drinking daiquiris," he replied. "I couldn't stop looking at you. Are you still pretty?"

She laughed and said, "I guess so. So . . . Cliff. What's going on?"

"Well, I thought I'd call and see if you were doing anything later on."

"Oooh," she sighed, her disappointment nearly genuine. "I have a date in like an hour. How bum!"

"Oh, that's OK. The thing is . . . remember we talked about how we both liked Emerson, Lake, and Palmer, and I said I had outtakes from where I work—the record studio?—and I thought that since I was in the neighborhood . . ."

"You want to come up now? Where are you?"

A nervous laugh. "Well, actually, I'm right across the street. In the phone booth."

Cute, she thought, calling from across the

street. It was thrilly and flattering, not the kind of thing an insurance junior executive would ordinarily do. Like in a movie.

"Just a minute," she said, and put the phone down. She skipped out to the hallway and looked out the hallway window. Her apartment faced the air shaft and this was the only way she could see out to Third Avenue. It was near dusk, a late Saturday afternoon, but she could see the figure in the phone booth three stories down. It was the guy.

She went back to her place and looked around. Reasonably neat. She picked up a skirt she had been hemming, threw it on a chair in the bedroom, and closed the door. She checked herself in the mirror in the living room, ran a brush through her hair, and tucked her shirt into her jeans. Then she picked up the phone.

"Come on up, then," she said. "But just for a little while."

When Art Dugman was angry he clenched his jaw so tightly that little round bunches of muscles, like grapes, stood out against his jawline, and thick veins popped out on his temples. In the Twenty-eighth Precinct they said that from the size of the veins you could estimate the degree of anger. To Lanny Maus they looked like firehoses ready to burst.

"Take it easy, Art," he said placatingly. "It ain't the end of the world."

"Boy, you don't know what the fuck you talkin about," Dugman shouted. "They treatin us like *fools*! How long you think we gonna last out there if the word get around we been fucked up the ass like this?"

"What're you talking about, fucked up the ass? The D.A.'s the one screwed up—they had a kid in there didn't know shit from Shinola . . ."

Dugman gave him a baleful stare. "The fix is in. It was set up."

"Wha-a-a-t! You saying the D.A.'s bent, and the judge too?"

"I don't know about the D.A., but if the score was tied with seconds left, and the coach pulled out Dr. J. and put in some kid who never shot a basket in his life, you probably might want to see if he was talking to bookies. The judge? Fuckin Nolan's been on the wire longer than Western Union. If it wasn't fixed, grits ain't groceries and Mona Lisa was a man."

From the corner of the squad room where he habitually sat, leaning his chair against the wall in the space between two filing cabinets, Jeffers asked, "If you right, why'd they spring him? He wasn't doin any talking."

"Why?" replied Dugman. "Why you think? This big, my man, *real* big, and real dark. We got serious players involved here. Sure, he wasn't talking, but then, he never been up on no murder charge either. They can't take that chance."

"Somebody's gonna hit him," said Maus.

"Now you detectin, baby!" Jeffers exclaimed. "You cookin good!"

"Fuck you, Mack," said Maus. Then to Dugman: "We gonna pick him up? Where's he gonna go?"

"Where you think?" Dugman snarled. "He ain't got but one place *to* run. His momma."

Ellen Wagner opened a beer for her guest and a Diet Pepsi for herself. They listened to the tape. Cliff seemed more nervous than she remembered him being, as if he were waiting for something to happen. When the tape ran out, Cliff rose to his feet to retrieve it. He slipped it into the pocket of his jacket.

"That was great," she said. "Can't I keep it? Or make a copy?"

"No can do: I'd get in trouble if they even knew I had it," he said apologetically. "Sorry."

"Oh," she said, beginning to get irritated. She didn't need two cautious guys in one day. She rose herself and plumped up the pillows where they both had been sitting. "Well, look, it's been real, but I have to get dressed, so . . ." She began to gather the glasses and cans from her coffee table.

"Let me watch you get dressed," he said softly.

She turned around abruptly, a sharp rebuke ready on her lips. It died there when she saw the expression on his face. Then she saw the knife.

Maus drove rapidly up Bradhurst Avenue, through the opening movements of Harlem Saturday night. It would start after suppertime, in the dusty twilight, first the little kids, running in screaming knots under the streetlights and through the schoolyards. Then the older kids would come out and hang in dense pockets around candy and convenience stores, blasting the night with boom-box music, yelling to each other, taunting, playing the dozens, going in and out of old unmuffled cars.

Later the older men and women would emerge, heading for the liquor stores or the clubs or the storefront churches, according to how they had decided to deal with life in Harlem. Last of all came the players, the pimps, gamblers, whores, runners, drug dealers, although there were getting to be so many of these that competition was driving them toward a continuous presence on the street. Maus drove by several places where drugs were being sold openly, circulating masses of young black men and women who talked little and shook hands with one another a lot.

Things were getting worse, according to Art Dugman, who had lived here all his life. Dugman had lovingly described for Maus Harlem as it used to be, full of sober, striving people constructing a dignified life in a world of unremitting hatred and contempt, blazing with music, lit by the genius of language.

"Crime and King killed Harlem," Dugman would say: crime for obvious reasons and King for leading the fight for civil rights and an end to segregation for those with the wit or luck to leave.

What was left was OK with Maus. Maus loved Harlem. To him it was like the *Arabian Nights* stories he had loved as a child—squalid, violent, exotic, exciting. This was not an opinion shared by many white cops from Long Island, which was why Maus was in the King Cole Trio and they were not.

"Turn right on Forty-four. It's 306," said Dugman.

Maus swung the blue Plymouth to the curb half a block east of where 144th Street joined Bradhurst, parking behind a hulk car up on cinder blocks. The hulk doubled as a playground for little kids, a party venue for teens, and a convenient rest stop for junkies on the nod. As the three cops left the car a party was getting under way; a dozen young men and a smaller number of girls were listening to music from a boom box set on the roof of the hulk, laughing, jiving, and passing around a fifth of sweet wine.

Dugman and Jeffers headed directly for the entrance to number 306, a classic five-story Harlem brownstone with broad limestone steps and balustrades, covered with graffiti and with inhabitants enjoying the early-summer evening. As the two cops mounted the stairs they seemed to bear before them an invisible cloud that suppressed casual conversation and caused the aversion of eyes.

They climbed three flights. Dugman flicked

his head and eyes upward. Jeffers nodded and continued up the stairs. Dugman turned down the hallway to the apartment where Mrs. Booth supposedly lived. Dugman would knock on the door. If Tecumseh Booth was there, either Dugman would grab him or he would go out the fire escape. If he went down, Maus would pick him up; if he went up, Jeffers would. The Trio had done this a lot.

Down in the street, Maus had become an object of interest to both the young people in the hulk car and the children circulating in the street. Half a dozen little kids asked to see his gun. Several times a corruscating gale of foul language would emerge from a tiny mouth when he refused to do so. Maus just smiled and flicked his eyes from one side of the cliff of buildings to the other, watching the windows, straining his eyes in the gathering dark. As the light faded, the party got bolder.

"Hey, po-lice! He long gone!"

"Hey, you momma in there, runnin' a train!"

"Yo, Jake! Gonna shoot another nigger, muh'fuck?"

A thin girl of about fourteen in a white off-the-shoulder blouse and her hair in corn rows strung with bright beads came dancing in front of him, her smile wide and mocking. "Hey, li'l whitey, they lef you all alone. You want company? You wann give me a ride in you' po-lice car?"

Maus said in a not unfriendly tone, "Chile, get outta my face. I'se working."

"Oh, listen here, the man's tryin to talk black," she sang out, a look of mock amazement on her face.

"How I s'pose to talk, chile? Ain I soul?" replied Maus.

"Shit, no! You whiter 'n rice!"

"How you know that? Is you my momma?"

At this, a little kid giggled and there was a sprinkling of laughter from the crowd on the stoop. The black man with white pretensions was a familiar figure of fun in the community; this was a twist that some were prepared to find amusing.

"Hey, Sherril, tell him to show you his dick!" someone shouted from the car. The thin girl grinned and said, "Yeah, you got one o' them white-boy needle dicks?"

Maus said, "Honey, if I flash my rod, you think I was God. The sight of my meat would make you drop in the street. But you can't see how I hung, 'cause you too damn young. I don' wanna take the chance, I might scare you out yo' pants."

At this, general laughter, and a voice called, "He soundin' on you, Sherril."

The girl's mouth dropped and she placed her balled fists on her hips, preparatory to returning fire, but at that moment Maus stiffened and moved away from the car. At the same time he pulled out his police ID card and clipped it to the front of his sweatshirt and drew his .38 from its belt holster.

The girl gave a little yelp of alarm and backed

away. The crowd followed the direction of Maus's gaze upward, to where a window on the third floor had opened. Tecumseh Booth was out on the fire escape and looking out heavenward.

Some people stepped out on the street to get a better view, and somebody must have spotted Jeffers' head poking above the roof parapet, because the crowd started yelling to Booth that there was a cop above him. Booth reversed direction and began to climb down the steel flights.

Maus moved into position to intercept him and suddenly became aware that, as often happens in Harlem, about a thousand people had appeared on the street in the past five seconds. A broad man with a beard and wearing a knitted green-red-and-black tam pushed in front of him, shouting, "What you want with him— what's he done?" Others in the crowd took up the cry. Someone yelled, "Get his gun!" Maus looked the man in the eye and said, "Hey, let me by, fella! I'm just doing the job here. We just want to talk with the guy."

The guy in question was stalled on the second-floor escape platform. Maus could barely make out the flapping glow of his white shirt. Some people were urging him to come down now, telling him he could get away, that there was only one cop on the street. Others were whistling and cheering. Maus heard a bottle smash behind him. His belly started to get tight.

Maus didn't hear the first shot. He saw Booth grip the platform rail and look around wildly. The second shot hit the platform itself and made it clang like a broken bell. The third shot ricocheted off the building, leaving a bright scar on the tan masonry. A woman screamed like a siren and the crowd went totally silent for a weird instant. Maus felt the pressure of a dozen pairs of angry eyes. "Motherfucker shot her!" shouted the bearded man.

Maus reached out and grabbed the man by his shirt and stuck the muzzle of his revolver under the man's nose. "Fool! Smell that gun! Did I shoot it?" The man's eyes went wide and he tried to back away. Maus gave him a push, which cleared a space in the middle of the crowd. He filled his lungs and shouted, "Somebody's tryin' to shoot him . . ."

The space disappeared as people swirled around him. His arms were pinned to his sides. He smelled sweat, perfume; he saw a huge black shape coming down the fire escape, shaking the whole structure; there were more shots, closer this time.

Maus fell, was trampled, he staggered to one knee. He saw Mack Jeffers lift Booth like a child up on his hip and fire shots down the street. People were yelling and running around in circles. Horns blared from the stalled traffic and there were sirens in the distance. Maus heard another shot and the scream of tires from a car tearing off down 144th Street.

*   *   *

"Someone's coming," she blurted. "My boyfriend . . ."

He waved the knife in front of her face. His smile was a terrifying parody of the social expression he had flashed moments before. "Your boyfriend will have to take sloppy seconds today, bitch. I'll make sure you're greased up good for him, you whore! Get into the bedroom and take your clothes off!"

She wasn't wearing panty hose under her jeans, of course. He made her take a pair out of a drawer. He wanted a dirty pair, but she didn't have any. That made him angry.

He made her lie on the bed, cursing her all the time, saying the foulest things in a quiet conversational tone. He wrapped the panty hose around her head and then made her lie back and draw her knees up to her chest so that she was fully exposed.

The telephone rang. With the blood pounding in her ears and the wrapping around her head, she heard it only faintly. It must be Seth, she thought. He always calls before he comes over and he's only fifteen minutes away. She felt a thrill of hope; whatever he did, it couldn't last very long. Maybe the phone would frighten him away.

But he leaned over her and placed the tip of his blade hard against her chest, under the breastbone. "Make a noise and I'll cut your heart out," he said, and then he answered the phone.

"Hello," he said. A pause. "This is the TV

repairman." She heard the faint burble of Seth's voice from the phone speaker. The knife pressed harder. She felt a tiny trickle of something wet roll down her ribs, but whether it was sweat or blood she could not tell. "No, I don't think she can come to the phone now. I heard the shower going. Uh-huh. Well, sometimes these new sets go on the fritz right away, y'know? OK, I'll tell her. Bye."

He hung up. She felt the bed move. Her legs were getting stiff in the exaggerated sexual position he had demanded and she tried to ease them down, but he saw it and it made him angry. He moved closer to her on the bed. She felt the knife running lightly over her genitals. He was speaking hoarsely now, obviously excited, "You cunt, slut, you want it, you can't wait for it, can you?" She heard his zipper open. She felt his weight on her. She was being raped.

Maus climbed to his feet, shaking with the aftereffects of terror. Whatever it was, the incipient riot, was over. People stood on the street in small clutches, talking, and every doorway and window was thick with watchers. Booth was sitting in the unmarked car, shaking, holding his face, which had been cut by flying brick. Dugman was in the front, talking quietly into the radio, telling the dispatchers that no help was needed.

"What the fuck was that all about?" asked Maus.

Jeffers answered, "Ask Tecumseh, here. I think your friends don't like you anymore, Tecumseh."

Maus said, "Son-of-a-bitch! Needless to say, the shooter skipped."

Jeffers nodded and pointed across the street. "He shot from the first-floor window of that vacant building. The tin over the window's bent back. He took four shots and he stopped when I started shooting."

"Any chance . . . ?"

"No way. He coulda gone out the back or up the roof. He coulda just walked out on the street and lost himself."

"How about that car that took off in a hurry? You think he was on board?"

Jeffers exchanged a look with Dugman, who put down his microphone and turned his attention to Tecumseh Booth.

"You know who it was, don't you?"

Booth looked at him mutely. Dugman reached into his pocket and pulled out a cigarette pack and matches, which he handed to Booth. The man lit one up and drew deeply on it. Dugman waited a minute or so and then repeated his question. Outside, the life of the street resumed as if nothing had happened.

Booth said, "Yeah, I guess."

"It was a cop, wasn't it?" asked Dugman.

"Yeah. He done the shooting. I jus drove, man. That's all I know."

"You gonna give us a name?"

"If I do, what do I get out of it?"

"If you don't, we'll be glad to put you back to your momma's house and wait for the man to come again. I bet next time he won't be shooting from cross the street. Figure the range be around two inches next time."

For the next few seconds Booth's face showed clearly the frantic working of his brain. At last he said, "OK, I'll tell you, but you gotta look out for me."

"Who?" Dugman asked.

Booth said, "It's you-all's boss. It's Fulton."

It had hurt worse than she had imagined, worse than the worst kind of cramps. She lay there silently, tears of rage and pain soaking into the panty hose wrapped around her head. He was arranging his clothes and pacing about the bedroom, not talking now. After a while she said, "Can I get up now?"

He didn't answer. He was thinking. He shouldn't have answered that call, but he couldn't resist, talking to the schmuck on the phone when he was looking up his girlfriend's cunt. There was a catch, though. Boyfriend could identify his voice; the girl knew his face. It was corroboration. Not good.

"What are you doing?" she asked, her voice thin and high.

He was wrapping the bedspread around her, tucking it in tightly on both sides, until she was like a mummy with its head wreathed in Tan Natural nylon.

"Please, let me . . ." she said. He straddled

her legs and held the knife over his head with both hands and drove it down into her with all his force.

"Wha-a-a-at!" cried Maus. "Lieutenant Fulton? Fuck you, scumbag! Try again!"

Maus turned his incredulous look toward Jeffers and Dugman, seeking support as to the absurdity of this statement, but the two other cops wore expressions of blank gravity.

"Hey, guys? You don't believe this horseshit, do you? Fulton?"

"Maus," said Jeffers sadly, "that car. Blue Trans Am with whitewalls. It was the Loo's car. And he was in it."

The rapist checked himself carefully in the full-length bedroom mirror. There was no blood on him at all, except on his hands, where he had gripped the knife. He looked at the shape on the bed. He couldn't remember stabbing her that many times. He must have lost track of time. Time! He checked his watch. Only eight minutes had passed since the phone call.

He went into the kitchen and rinsed his hands and the knife and put the knife away in his jacket pocket. He brought the beer can and the glass he had used back to the kitchen, wiped both of them off, rinsed and dried the glass and tossed the can in the trash. Then he wiped the tap handle off.

Twelve minutes. Another wipe on the stereo where he had touched it. He walked toward the door. He felt good, as usual, except that his underwear was wet and sticky. He had experienced another, more intense orgasm as he was taking care of the girl. Two for the price of one, he thought, and then had an even more amusing notion: the police would think it was a nut case, all that stabbing. It was a different pattern. No one would ever associate it with him. He was not, after all, a nut. The rapist opened the door, his hand wrapped in a handkerchief, and let himself out.

The three detectives and their guest drove south through the increasingly noisy evening. Each of the cops was chewing over Booth's revelation in private. Maus broke the silence.

"It still don't figure," he said. "Why are we taking this mutt's word for it?"

"It ain't just his word," replied Dugman from the rear seat.

"What, then? What! Rumors? Street bullshit?"

"It adds up. The street know something's goin down. Here, I'll show you. Maus, see that line of cars waiting to buy dope? Get in line. Mack, grab us one of them skells."

"Which one?"

"Any damn one. We doin a scientific sample."

Maus pulled the car over to where a dozen or so men were crying their wares. A thin brown man in a lavender T-shirt and a Mets baseball cap came up to the passenger window and put his hands on the sill, saying, "What you want? I got it all an' the price is right. I got weed, pills, smack, skag, coke . . ."

Striking like a cobra, Mack grabbed the man by an upper arm and jerked him through the window. Maus hit the gas and they roared off down the street.

Mack flipped the man around so that his head and shoulders were resting on his own lap, while the pusher's legs were flapping out the window. His massive forearm rested gently against the pusher's throat.

"Wha', wha' . . . wha' the fuck goin on! Leggo me!" the pusher began. Mack increased the weight of his arm and the cries choked off.

"Listen up, my man," said Mack softly. "We just want to know one thing. Where you getting your stuff. Not the mutt you get it from, the big slick. Who's the Barnes Man?" He raised his arm a hair.

"Dunno what you talkin about, man. What stuff?"

Mack dropped his arm again. When he raised it, the pusher gagged and coughed for a long time. Mack repeated the question and this time the pusher croaked, "Choo-choo."

"Choo-choo Willis, huh?" said Mack. "OK, who else still in business?"

"Blade still movin it. Some Jamaicans. Some spics. Willis been doin good since they aced all those guys."

"What's out on the street about who's doin the hits?"

The man's face clouded, and he hesitated.

From the rear seat Dugman said, "Don't worry, it ain't us. Just tell what you heard."

The man coughed hard and then said, "I heard it was cops."

"That's what we heard too," said Dugman. "You hear any names?"

The man shook his head vigorously. "No, I didn't hear nothin else. It just street jive anyway, you know?"

"The name Fulton mean anything to you? Clay Fulton?"

The man screwed up his features, showing thought superimposed on terror. "Yeah. Couple of days ago, my man Socks say somepin about some Fulton. Like he was connected, wired. Big dudes want to know anybody saw him aroun'. Some shit like that."

Mack looked back at Dugman, who nodded. Mack said, "Pull over," and when Maus did so, he flung the pusher out the window like a piece of trash.

Half an hour later Booth and the three detectives were sitting in a luncheonette on St. Nicholas Avenue having coffee and arguing about what, if anything, to do.

"I say, confront the man," said Maus. "We go up there, we say we saw you when somebody was trying to ace Tecumseh here, the word on the street is you're dirty, so what the fuck, Loo? That's the right thing to do."

Dugman shook his head. "Yeah, it would be, if Fulton was playing straight with us. But he ain't. Which means he thinks he's covered some way. So what's he gonna say? Either yes, I'm bent, and what the fuck you gonna do about it. Or no, and fuck you for accusing me. Either way we're fucked in the ass. But . . ."

"But what, Art?" asked Jeffers.

"Like I said before, there's somethin deep goin on here. We ain't got near all the story, and this old nigger ain't about to go jumpin into somethin deep when he don't know the whole story."

"So what do we do?" asked Maus, a note of tension straining his voice. "We can't just go on working for the man, pretending everything's cool. Maybe *you* all can, but I'm not made for this happy horseshit. I got to know who I can trust, you know? OK, the Loo is bent—fuck me for a chump, I thought he was a class act. But now, I'll tell you right now, I'm gonna transfer out of here. I'm no fuckin virgin—plenty of guys on the take are standup cops. But not pulling jobs, killing people, even if they *are* scumbags. How can you trust a guy like that, if it's true?"

"Play along, Maus," said Jeffers. "Game ain't over yet."

"Yeah, but we got no cards," replied Maus glumly.

At this remark, a smile, and a not very pleasant one, broke out on Dugman's face. "Uh-uh, you wrong there, Maus. We got us the biggest card in the deck. We got us the *ace*." And he looked at Tecumseh Booth. The others did too. Booth shifted nervously in his seat.

"What you gonna do?" asked Booth.

"That is the question," said Dugman reflectively. "What indeedy?" Here he paused and lit a long Macanudo cigar, and watched the sweet smoke rise to the tin ceiling above. "What we require," he said, "is, one, a place to stash our hole card. Mack, my thinking is it might be a good time for you to take a week off, take your cousin Tecumseh fishing over in Jersey. Tecumseh probably don't get in as much fishing as he'd like, driving hit men around all hours.

"Two, we need a connection, a pipe to the outside. This too big for just the three of us."

"You don't mean the snakes?" said Maus, shocked.

Dugman wrinkled his nose in contempt at this reference to the department's Bureau of Internal Affairs. "Shit, no! I meant somebody with some clout, but not under Fulton. What about that guy you were in court with when they sprung Tecumseh, the task-force guy."

"Manning?"

"Yeah," said Dugman, "Manning could be the one."

NINE

"So what do you think?" Karp asked. "Do you like the boyfriend?"

Guma wriggled in his chair and chewed thoughtfully on the stump of a dead black cigar. "Not particularly," he said. "The cops, of course, *love* the boyfriend."

"They always do," Karp agreed. "It's convenient and it's usually right. Why don't you like him?"

"Coupla things. One, the guy calls 911 from the girl's apartment, and when the cops get there, the body's still warm. So either he did it, or whoever really did do it must've practically passed him in the goddamn hallway going out.

"So if there's not another guy, we have to believe that this white-bread insurance exec with no priors and no history of violence shows up for a regular date with his sweetie, rapes her, wraps her up like a mummy, and stabs her thirty-nine times."

"It's happened," Karp observed.

"Everything's happened, Butch. Ponies

have come in first at forty to one, but that's not the way you bet. Oh, another thing: the boyfriend, what's-his-name, Allman, he claims that he called the girl before he came over and that a man answered the phone. The man said he was a TV repairman, which Allman thought was strange, because he had just helped the Wagner girl pick out a new RCA last week. The man said Wagner was in the shower, which Allman also thought was weird because he was only fifteen, twenty minutes away, and they had tickets to a show, and if she was just taking a shower, she wouldn't be ready to go. So he hauled ass over there and found her dead.''

"Do you believe him?"

"Mmm, I sort of do. There was no sign of forced entry; the girl let the killer in. According to Allman, she occasionally dated other men. He knew about it; didn't like it, but he could handle it, he says. Not a jealous type, he says.''

"Any hard evidence?"

"A little, but also strange. They searched the garbage and found a couple of cans on top of the bag. One Diet Pepsi with her prints on it and a can of Bud with no prints at all—wiped clean, as a matter of fact. Tends to confirm the boyfriend, no?''

"Could be," said Karp distantly. Something was tugging at the edge of his mind, but it wasn't a murder case. After a bit, he asked, "So where are we taking this? Since you don't like the boyfriend."

"Look at the patterns, round up the usual weirdos."

"You're thinking weirdo?"

"I'm looking at thirty-nine stab wounds, a rape, and Mr. Neat, Mr. Cool talking on the phone when he's raping the girlfriend. Cleaning up too—a supercareful son-of-a-bitch. We got a sociopath for starters. Maybe he did it before. I wouldn't want to take your money if you're betting he won't do it again. I hope . . . you know . . ."

"Yeah, that we can get him before," said Karp. It tugged at his mind again, a similar case, a similar conversation. But there were so many cases and conversations.

The phone rang, and the train of thought was gone. With an apologetic glance at Guma, Karp snatched it up and said, "I'm in a meeting, Connie."

"I know that," said Trask. "But it's a Detective Manning and he says its urgent."

Karp placed his hand over the mouthpiece. "Goom, was that it? I got to take this call."

Guma stood up. "Yeah, you got the whole story. I'll be in touch, especially if we get another one."

JoAnne Caputo had been calling Marlene about once a week to see how things were going. Marlene began to dread the calls. In fact, nothing was going on, and she was going to have to tell Caputo that face-to-face, because the woman had insisted on coming in this afternoon with what she claimed was a new insight into the rape-victim data, and Marlene hadn't the heart to turn her down.

Karp had said he would talk to the cops about her pattern rapist. She didn't know whether he had or not, and was not inclined to nag him about it, because of the business about nepotism, and the silly tantrum she had thrown.

On the other hand, he was supposed to check the severance thing out too. She looked at her watch and saw that she had fifteen minutes before Caputo's appointment. Enough time to see Karp, find out about the bureaucratic bullshit, and maybe put a zinger in about the rape business.

"He's on the phone," Connie Trask called as Marlene breezed by her desk. Marlene ignored the warning, as she usually did, and stuck her head in the door. Her bright smile froze when she saw Karp's face, which was the sort worn when you get the call that your whole family has been wiped out in a head-on. He saw her, and shook his head, and made a little shooing out motion with his hand.

Marlene shooed, and closed the door hard enough to rattle the glass. Everyone in the office, all the secretaries, clerks, and hangers-out, looked up. Marlene felt a flush move over her face. She stomped over to the battered office couch and pretended to read a six-month-old copy of *Government Executive*.

After five minutes or so, Connie Trask cleared her throat meaningfully and nodded toward the bureau chief's office. Marlene walked with frosty dignity across the office and through the door.

Karp still had that look. Marlene sat down and lit a cigarette. "Who was that, your girlfriend?" she asked nastily. "Is she pregnant?"

Karp rubbed his face. "Marlene, please. I don't need this."

"What, I can't listen to your secret phone calls?"

Karp started to say something, stopped, and merely shook his head.

"It was that cover-up thing?"

Karp nodded.

They were silent for a few moments. In Marlene, feelings of sympathy fought with her suspicions that if she were one of the boys Karp would have confided in her. At last she said, with false brightness, "Well, on a lighter note, what's happening with this nepotism crap? Did you fix it?"

"I did not fix it, Marlene. It can't be fixed. There's a loophole that allows you to extend the time allowed so you can close out current cases—for the good of the office, as they put it. But after that you're out."

"Bloom said that?"

"I didn't go to Bloom, Marlene. I checked the

regs and called a guy I know in the AG's office in Albany. No hope."

"With all the stuff you've got on Bloom . . . ?"

"You're not listening, babe. I got stuff on Bloom because he broke the law, and he knows I know it, and if he tries to break the law again, I might use it. But I'm not going blackmail *him* into breaking the law on my behalf. Or yours."

"No, but you're doing some kind of great coverup for one of your asshole buddies. *That's* OK!"

Karp's jaw tightened and he leaned toward her across the desk. "You're being a prick, Marlene. Now, cut it the fuck out!"

Marlene shot to her feet. "*I'm* being a prick? *Me*?" she shouted, and she was working her mouth around some particularly vicious thing to say when the situation suddenly became too much for her to bear. She fell back into her chair with tears starting. I will not cry, she told herself sternly, and by dint of some strenuous lip-biting and facial contortions she was able to compose herself.

"You're right. I'm sorry," she said flatly. "What about the cops? On the rape thing."

"Yeah, I talked to Dworkin this morning."

"Dworkin? Come on, Butch, Jerry Dworkin? The guy's a broom. He hasn't had an idea since 1953."

Karp sighed. "No, he's not a rocket scientist, but he is the D.A. squad chief and he's the guy I have to work with."

"And what did he say?"

"He said, 'Great, but what am I supposed to do with it?' Or words to that effect. What he meant was, if they catch a guy wrapping panty hose around a rape victim, your stuff helps to make a better case. They could bring the other women in and get an ID on the guy. But until then . . ."

Marlene stood up again. "Until then he's not going to budge his fat ass."

"Marlene, you're gonna kill me, but the guy's got a point. What do you want the cops to do? Check out every date made in every singles bar in New York? They don't have the troops. Look, Guma was just in here with a rape-*murder*. The bastard got away clean as a whistle, and we don't have lead one. A psycho this is, wrapped the girl up and stabbed her thirty-nine times, nice girl, nice building. *That's* what the cops are going after, not some—"

"What did he wrap her up in?"

"What? I don't know, some sheet or something. Why?"

"Was she slender, dark-haired?"

"Marlene, *I* don't know. Guma's got the case."

She moved toward the door, excitement starting to flow through her. Karp said, "Hey, are we OK now?"

She flashed him a quick smile. "Yeah, sorry I snapped."

"OK, remember we have a date tonight. My aunt."

She waved in acknowledgment and was gone.

JoAnne Caputo was waiting in her office when she returned. The woman was wearing scruffy jeans and a leather car coat too warm for the weather, as a kind of armor. Her dark hair was dirty and pinned back and she still had smudgy circles under her eyes. She wore no makeup.

"Something going on?" Caputo asked. "You look excited."

"Yeah, something might be," said Marlene. "There's a chance our boy killed somebody with his knife."

"Oh, Christ! Who?"

"I don't know yet. Let me make a phone call."

Marlene dialed Guma's number and was told he was on the phone.

"He's in. Let's go!" said Marlene, and hustled Caputo out.

Guma was out again by the time they got to his office, but they tracked him down in a busy corridor outside a tenth-floor courtroom.

"Goom! We got to talk," said Marlene.

"Hey, sweetie," said Guma with a wide grin. "I'd love to, but I'm in court like five minutes ago. Hey, tell me, what's the difference between a lady lawyer and a pit bull?"

"Lip gloss," said Marlene, rolling her eyes.

"Oh, you heard it already." Guma looked more closely at JoAnne Caputo. "Who's your friend?"

Marlene made the introductions. "Goom, Jo-Anne's a . . . witness in a case you just picked up, a rape-murder?"

"Yeah, the Wagner thing. Bad shit. A witness?"

"Not exactly. But we won't know unless we see the case file. Where is it?"

"My girl's got it. Under Wagner, Ellen. Feel free." He looked more closely at Caputo and smiled. "Don't I know you from somewhere?" he asked her.

"For Chrissake, Guma!" cried Marlene.

But Caputo's eyes had gone wide. She cried out and pointed her finger at Guma.

"You! You're the guy from Adam's!" she called in a shrill voice.

People in the hallway stopped and looked. Guma's jaw sagged and his face took on a stricken expression. Oh, no, Marlene thought in a panicked instant, she's cracked up. She's going to start accusing people at random. As gently as she could, she said, "Ah, JoAnne, I really don't think that Guma here could be . . ."

Caputo shook her head vigorously and said in the same excited tone, "No, he's not the *rapist*! He was hitting on me the night I met him. At Adam's." The crowd became more interested and there were chuckles from one or two of the regulars.

Guma held up his hand in a protective gesture and backed away. "Uh, ladies," he said, "it's been a pleasure, let's have lunch, but . . ." He scuttled away and was gone through a courtroom door.

Marlene looked at Caputo in amazement. "Guma was there? He hit on you that night?"

"Yeah, the fucker was all over me. Sorry, I hope he's not a friend of yours."

"As a matter of fact, he *is* a friend of mine, but he's also a chauvie, horny scuzzball when it comes to women, and he knows I know it. It's OK as long as you regard him as a separate, though exotic species, in a *National Geographic* kind of way, like a spiny anteater."

Caputo grinned broadly at this, and it struck Marlene that this was the first time she had ever seen the woman smile. It lit her face through the ever-present mask of pain, like a photoflash behind filthy glass.

They went quickly to Guma's secretary, retrieved the Wagner case file, and repaired to Guma's private office to examine it. In a few minutes Marlene let out a sharp yelp of triumph.

"It's *him*! No forced entry. He left the panty hose wrapped around the victim's head. It's him! We got him!"

"What do you mean, 'we got him'?"

"Oh, shit, JoAnne—it's horrible, but the murder puts your case into a whole new category as far as the cops are concerned. It's a violent murder. It's big-time. Assuming . . ." She paused speculatively.

"Assuming what?"

"Assuming we can convince them that it's the same guy."

"That's hard?"

Marlene frowned and scratched her head with a pencil. "It could be. Cops don't like advice. They like to figure it out for themselves. They like clues and witnesses and snitches. They might take some convincing that a serial rapist who never stabbed anybody would all of a sudden turn into a crazy slasher. I don't know . . ."

They were silent for a while. Then Marlene said, "You said you had something to show me. On the data?"

JoAnne nodded and pulled some folded paper out of a large leather bag.

"Yeah. I was thinking about disguises, the ones the guy uses." She spread the papers on Guma's desk. "Look, there are nine pantyhose rapes, but only five descriptions. It makes sense in a way. It's probably a lot of work to get the disguises right. I mean, think what it would take for you to pretend to be five different people. Also the pickups all took place at one of five singles clubs, and the rapes occurred at intervals of three to four days afterward. So I was trying to see if there was some kind of pattern to the disguises and the clubs."

The paper laid out on the desk showed four columns:

Case	Club	Date	Descr.
1	D	12/15	v
2	C	1/03	w
3	A	1/17	x
4	O	2/01	y
5	T	2/15	z
6	C	3/12	x
7	T	4/25	v
8	C	5/24	y
9	A	6/07	z

"What does it mean?" Marlene asked.

"OK, it's in chron order, of course. The second column is the name of the club. D is Dreamland, C is Clancy's, A is Adam's, O is the Omega Club, and T is Tangerines. All big noisy places, dark, and so on. Then the date when they met the guy, and the right column is the code for the disguises." She passed Marlene another piece of paper:

V = 5'10/blond short/blue/white jeans
windbreaker

W = 5'8/dark long/brown/bump nose/
casual/avi-glasses

X = 6'1/sideburns-red med./brown/
sm nose/scar/cowboy

Y = 5'10/thin brown/hazel/hornrims/
3-piece suit

Z = 5'8/blond curls/blue/cleft chin/
glasses/finger miss

"Five different guys," said Marlene. "I'm still amazed! What do you think about the finger on Z?"

"In the Z disguise he's missing the pinky on his left hand. Or so it appeared to the victim. He even brought it up, so she'd be sure to notice. Want to bet it's phony?"

"No bet," said Marlene. "So what does it all mean?"

Caputo shook her head glumly. "I don't know yet. But somehow he's got to have a system to keep the disguises straight with the different clubs when he makes his hit. But there's no pattern. He goes Dreamland, Clancy's, Adam's, Omega, Tangerines, then Clancy's, then Tangerines, then Clancy's *again*, then Adam's."

"Maybe he didn't like the band at Dreamland. Maybe he got spooked at Omega and dropped it. Or maybe there's no pattern. Except that, as I read it, he never repeats a disguise at a particular club."

"Yeah, that's his point, that's what he can't afford to do on nights when he meets his victim. But there's *got* to be a pattern. This is a pattern guy. I know it's there, if I could only—"

The door opened and Guma walked in. He raised his eyebrows at the sight of the two women. "Well, girls," he said, "what are we doing? Playing the pools?"

"No, we're finding your killer," said Marlene. "Come here and look at this."

Marlene quickly filled Guma in on the theory that the man who killed Ellen Wagner was a serial rapist, based on Marlene's case histories and the computer analysis. When she was done, he wrinkled his face into an expression of doubt and said, "I don't know, Marlene. It's fancy, all right, but what does it get us? You know? I go to the cops with this, they'll laugh in my face. The only real connect you got between all these cases is the panty hose on the head. Interesting, but not conclusive. Disguises? In the movies, maybe. Let me see that sheet again."

Guma studied the columns on Caputo's printout for a moment and then flicked the paper with a finger and shook his head. "I see five guys, five joints, random times. It starts every two weeks, fine, but look at March, here. What, the guy took a vacation? He took his panty hose to San Juan?"

He tossed the paper onto his desk and shrugged. "Don't even think cops, kid. Say we finally *get* a suspect. Think jury. Think reasonable doubt. Imagine convincing twelve people that nine people who ID five different descriptions were raped by the same guy, and that the same guy, who never broke skin on nine, decides to tear number ten to shreds.

"No, we'll get this asshole the usual way. Canvassing the area. Snitches. He'll make a mistake—"

JoAnne Caputo suddenly leapt to her feet and slammed her fist on the desk. "That's it! That's it! I'm so dumb!" She slapped her forehead with the palm of her hand and then retrieved her printout. She sat down again and began scribbling rapidly on it.

"What's going on, JoAnne?" asked Marlene cautiously.

Caputo wrote for a half-minute longer before answering, then threw her pencil down and sat back with an expression of fierce triumph. "There! It's perfect!"

Guma and Marlene moved around the desk to look over her shoulder as she explained. On the paper before her, she had penciled in five additional lines:

Case	Club	Date	Descr.
1	D	12/15	v
2	C	1/03	w
3	A	1/17	x
4	O	2/01	Y
5	T	2/15	z
6	D		w

7	C	3/12	x
8	A		y
9	O		z
10	T	4/25	v
11	D		x
12	C	5/24	y
13	A	6/07	z
14	O		v

"Mamma mia! There's the pattern," Marlene exclaimed.

"Yeah," said Guma, "the clubs repeat, but what about the X and Y business?"

"That's how he keeps the disguises straight," Caputo explained. "He can't afford to repeat a disguise in a club where he's made a hit. So he runs the disguise sequence out of sync with the club sequence. Look—at number six, the beginning of the second sequence, instead of starting with Mr. V again, he starts with Mr. W. The next sequence starts with Mr. X, and so on. He can keep that going for twenty-five hits. At twice a month, that's a whole year."

Guma knotted his brow. "It's still hard to believe. I mean, there's a zillion clubs. Why does he bother with this?"

"Because it's part of his thrill," Caputo answered with passion. "It's elegant, it's clever, and he figures no one will ever catch on. Also, the guy's a nut. Maybe he feels more in control this way. Maybe he's nervous in a completely strange place. Who the hell cares? We got him."

Marlene was studying the altered chart. "Jo-Anne, what's number fourteen? Why did you add one at the end?"

"For Wagner. I bet if you check at the Omega Club you're gonna find that the third weekend in June she was talking to a guy five-foot-ten, short blond hair, blue eyes, in white jeans and a windbreaker."

"I'll get the cops moving on it," said Guma, showing real excitement at last. "This, they can understand."

"What can I do for you, Butch?" asked Chief of Detectives Denton. The receiver of the phone was uncomfortably warm and slick against Karp's ear. He thought, what you can do for me is to get me out of this goddamn situation, say it never happened, say Clay Fulton is back among the decent living souls instead of wherever he is, say that the line between the good guys and the bad is still bright and shiny.

What Karp actually said was, "I got a call from Manning. You know, the cop on Bloom's task force?"

A pause. Then, "Yeah?"

"Yeah. He was full of news. It seems somebody tried to assassinate Tecumseh Booth at his mother's apartment house."

"I thought Booth was in custody," said Denton.

"Sprung on a technicality."

"Couldn't you stop that?"

"I wasn't sure I wanted to. I figured Booth in play on the street was a better bet than Booth with his lip buttoned in the cells. Not to mention that Rikers is not the safest place in the world if somebody wants to do you. And I was right, as it happened. It brought them out."

"Did anyone see the hit man?"

"Yes, well, as a matter of fact, Manning said the shooter was identified leaving the scene. According to the cops there, who happened to be his own men, it was Clay Fulton himself. Speaking of whom, when your detectives pressed upon Mr. Booth the basically unsafe nature of his position, and that if he wanted police protection he was going to have to come up with some names, the name Mr. Booth came up with was Clay Fulton."

An expletive that Chief Denton did not ordinarily use hissed over the line. "I agree," said Karp, "but what are we going to do about it?"

"Do about it? Not a damn thing. So some mutt named him. We know it's not him, and who can figure what a mutt is going to say? I could give a rat's ass. As for the other thing—

hanging out near the shooting—it's part of the plan. Fulton can handle himself.''

Karp took a deep breath, waited, and said, ''Yeah, I guess. Look, Chief, you remember a couple of years back we had a bunch of Cubans running around killing people? I recall these guys got their start infiltrating terrorist groups for the feds, and in order to, like, prove they were the real goods, they would pop a couple of people, show their good intentions. Now, do you think it's in the realm of possibility that Clay is doing the same thing? Showing he's a friend by wasting this mutt?''

A silence on the line. Then, ''I'll check it out.''

''Please,'' said Karp. ''And for the record, Chief—if that's the game plan, official or unofficial, I'm gone. I'm off the court. It's wide open, no deal, whatever falls out. Sorry, but—''

''I understand,'' said Denton curtly, and hung up.

''How was your day?'' asked Marlene. They were in a cab, traveling north toward Karp's aunt's apartment.

''Hell on earth,'' replied Karp in a tone that did not encourage exploration. ''How was yours?''

Marlene shrugged. ''Nothing much. Putting asses in jail.''

''Where did you run off to in such a hurry?''

"Oh, just had to see somebody I forgot about. Nothing special."

She was disinclined to share with Karp the revelations of that afternoon concerning the panty-hose rapist—or the panty-hose killer, as he now was. Karp was being withdrawn and sullen. She could play that game too, although she knew it was stupid and infantile to play back to him what he was putting out. Why should she always be the one to jolly him back to humanity? She was running a major jollying deficit herself, which she did not intend to keep doing into the indefinite future.

Nor did she quite trust him to share her enthusiasm on this case. It wasn't Karp's kind of case, and he would be annoyed to see her plunging into something new when he expected her to be leaving the D.A. in a few weeks. She would drop it in his lap only when it was good and ripe, when they had the guy, and the loose ends were sewn up.

After a few minutes Karp said in a dull voice, "I guess you're starting to close things down, right? Since you're leaving and all."

"Right," said Marlene, intending no such thing.

Silence reigned for the rest of the ride. Karp slouched in the corner of his seat, exhausted, the despair growing in him. He'd burned his bridges with Denton, that was for sure, however this mess turned out. He was surprised at how acutely he felt the loss. Perhaps he had imagined the extent of feeling in the relationship. What was he to Denton after all? A chip on the table? A useful tool?

Faces flashed before his mind's eye as he subjected various relationships to the skills honed at a thousand Q&A's. Garrahy, a man absolutely himself, a model. How did you *get* that way? Where did the sureness come from? Denton. In the Garrahy mold, but . . . maybe it was that Karp was older, more experienced. Maybe he would have seen the same duplicity of motive in Garrahy if . . . No, that was crazy. Garrahy was all right. Denton was OK too. Fulton. Impossible to believe he was corrupt. There must be some mistake about shooting Booth. Maybe. Maybe nothing was as it seemed. The image of the lawyer Rich Reedy floated into his mind. A rogue, maybe, but an honest rogue. No pretenses. Maybe that was the way to survive. No illusions, no hypocrisy.

Karp felt again a familiar painful emptiness. He defined it to himself as missing Garrahy and the ability to speak his mind frankly to a man he respected, but at some level he understood that it was more than that, something injured and missing behind the deepest defense. Now, and unusually, he thought of his father. He would have to do something about his family. He was getting married, after all.

He imagined visiting his father, and his father's hot young wife, and telling them. His father would take him aside. "They got any money?" he would ask confidentially, meaning Marlene's family, feeling for the business possibilities. No? Then he would grin conspiratorially and say, "She's a good piece of ass, huh?" Money and sex, the twin poles of existence. He might also say, "Schmuck! Rich girls got pussy too," one of his favorite expressions.

Dan, the younger of Karp's two older brothers, would say the same thing, probably in the very same words. He had abraded his own personality into a pathetic clone of the old man's, in a suicidal search for a morsel of attention. Richard, the eldest, had gone off the other end, seeking purity in a return to the faith. Assuming that Rabbi Richie could even bring himself to see Butch the Apostate, Karp imagined himself sitting in his brother's musty living room, in which even the thick air had been passed as strictly kosher, and telling him that he was—the final infamy—marrying a shiksa. They would hear the blast in Tel Aviv.

So much for family. Karp shook his head, as if clearing it after a physical blow. Why did he have to be alone like this? He was going to be a father soon, for God's sake! What the hell did he know about being a father? What could he teach the kid? Shooting hoops? Cross-examination? *He* was the one who needed a father.

But this thought, which might have occasioned much profitable internal dialogue, and also explained a good deal about Karp's career thus far, was cut short by the arrival of the taxicab at its destination, a large apartment house on Central Park West.

"That's four-eighty," said the cab driver.

"Ground control to Butch," said Marlene. "We're here."

Karp snapped to, fumbled for his wallet, paid, and left the cab. Marlene looked up at him, a worried expression on her face, and squeezed his arm. "Where were *you*?"

Karp shrugged. He really didn't know. "Just tired, I guess. Let's go up."

TEN

The woman who opened the door was half Karp's size, and to Marlene's eye Sophie Leonoff bore scant resemblance to her grand-nephew. Karp immediately swept her up into a hug that raised her shiny little shoes several inches off the ground. She kissed him loudly on both cheeks.

"Uhh! What a monster!" she cried. "My ribs are broken. Come in, come in!"

She ushered them out of the dim hallway and into a large brightly lit living room. Karp made the introductions, and Marlene could now examine her hostess more clearly. The face bore the deep lines and pouches of seventy or more years, but the huge black eyes that shone from their deep nets of wrinkles seemed younger, humorous and sharp. She was heavily but carefully made up. Her hair was dyed dark red, and she wore it in a tight nest of permed curls.

On her thin frame she wore a marvelous dress of black silk, netted across the front and decorated with sequins, the kind they sell in the little appointment-only dress shops that dot the Fifties off Fifth Avenue.

Aunt Sophie also wore a simple string of pearls and a clinking assortment of bracelets and jeweled rings. A rich New York matron in a remarkable state of preservation, thought Marlene, and was preparing herself to undergo an evening in her patented nice-to-old-ladies persona, when she became aware of being subjected to a scrutiny sharper than the one she herself had applied.

Aunt Sophie had cocked her head back and was examining Marlene through shrewd and narrowed eyes, a quizzical smile playing on her lips. She fondled the material of Marlene's suit jacket briefly, felt the lining, then made a little turning motion of her hand, jangling her bracelets. "Turn around for me, dolling," she said.

Marlene rotated obediently. "A nice five," said Aunt Sophie. "Very nice. So tell me, when you're expecting?"

Marlene blushed and uttered an astounded laugh. Aunt Sophie patted her arm reassuringly. "Dolling, pardon me I'm calling a cat a cat. I was in the business. I made more wedding gowns than I got hairs left. You ain't the first, believe me."

Marlene looked at Karp, who was standing like a phone booth, examining the ceiling. "December," she said.

"That's nice," said Aunt Sophie. "I'll be a great-great-aunt, I should live that long." She clutched Karp by the elbow. "You, *momser*, come with me to the kitchen, you can help take out from the oven. I don't like to bend down so much, I maybe can't stand up straight again." To Marlene she said, "Make yourself comfortable, dolling. There's a bar there, have what you want. You could make me a little Scotch and soda with ice, denk-you."

The tiny woman hauled Karp away and Marlene walked over to the bar, taking in the living room as she did so. It was furnished in the taste of the late thirties, art-deco-painted furniture in beige and pale gray, bas-relief plaques featuring sharp-eyed women with their wooden hair carved in buns, a white baby-grand piano covered with photographs in silver and wooden frames.

The thick carpeting was beige, as were the walls, which held two large lithographs, framed and signed, one by Ben Shahn and the other by Picasso. Everything shiny and well-cared-for, without mustiness or fuss, as in the kind of museums where people actually live in costume among colonial antiques.

The bar was also a reminder of an age when the upper middle classes poured enormous quantities of hard liquor down their throats at every occasion in which more than two people were in a room for more than three minutes. Marlene made a Scotch for Sophie and a Coke for Karp. She restricted herself to a white wine, in deference to the Little Embarrassment.

Sipping her wine, she inspected the pictures on the piano, at first idly, then with fascination, as she realized they cast a hitherto unavailable light on the mysterious stranger to whom she had bound herself. Here were Aunt Sophie and another woman, in their twenties. Sophie, lovely as a young bluebird, was laughing, while her companion, less well-favored but still handsome, looked out at the camera suspiciously with a face full of unerring righteousness: Karp's ferocious late grandmother.

A wedding portrait from the thirties: a tall man, looking determined and confident, bearing Karp's wide cheekbones, and a beautiful woman with Karp's gray eyes, eyes that were not at all confident, in a beautiful, gentle, and introspective face. The dead mother and the estranged father. The thought exploded into her mind that *all this* was now growing within *her* body. It rocked her like the surf and she grew momentarily dizzy.

Her vision cleared, and she reached for another frame. Three boys, aged about eight, ten, and twelve, the youngest her own lover. The other two were showing the false smiles encouraged by commercial photographers; little Butch, in contrast, was holding out, just the ghost of a secret smile on his lips and his little chin defiantly raised. Unaccountable tears stung her eyes.

She dabbed at them and went on. A portrait of a continental-looking man with a pearl tie pin and an Adolphe Menjou mustache. Husband? Brother?

In a black ebony frame, a small sepia photo

taken before the turn of the century, a large
family in front of a farmhouse in summer, the
men hatted and heavily bearded, the women in
long white dresses, the boys in sidelocks, the
little girls in pinafores. The Old Country. Marlene's grandmother had stacks of pictures like
this one, from another Old Country. For the
first time since she had begun with Karp, it
came home to Marlene that the difference
might be important.

The rest of the photographs showed a
younger Sophie with other people, dressed ele-
gantly in the fashions of the twenties and thirties, usually at café tables covered with food
and bottles, and in the street, in trios and couples, clutching one another and laughing at the
camera. The streets were in Europe somewhere—ah, it was Paris—the signs in French, a
typical Métro entrance in one background.

Marlene smiled and inspected one of these
photographs more closely. In this, Sophie was
holding the arm of a sharp-faced woman with
large intelligent eyes. With a start, Marlene recognized Colette.

Thus was Marlene's curiosity unbearably
piqued, and after the excellent dinner, during
which two bottles of an unearthly Montrachet
followed the *suprême de volaille* down the hatch,
oiling the tongues of the two ladies, while re-
ducing Karp to grinning stupefaction, she
brought up the subject of Sophie's speckled
past.

"Colette, yeh," laughed Sophie. "Another

size five. Yeh, yeh, of course, dolling, I knew them all. We was in New York, from Poland, me and my sister may she rest in peace, five years sewing, and I run off with a dencer. A bum, but from gorgeous, *quel beau*, you never saw. Then after—who knows?—a year, he ran off with a *putain*, who knows where?

"So, nu, I wake up, I'm in Paris, with no money, what I'm gonna do? Thank God, I could use a needle. I worked for Worth, for Mainbocher. Also, later, I had my own place on Rue Champollion.

"They all came to me, the actresses, the girl-friends, the writers. Why not? I was good and I was cheap. *Ma petite juive*, they used to say."

She giggled. "You know what I done? I had a friend, fancy-schmancy, *très beau mondaine*, *versteh's*? A very fine lady. We used to go to the salons for the shows. I was the servant, the little mouse in the back. I would see the dresses. Then I would run back and buy mate-rial and take it to the shop and make the dresses. For my friend and her friends."

"You made them? From memory?"

"Of course, from memory—what you think? Every stitch, better than Dior and half the price. You couldn't tell the difference. That's how I met Max. Max, my husband, he should rest in peace. He had businesses in New York. When he found out what I did, he said, 'Sophie, this is millions here, what you can do. Make the dresses, cut patterns, I'll send them to New

York, I got there people can make thousands with machines.'

"So I did, and he was right, we got rich. *Cousu d'or!* Every year, I would go back and forth, back and forth, boats, airplanes. All first-class. In Paris, at the George V all the time. And we got married. He said, why not mix business with pleasure? A mensch, *aimable*! That was Max. You would've loved him. Roger, you remember Uncle Max?"

Karp stirred, mumbled something, and resumed his grinning stupor.

"Our first season, he gave me this." Aunt Sophie stretched her arm across the table to show Marlene a bracelet on her wrist. It was a thick wide band of gold in the art-nouveau style, decorated with a line of jaguars running through a jungle. The jaguars' eyes were diamonds and the jungle was constructed of close-packed emeralds. Marlene examined the bracelet. "It's incredible," she exclaimed and then froze briefly. Just above the bracelet on the thin wrist was a line of blurred blue numbers: 75955. Below these, a tiny solid heart had been tattooed in red.

Aunt Sophie caught the change in expression. "Yeh, that. He begged me, he said, 'Sophie, don't go this year, I got a bad feeling. But me, what did I know from this? I forgot I was Jewish already. I went for the spring show in 1940, and bang, comes the Nazis. I'm caught. Two years I'm hiding. I'm sewing, I'm starving. Then I get picked up—don't ask! *Un tour de cochon!* I was in the camps two years, four months, thirteen days. I don't know the minutes. Also sewing, for the Nazis, they want nice clothes for the girls too.

"So. I got on my wrist a souvenir. I come back on the boat, Max is there. 'In my heart I knew you would come back,' he says to me. He wants me to get rid of this, but I say, no, we should never forget. But I put in this heart myself, to cover up, you know, the swastika.

"Roger, here, he was always interested, so interested. His mother, she should rest in peace, would say, 'Leave Aunt Sophie alone, she don't want to remember these times,' but he would ask. One time, cute! You could die from it. He brought out a little wet rag and soap. 'I'll clean it off, Aunt Sophie.' So he was scrubbing, scrubbing, and the more he was scrubbing, the more it wouldn't come off, and he was crying and scrubbing. You remember that, Roger?"

Marlene saw that Karp was now alert, not smiling, grave. "Yes, I do," he said.

Sophie went on. "He would ask me, how come they put the little mark across the seven like they make, and I would tell him, they're very careful, the Nazis, they don't want to mix it up with a number one, God forbid they should kill the same person twice." She laughed and shook her head.

"So, dolling . . . *quel mignon!* You was going to grow up and get those Nazis for your old Aunt Sophie. So tell me, Roger, what do you hear from Daniel and Richard? I never hear from them."

Karp and his great-aunt began speaking of family, reminiscences mixed with news of births, deaths, college graduations, professional success or failure, speculation about missing persons, the occasional maledictions on the clan's bums. Marlene sucked on the remains of the wine and listened to the hearthfire legends of the paternal Karps and the maternal Gimmels. It had not sunk in on her until this moment that Karp sprang from the same sort of limitless immigrant circus from which she herself had sprung, with its stars, its clowns, its humble shovelers-up after elephants.

That Karp had depths, she knew; she had never glimpsed before this evening the creatures that inhabited them, and was by turns fascinated and frightened, as she had been when studying the pictures on the piano.

Karp seemed so isolated as a man, so himself, a creature *sui generis*, that Marlene had let herself imagine that Karp's origins meant as little to him as they did to her: an interesting fact, an exotic spice; occasionally, as with the wedding preparations, a mild pain in the ass. She saw Karp as a perfectly melted New Yorker, as she was. Now it began to dawn on her that there might be a chunk of some more refractory metal buried in the melt, something ancient and hard as diamond.

Aunt Sophie was running down, the pauses between her remarks getting longer, her voice fading into whispery hoarseness. Karp and Marlene cleaned up the supper things and, with many a sincere promise to return often, made their farewells.

Out in the street, searching for cabs on Central Park West, Karp seemed to have dropped some of the defeated sullenness that he had worn on the ride uptown. He put his arm around Marlene's shoulders and asked, "So how did you like my Aunt Sophie?"

"I loved her," said Marlene with feeling. "There's a lot of her in you."

"You think so? She's a tough old lady. I could use all I can get."

A cab appeared and Marlene stopped it with her ear-cracking two-fingered whistle. As they started their downtown drive, Karp remarked, "Yeah, she's something. When we were in the kitchen, she took one look at me and asked what was wrong, I had such a long face. I looked at her and, I don't know, I started to feel better. And it's funny, I remembered she had the same effect on me when I was a kid, when I was miserable. Like when my mom died. There's worse things dolling,' sympathy, but . . . it somehow put everything in proportion, because you knew that whatever you were going through, it was bullshit compared to what *she* went through. And there she was, this funny, happy lady.

"And that business with the tattoo . . ." Karp laughed. "I could never get over the cross mark on the seven. So they wouldn't mix up the corpses. God! I haven't thought about that in years, it's like . . ." Karp suddenly stopped short and sat up rigid in his seat. He looked at his watch.

Marlene felt the motion and asked, "What is it?"

Karp leaned forward and gave the driver a new address. The cab swung into a left turn and soon was heading north and west.

"We're not going home?"

"No," said Karp. "We're going to a club. Listen to some music. Live a little."

"Butchie, what a treat!" cried Marlene. "Let's hear it for Aunt Sophie! Where are we going?"

"A little joint uptown. Pepper's," said Karp.

"Jesus, Butch, I didn't know you knew about places like this," said Marlene, peering through the smoky darkness of Pepper's. "What an evening of revelations this is turning out to be!"

Settled at a table the size of a dinner plate next to the toilet door, Marlene remarked, "God, they really know how to treat white folks here. Fuck-a-duck, Butch, I haven't come uptown to hear music since high school."

"Takes you back, does it?"

"Yeah, ply me with sweet drinks and I might let you feel me up in the cab."

"Not all the way?"

"Well, perhaps just the tip, if you're super nice. Not a bad band, by the way. Who is it?"

"I don't know the official name. Recognize the piano?"

Marlene put her glasses on and squinted. "Looks like . . . Clay Fulton?"

"Yup, that's him."

Marlene gave him a suspicious look. "The plot thickens. Could it be that we're here for something other than careless gaiety?"

Karp shrugged and ordered a couple of beers from a passing waitress. The band finished its set, and a few minutes later Clay Fulton walked by their table on the way to the men's room. Marlene was about to hail him but Karp held a finger to his lips and shook his head. Fulton went through the swinging door and Karp stood up. "Be back in a minute," he said.

Fulton was standing at the single urinal. Karp waited for him to finish. He said, "Hey, Clay."

Fulton spun around. His face was tight, and he had dropped a few pounds since Karp had seen him last. "What're you doing here, Butch?" he asked curtly.

"Listening to music with Marlene. Thought I might talk to you while I was up here."

Fulton pretended to look at his watch. "Yeah, well, I'd like to shoot the shit with you, but I got to make some calls."

Karp didn't move from his position in front of the door, and it was clear from his stance that he didn't intend to.

"Let me by, Butch," said Fulton, a stiff smile on his face.

"In a second, Clay. I just need to know something. The word is you took a couple of shots at Tecumseh Booth the other day."

Fulton's smile vanished. "I don't know what you're talking about," he snapped.

"Yeah, you do. Somebody tried to kill Booth at his mother's place, and Dugman's bunch saw you driving away, and I just wanted to—"

"What the fuck is this, Karp? *I'm* the cop. *I* ask the questions. Don't bother me with this horseshit! Now, get the fuck out of my way!"

"You're being set up, Clay. And I know what you're doing and you're fucking it up."

For an instant Fulton went rigid, gaping like a gaffed cod. Then his jaw tightened, he uttered an inarticulate growl and tried to force his way past Karp by main force. Karp gave him the hip and pinned him up against the plywood wall of the narrow passage leading to the door.

"Listen to me! I'm your friend, goddammit!" Karp yelled into his ear. "You owe me three minutes without bullshit. And if I have to grab you in a fucking john, that's your fault, not mine."

Karp felt the tension in Fulton's body relax slightly, and he pulled back. There was still less than a foot of space between their bodies. Fulton's face glistened like damp dark wood in the unforgiving light of the naked bulb.

"OK," said Karp, "I'm gonna lay out what I know, just the way it came to me. One, you come in and tell me these dope-dealer killings are connected and you're trying to get put in charge of all of them. Two, I find out Bloom is organizing a task force to look into them, to which you're not invited. I go to the first meeting, and I find out that the official representative of the police force thinks you're poison. Three, you drop out of sight. There's rumors flying around that you're dirty. Four, Tecumseh Booth gets sprung on a technicality under suspicious circumstances. Somebody with serious clout was using it, on a judge.

"Five, I'm worried about you, so I call the C. of D. I get completely stonewalled. This sets me wondering. I'm pretty tight with the chief. I'm pretty tight with you. Why doesn't anybody want to talk to me about these murders? What could it be? Is Denton taking bribes in his old age, a guy who never took a free cup of coffee in his life? Clay Fulton is dirty? It's like the pope saying, hey, I already got the yarmulke, I might as well get circumcised and move to Crown Heights. It doesn't figure, except for one possibility. One possibility would make Denton and Fulton act this way. What is it, Clay? You gonna tell me?"

Fulton looked into his eyes a long minute. Then he sighed and said, "I can't tell you, Butch—believe me, I would if I could, but—"

Karp held up his hand. "OK, OK, I understand. Let's be hypothetical, then. Let's say we got the chief of detectives and his ace lieutenant investigating a series of drug-pusher killings. The lieutenant thinks they're all connected. So what do these ace detectives do? Do they bring their evidence to the task force that the D.A. has started to investigate these selfsame killings? Do they launch a serious public investigation of these killings? They do not. They work in secret. They don't even talk about it to their close personal friend who happens also to be a D.A.

"So this friend starts asking himself, why the secrecy? What's the answer here? The envelope, please. Ah, here it is. The *one* thing that would cause this kind of shutdown. What if our two detectives have concluded that the only way the killings could have been done the way they were done is if they were done by rogue cops? Something snapped somewhere and you got a couple of guys out trying to clean up the city. Clint Eastwood in real life—they're shooting dope pushers.

"See, it's like your pattern that wasn't a pattern. You get two good honest cops like you and Denton acting in this way, and somebody who knows they're good and honest *has* to guess what they're doing.

"Because, being good cops, they have this problem—crazy cops, it's bad for the force. It's one thing in the movies, but in real life it's another story: they're looking at a long, messy trial, a scandal, and so soon after the Knapp Commission? So maybe they can handle it privately. Grab the guys, a quick ticket out of town, case closed. And the victims are scumbags, nobody gives a shit about them anyway."

Karp paused and looked searchingly at his friend. Fulton gave him a long flat stare. At length, some little flicker around the eyes showed Karp he had gotten through, a mental transmission had clunked into a different gear. Fulton nodded slowly. "Go on," he said.

"So they're looking for wackos. The lieutenant goes underground, they start spreading stories he's dirty. Why? He wants access to the underworld. He wants to be approached. Now he's a guy who takes dirty money, he beats up people. Maybe his new mutt friends will let something drop, maybe he'll hit the jackpot, he'll get contacted by the actual guys: 'Hey, Loo, want to ace a pusher—it's fun!' "

Fulton was growing restless. A man pounded on the locked door to the toilet. Karp understood he had less than a minute to finish.

"Get to the point, Butch," said Fulton.

"The point is, they're wrong. You're wrong. It's not a couple of crazies. They're connected. They're not free-lancing. They're doing it *for* somebody, and whoever it is has a shitload of clout."

"How do you know that?"

"Got you interested, didn't I? It was the judge who sprung Booth that got me thinking. Why would he do that? A judge conspiring with crazy cops? Maybe, if it was a certain kind of judge, but not the Honorable Mealy Nolan. This is a lightweight: intellectual and moral. And a *criminal* lightweight too, which is my point. On the pad since the year one, but safe.

"Not a sticker-out of the judicial neck, you know? Little fixes a specialty, for a consideration, but no fat envelopes. Somebody calls him, says, 'Terry, me lad, I just heard IBM is about to split and I took the liberty of picking up a hundred shares for you. And by the way . . .'

"That's how it would go. But a cop walks in, says, 'Judge, we been waxing these dope dealers, cleaning up the streets for the citizens, and now we'd like you to spring the only witness so we can wax him too.' No fuckin way, boss!"

"Who's the guy, then?" Fulton asked, going instantly, as Karp had feared, to the key weakness of the hypothesis.

"The guy who called Nolan, you mean. This I don't know."

Fulton seemed to let out a long breath. He shrugged and walked toward the door. This time Karp did not block him. Fulton said, "It's a nice story, Butch. Hypothetically speaking. I don't know what you plan on doing with it, though—"

"But I know how to find out," Karp interrupted.

"How?"

"I'm going to ask Tecumseh. He leads us to the cop, and the cop leads us to the guy."

Fulton grinned broadly and shook his head. "You don't give up, do you? What makes you think Booth will talk? He never talked in his damn life, except to tell a lie."

"He'll talk to me," said Karp, and even as the words formed in his mouth, the plan for making them true leapt all complete into his brain. He said, "Come and watch us play ball tomorrow. I'll set it up."

Fulton said, "You better not tell Dugman that

I'm gonna be around. I don't think he trusts me around Tecumseh anymore."

"No, I'll fix it up so there's no contact," said Karp. "By the way, I should call him now. You happen to know where he is?"

"Yeah, he's got the graveyard shift tonight, at the precinct."

"OK, I'll call you tomorrow after everything's set."

Fulton nodded and left.

Karp went to the pay phone and called Dugman. After some preliminary fencing, Dugman became extremely cooperative. The detective had grown increasingly nervous about his position: he was working for a lieutenant he thought was involved in the very murders that lieutenant had ordered him to investigate; he was holding a private prisoner who might be a key witness in those murders; and he sensed that there were big wheels moving somewhere behind all this, wheels that could squash a fifty-five-year-old black detective without even slowing down.

Fearless on the streets, Dugman felt helpless before the forces of bureaucracy; he was looking for shelter and when he discovered that the D.A. was going to provide it, he was unabashedly grateful.

After the call, Karp walked back to Marlene, who had ordered another set of drinks. "Hi, sailor," she said. "You were in there long enough for a blowjob."

"What's a blowjob?"

"Fifteen dollars, same as downtown," she shot back.

Karp looked at the drinks in a meaningful way. Marlene caught the look.

"It's a wine spritzer, Doctor," she said defensively. "I have cut down smoking and drinking as much as I am going to, and if you think I am going to become a granola fascist because I'm knocked up, you have another think coming. My mom drank a pint of wine and smoked a pack of Pall Malls every day of her six pregnancies, and we're all perfectly normal."

"Present company included?" asked Karp.

"Besides me, I mean," said Marlene, cracking a smile. "But really, what's going on—with Clay and all?"

"Just office stuff. Catching up on things," said Karp evasively.

Marlene pouted. "OK for you, buster—in that case I'm not going to tell you *my* secret. Oh, good, they're going to do another set."

Fulton and his trio had come back to the tiny stage, and without preamble burst into a lively upbeat tune.

" 'Tinkle Toes,' " said Marlene. "Lester Young." They listened. After, she said, "Hey, Clay's not bad. And the sax. Not that I know much."

"Lester Young," said Karp. "Pres."

Marlene looked at him in amazement. "That's an impressive piece of cultural information, for you. He has an aunt who knew Co-

lette, he drinks, he clubs, he jazz-aficionados
. . . it's a whole new Karp."

"Oh, and what was wrong with the old
Karp?"

"Nothing, dear, nothing—you were perfect
then and you're even *more* perfect now,"
breathed Marlene in her best phony Donna
Reed voice. "Let's just listen to the music."

They left at two. The magic of the evening
was capped by their fortune in finding an on-
duty cab in Harlem.

"We'll never get to work tomorrow, and I
don't care." Marlene yawned. "Let the wheels
of justice grind to a halt."

"Yeah," said Karp, "what's a few less asses
in jail?"

Marlene looked him full in the face. "You're
such a phony baloney, Butch," she told him
sternly. "The line you lay down about it all
being a game—putting asses in jail. It's that
number seven, isn't it? That drives you. You
can't stand for anybody to get away with it.
That's why you're such a fanatic."

"Yeah, right. If you say so," Karp retorted,
feeling defenseless and more vulnerable than
he liked to feel. "You're in charge of that deep
stuff." Marlene was about to answer this, but
found she lacked the energy required for another bout of mutual introspection. She snug-
gled into Karp's chest and immediately fell
asleep.

Karp watched the traffic lights shine through
the steam from the manholes, and reflected that

he had not felt this good in weeks. He had managed to scoop Fulton in with a net of plausible lies, all whiter than white, revealing his own knowledge of the affair to Fulton without breaking his promise to Denton. It was unlikely that Fulton would tell Denton about this conversation; it would be close to admitting that Fulton had let Karp in on the deal. As Denton had in fact.

Fulton was now no longer entirely outside the cover of the law, nor was he pursuing the phantom of a mentally deranged-police-officer cabal. He was ready to listen, and if he rolled, Denton would roll too. The kid had dribbled through the zone, he had paint underfoot, and tomorrow he would take his one and only possible shot.

ELEVEN

Karp and Hrcany, dressed in sweats and sneakers, and carrying duffel bags laden with softball equipment, walked out of the Criminal Courts Building and toward Hrcany's car, which he had stashed in the special judges-only parking on the Leonard Street side. It was five-fifteen on a Friday, and every judge in the world had been safe at home for hours.

They drove north toward Central Park and its tracts of softball fields. The D.A.'s team was playing their traditional rivals, a team from the Legal Aid Society, called the Bleeding Hearts. The D.A.'s team was called the Bullets, from the slang term for a year in the slams.

Karp seemed nervous and distracted. He kept looking out the window, checking both sides of the street, as if searching for an address. Hrcany said something, which Karp missed.

"I said, we should wrap up Petrossi next week," Hrcany repeated.

"Good, that's great," said Karp absently. Then he tapped Hrcany's arm and asked him to pull over.

"We got beer already," said Hrcany.

"No, I got to stop in at that travel agency. I'll just be a minute."

Karp returned holding a ticket folder.

"Where're you going?" Hrcany asked.

"Nowhere. This is something else." He stuffed the ticket in his sweatshirt pocket and said, "So—Petrossi. We gonna win?"

"You have to ask? It's a lock. By the way, any progress on this drug-lord business?"

Karp stiffened, but kept his voice casual. "Not much, I guess. Schick handles the day-to-day. Why?"

Hrcany looked sharply at his companion for a second, then turned his attention back to the rush-hour traffic. "Oh, I've been hearing stuff."

"Who from?"

"Oh, around the hallways. Cops bullshitting. You know. Word is they're looking at a cop for the shooter."

Karp looked at him sharply.

"Yeah, I figured you'd be interested. Number one on the charts is your buddy Fulton."

Karp looked away. Hrcany continued. "So what do you think? You know the guy. Could he be bent?"

"Anybody could be bent, Roland. But it's a big jump between 'could-be' and bringing a case."

"But you have your doubts."

"Yeah, I've got to say I do. He's been acting funny. He's been hanging with some dirty people. And he was seen running from the scene of an attempted murder of a witness in the case."

Hrcany said, "It's a funny business. Considering the scumbags he's knocking off, maybe they should give him a medal. Some of the cops I talk to think that."

"How about you, Roland? You think that too?"

Hrcany paused significantly before answering. "There are days . . . but let's face it— what *we're* doing isn't having much of an effect. A little police terror might calm things down."

"Just like Hungary, huh?"

Hrcany flushed, and snapped angrily, "That's not the fucking same thing at all!"

"No, I guess not, from our point of view. Maybe they feel different up in Harlem. In any case, there's enough people on the lookout so that if it *is* Fulton, they'll eventually nail him. A real shame too—he probably cracked up from the strain. It'll be a hell of case to try, though."

"Yeah. Are you sure that kid Schick is up to it?"

"He'll learn," answered Karp dismissively. "Meanwhile, I'm more concerned if he can pull the ball to right field."

As it turned out, Peter Schick did pull the ball for a single and a nice double, scoring once. But the Bullets lost the game, 10–7, to a team that had as members a surprising number of

Dominican hotshots, purported paralegals, but, to the disgruntled Bullets, patently clients and other semipro ringers.

Karp went one for four and missed an easy out at first base. He was not playing with anything near his usual concentration, and the reason for the lapse was sitting in a dusty tan sedan parked up on the grass verge of the access road. When the game was over, Karp slipped away from the noisy crowd of players clustered around the beer cooler and walked over to the car.

"Thanks," said Karp to Dugman, who was sitting in the car's front seat. "I'll bring him right back."

Dugman said, "Go with the man, Tecumseh."

Tecumseh Booth got out of the back seat and stood blinking on the grass. "What is this?" he said, looking back at Dugman as if the cop were his own momma.

"Man just want to talk with you, man," said the detective. "Don't worry, we gonna stay right here."

Karp walked Booth along the verge until they came to a pedestrian path, at which they turned and walked north for a distance in the direction of Sheep Meadow. Karp sat down on a bench placed before a pile of glacial boulders and motioned Booth to sit as well.

"I hear you had a narrow escape," said Karp conversationally.

"Who are *you*?" demanded Booth.

"My name's Karp. I'm with the D.A."

"I don't need to talk to no D.A. I got a case-dismissed."

"OK, suit yourself." Karp leaned back and breathed deeply. The air was cool and scented with mown grass and orange rind.

"Sure is a nice day," Karp observed. "You should enjoy it. It's probably going to be your last." He turned and looked Booth full in the face. Booth wore his usual stubborn passive mask, but there was something twitchy around the eyes. Being shot at, with the prospect of more shooting to come, will do that.

"See, the problem we got here is, you're no good to me anymore as a witness," Karp resumed. "You got off, as you point out, and you won't testify against whoever got Clarry, because you're a stand-up guy. I need a cooperative witness.

"Now, what do you get for being a stand-up guy? You saw what happened. They tried to kill you. And they're going to keep on trying."

There was no reaction. Booth continued to stare mutely at him. This wasn't working.

"The penny hasn't dropped yet," said Karp, more urgently. "You're still thinking this is just another job—you drive for some guys knocking over a liquor store, and the cops catch you and you keep your mouth shut. That's natural. We understand that. But you're in a whole different game now. There's big guys involved, very big guys—cops too. Look, you see those ants down there?"

Karp moved his foot to indicate a swarm of the insects mining some strewn Cracker Jack. "They've got a code too. They stick together. Maybe there's another kind of ant tries to move in on their turf, they gang up on them. Who knows, maybe they make deals. Maybe there are stand-up ants and rat ants. Whatever. But what you're into is this!"

Karp brought his sneaker down sharply, with a savage twist, crushing the ants and their food into a damp smear. A couple of the surviving ants went scurrying off in different directions. Booth was watching the demonstration with interest.

"The ones running are the smart ants, Tecumseh," Karp said softly. "They know when they're licked and they get small real fast. OK, I don't want to waste your last day on earth, so I'm going to make it short. One of two things is going to happen right here and now.

"One is, I'm going to ask you what you know about these killings and you're going to keep quiet and I'm going to get up and walk back to that car and we're going to drive away. That's it—sayonara, Tecumseh.

"You figure the odds. Think you can get out of town on your own? Think you can get out of the *park*? Want to bet we're not being watched right now?"

Booth was not able to suppress an involuntary searching movement of his head. The trees and bushes rustled and crackled in a way that suddenly seemed menacing. It was not like the warm security of a police station or an interrogation room. Booth felt hideously exposed. His breath came shorter and Karp pressed on.

"On the other hand, you could talk, and I'd give you this."

Karp took an airline-ticket folder out of the belly pocket of his sweatshirt and handed it to Booth.

Booth looked at it as if it were a crossword puzzle in Amharic. "What's this about?" he asked.

"It's an open ticket to L.A. in a fake name," said Karp. "You answer a few questions, and then we both go back to the car and the detectives drive you to La Guardia. They'll give you some cash and kiss you good-bye. You're on the next flight to L.A. with two hundred dollars in your pocket. A new life. Or maybe I should say the only life you're likely to have."

Booth took the ticket out of the folder and read it slowly, paging through the counterfoils, as if it were a letter from an old friend, full of sage advice. Booth tried to think it through, to figure the angles, but he was unused to thought. Other people made the plans. He just drove and kept his mouth shut. Hesitantly, and in a near-whisper, he said, "I just tell you? No court? I don't sign no papers?"

"Just me, and right now. And you're gone."

Booth released a long, soft sigh, like the last breath of an old, sick man. "Yeah, what the fuck," he said. "Whatever you want."

Twenty-five minutes later, Karp sat on the bench and watched Tecumseh Booth walk rapidly away down the leafy path. Two minutes after that he heard a car door slam and the sound of a car accelerating. For a while he sat quietly in the breezy silence. Then in a loud voice, he said, "Home-free all!"

Steps crunched on ground litter behind him, and Clay Fulton came out from behind the boulders, brushing grit off his suit coat and trousers. He had a small Nagra tape machine hanging from a shoulder strap and a gun microphone in his hand.

"Did you get it?" asked Karp.

"Yeah, I did," said Fulton, sitting wearily down next to Karp. "Helluva thing. It never fucking occurred to us." He shook his head, flabbergasted.

"I know. I've had the same feeling about the D.A.'s office from time to time. It makes you wonder."

"It do," said Fulton. And after a brief silence: "So where do we go from here?"

"Well, now that we have names and places, we can start building a real case. If you're up for it, I figure the best thing is to keep on with what you're doing. You're getting an evil reputation, my man. Anybody interested in hiring bad cops, you'd be right up there with the real bad boys."

Fulton offered a smile without much humor in it. "Yeah. The bad boys. Son-of-a-bitch. I still can't get my head around it. Cops taking money—sure. Maybe pulling burglaries even— we had that a lot. Lifting dope and selling it. But contract murder?"

He shook his head hard, as if trying to dispel a bad dream. "And Manning. The inside guy, the *task-force* guy. Son-of-a-bitch!"

"Yeah, Manning. That'll have to be your end. But I'd watch one thing."

"What's that?" Fulton asked.

"I've been thinking. Manning was a little too enthusiastic in blackening your reputation."

"Blackening. I like that."

"So to speak. I'd also bet that he's been clocking overtime accelerating the rumors around town. Why would he do that? One reason might be that it's getting hot. He hears the hounds baying across the bayou. Whatever. So wouldn't it be neat if he, Manning, was to bring down the notorious Fulton, who turned out to be the black killer cop that's been popping all these drug dealers?"

"I like it," said Fulton after a moment's reflection. "I'd have to be dead, of course."

"Needless to say. So watch your young black ass."

"How?" Fulton said, and then he laughed, a rich loud sound that echoed off the rocks.

Karp saw that it was genuine release of tension. Fulton was glad, at least, to be no longer alone in the chase. Then Fulton said, "OK, but I'm gonna have to get close to them, and stay away from you. We'll have to figure something out." He thought for a moment and then snapped his fingers. "Perfect!" he said. "I just wasted Tecumseh. He's in a car trunk in the Jersey meadows. That's the story. It's my ticket in."

Karp grinned in appreciation. "Very good. I love it. It's sneaky and clever. You're sure you're not Jewish?"

"I am. This black horseshit is just for affirmative action so I could make lieutenant. Yeah, it should work, unless Manning is down at La Guardia seeing his momma off on a plane. What'll you be doing meanwhile?"

"Somebody hired them. That's who I want."

"Hired them? But we already know that. Booth said they were working for Choo Willis."

"No, he didn't—not exactly. Sit down for a second, I want to play some of that tape."

The two men sat on the bench and Karp fiddled with the Nagra, rolling the tape back and forth until he had the section he wanted. "Listen to this carefully," he said.

The voice of Tecumseh Booth was thready but the words were clear enough: ". . . an then we went down to that club, you know? Club Mecca. An Manning, he tol' me to wait outside, in the club while him and Amalfi went inna back. So then he come out an he have a big envelope, an he peel off my end from a roll of cash, thick as shit. Motherfucker got paid, you know? So then, I say, who back there? An he say, you don't got to know that, you just got to drive.

"So later, I'm out in the car, drivin, an I go by the club, an there's Choo Willis standin with some of his homes outside, an I figure that was him, cause Choo bout the biggest dealer we ain't killed, an he hang there all the time. We doin it for him, dig? So then . . ."

Karp clicked off the tape. Fulton shrugged and said, "So? That's what I said—it's Willis."

"Yeah, they're doing it *for* Willis. He's the immediate beneficiary. But Willis didn't organize this. No way. And I doubt he was the only one in the back room with the cash."

"How do you know that?"

"Look at it! This whole thing stinks of heavy cover. Would cops work *for* a Harlem dope pusher? They might help him, but they're not going to take orders from a mutt like that. Would Willis have the clout to roll Nolan? I told you, Nolan isn't a fat-envelope guy. No, there's somebody else, somebody big."

Karp pondered for a moment. "Tell me something: what's your take on Fane?"

"The congressman? Shit, Butch, what do I know about those kind of people? He comes on like a regular politician. You think he's involved?"

"No, just wondering," Karp said. "It could

be, though. He's supposed to be smart enough. And everybody likes money, especially pols. But it's somebody *like* that. Somebody who knows how to move money and move the system. Just you do your end and I'll look into it."

Karp walked slowly back to the ballfield. The post-game party had thinned out and the beer was almost gone. Karp put his hand on the shoulder of a small wiry man and said, "V.T., we need to talk for a minute."

Vernon Talcott Newbury looked around and smiled when he saw Karp. His smile was perfect, white and even, and his face was perfect too—classical features and dark blue eyes with long lashes. He wore his blond hair long and swept back.

Karp picked up a Coke from the cooler and V.T. grabbed a beer and they walked over to sit near first base. "I need some advice, V.T."

"Sure, Butch. Is it that sexual-dysfunction thing again?"

"Fuck you," said Karp with a laugh. "No, it has to do with the drug-dealer killings. I need to run some financial traces."

"Aha. And you thought to yourself, think money, think V.T. Newbury. Why go through the messy business of subpoenaing records and causing a fuss when you knew that V.T., with his elaborate connections in the financial community, could gather much the same information, et cetera?"

"Something like that. And your vast personal wealth, so that if you got caught and got fired, you wouldn't suffer."

"My vast personal wealth is so tied up in trusts that I have to struggle to make ends meet. My wine merchant is now asking for *cash*, if you can believe it. Who's the malefactor?"

"Marcus Fane, and maybe some other people," said Karp.

V.T.'s eyes widened. "Representative Fane . . . so he's been killing the pushers. I admire that. More congressmen should cut through the red tape and bureaucracy to rid our streets of these villains, et cetera. Of course, it's not the kind of thing you can use in a campaign speech . . ."

"Be serious, V.T. I don't mean he's doing the killings. I'm not even sure he's involved. I'm just covering bases."

"Literally, for once," observed V.T. Karp was sitting on the first-base sack. "So what sort of dirt do you want? Just the basic model, or with air conditioning and whitewalls?"

"I don't know, V.T., you're the expert. Is he richer than he should be? Is his wife? Has he got Krugerrands salted away in Bimini? Also, I'd like whatever you can find on the ownership of a Harlem nightclub called the Club Mecca, and, let's see . . ." He thought for a moment more. "Oh, yeah—Judge Terence Nolan. See if you can find out whether anybody's done him any financial favors lately."

"Right. Fane. Mecca. Nolan," said V.T. "That shouldn't be hard. Matter of public record, most of it. I won't hardly have to use any illegal sources, except maybe for about the judge."

Karp placed his hands flat over his ears. "I don't need to hear about how you do what you do, V.T. Just do it," he said, "and soon."

On Monday, Marlene caught Guma outside the grand-jury room on the sixth floor of the Criminal Courts Building.

"You've been avoiding me," she said flatly.

"Marlene!" said Guma brightly. "How could I be avoiding you? Everybody seeks you out to bask in your charming personality."

"Cut the crap, Goom! What went down this weekend? Did the cops check out the Omega Club?"

Guma seemed nervous, darting glances down the hallway in both directions. "Well, yeah, they did, and, uh . . ."

"And what? What are you looking around like that for? Somebody's husband chasing you?"

Guma laughed insincerely. "I only wish. Yeah, look, Marlene, it's a shutout on that. They got zip."

"Zip? How could they get zip?"

"Easy. The place is dark as a well-digger's ass, for starters. They got strobe lights there, everybody's blinking and faces look like a fucking fun house. Also they run two thousand people through there on a good weekend. How the hell do you expect a bartender to remember one chick talking to one guy, much less what the guy looked like?''

"Fuck!" said Marlene, loud enough to draw stares from the passersby. "OK, so what now? Where do we take it from here?"

Guma shifted nervously. "Well, really, nowhere, kid. The regular dicks have washed their hands on it. I mean, they might do a couple of sweeps, talk to some people, but . . . Oh, crap!"

Guma was staring in horror down the hallway. "Marlene, listen," he said in a low, urgent voice, clutching her arm, "just play along with this. I'm in serious deep shit here."

Marlene was about to ask what was going on, when a tall handsome woman in a tailored suit, with a face that Marlene vaguely recognized, walked up to them, smiling.

"John," she said to Guma, "what a nice surprise!"

Guma smiled in return. Marlene could see small trickles of sweat running down from his thick sideburns. "Hi, Sylvia," said Guma. "I guess you know my sister, Marlene. Not socially, of course."

The two women nodded politely to one another and smiled at this pleasantry. Guma said, "Gee, Sylvia, you know, I been meaning to call you, but I've been swamped. It's all these immigrants—Chinese, Cambodian, from Central America. The first thing they do they get a little money, they're making it in the USA, bang!—the kid's got to have straight teeth. I'm thinking of taking on another man, in fact."

"Well, at least you're coining money. How you get away with charging what you do, I don't know," said Sylvia Kamas.

"Yeah, Judge," said Marlene, "maybe we have a grand-larceny case here."

They all laughed, none louder than Guma. "That's good, Marlene," he chortled. "Well, at least I have a friend in court." He squeezed Judge Kamas' arm. Then he made a show of looking at his watch and striking his forehead. "Oh, my! It's almost two. I'd love to hang out with you ladies, but I got to fit a . . . a . . . a retainer at two-fifteen." He kissed Marlene on the cheek, patted Sylvia's arm again, and tore off down the hallway.

They watched him go. Judge Kamas turned to Marlene and said, "Your brother—what a sweet man! And a cutup! I've never met anyone who made me laugh more. He must have been a real handful at your house."

"Not really," said Marlene pleasantly. "We didn't even know he was there."

Marlene finished her business with the grand jury in short order and headed directly for Guma's office, at the trot. The door was locked and the light was off, but Marlene, pressing her ear against the frosted glass, heard the telltale rustle of paper and the creak of a chair in use by a portly body. She rapped sharply on the glass. "Guma! Open up! It's your own sis!"

Silence. Then, cautious steps, the snap of the lock, and Guma peering out through a narrow slit like a Maquisard on the lookout for the Gestapo. "For Chrissake, Marlene, keep it down!"

Marlene shouldered her way past him into the office and sat down. "OK, Mad Dog, let's have it. The whole story."

Guma gave her the whole story. "Honest, Marlene, it just happened. I didn't plan it," he concluded. "It was just one of those things."

"Yeah, a trip to the moon on gossamer wings. Does Butch know?"

"Yeah, I had to tell him. To get off Petrossi."

"Ah, I wondered about that. So, what are you going to do about it? You can't spend all day with your head in a bag. Maybe the witness-protection program can help—give you a whole new life in El Paso?"

"Come on, Marlene, it's not funny. If this gets out, I'm fucked forever."

Marlene thought for a long minute. Then she said, "OK, Goom, here's the deal. I'll cover for you, if . . ."

"Anything!" Guma exclaimed, his face lighting up.

"I want Wagner," she said.

Guma looked puzzled. "Wagner? Sure, but what good's that gonna do you? You're out of here in a week is what I hear."

"Not if I have a continuing case. That's the exception. And I want this guy."

"Yeah, but that won't hold up, Marlene. You can't keep *adding* cases after you get the severance letter."

"No!" said Marlene forcefully. "It's not an add-on. Wagner is the same case as the serial rapist I've had for months. It's another element in the same case, which means I can stay until it's finished."

Guma looked doubtful. "You can convince Butch of that?"

"Ve haff our vays," said Marlene with confidence. "And, Goom? Let me tell him. Keep this under your hat."

Guma shrugged and held out his hand, palm up, and Marlene slapped it.

"Done deal," he said, "but let me tell you, the cops ain't gonna be so easy. I don't know who you're gonna get to follow up on it."

"Don't worry," said Marlene. "I'll think of something."

Back in her office, Marlene dialed a familiar number and was relieved to hear it answered by a familiar voice.

"Detective Raney," said the voice on the other end of the line.

"Jim? It's Marlene."

"The roller queen? How the hell are ya?"

"Fine. Great. But I need your help on a thing. How would you like to be in on a hot collar?"

A pause. "Uh, to tell the truth, Marlene, I'm still sort of on light duty. The last time you got me in on a hot collar I almost got canned. The up side was I also got the shit beat out of me by King Kong."

"This isn't like that, Jim. This *is* light duty. It's just going to a place, a singles bar, with me and a witness, and picking up a guy."

"And what guy would this be?"

"A serial rapist. He killed his last victim. It was that slashing case in the One-seven."

"Yeah? And what about whoever caught it in Zone Five homicide? They too busy for a hot collar?"

Marlene had anticipated this objection and had decided that her only recourse was the truth. Detectives were notoriously sticky about stepping into the turf of other units. Raney was assigned to Detective Zone Four on the West Side of Manhattan and would hesitate before stepping into a case originating in another zone.

"No," she said, "to be perfectly honest, this is something I figured out for myself. The connection between the rapes and the murder—the D.A. cops and zone homicide don't buy it."

"Intuition again?"

"No, goddammit! I got a pattern. The guy repeats himself. He picks up women in singles bars, finds out where they live, shows up at their places, and rapes them. The last one went sour and he killed her. But it's the same guy and I can prove it. I got evidence, I got a consistent M.O. in all the cases."

A longer pause. "Ah, Marlene, as much as I'd like to help you out . . ."

"Oh, come on, Raney! It's no big deal. Look, we'll keep it unofficial: just a lonely cop out on a date with a couple of classy Italian ladies."

"A couple? Who's the other one?"

"JoAnne Caputo."

"Does she put out?"

"For Chrissake, Jim, she's my rape victim. I think she can ID the bad guy."

"A rape victim, huh? It sounds like a real fun evening. What's the boyfriend say about this?"

"The boyfriend doesn't know, not that it's any of your business."

"Ah-hah. This is sort of a little fling before the wedding bells chime."

"Oh, shit, Raney! Be serious! I'm trying to catch a real bastard here, and I got nobody to help me. Except you. Now, *please*, will you do it?" Marlene felt her voice shaking. Raney heard it over the wire and changed his tone.

"OK, sorry," he said. "What about this mutt? He gonna put up a fight?"

"You'll do it?"

"I'll give it a shot, as long as it's, like you say, unofficial. Besides, I'd like to see you. What about the guy?"

"No problem, I'd say. He won't expect it, he

won't be armed. He's out to cruise women, not hassle cops."

"OK. Where and when?"

Marlene gave him the address of Tangerines and they arranged to meet at eight-thirty that Friday night. "Any other questions?" she asked.

"Yeah, do I at least get to cop a cheap feel off you on the dance floor?"

"Sure, Raney. Just keep it professional," said Marlene sharply, and hung up.

TWELVE

When Clay Fulton walked into Logan's, people glanced up, as they usually do when a new person comes into a small dark saloon. Then they all looked purposefully away. Nobody offered to buy him a drink. Logan's is a cop bar on Amsterdam near 145th. Everybody in the place when Fulton entered worked for the police, except the bartender, who was a retired cop, and the scattering of women, who were there to meet cops. People from the Twenty-sixth and Twenty-eighth precincts drank there, and also some from the Thirty-second, to the north. Dick Manning drank there, and was drinking there now, which was why Fulton had come.

Manning was sitting in a booth with his partner, Sid Amalfi, joking with a tan woman wearing skintight electric-blue toreador pants and a blond wig. They fell silent when Fulton walked over to them.

"Hello, Dick, Sid," he said. "Can I buy someone a beer?"

"Not today, Fulton," said Manning, scowling.

Fulton ignored this and slid into the booth next to Amalfi. "You know, that's a shame, because I think we have some business to discuss."

"We got nothing to talk about with you, Fulton," said Amalfi.

"Who's your friend, Sid?" the woman asked.

"He ain't no friend of mine," snapped Amalfi.

Manning stared hard at Fulton, who responded with a wide shit-eating grin. Manning turned to the woman. "Say, Doris? We got some business to discuss here. See you later."

The woman sniffed and made off for a more congenial corner. Manning said, "What the fuck are you doing, Fulton?"

Fulton said, "What, I can't have a drink with my brother officers? Especially since we're in the same line of work."

"What're you talking about?"

"Your moonlighting job. I just had a little chat with a friend of yours—Tecumseh Booth."

"I don't know any Booth," said Manning.

"Yeah. Yeah, you do," said Fulton. He took a tape cassette out of his jacket pocket and placed it on the table. "I got it all here. The Clarry hit. Springing him from jail. Choo Willis and the other hits. Club Mecca. It's quite a story. Sort of old Tecumseh's last will and testament, as a matter of fact."

Amalfi's face had gone dead white. "For Chrissake, shut the fuck up, Fulton! You can't talk about it *here*—"

"Shut up, Sid!" Manning snarled. Then, to Fulton, "You want to show us some evidence, let's go someplace where we can take a look at it, discuss things—"

"Cut the horseshit, Manning," said Fulton, raising his voice. "What I want is *in*. You guys got a gold mine working, I got a key to the door, and I want my piece."

Heads turned in the bar. Manning held up his hands placatingly. "OK, OK! Look, no problem—but let's go where we can talk."

They went to Manning's car, a loaded white Trans Am. "This is pretty nice, Manning," said Fulton when the doors were closed. "I might get me one of these, or maybe a Benz."

"I like American cars," said Manning. He started the engine, gunned a couple of times, and peeled off up Amsterdam. "You can't beat the pickup."

"That's a point," agreed Fulton. He pulled the cassette out of his pocket. He said, "By the way, in case you're thinking what you might be thinking, this ain't the only one of these, you know. You guys better pray I stay in good shape, if you catch my drift."

From the back seat Amalfi said, "How do we know you ain't just blowing smoke?"

"Listen," said Fulton. He slid the tape into the cassette player and they listened for a while to the voice of Tecumseh Booth.

Manning ejected the tape. He pulled the car over and parked on a side street. "That's enough," he said. "How did you get him to talk?"

"I shot him in the knee. Then I said the next one I'd blow his pecker off. He came around pretty quick."

Manning chuckled. "You're quite a fuckin' piece of work, Fulton. I never would of figured you for a stunt like that. It goes to show you, you never can tell. So where is Tecumseh now?"

"Well, I didn't lie to him. I put the next one in his ear. He won't be making any more tapes."

Manning and Amalfi both laughed. "You got rid of him OK?" asked Manning. "They can't connect you?"

"No problem. I picked him up from where my guys had him stashed and I told them he ran. He's in a trunk in a crusher yard out in the Meadows. So, am I in?"

"I guess you are. How about your boys?"

"No, I don't want nobody else in this. Keep it simple. And keep the cash." Fulton put an expression of avid greed on his face. "And about that—what does our end come to?"

"We get fifty large a hit," said Manning.

Fulton whistled. "Very nice. But I guess the price gonna go up. Now you got an extra mouth to feed, I mean. I don't want to put my partners out any."

Manning smiled. "No. No problem. You got no idea how much cash is floating around in the coke business. It's like fucking Monopoly money. Makes smack look like kids selling lemonade. But I got to talk to my man about it."

"Who is . . . ?" asked Fulton.

Manning waved a cautionary finger. "Uh-uh. You in, but you ain't *that* in, man. I'll talk to the man tonight and get back with you tomorrow."

Fulton frowned and thought for a moment. "OK, that's cool," he said. He got out of the car. "See you around, partners," he said, and sauntered away.

Amalfi got out of the back seat and dropped down next to Manning. His face was flushed and angry. "What the fuck, Dick! You really gonna let that shithead in on this?"

"Cool down, Sid," said Manning. "He ain't gonna do nothing without us, and I need time to figure. That tape is bad news."

"Yeah, but we could grab him and make him tell where the other copies are. Like he made Tecumseh."

"We could," agreed Manning. "But I'm also thinking he could come in handy another way too."

"Like what?"

"Like I'm starting to like Lieutenant Fulton for these killings we're investigating," said Manning.

After a moment, a smile grew on Amalfi's face. "Yeah," he said, "now that you mention it, so do I."

Dressed in the trousers and shirt of a rented tuxedo, Karp bent and twisted before the cheval mirror near Marlene's bed, attempting for the fifth time to get the bow tie right.

From her position on the bed Marlene gave him irritating advice. "No, you still didn't hold the fat end with your thumb. And don't fling it down like a three-year-old and glare at me like that! If you can't tie a bow tie, why didn't you get one of those clip-on thingees?"

"Because," Karp replied, retrieving the offending item, "only nerds wear clip-ons. And if you're so smart, why don't you tie the goddamn thing?"

"All right, I will," said Marlene, bouncing off the bed. She stood in front of Karp, dressed only in a ragged Let-It-Bleed T-shirt and blue satin underpants, and tied a perfect bow in five seconds flat.

"How did you *do* that?" asked Karp, amazed.

"I have three brothers, all as ham-handed as you, and not nerds. What are you doing?"

Karp had wrapped his arms around her and pulled her close, running his hands under the elastic and clasping a haunch in each one.

"I really know how to tie a bow tie," he said into her ear. "It was just a ruse to get you close so I could do this."

"What a liar, and if you keep doing that I'll never let you out of here, and you'll be late, and all the bigwigs will spot the stains on your pants and make fun of you."

"Let them," said Karp. "I'm not proud."

After considerable kissing and fooling

around, Karp said, "I have to go before I come, so to speak."

Marlene said, "I knew it! Get a girl to the absolute squish point, and run off. I guess your career comes first. Dear. Not-quite-wifey will have to rub it off against glossies of Bruce Springsteen while you cavort with the great."

Karp laughed. "Yeah, right—the career. Reedy invited me to this political wingding. The old farts have to check out the new kid, make sure I don't have horns."

"How noble of you to suffer for your little family! Why don't you admit you're ambitious? You'd *love* to be D.A."

Karp stood up, adjusted his clothing and smoothed his hair in the mirror, then put on his dinner jacket.

"I'd love it, sure," he said, "but whether I buy it depends on the price tag."

"Is there a price tag?"

"Sure. Just like in Macy's. I just haven't been told what it is yet. How do I look?"

"Like a young fart," replied Marlene grumpily. "No, actually you look gorgeous. Have a good time."

He leaned over and kissed her lightly. "Don't wait up."

"I won't," said Marlene, feeling guilty.

She heard the hollow slam of the downstairs door and checked the bedside clock radio for the time. Six-thirty. Still hours to kill. She went down the ladder from the sleeping loft, turned on the TV, watched the beginning of a movie, lost track of the plot, switched it off, made an omelet and toast, ate desultorily, fed most of it to the cat, paced the length of the loft, the butterflies growing more huge in her gut. She went down to the gym end of the loft, laced on a pair of light gloves, and slapped the speed bag around until her arms were limp. Seven-thirty.

She peeled off her sweat-sodden clothing, folded back the cover of her bathing tank, and plunged in. She waited for the warm water to relax her, gave up, emerged, dried and powdered herself.

She dressed and made up carefully in the style she thought of as classy-but-available: lots of eye makeup, false lashes, and crimson lipstick. She brushed her heavy black hair, then combed it across the bad side of her face, Veronica Lake style to obscure her glass eye. She put on a long black skirt with buttons up the front, the bottom six undone, and a Chinese raw-silk shirt in red over bare skin—the top three buttons undone.

She checked herself in the mirror: a dark, smallish, pretty woman showing definite nipples. She looked like all the victims. She grabbed her bag and left.

Tangerines was housed in a narrow tan building on Madison in the Sixties. Its name was drawn in neon of the appropriate color in the curtained window. Raney was not there when

Marlene arrived, and neither was JoAnne Caputo. She paced outside for ten minutes, spurning half a dozen pickup attempts. Finally she turned with a curse and went inside.

There were around two hundred people in the place, most of them members of a youngish crowd who lacked the fame and money to go to the big see-and-be-seen places and who considered themselves too sophisticated for the ignominy of standing behind the velvet rope with fat people from the burbs, gaping at the gilded folk. There was a long bar along one wall, separated from the main room by a low planter and trelliswork, packed with climbing philodendrons, ferns, and aspidistras in pots.

The aisle thus formed was jammed with standees holding drinks—the meat market itself. On the other side of the greenery was the cabaret, a room of twenty or so tables, each lit by little orange globes, a tiny stage, and a dance floor not much larger in front of it. The stage was occupied by a trio and a singer, doing sixties stuff and some contemporary music, with a bias toward the romantic. Couples clutched one another and rocked gently on the dance floor. Contact dancing was back at Tangerines.

Marlene checked out the cabaret briefly, went back to the bar, muscled her way through the crowd, and scored a tonic and lime. She felt a tap on her shoulder and turned.

For a moment she failed to recognize her. JoAnne Caputo was decked out in a platinum wig and violet lipstick and wearing what looked like an army-surplus tent in mustard brown.

"JoAnne!" Marlene exclaimed. "You look . . . different."

Caputo's expression was vacant and disturbed at the same time, as if she had just awakened from a nightmare. There was a knotted and ferocious look around her eyes. "I look like shit," she said tonelessly, "but I don't want him to recognize me. Is the cop here?"

"Not yet, but he'll show up. Have you spotted anybody who looks right?"

"No, but I just got here. What do you want me to do?"

Think fast, Marlene, Marlene thought. She hadn't counted on the place being so crowded or on the lines of sight being so constrained. Catching someone in this crowd was a job for half a dozen men.

"OK, here's the plan," she said at last. "You stay in the bar and sort of drift back and forth through the crowd. That's where it's most likely he'll be. If you spot him . . . um, stick your head through those plants over there and signal. I'll be in the main room over by the far wall. I got to watch for Jim. For the cop."

JoAnne nodded agreement, and took a deep swig of her drink, which Marlene doubted was nonalcoholic. As she left, she saw JoAnne signaling strenuously to the barman for a refill. That's all I need, she thought: an identification by a drunk witness. It was starting to look like not such a great idea.

The far wall of the main room supported a narrow padded shelf running almost its entire length, against which standees could lean and rest their drinks. Marlene leaned and took in the room. To her right were the dance floor and bandstand of the cabaret and to her left was the street wall with its curtained window, glowing pale orange. The barrier of plants stopped just short of this wall, and the passageway thus formed was guarded by a velvet rope. She could just make out the door to the outside around the end of the fernery.

"Come here often?" asked a voice to her left.

She turned to it. He was medium tall, of medium build, wearing a leather jacket over a black T-shirt and black jeans. His dark hair was collar-length and swept back over his ears. His eyes were dark and his features were even, except for his nose, which was long and marked by a lumpy ridge down its center. She looked down at the floor. He wore woven loafers with no socks.

The man smiled winningly. Marlene felt herself smiling back. She said, "Not really. This is my first time," trying to keep the tension out of her voice as she realized that it was the guy.

Karp sat in his unfamiliar dinner clothes with two dozen similarly dressed men, all with real bow ties, in a suite of a small, expensive midtown hotel, listening to Congressman Marcus Fane finish his speech. He sipped his coffee, but passed on the little snifter of brandy set before him. It had been quite a meal: Scottish smoked salmon to start, a cream soup with oysters and crab, an enormous slab of prime rib, decorated with potatoes and mushrooms carved into fanciful shapes, a salad made of some unknown sour greens and yellow flowers, and baked Alaska for dessert.

Karp had never had baked Alaska, nor had he ever dined with a group such as this, one of the little bands of prosperous men who called the shots in the cities of America. He looked down the table at the smooth attentive faces, some of them famous, others obscure, but all radiating confidence and power. They represented the City's largest banks, the big real-estate holdings, a few of the megacorporations that were still headquartered in New York, the insurance industry, the stock market, the state, the newspapers and the TV networks, the archdiocese, the Jewish community, the unions, and the two political parties. Fane represented the downtrodden masses and the federal government.

He was a good speaker, Karp thought. He spoke extempore, and seemed both confiding and blunt. Karp agreed with the burden of the speech, which was that crime was bad and ought to be stopped, and applauded politely with the others when it was over. The party rose. Apparently they were going to adjourn to the other room of the suite, there to indulge in yet more of the secret rituals of the rich and powerful.

Karp joined the flow, and as he did, he felt

a hand on his shoulder. It was Richard Reedy. "Enjoying yourself?"

Karp smiled and answered, "Nice feed. Uplifting speech. I'm waiting for when they bring out the coffers full of gold and we all let the coins run through our fingers and cackle."

Reedy laughed out loud, threw a companionable arm around Karp's shoulder, and carried him into the next room, which was stocked with comfortable chairs and waiters circulating with more after-dinner drinks. "I want you to meet Marcus," Reedy said. "He's a good man to get to know."

Marcus Fane was talking to an elderly man in ecclesiastical costume and a portly man with a red face. Reedy signaled to him in some subtle way that Karp missed and Fane excused himself and walked over to them. He was a stocky man with a smooth medium-brown face and straight oiled hair worn in the fashion of the late Adam Clayton Powell. He grinned his famous and photogenic grin as he shook Karp's hand.

"Well, well, Mr. Karp! Rich here has told me so much about you."

"And what was that, Mr. Fane?" asked Karp blandly.

"Please, it's Marcus," said Fane. "And you're Butch. Why, he's told me you're just the man to inject a little vigor into our criminal justice system."

Karp glanced at Reedy, who winked in his

merry way and smiled. Karp nodded and smiled, feeling vaguely uncomfortable.

"You have political ambitions, I hear," said Fane.

"Well . . ." said Karp hesitantly.

Fane took in the occupants of the room with a broad gesture. "And you've come to the right place. This is where political ambitions are fertilized, sir. With money." He winked broadly.

Karp smiled conventionally at this wisdom. Reedy said, "Maybe we can set up a meeting later in the month, Marcus. Butch, here, and a few key people. Maybe form an exploratory committee?"

"Good idea, Rich. Never too early to dig worms, ha-ha! Call my office and set it up."

Fane was edging away, obviously responding to another invisible signal emanating from one of the other groups of men that had coalesced in different parts of the room. He shook hands with Reedy and Butch again. "Excuse me," he said. "Old pols can't resist working the room. Rich, on that Agromont thing, consider it a done deal."

Fane left and Reedy said, "Well, that's that."

"What's what?"

"He likes you. You're a plausible candidate." Reedy moved over to a coffee setup and drew a cup of black coffee from a silver urn. Karp followed him.

"How does he know that? I barely opened my mouth."

Reedy carefully rubbed a bit of lemon rind

around the rim of his cup and sipped. "He knows. You're tall, you have an honest face. Jewish, but not *too* Jewish. Your record is fine, not that anybody gives a rat's ass. A bad record can sink a candidate, but a good record's not enough to win."

"What is enough?"

"Money. What else? Half a mill should do it, for starters." He looked sharply at Karp. "You haven't got any, have you?"

"Not so you'd notice. My penny jar is pretty full, but I always forget to stop by the bank for those little paper tubes. I guess you don't have that problem."

Reedy grinned. "Don't joke about money, Butch. Money is always serious, especially among our present company."

"I'll remember that. Speaking seriously, then, what about Fane? Is he rich too?"

"Oh, I imagine he's well-off," Reedy answered casually. "He's got some nice income property uptown. Some investments too. People like to give stock tips to congressmen."

"And maybe to judges. You know a judge named Nolan?"

"I know the name. Why?"

"Just wondering. In these drug killings we've been investigating: Judge Nolan released a witness on what, for him, seemed an excess of constitutional zeal. The guy walked out and somebody tried to kill him. Then he disappeared."

"You think he's dead?"

"I wouldn't be surprised. Whoever's doing

these killings is pretty slick. It might be interesting to find out if anybody's passed any lucrative information to Judge Nolan in the last week or so."

Reedy nodded. "You'd like me to look into that."

"Yeah, I would, if it's not a problem," answered Karp gratefully, while thinking, ungratefully, that whoever had done it was probably the type who inhabited meetings like this one. Or this one itself.

"So, tell me, Marlene," said the guy, "what's your racket?" His name was Glenn. He was a Capricorn, he lived in Inglewood, he liked the music.

"You mean what do I do? I work for the D.A." Marlene watched his face carefully. No rush of sweat to the brow, no wild rolling of the eyes. Instead, mock wariness: "Uh-oh. I better watch my step around you. What are you, a paralegal?"

"Um, in a manner of speaking. How about yourself?"

"I'm in TV," he said. "In production at ABC."

"That's impressive," said Marlene, remembering her cards. "Do you mingle with the stars much?" Keep him talking. Keep him interested. The guy had moved around so that he stood between Marlene and the doorway. She tried to crane her neck unobtrusively, so as to keep the door in view, while at the same time darting glances at the fern wall to see if she could spot JoAnne.

"Looking for someone?" the guy asked.

"Huh? Oh, no, not really."

"You keep looking at the door," he said.

"Oh, well, I was supposed to meet a girl-friend here later."

"Not a boyfriend?"

"Isn't that why I'm here?" replied Marlene as coquettishly as she could manage. Smile. Lean. Show some tit.

Encouraged, the guy moved closer. She could smell his cologne and the leather of his jacket.

"So. Wanna do something?" He touched his nose meaningfully.

"Um, like what?"

He laughed. "You know, blow. Do a coupla lines in the can. Get in the mood."

Marlene did not lead a sheltered life, but she had never been offered cocaine socially by a stranger before. She hadn't expected the guy to do it, and it threw her out of character. She shook her head spontaneously and vigorously in refusal.

This was apparently not the response expected of Tangerines bimbos. The guy's glib smile faded and he shrugged.

"So. Wanna dance?" he asked.

"No," she said. On the floor she would never be able to watch the door for Raney. Then, seeing his smile vanish completely, she added, "I, uh, hurt my foot playing racquetball. I'm practically crippled."

Smile again. "Hey, I play too. Where do you go?"

"Um, you know, all around."

"Like where? Tenth Street? Midtown Courts?"

"Yeah, those. And, um, you know, the Y." The guy looked at her peculiarly, his expression losing any enthusiasm. *He thinks I'm lying. He thinks I'm trying to dump him.* This wasn't working. She had to get JoAnne. "Look," she said, "I got to run to the ladies'. Why don't you order me another drink for us. I'll be right back. Don't go away now!" She tried to inject a flirtatious note into her voice. He nodded and she went off, remembering to drag a foot behind her, like Quasimodo.

The rest rooms at Tangerines were located off a long narrow hallway that led from the corner where the main room met the aisle of the bar. Marlene entered it, turned to make sure she wasn't being followed, and then went back into the crush of the meat market.

It was even more crowded now, at the peak of the Friday-night follies, and loud with fevered chatter. Despairing of finding JoAnne in time, she elbowed her way through to the bar and stood up tiptoe on the rail, hoping to spot the preposterous wig. To her vast surprise, she found herself staring down at a familiar head of strawberry-blond curls. It was Jim Raney, dressed for disco in a chino suit and an open-necked blue shirt.

"Raney," she shouted. "Dammit, where have you been!"

He looked up at her in amazement. "Where was *I*? Where were *you*? I've been here nearly an hour."

"Never mind that—I've got him," she said. "Follow me!"

She grabbed his sleeve and led him back into the main room. The band was, inevitably, doing "Saturday Night Fever" and showing they could play it loud. Marlene's eyes went to the wall where she had left the guy. The two glasses they had used remained on the little shelf; the man himself was gone.

Marlene clenched her fists and uttered a screech of frustration. Raney asked, "What's up? Where is he?"

"Where is he? He's fucking flown, Raney, that's where he is."

"Could he be in the john?"

"No, impossible! He would have had to get past me there, and he didn't. Shit! He must have skipped. There's a way out around the front."

Raney followed her quickly through the crowded cabaret, stepped around the ferns, over the velvet rope, and out into the street. "There he is!" Marlene shouted. Raney looked in the direction of her pointing finger. A man with a leather jacket stood on the curb, trying to flag down a cab.

Raney walked toward the man. "Hey, buddy," he called, "could I see you a minute?" The guy looked over his shoulder, saw Raney, saw Marlene. His eyes widened as he recog-

nized her. He backed away. Raney took his
leather shield holder out of his jacket pocket
and flipped it at the guy. "Police," he said, and
the guy ran.

Marlene was after him like a dog on a rabbit,
across Madison. Raney cursed and followed,
but the light on the cross street had changed
and he found himself trapped briefly between
the lanes of honking traffic.

Marlene was running without thought, concentrating only on the flapping crow shape of
the leather jacket as it flickered, caught in one
streetlamp after another.

She chased the guy north on the west side of
Madison, about ten yards separating them. The
foot traffic on Madison was sparse, mostly couples working the bars and panhandlers. They
flicked by, barely noticing the chase. Marlene
was wearing low heels, a disadvantage, but her
quarry was wearing loose slip-ons, which kept
flapping off his feet as he ran. Every twenty
paces or so he would have to make a little skip
to jam them back on, and Marlene would close
the distance. Then his longer legs would tell
and he would stretch it out again.

Marlene could hear his breathing become
louder and more ragged. She was in better
shape, she thought: raping probably wasn't all
that aerobic. He wouldn't last another three
blocks. With relief she heard Raney coming up
behind her.

The guy suddenly veered left up a side street.
When Marlene turned the corner, the guy had

slowed to an odd stumbling trot. He had his
right hand jammed into the pocket of his jeans.
He was struggling to get something out of his
pocket. Marlene thought: *Knife!* Jesus, he
brought his knife.

She couldn't stop. She was almost on him.
She heard Raney shout, "Hold it, hold . . . !"
The hand came out of the pocket and something shiny flew from it and skittered on the
street.

He tried to accelerate again, but Marlene was
on him, her fingernails digging deep into the
leather of his jacket. He jerked his body violently and nearly pulled her off her feet. One
of her shoes went flying. She felt several nails
crack off. He swung an arm around, grabbed
the front of her shirt, and heaved her around
to face him. The shirt tore down the back and
her grip on the jacket was broken.

She could see his face now, the sweat-slicked
hair, the features red and contorted with rage
and fear. He set his feet and aimed a back-
handed right at her face.

Marlene crouched and ducked, but his
knuckles still slammed against the side of her
skull, reddening her vision. He hauled at the
shirt, to set her up for another blow, but Marlene came with it, bringing her hard little right
fist up from nearly pavement level, putting the
full 110 pounds behind it, sinking it up to the
wristbone in his crotch.

He let go of the shirt with a shrill cry and
bent double. Then Raney was there in a long

flying leap, whipping his big Browning pistol down on the guy's head with a sound that echoed from the buildings like a gong.

The guy crumpled without a sound. Marlene collapsed and sat on the pavement, sucking air, clutching the tatters of her shirt to her naked breasts. She felt the sweat drying on her back.

Raney checked the guy's pulse, cuffed his hands behind his back, and knelt down beside Marlene.

"You OK?" he asked.

"Yeah. Fine."

"Light duty, huh?"

"OK, OK, OK," she gasped. "It was a screwup. I didn't think it would go down like this."

"Yeah, well, it happens. By the way, that was quite a shot to the nuts. Characteristic, if I may say so."

"Thanks, Raney," said Marlene sourly. "Hey, can I borrow your jacket? My tits are hanging out here." Raney shrugged it off and she slipped into it, grateful for its warmth as well as the protection it afforded from the gapers in the small crowd that had gathered around them.

Raney stood up and helped Marlene to her feet. She recovered her shoe and leaned against him to put it on. She was still wobbly and dizzy with adrenaline and fatigue. Raney said, "Look, we got to call this in." He pulled a card out of his wallet. "There's a booth on Madison and 66th. Call this number. Ask to talk to Detective Franklin. When you get him, explain the situation and tell him we need a blue-and-white and a bus."

"A bus?"

"Yeah, you know, an ambulance. Hey, are you sure you're OK?"

"Uh-huh. Just a little shook."

"OK, then meet me at the two-oh and we'll book him. What's the charge, do you think?"

Marlene sighed. "Better make it possession for now."

"Possession? What're you talking about? I thought this was the Wagner killer."

"It is. I think. But my witness never got a look at him and I don't know him from Adam. He just fit what we were looking for, in general. Meanwhile, he offered me coke in the place there, and he tossed a vial during the chase. You should find it in the street. It's enough to hang on to him with until I can get JoAnne there and ID him."

"Holy shit, Marlene!" Raney yelled. "You mean to fuckin' tell me—"

"Don't, Raney. It'll work out OK—trust me. Let me make that call now. You got a quarter?"

The guy was loaded and shipped, leaving a small round bloodstain on the sidewalk. The cops found the vial the guy had dumped, half-full of white powder. Raney and Marlene walked back to Tangerines in silence.

The noise of an excited crowd greeted them when they were half a block away from the club. Marlene buttonholed a chubby young woman in a fringed white dress.

"What's going on?"

"It's crazy!" the woman replied. "Some chick with a big knife got this guy cornered in the hallway by the john. She's yelling he raped her and she's gonna cut his business off. It's wild! I'm going home to watch it on TV."

Marlene felt a thrill of despair. "What kind of woman?" she croaked weakly. "A blond in a dark tent dress?"

"Yeah, frosted blond. But it was a wig. She pulled it off and threw it at the guy. It was just like the movies!"

The woman hurried off down the street. Marlene started to run toward Tangerines, but Raney grabbed her arm.

"Marlene, what the fuck is happening?" he cried.

"It's JoAnne. My witness." She broke away from him and trotted heavily down the street to the club, her belly roiling, her heart popping against her breastbone. Fifty or so people were milling around outside and more were flowing out of the door. Marlene pushed vainly against the tide. Raney caught up with her, put his arm around her, hoisted her up on his hip, and, waving his shield and shouting, "Police! Coming through!" forced their way into the bar.

Someone had turned the cleaning lights on, giving the interior of Tangerines the charm of a raddled whore at noon: stained carpet, rusty tin ceiling, overturned chairs and tables, pools

of spilled drinks and melting ice. Marlene and
Raney moved along the length of the deserted
bar, broken glass and ice cubes crunching
under their feet.

In the corridor leading to the rest rooms
stood three men, two large in white shirts and
bow ties, one small in a sports jacket. Raney
approached the jacket, flashed his shield, and
said, "Police. What's going on?"

The jacket backed out of the way and pointed
down the corridor. "Bitch is crazy, man. She
took this guy hostage. We haven't been able
to get near her—she's got a fuckin' sword in
there."

Raney and Marlene both looked where he
was pointing. JoAnne Caputo was crouched in
the corridor. She was muttering and snarling at
a man cringing a few feet from her, backed into
the corridor's dead end. In her right hand she
held a K-bar knife, Marine issue, which she
waved and poked at the man. Marlene noted
with horror that the man bore a striking resemblance to the guy they had just arrested. He
was bleeding from several cuts on the arm and
his face was drawn and frightened.

"Yeah, I see," said Raney. "You the manager?" he asked the sports jacket.

"Yeah. You gonna shoot her?"

"No, I don't think so. You called the police?
Good. Look, take your people and clear the
area. If any more cops show, send them back
here."

The manager seemed relieved and did as he

was told. When they were alone, Marlene said, "Raney, let me talk to her."

"Uh-uh. This is police business. You oughta wait outside."

"Bullshit!" cried Marlene, and moved toward the corridor. Raney stuck his arm out to block her, but at that moment heavy steps sounded in the bar and a TV crew—camera with blazing lights, a soundman, and an intrepid local news reporter—came charging in.

"Get out of here! Are you crazy?" shouted Raney at the crew.

Marlene used this distraction to break away from the detective. JoAnne too had turned at the sounds. The TV light dazzled her. She held up her free hand to shield her eyes. She saw someone coming toward her out of the halo of unbearable light. She struck out wildly with the knife, felt it catch in something, heard the ripping of fabric. She saw a face inches from her own, a familiar face. She tried to shake the fog of a dozen drinks out of her mind. Arms wrapped around her, pulling her close to a body slick with sweat, a woman's body.

"JoAnne!" a voice cried. "It's Marlene! It's OK, you got him. It's over." JoAnne Caputo started to wail, horrible screeching cries, the violation of the body at last finding its own voice. Marlene held her, swaying, saying inane and calming things into her ear. The big knife clunked on the floor.

She saw the guy come out of his corner, saw him run past, heard curses and the crash of bodies. She looked over her shoulder and saw Raney wrestle him to the ground. Suddenly the place was full of cops. It *was* over, but only in real life. There was still the television.

THIRTEEN

Karp was sitting in the darkened living-room section of the loft, staring at the gray flicker of a late movie, when Marlene crawled in at two A M. He looked up bleakly as she entered.

"Are you going to say, 'Where have you been, young lady?'" she asked.

"No," said Karp. "I'm not your father. And I know where you've been. It was on the late news."

"Ah, *shit!*" cried Marlene. She went to the cupboard and brought out a bottle of red wine and a glass, filled it, lit a cigarette, and threw herself down on a rocking chair, facing Karp. She was still wearing Raney's jacket, its lining hanging out where the blade had slashed it.

"So. How did I look?" she asked belligerently.

Karp shrugged. "Like everybody else on TV. Like an asshole."

"We got the guy," she said.

"That's nice, Marlene," said Karp flatly, still staring at the screen.

She finished her wine in two gulps and put

the glass down on the old door set on concrete blocks that served the loft as a coffee table. She clutched the jacket more tightly around her. "That's it? No congratulations on a job well done from my leader?"

"No. Because it's not your job. It's not your job to go running around after suspects. It's not your job to tackle crazy women waving knives—"

"She was my witness and she's not crazy."

Karp brought his fist violently down on the coffee table, bouncing it askew and toppling the glass. The dregs of the wine spilled over the white surface like blood from a wound. "Shut up!" he shouted. "Don't *argue* with me! Don't make *excuses*! This isn't fucking *court*! I'm not your goddamn *parole officer*."

"I knew you'd do this," she snarled. "You can't stand it when I'm not a good little girl. Well, if you'd gotten off your ass and gone to bat for me with the cops, I wouldn't've had to chase the fucking bastard down myself."

Karp was up on his feet, facing her, screaming. "What the fuck are you talking about! I *did* go to the cops. And what the hell does that have to do with anything? Don't you get it? Even PW's go on light duty when they get *pregnant*! You could have lost the *baby*!"

Marlene shot up too, knocking the rocker backward. Their faces were inches apart. "Oh, *that's* what it is. The baby!"

"You don't think I should be concerned?" Karp cried. "This is the second time this year that you've got yourself involved in a situation that required you to run around the streets with your clothes off because you insist on being Nancy fucking Drew and the girl commandos. And you promised me, you *swore* to me that you would take it easy. And then you go on this . . . I don't know . . . *crusade*—it's insane when you're carrying a child."

"There it is! Not *me*, not what *I* want, just your precious bloodline. Well, fuck you, Jack, and fuck the baby too! You think I'm gonna sit on my butt and knit booties and smile like the Mona Lisa for the rest of my life? Think again! I'm gonna live my own life *exactly* as I please. And that includes doing whatever I have to do to get my job done, as *I* decide. Not you, and not some fetus. It'll have to take its chances, the same as everybody else in this goddamn city."

"What job? You don't have a job after next week," Karp shouted.

"Oh, yes I do! I'm gonna take this case down to the wire."

"You can't! You're out!"

"No, I'm not. I get to stay for continuing cases, and this guy is the same guy who's been doing the rapes I've been working on for months, so it's the same case."

Karp opened his mouth to speak, to scream in fact, but was suddenly affected by a feeling of inutility and despair. He sank back on the couch, shaking his head. "I can't believe it," he said. "You're crazy. Out of your fucking mind."

"I'm always 'crazy' when I don't do what you want."

"Right, Marlene," Karp said with a sigh. "Whatever you say."

"Now you're going to get all depressed for days," said Marlene. "I wish one time we could just have a good fight and clear the air." She shucked out of the jacket, stuffed her rags of shirt into the trash, and vanished behind the screen that divided the living area from the bathing tank.

Karp had averted his eyes from her naked-ness. What Marlene wanted, he knew, was a slam-bang battle, including blows, a long blub-bering cry, and a good fuck to top it off. Karp wondered why he couldn't do it. But he could not; some deep knot of resistance to such a re-lease tied him into this angry passivity. He was right and she was wrong.

Karp's parents had never fought, that he re-membered. Father knew best. He laid down the law. Mom smiled bravely under the cold and sarcastic logic with which he did so, right up to the doors of death. Maybe she cried secretly, her head jammed under two pillows. Did he remember that?

Karp got up, drank a glass of water at the kitchen sink, and slipped into his sneakers. Marlene was splashing and humming to herself in the bath. Humming! *She* was fine. *He* was left holding the bag, the anger, the sense of betrayal. Karp muttered a curse and walked out, slamming the door behind him.

He knew he would walk the streets until three-thirty in the morning, wondering whether the next thirty years were going to be like this, feeling angry at, and sorry for, himself at the same time. And he knew he would crawl back between the sheets with Marlene and hope for it all to have blown over by the morning, or the next day, or the next. In any case, in the morning he could at least go to work and take it all out on the felons.

Roland Hrcany was not ordinarily sympathetic to the struggles of the younger ADA's. Like Karp, he had been bred in a hard school by the old guys of the former Homicide Bureau; unlike Karp, he saw no reason why he shouldn't give back what he had got, with interest. He was, in fact, the very last of the senior attorneys to whom a rookie would go for advice and counsel, so that the presence of Peter Schick in his office, wanting to talk, aroused his curiosity, if not his sympathy.

"So," he said, leaning back and cocking one foot up on his desk. "You're here. Spit it out. By the way, you look like shit."

Schick flushed and grimaced. "Yeah, well, I guess I'm not sleeping too good. Um, I don't know exactly how to put this, but, um, it's driving me up the wall. It's this drug-killings task force . . ."

"Yeah? What about it?"

"Well, there was a meeting this morning. Manning was talking about how they couldn't find this witness, Booth, and that he had information from a reliable informant that Clay Fulton was involved in the disappearance. You know they saw him leaving the scene of the attempted homicide?"

"Yeah, I heard. So what did Bloom say?"

"He got all excited," Schick said. "He wanted a full-scale investigation started on Fulton. And he kind of looked at Karp real hard, because he knows that Karp is, like, close to Fulton and he always defends him. But this time Karp just shrugged and said he'd set it up.

"Then, later, I went to him and asked him how we were going to proceed on the Fulton thing, and he said to forget it, he was just blowing smoke. Then I asked him about Booth and what he thought about the Fulton connection, and he said he didn't think there was anything in it."

"But you think there is?" asked Hrcany.

Schick looked away, embarrassed. "Yeah, I *know* there is. Um, that's why I had to talk to somebody about it. Before I went to Karp. I mean, I'm way over my head here."

"So, talk! Why do you know there's a connection?"

"Because I saw it. Last Friday, when we were all playing ball in the park—a couple of us were hitting fungoes, just farting around, you know, a little bombed. Somebody got off a good shot and the ball went into the woods along the left-field line. I went into the woods looking for the ball. So I came over this little rise, I'm down on my hands and knees looking, and I lift my head over the bushes and I can see the path and a bench in front of some rocks. About twenty yards away, Karp is sitting on the bench with a black guy, and I look again and I see it's Booth."

"How did you know it was him?"

"For cryin' out loud, Roland! I've been practically sleeping with the guy's jacket for the past month. It was him. I wasn't close enough to hear what they were saying, but after a while Karp gives Booth something, like a little envelope, and Booth gets up and walks away. Then Karp yells out something and Fulton comes out from behind some rocks. Fulton's got a tape recorder. They sit down and listen to the tape and talk for a little while, and then they shake hands and walk away."

Hrcany was staring directly at Schick as he related this, and after he fell silent the intensity of the pale-blue gaze did not diminish. Schick met it uncomfortably, swallowing hard. After some moments of this, Hrcany seemed satisfied. He considered himself an expert on lying and was convinced that the younger man was relating the truth. He nodded and pursed his thin lips. "So. What's your take on all this, Schick? What's Karp doing?"

"I don't know. I think he's protecting Fulton—that's the general plan. What he's doing with Booth . . ." He shrugged helplessly. "Like I said, it's way over my head."

Hrcany dropped his foot and sat upright. "Yeah, it is. OK, I'll take it from here. You know to keep quiet about this."

Schick nodded. Relieved of his burden, he felt like a new man. "Um, if I can help—" he began.

Hrcany made a dismissive gesture. "Yeah, I'll call you. Meanwhile, you keep in touch if you learn anything else in the same line."

After Schick had left, Hrcany sat awhile in thought, occupying himself by lifting the front of his desk off the floor, in a series of slow curls, stretching the fabric of his shirt across his coconut-hard biceps until it creaked. Hrcany considered himself Karp's friend, as friends were counted in his bleak view of human nature at the New York D.A.'s office: someone you could depend on most of the time and who would probably apologize if he screwed you unusually hard.

Hrcany, in fact, admired Karp, and the people that Hrcany admired comprised a very small club. Karp was the only criminal lawyer in the D.A.'s office that Hrcany considered his peer, and perhaps, if he were to be completely honest, something more than a peer—the best.

His admiration was, however, crusted with just the faintest patina of contempt; Karp was a great lawyer, sure, but after all, something of a Boy Scout, not enough of a street fighter. There was the problem. That Karp had not told

him about what he was running with Booth
and Fulton, that he had, as it now appeared,
maneuvered, *manipulated*, Hrcany out of the
drug task force so that he could put a raw
know-nothing in there and thus become free to
play whatever game he was playing, disturbed
Hrcany more than he was willing to admit. It
struck him at the heart of his own self-esteem—
his status as resident master of dirty pool.

He did not, of course, wish to hurt Karp in
any way. Karp was a buddy. But if someone
flicked you with a wet towel in the locker room,
you had to flick him back. Hrcany reached for
the phone.

He dialed the number of the Twenty-eighth
Precinct and talked briefly. Then he hung up
and dialed the Thirty-second. He talked with
two cops there. An interesting picture started
to emerge. He made a few more calls. Hrcany
knew cops. More to the point, he had stuff on
a lot of cops, small stuff, most of it, but
enough, in the atmosphere of paranoia that had
affected the NYPD after the Knapp corruption
scandals, to give Hrcany a way to get information that few men outside the department were
able to acquire.

After the fourth call, he stretched, again
flexed his collection of large muscles, and studied the yellow sheets of legal bond he had covered with notes. His technique had been
simple. What about this Fulton, I hear he's real
dirty. You heard that too? I hear you used to

hang around with him. No? Good. Who's he hanging with, then?

Hrcany knew that the famous Blue Wall had its little chinks and cracks. Cops would not rat on a brother officer, but while one of them was under serious investigation they liked to keep their distance, maintain a discreet separation from the diseased member of the pack, especially off-duty. Even those under suspicion knew this, and it was considered good form for them to restrict their contacts during the active phase of an investigation.

Hrcany also knew that if Fulton was involved in the drug-lord killings, he had not worked alone. Either someone in his command had helped him or he had gone outside, which would have been a smarter move. Still, he was surprised at what he had learned. You had to admire the guy's balls. Who had Fulton been seen with repeatedly over the past few weeks? Who were his new drinking buddies? The very cops who represented the department on the drug-killings task force: Manning and Amalfi.

So, were they setting Fulton up? Were they running their own investigation? Another call, this time to police headquarters to a deputy chief in Internal Affairs, who owed Hrcany a favor. More and more curious. Manning and Amalfi were not investigating Fulton. In fact, despite the persistent rumors about Fulton, there was no active investigation of him going on at all. The deputy chief hinted darkly that this was on orders from way upstairs. From whom? The chief declined to say.

That was OK. Karp's close relationship with the chief of detectives was well-known. An obvious cover-up. The only remaining puzzle was the business with the tape in the park. Why would Fulton and Karp be making a tape with Tecumseh Booth? He thought for five minutes. Ah, that was it! Now it all made sense. He picked up the phone to make another call, then reconsidered and put it back again. What he had to do couldn't be done on the phone.

Karp rubbed his eyes and looked up from the thick case file that Marlene had assembled on the panty-hose rapist who had graduated to murderer. He now had a name: Alan Meissner, a nice Jewish boy from the Bronx, no less. A college graduate, a mid-level executive with the phone company, nice to his mom, a real shock for the neighbors. Meissner's hobby and chief outside interest was, needless to say, amateur theatrics.

Karp yawned and went back to reading. He had not slept well during the past week; he never did when Marlene and he were having a period of excruciating and loveless politeness. He wondered yet again whether this was it, a preview of the next thirty years or so. He was missing something, he knew, Marlene wanted something from him, but he couldn't figure out what it was. He just hoped that she'd tell him, lay it out so he could play by the rules henceforth.

Back to the file. It was a good case, he thought. Despite her extracurricular ditziness, Marlene was a first-class prosecutor. She had marshaled the rape victims one by one, and each had picked Meissner out of a lineup. They had searched his apartment after the arrest and found the elements of all the disguises he had used: wigs, makeup, contact lenses, and the lifts he had used to manipulate his height. They had found a little address book with the names and addresses of the victims—including the murder victim—written down in Meissner's hand. They had played a tape recording of Meissner's voice for Seth Allman, and he had identified it as the voice he had talked to at the time of the murder.

All good stuff and all properly warranted. It would hold up. But the core of the case, of course, was the panty hose. Five women, all standing up individually in court and describing how their rapist had wrapped panty hose around their heads, when combined with the crime-scene photos of Ellen Wagner's punctured body and wrapped head, would be devastating to the defense. The law called it "a common scheme, plan, or design," and Karp knew that it was particularly convincing to juries. Juries might not know much, but they understood things they could recognize in themselves. They all knew what a habit was, and a lot of them knew what an obsession was.

He started to call Marlene, to have her stop

by and discuss some of the details, to tell her she had done a good job. But he put the phone down. He couldn't face her across a desk. Instead, he signed the transmittal letter as bureau chief and tossed the package in the tray for the district attorney. With Bloom's signature on it—a matter of form—Marlene would take the case before the grand jury, who would bring in an indictment—also a matter of form. Karp yawned again and picked up the next case file.

Sid Amalfi lived in a respectable Queens neighborhood made up of large two-story houses on maple-lined streets. It was inhabited largely by mid-level civil servants and skilled workers and was nearly crime-free. Amalfi's house had a late-model white Caddy in the garage and a big Bayliner inboard on a trailer parked on the street outside. A little unusual for that neighborhood, but not altogether unknown; guys gambled on sports and out at Aqueduct, and people got lucky. After all, there had to be some winners, right? Amalfi, however, also had a condo at Queen Cay in the Bahamas, with a boat floating in front of it that didn't fit on a trailer. This was not only unusual, but impossible, which was why it was recorded in his brother-in-law's name.

It was eight and just getting dark when Amalfi pulled his battered cop Plymouth into his driveway. He was still nervous about how this thing with Fulton was going to play out.

He was the nervous one; he had a family and a lot more to lose. Manning was the cool one, and although Amalfi had difficulty admitting it to himself, also the leader of their scam. Things had changed in the job, but Amalfi still had problems taking orders from a black guy. And now there was this other dinge in on the thing.

He locked the car and walked across his lawn, carefully stepping on the fieldstones placed there. A couple more jobs—another fifty large— and he would have enough to hand in his tin and get out, never have to worry about money again, the kids provided for, fish all day, drink all night . . .

A car door slammed on the quiet street. He heard footsteps behind him and his stomach jumped. He was starting to reach for the pistol under his arm when he recognized the first of the two men coming up the path as Roland Hrcany. The other man was a thin fellow with a heavy jaw. Amalfi didn't recognize him, but knew that he was a cop.

Hrcany said, "Detective Amalfi, we'd like to speak with you."

"What's this about, Hrcany? I'm off-duty." Amalfi looked inquiringly at the other man, who took an ID card from his jacket and flashed it. "Sergeant Waldbaum, Internal Affairs," he said.

Amalfi held out his hands and forced a smile onto his unwilling face. "Hey, guys, what is this? You gotta come to my home, at night?"

"We thought it was advisable. The fewer people aware of this at this point, the better," said Hrcany.

"Aware of what?" said Amalfi. "Am I under some kind of investigation?"

"The investigation is over, Amalfi," said Hrcany. "We got the tape."

Amalfi's face twitched involuntarily. "What tape is that?"

"The tape, Amalfi," snapped Hrcany. "Booth's tape. Fulton's tape. It's over. The drug-pusher killings. We know the whole story. The only question is, who's gonna take the fall?"

"I don't know what the fuck you're talking about, Hrcany," Amalfi said, fighting to keep his voice level and conversational, fighting the bubble of panic souring the back of his throat. "And I don't have to listen to goddamn insinuations on my own front walk. You want to charge me with something, go ahead, but I want my lawyer and my PBA rep standing next to me when you do."

Hrcany smiled unpleasantly. "Fine, Sid. You want to play it that way, it's OK by me. But let me tell you something—the others are going to walk on this. Fulton and Manning are laughing at you right now. Figure it out, asshole! Two brothers, the game is falling apart—who the fuck you think they're gonna pin it on? One of them? Think again! Tapes can be edited, you know. Coupla days maybe, they'll find you with one in the ear, and a tape from old Tecumseh saying you and him did all those jobs."

Amalfi shouted, "I don't have to listen to this horseshit," then spun around and stalked up his walk to his front door. He slammed it behind him, and then ran, knees trembling, to the downstairs bathroom, where he knelt, retching for a good ten minutes.

Amalfi knew what Hrcany was doing, had done it himself a thousand times. Break up the group; sow distrust; the first step in cracking a gang. The problem was, it didn't matter that Amalfi knew what was going on; the thing still worked.

Hrcany and Waldbaum walked back to their car, got in, and sat in silence. Hrcany lit a small cigar and contemplated the glowing tip as deep twilight fell on Queens.

"What the *fuck* was that all about?" Waldbaum asked.

"It's funny. When I walked up that path I didn't know shit. Now I know just about all I need to. He's dirty. God, is he dirty! He's *in* it with Fulton. And Manning too, of course."

"What, they've been shooting these pushers?"

"Yeah," said Hrcany, "so it seems. But I don't know that, since I haven't heard the tape."

Waldbaum's jaw dropped. "You were bluffing?"

"Yeah, but he bought it," answered Hrcany.

"I didn't see much there, Roland. He looked pretty good."

"I saw his eyes, Joe. He looked bad. He's heard about the tape and it scares the shit out of him. All the schmuck had to do was look puzzled and act friendly and say he was working Fulton because the rumor mill said he was involved. Then we would've been dead in the water. I mean, it would've been a hell of a lot more plausible than believing he was in with Fulton."

Waldbaum nodded. It made a kind of crazy sense. "So what now?"

"Nothing, tonight. Let him cook for a while. The next time we roust him out, he'll be done."

"Shit, Roland, if you're right, this is the biggest thing going and I'm hanging out by my shorts here," said Waldbaum. "I can't fucking accuse a cop of murder without clearance from the unit captain."

"As I recall," said Hrcany, "you didn't accuse him of anything. Neither did I. I just said we had a tape and that he was gonna get set up."

"But we don't have a tape. We don't even know what's on the fucking tape."

"Yeah, we do. Look, what else could it be? Karp knows Fulton is dirty, so he figures a way to protect him. He gets Fulton to tape Booth telling his story."

"What good's that gonna do Fulton?"

"I don't know exactly, but trust me: if Karp's involved, you can bet it's clever. Maybe they'll doctor the tape some way. Even better, they give Booth a script exculpating Fulton. Maybe other people are involved. Karp's game has to be stopping the killings, getting the heat off his friend. I mean, once they stop, that's it—nobody gives a rat's ass a bunch of pushers got killed, as long as they don't keep rubbing our faces in it. So the tape could be a threat—Fulton telling his boys, they got us, time to close up the store."

"But you don't know any of this for sure," Waldbaum observed.

"No, I don't," Hrcany said grimly. "That's why we need a fucking tape of our own."

"How was the grand jury?" asked Karp.

"It was grand, as advertised," Marlene replied. "No problem with the indictment. We arraign this coming Tuesday." They were in the loft, sitting side by side on the couch, eating pizza off the coffee-table door, and watching the news on TV with the volume turned almost all the way down. They were not interested in the news from anyplace else but each other, but this had been delayed for technical reasons. The air had not cleared between them; rather it lay like a chill and sticky mist, permitting the passage only of polite conversation.

"Who's on D.?"

"Mr. Motion," said Marlene.

"Polaner? That should be fun; the man gives a whole new meaning to 'justice delayed is justice denied.' Your mutt has good judgment, anyway. The longer he can stretch this out, the less convincing the witnesses are going to be, and Mr. M. is the boy for that. What's he like, the mutt?"

"He's charming. It's all a terrible mistake, but he doesn't hold it against me personally. He's going to look damn good in court."

"Well, Polaner will never call him. Why should he? His game is to impeach your witnesses, not give you a shot at his boy. Are there any more slices without anchovies?"

"No, because you eat twice as fast as I do and you don't like anchovies, so you always scarf up the pepperoni slices," said Marlene.

"But you're eating a pepperoni."

"Yes, 'cause if I don't start with a pepperoni, I never get *any* pepperoni, on account of the aforesaid difference in eating speed."

Karp sniffed, and began delicately to pick anchovies off a slice of pizza. "That may be true," he said, "but it doesn't seem fair. We should be able to order pizza that's precisely adjusted to our individual topping preferences and eating rates."

"It's not the pizza guy's problem, Butch," said Marlene. "Have you considered that the answer might lie in personal growth and change? Perhaps slowing yourself down. Perhaps learning to savor the healthful anchovy."

"I have considered it," said Karp. "I've also considered that whenever personal growth and change enter the conversation, it's always me that's targeted for personal growth and change."

"Perhaps it's because Marlene, by dint of exhausting struggle and introspection, has moved closer to the goal of earthly perfection than you yourself have. And by the way, for the record books, I believe this is the most inane conversation we've had this year."

"I'd have to agree on that, although the year is still young," said Karp, finishing his slice and wiping his hands and face on a paper towel. "Also, I like 'by dint.' It's a phrase we don't get enough of nowadays. Speaking of which."

"What are you doing, Butch?"

"Checking to see if you have any panties under your kimono. I make it a point never to wax philosophical with people who have neglected their panties."

"And?"

"Nothing so far," said Karp, "but I'll be able to look better if I get your legs arranged sort of across my lap. Like this."

"You know," said Marlene, letting herself be shifted, and sinking back into the velvet cushions, "I have to confess, I occasionally go to the office in the summer without anything on under my dress. Do you think that's too slutty?"

"I wouldn't presume to comment. It hasn't affected your professional performance that I can see."

"Thank you," said Marlene. A long silence,

humming with the Lebanese situation, and then a series of soft groans and cries. "Oh, my!" she said. "That took her by surprise. Could you feel that?"

"Yes," said Karp. "It felt like an escaping anchovy. What are you doing with your foot?"

"You mean the foot I have inveigled inside your sweats? This is called the Sicilian Rolling-Pin Maneuver."

"Sicilian, eh?"

"Yeah, and we're not really supposed to perform it until after marriage. Along with the Palermo Pout, it's the main reason our little island has been invaded so many times in history."

"I can see why," said Karp huskily. "Anyway, I guess we're back together now. I'm sorry I got mad at you and moped."

"That's OK," said Marlene. "I realize I'm hard to live with. Someday I'll settle down. And don't worry about the baby. She's half an inch long and hard as nails. So, are you going to jump on me, or what?"

"You seem ready for it."

"Ready? I'm frothy. It's blowing tiny bubbles." She squirmed deliciously on the seat cushions, sliding flat and hoisting one leg on the back of the settee.

"Wait a second," said Karp, after wriggling out of his sweatpants, "you got pizza crusts under your ass."

Marlene grabbed him by the front of his sweatshirt and yanked him onto her. In an instant he was firmly socketed, sinking into her like a pipe wrench dropped into a crock of warm chili. She heaved and bit his ear and whispered, gasping into it, "We can . . . eat them . . . later. Or cut them . . . into little cubes and . . . serve them to . . . special guests."

"Stop talking, Marlene," said Karp. Which she did.

FOURTEEN

Detectives Lanny Maus and Mack Jeffers were sitting in the back of an old Ford van on 143rd Street in Harlem, waiting for a murderer to arrive so they could arrest him. The van was hand-painted a dull black and it was hot inside. By an arrangement of the van's rearview and side mirrors they had the entrance to the apartment house under indirect observation. The two men reclined on scraps of old carpeting and munched on doughnuts, washed down with quantities of iced Coke from a cooler. This was one of the penalties the King Cole Trio paid for being famous in Harlem, that in order to observe unnoticed, they had to hide in uncomfortable places.

"We should call in," said Maus.

"Fuck that," said Jeffers. "He show up, we call in."

"But Art said—"

"Fuck him too," said Jeffers, shifting his bulk and rocking the van on its worn springs. "Man got the rag on all week, and he takin' it out on us."

Maus nodded. "You think he's still pissed about how the Tecumseh thing went down?"

Jeffers glared at him. "No, *I'm* pissed about *that*. Fuckin' little mutt get a free trip to L.A., gets to lie around in the sunshine, while we sweatin' our ass off in some damn van. The fuckin' Loo what give Dugman a hair up his ass."

"What, he thinks the Loo is dirty too?" asked Maus.

"I don't know if he think it, or he know it, but that's it, man."

"So, hey, so he's dirty," said Maus. "I never figured it for him, but it could happen. There's a stink, the snakes'll be in and hang his ass. Why is that skin off Dugman's butt?"

"You don't know much, son, if you got to ask that," said Jeffers.

"Yeah? So I'm a dumb maggot. Tell me why. Is it because Art's in on the dirt?"

Jeffers scowled at the other detective and rolled his eyes in disbelief. "Not that kind of dirt. Look, Dugman a cop for what? Goin' on thirty years. You got any idea what being a black cop in Harlem was like thirty years ago? We talking just after the war. They was still lynching folks down South. Cops up here'd think no more about wasting a bad nigger than giving a god-damn parking ticket. Shit, *less*.

"But a *black* cop, a black cop was like a fuckin king up here, you understand? Power of life and death. Money coming in from the whores, from numbers, liquor violations. Fuckin dude hasn't bought a meal or a suit of clothes or a bottle of J&B in Harlem in all that time. Shit, fuckin Dugman used to perform *weddings*. Get the picture?"

"Yeah," said Maus, "kind of." He shifted on his knees and checked the mirrors. There were half a dozen young men and a couple of girls lounging on the steps leading to the house they were watching. An old woman in black climbed painfully up the steps dragging two shopping bags. Without stopping his observation, he said, "By the way, what makes you so sure this sweetheart is gonna show today?"

"His girlfriend live there. Also this the end of the month. Tomorrow welfare Tuesday—jingle day in the ghet-to, you dig? He gonna slip in there, get her pussy feelin good, and also make sure nobody else there for the payday."

"Wait a minute—I thought this guy shanked his girlfriend; that's why we're chasing him."

Jeffers smiled pityingly. "That was a different girlfriend. Take a couple, three mommas to support our boy in the style to which he has been accustomed. What's the matter, you disapprove of the life-styles of the poor and soulful?"

"Hey, no shit, I love all you people," said Maus, straight-faced. "The sense of rhythm, Harry Belafonte, Martin Luther King, watermelon, chitlins—the whole nine yards."

Jeffers grimaced and flicked icy water from the cooler at his companion. Maus laughed and said, "But go on about Dugman and the Loo.

You're saying that old-time Harlem had something to do with why Art's pissed off?''

"Yeah. OK, so Art's dirty, but it's clean dirt. There's a line he draws. The skells, the bad niggers, the drugs—especially the drugs—are on one side. He's on the other. He gonna shoot people, but nobody *else* gets to shoot people. Not on his stand. Like that. And the paddies downtown think that's just great; as long as he keep passing along a piece of the pad from his action, keep the brothers from running riot up here, he's golden. He's never gonna make higher than sergeant, but what the fuck, he's a dinge, right?

"So then comes Knapp. Turn on the lights in Harlem and people running around like roaches. Art's shakin—he's going down. And who saves his black ass?''

"Fulton?''

"Yeah, Fulton. This was just before you got here. You never heard this story?''

"Yeah, I heard. They were getting charges ready on Art, and Fulton cashed in some chips.''

"Yeah, that's how it went. But, dig it, it was more than that," said Jeffers. "Look at it from Art's point of view. Here's this black guy and he's everything Art ain't. College graduate. One of the first black detective loos in history. The guy's platinum. Besides, the dude is one tough motherfucker street cop—first guy through the door, wounded in action twice, police medal of honor, commendations up one side and down the other. So afterwards, when they drop the charges, he lay down the law to old Art; things has changed. I cover your ass, I ain't gonna hassle you about no chickenshit, but no fuckin cash better change hands no more.

"And Art buys it. What, he's only got three, four years max he's gonna stay. You got it now?"

"I got it," said Maus thoughtfully. "What you're saying is that if Fulton is really killing guys for pay, for pushers, Art is like the asshole of the century."

"Yeah, man. And Art can't afford to look like no asshole in Harlem. It's his fuckin neck on the street. And you know something else? Underneath, what hurt him worse'n even that— Art love that boy. Seeing a black kid gettin over like that—"

"Hey," Maus interrupted. "Check this out!"

Jeffers slid forward and looked at the mirrored image. Maus said, "The dude in the blue track suit talking to the mutts on the stoop. He looks good."

Jeffers nodded. He picked up an Ithaca pump gun and jacked a round into the chamber. "Yeah, that's him. Wait'll he goes inside. We'll get him on the stairs."

Marlene sat at the prosecution table of Part 30 waiting for the court officer to call *People* v. *Meissner* so that the panty-hose killer could be arraigned on the grand jury's indictment. She glanced sideways across the aisle at her opponent and his client. Henry Polaner was a small man with a large head decorated with an abundance of pepper-and-salt hair through which prominent ears peeked like inquisitive jungle animals. His eyes were dark and heavy-lidded, his nose bulbous, and his infrequent smiles showed a rank of perfectly capped teeth. His favored expression was bored amusement, as if to challenge anyone's serious belief in the farrago of legal nonsense brought by the prosecution.

His client, now undisguised, was an unprepossessing man of about thirty. His hair was medium brown, his eyes were pale hazel, his build was average. His features were even and conventionally handsome. His nose was straight and long, without bumps, and he had all his fingers. The only remarkable thing about him was his expression, and that only remarkable in a man facing trial on a charge of murder. He seemed like someone about to watch a play or a sporting event, long-anticipated and promising pleasure. He liked to smile, and his smile was that of a mischievous little boy caught at some trivial misdemeanor by an indulgent parent.

The case was called. The formal reading of the indictment was waived; in calendar courts in New York County, briskness is all, as is repetition. The average felony case makes fourteen court appearances before disposition. The judge asked for the plea.

Polaner stood and said, "Not guilty, your Honor, and may I say that I believe we have an excellent motion to dismiss based on the content of the grand-jury indictment. Apparently a good deal of evidence was presented that was both irrelevant and highly prejudicial to the case."

The judge looked over at Marlene. "Miss Ciampi, was all evidence in this case presented to the same grand jury?"

"Yes, your Honor," said Marlene. The question struck her as odd. Evidence in complex major cases had often been presented to grand juries composed of different people on different days, and indictments had been struck down because of the practice. The law said that the actual jurors bringing an indictment had to have heard exactly the same evidence. But it was defense attorneys, not judges, who were supposed to bring that question out in court. Marlene felt the first presentiment that this was not going to be a routine arraignment.

Polaner said, "Your Honor, at this time I ask for access to the minutes of the grand jury. I believe such access is warranted in order to demonstrate the prejudicial nature of the evidence presented."

Marlene said, "Your Honor, it's been the practice of the court to turn over grand-jury minutes only after the appearances of the relevant witnesses at trial."

The judge looked down at Marlene and frowned. "Young lady, don't tell me what the practice of the court has been! The practice of *this* court is whatever *I* say it is. I'm not going to lay myself open to reversible error just to suit your convenience. Now, counsel has argued that the grand jury has been prejudiced by the nature of the People's evidence, and he needs those minutes to establish prejudice. I want you to turn those minutes over to the defense forthwith."

"Yes, your Honor," said Marlene meekly. Inside she seethed: something was wrong, terribly wrong. This should not be happening in a calendar court.

"Move thirty days to prepare motions, your Honor," said Polaner.

"Granted."

"And as a final matter, your Honor, I ask that a reasonable bail be granted in this case. My client has lived in this community all his life. He is a college graduate, gainfully employed in a professional position. He has strong family and neighborhood ties and is additionally the sole support of his widowed mother."

"Your Honor, we strongly object to setting bail in this case," said Marlene with a sinking heart. "We have an overwhelming case on the evidence, and the charge is murder. Both these elements make flight before trial a distinct possibility."

"Yes," said the judge blandly, "but there seems to be some doubt about this so-called evidence. Bail is set at twenty-five thousand dollars." The gavel came down. Polaner turned to his client and shook his hand and clasped him on the shoulder. But Meissner wasn't looking at the lawyer. He was looking over Polaner's shoulder, directly at Marlene. He smiled at her, a confident and mocking smile. He winked.

"Next case," said Judge Nolan.

Marlene gathered up her papers and walked out of the courtroom, feeling as if she were wading in taffy. The press was there in force, people shoving mikes and cameras in her face. She put her head down and no-commented her way to the elevator. Her face seemed larger and hotter than normal. It was a nightmare. The guy walked!

"The guy walked," Marlene wailed as she burst into Karp's office.

"Who did, babe?" asked Karp, alarmed. Marlene's face was blanched and her good eye was wild in its socket.

"Meissner. The fucking judge walked him on twenty-five K, *and* he made me turn my grand-jury minutes over to him."

"What!"

"Yeah. According to Mr. Motion, the evidence presented at the grand jury, meaning the five rape cases with the panty hose, was prejudicial and irrelevant."

"And the judge bought it? What was he, senile?" Karp asked this not at all facetiously.

Marlene shook her head. "Not so you'd notice. It was Nolan, for God's sake! Oh, and he was all of a sudden concerned about reversible error. Yes, well you may gape—Judge Nolan, who has been reversed so many times he has a gearshift stuck up his ass. Here's a bastard who never walked an accused homicide in his life, and you would think, wouldn't you, that when he finally gets a chance to show it's not just black and PR thugs who get put away, he'd . . . What's wrong?''

Karp was biting his upper lip and staring at the floor in thought. "Nolan," he said. "It's not the first time he walked one. He did it on Tecumseh Booth too."

Marlene wrinkled her brow in confusion. "What're you talking about? What does Meissner have to do with the drug killings?"

"Nothing, I don't think," answered Karp. "Except for the honorable Nolan. I'm pretty sure that somebody told him to spring Booth. Springing Meissner might have been a freebie."

"But why? On a case like this? It can't make him look good."

"Judges don't have to look good," said Karp. "Besides, he was just protecting our precious civil liberties. *We* have to look good. Bloom does and I do, assuming . . ."

"Assuming what?"

"Assuming I'm interested in running for D.A. anytime soon. Meissner is a hot public case. Maybe somebody's sending me a message. Like, lay off Nolan."

"I didn't know you were *on* Nolan," snapped Marlene, her anger shifting, as it often did,

from the issue at hand to the person of her own
sweet lover.

"I need to know who put the fix in on
Booth," said Karp. "I asked V.T. to look into
Nolan's finances, see if maybe there was a connection to Congressman Fane or somebody like
him. That was it. Word must have got around."

"Yeah, well, if that happened, it seems to
have royally fucked up my case. Christ! What
the hell am I gonna tell the women?"

"Tell them we get shafted sometimes but
we're not out of the game yet. You'll do a great
job responding to Polaner's motions, and
meanwhile things could change all around.
Also, I'll check out what's going on with my
newfound friends in high places."

"OK," said Marlene grumpily, "but anybody
who fucks with me on this one is dead meat."

Dick Manning had a small but elegant apartment off West End Avenue in the Eighties. He
had decorated it in masculine modern, full of
the type featured in *Playboy* magazine: the furniture covered in pale or dark leather, the
lamps of spidery black metal, tables of glass
and gilt steel. He had African masks on the
walls and some colorful primitive paintings he
had picked up for a song on a Haitian vacation,
and which were now, he had heard, appreciat-
ing nicely in value. His stereo and TV were
large and expensive, with immense flattened
speakers reaching halfway to the ceiling. One
wall was covered with gold-flecked mirror

squares; another wall was windows, looking out over the avenue.

Manning sat in a large leather armchair. Fulton was on the Haitian-cotton couch opposite and Amalfi was in a chrome-and-leather sling chair off to one side. It was Fulton's first visit, and he regarded it as a good sign, the only good sign in a period of intense frustration. Six weeks had passed since he had revealed Tecumseh's tape to Manning and Amalfi, weeks devoid of action. All the remaining dope dealers were healthy. Fulton had no play except to sink deeper into his persona as a bad cop. As a result, no cop would talk to him unless he had to. Even the King Cole Trio was giving him furtive, hostile stares and responding to his orders with sullen obedience.

Manning poured Hennessey and orange juice into glasses and handed one to Fulton. Amalfi came over to the coffee table and got his. Manning said, "Drink up, Fulton. You look like you could use it."

"I'm psyched," said Fulton. "Long time, no action."

Manning lifted an eyebrow. "You think there's gonna be action?"

"Yeah. You didn't drag me up here to, ah, solidify our close friendship. So what is it?"

A broad smile spread over Manning's face. "You sharp, Clay. They told me you was a smart mother, and it's true. Ain't it, Sid?"

Amalfi said unenthusiastically, "Yeah, Dick, he's a sharp one, all right."

"Yeah, we do have a little job for you to-night," Manning continued. "You know Nicky Benning?"

"What about him?"

"We're taking him down," said Manning.

Fulton snorted. "Benning? With what army? Fucking guy runs half the dope in Harlem and all of it in the South Bronx. There's fifteen layers of operation between him and the street. Nobody's even *seen* him on the street for years. How the fuck you gonna get close to Benning?"

"Easy," said Manning. He took a sip from his glass and lit a cigarette, enjoying the pause and the attention it generated. "Brother Benning is in the hospital. Seems his ulcer bust day before yesterday. Must be a tense business running all that skag through town. So he's in a private room at Roosevelt under a phony name. No guards. It's a easy hit."

Fulton said, "How did *you* find out about it?"

Manning grinned. "I got a little bird, tells me stuff. So—you wanted some action. You in on this, or what?"

"I'm in," said Fulton. "What, you figure I go in alone?"

"Uh-uh, we don't work alone," said Manning. "Sid'll go with you."

"Yeah, OK," said Fulton carefully. "You staying?"

"No, I'll go out with you. I got some business uptown. Lemme get my jacket."

Manning went into the bedroom. Fulton stood up. The mirrored wall dimly reflected the inside of the bedroom. Fulton saw Manning take a pale sport coat and a shoulder holster from a closet. He put on the shoulder holster and took an automatic pistol from a bureau drawer and stuck it in the holster. Then he took a small revolver from the same drawer and, propping his foot up on the bed, placed it in an ankle holster strapped to his right leg. He put his jacket on and checked himself in a long mirror. As he emerged, Fulton turned quickly away from the mirror and noticed Amalfi staring at him. Amalfi looked peaked and gray. There was a twitch in one eye. Fulton had a good idea why he was nervous.

Roosevelt Hospital, on Ninth and 59th, was only ten minutes from Manning's apartment. Fulton and Amalfi parked Amalfi's old car near the emergency entrance. Amalfi handed Fulton a brass key. "This'll open the fire door from the outside. He's in room 523."

"I gotta walk up five flights?"

"Unless you want to go up the elevator with a bunch of witnesses. The room is between the fire stairs and the nurse's station. You should be in and out in three minutes. Wrap the gun in the pillow."

"Good advice, Sid," said Fulton. "I can tell you're the brains of the outfit. You gonna stay here?"

"Yeah, it's a one-man deal."

Fulton nodded and got out of the car. He found the fire door, opened it with no problem, and walked quickly up to the fifth floor. Nicky

Benning was where he was supposed to be, draped with various tubes, sleeping, unguarded.

Fulton went back to the fire stairs and waited on the landing for a few minutes. Then he went back to the hallway and took the elevator down to the ground floor. He went through the emergency room and paused in the shadows by the doorway. He could see Amalfi's car clearly. As Fulton had expected, Amalfi was no longer in it.

As he walked back to the fire door, Fulton wondered how they planned to do it. They couldn't just shoot him in the back, not a detective lieutenant. It would have to be a confrontation. They would get the drop on him and set it up. A couple in the chest and then his gun pressed into his own dead hand and a shot fired. Sorry, but I had no choice. I caught him red-handed after he killed Benning, he shot at me and I dropped him. It might have worked, Fulton thought, with a realization that chilled him. Karp would bitch, but he couldn't do much without the cooperation of the police. And of course the investigation would be handled by guess-who. Even Denton couldn't do much, without destroying himself. The other brass would go along with it, if the killings stopped and Manning and Amalfi left the country. To protect the department.

Slowly he inserted the key in the lock with his left hand. He pulled and cocked his .38 Airweight. There were two good places for an ambush. One was up on the fifth floor, to the left of the fire door. The other was in the little blind corridor to the right of the first flight of fire stairs. Fulton didn't figure Amalfi for a man who would walk up five flights unless he absolutely had to.

He took a deep breath, snapped the lock, flung the door open, and leapt in, crouching, his pistol pointing rigidly down the little corridor. It pointed straight at Amalfi, who stood there flatfooted and amazed, with a flat pint of vodka halfway to his lips, his gun in its holster. The bottle dropped and shattered, filling the landing with an appropriately medical smell.

"Uhhh, no!" Amalfi croaked. His face sagged in terror. Fulton darted forward, spun the unresisting man around, shoved his face up against the concrete wall, and patted him down. He pulled out and placed in his own pockets Amalfi's gun, his handcuffs, and a nasty little blackjack. As his fingers searched the small of Amalfi's back, he stopped abruptly and cursed.

"You're wearing a fucking wire!" he shouted. The sound echoed like an accusation from heaven in the stone vault of the stairway. He grabbed Amalfi's jacket and whipped him around again so that they were face-to-face.

"Talk!" Fulton ordered. "What's going on?"

"Don't kill me! I got money—"

"I'm not going to kill you, asshole. Who're you working for? Internal Affairs?"

Something clicked in Amalfi's mind then. An "aha" from some hitherto untapped reserve of insight, brought forward by fear of death. For the first time in the weeks since his life had gone in the toilet, since he had heard Fulton's tape, since Hrcany and the shoofly had visited him, he was thinking clearly. He breathed deeply and relaxed. "Yeah," he said. "You too?"

"No, but close," said Fulton. "They turned you, did they?"

"Yeah."

"Who are they after? They got you and Manning already."

"They want who Manning . . . who we're doing it for."

"You mean Choo Willis?"

"Not just him. Fane."

"The congressman? He's in on this?"

"Yeah. He's deep in. Willis works for him. He owns the Club Mecca. There're other heavies involved but, ah, we don't have anything definite on them yet. Manning knows the whole story, but he keeps it close."

Fulton uncocked his pistol and was silent for a while. He made no move to give Amalfi back his gun. "How the fuck did this all get started?" he asked.

Amalfi shrugged. "One thing led to another. Me and Dick was chasing this skell across the roof one night. We cornered him and he shot at us and we wasted him. He had a pile of cash on him and we split it up like we always did. Dick took a little coke off him too. I never did that, but Dick always could move dope. Then we were talking about what a pain in the ass it was gonna be, shooting this shithead, and all the investigation and the fucking paperwork, and Dick said, 'You know, if we was smart, we wouldn't be chasing these assholes across the roof. We could ace them at our convenience and get paid a shitload of money for it.' That was the start. Then we started doing jobs. Dick did the actual . . . you know, the work. I never did any of that."

"But you took the money."

Amalfi nodded. "Yeah, I took the money. Shit, man, they're dirtballs, what the hell, right?"

"Wrong. I don't know what deal you cut with Internal Affairs, but I'm going to let that slide for now. Just do what they tell you. But whatever goes down, it's got to go down fast. Tomorrow or the next day Manning is gonna find out I didn't ace Benning and the shit's gonna hit the fan. By the way, what did you intend to do, laying for me here?"

Amalfi said, "They, ah, wanted me to bring you in. Put the squeeze on you. Get a wire on you too. They figured you took out Tecumseh."

Fulton smiled without amusement and shook his head. "Can't trust nobody nowadays. Look, tell those assholes I'm the good guys. If they don't believe you, tell them to go to Chief Denton. We were trying to keep the lid on this, but it's blown now. Asses'll be frying like bacon downtown when this gets out."

Fulton opened the door. Amalfi said, "Hey,

how about giving me my stuff back?" He tried to meet Fulton's contemptuous gaze and couldn't.

Fulton said, "I'll toss them under your car," and slammed the door behind him.

Marlene had put nearly fifty hours of work into answering the motions in *People* v. *Meissner*. It all went up in smoke in less than three minutes. When the case was called, Nolan shuffled the papers before him, cleared his throat, adjusted his reading glasses, and said, "On reviewing the defense motion to dismiss, I find that the presentation of five individual cases of alleged rape to the grand jury was in fact prejudicial. The alleged rapes are separate and distinct crimes and cannot be used as evidence for predisposition to this particular homicide. Thus, the People's attempt to demonstrate a common scheme, pattern, or design cannot be sustained. As there is insufficient other evidence to support the indictment for homicide, that indictment is dismissed. The People may make a separate submission to the grand jury in this case, if additional evidence sufficient to support an indictment of homicide can be obtained."

Marlene was not surprised by this judgment. Nolan had telegraphed it clearly enough by his acceptance of Polaner's initial motion. No more would she have been surprised by the death of a relative long in decline; but, like such an awaited death, the loss hurt her deeply nonetheless. The greater pain, however, was attendant on what she now had to do: call up the women involved and tell them that their tormentor really had slipped the clutches of the law.

She put this duty off until the end of the day. She wanted to call them at home rather than at work, a little considerate touch, and all she could offer. It was dreadful nevertheless. Screams. Crying. Accusations of incompetence. Curses.

From Caputo there was a cold and quiet acceptance that was more chilling than any shriek. Caputo was now a defendant herself, on an aggravated assault charge brought by Meissner. It occurred to Marlene that she might be planning to finish the job. She said, "Jo-Anne, believe me, he's not going to get off. Somehow, we'll get him. We'll go over the evidence, hit the bricks again . . ."

Marlene barely believed this herself and Caputo was open in her disdain. "Sure, Marlene," she said. "That'll be great. Call me when it happens." She hung up.

There followed five minutes of blank time. Marlene tried to think of some reason for ever moving out of her chair again, and failed. She would stay there like Miss Havisham at the wedding feast, while spiders wove their webs in her hair and her clothes rotted. No, actually, she was going to get married and have a baby, preferably in that order. So she had to move. She tapped "Yellow Rose of Texas" on her teeth with the back of a Bic pen while the seconds ticked off on her little desk clock.

When the phone rang it jerked Marlene to attention like a shocked frog. The voice on the phone was muffled and accompanied by the sounds of chatter and music, as if the man was calling from a pay phone in a noisy lounge.

"Hey, how you doing?" it said.

"Who is this?" she asked.

"Who do you think?"

Her belly trembled. "Meissner?"

A laugh. "That would be telling," said the man. "Let's say I'm a friend of the court. Let's say I'm just a guy sitting in a bar checking out the foxes."

"You filthy little shit—"

"Uh-oh, you're sounding like a sore loser, Marlene. You ought to learn to take your lumps like a man. Face it, you were outclassed, baby. You didn't have a chance in hell of getting a conviction with that bullshit case. And do you know why?"

Marlene resisted the impulse to slam the phone down. Something in the gloating tone made her keep listening. She had heard it often enough, from criminals more interested in impressing with their cleverness than protecting their skins. That cast of mind was the prosecutor's best friend.

"No, why?" she said evenly.

"Oh, she's interested. She thinks maybe he'll make a damaging admission. No fucking way, babe. I'm not going to, and even if you get this on tape, there's no way you could ID my voice in this noise. Am I right?"

"I guess so," said Marlene. "Looks like you thought of everything."

"Yeah, I did. So, you want to know why you lost? I'll tell you. It's the system. It's designed to catch assholes. Hey, it's *run* by assholes. You know it's true. Nobody with anything on the ball ever gets caught. You think you'll ever touch the guys who are raking in millions—drugs, whores, stocks, real estate, contracts? No way. So, if somebody wanted to just, say, figure out the system, so he could get a little pussy the way he likes it, the system can't touch him. It only takes about forty minutes of real thought on the part of anyone with serious brains."

"Nevertheless, we caught you," she said.

"A minor flaw in the plan. It will be corrected, never fear. And don't bother trying to figure it out, either, you pathetic cunt. It's far too complex for your puny mentality. I suggest you confine yourself to nigger sneak thieves—they're just your speed."

He hung up. Marlene lit a cigarette and watched the smoke rise in a corkscrew spire. After a while her hand stopped trembling and the smoke rose straight through the close air of the little office. Something had happened during the conversation; something had changed in her mind, although she could not say exactly what it was. Remarkably, she felt better, even chipper. The defeat now stung less because she realized that it was only temporary. In some deep way he was vulnerable, or she could make him so. He wasn't as smart as he thought he was; if he were, he wouldn't have called her. She would have him, after all, somehow, and in a way no error could reverse. She grabbed her bag and went out, looking for Karp.

FIFTEEN

"I can't believe it!" Karp exclaimed when Marlene told him.

"Believe it," said Marlene, picking listlessly at her almond chicken. They were eating Chinese out of white cardboard boxes in Karp's office. The building was largely deserted at this hour, except for the arraignment courts and the operation of the complaint room on the fourth floor.

"Nolan was bound and determined to let him go, the fucker. I guess your bigwig friends wouldn't do anything about that."

Karp shrugged. "Who the fuck knows? I'm playing out of my league there, to be real honest. I mean, what could I say? Call Reedy and tell him to roll his tame judge? I don't even know that Reedy has a squeeze on Nolan."

"What did he say? Reedy, I mean."

"I told him that I thought Nolan was throwing the case because he had a hard-on for me because I had set the hounds on him because of the Booth thing. And I asked him what he thought."

"And?"

Karp smiled. "Well, it's sort of funny. He kind of hemmed and hawed and said that Nolan was a guy a lot a people gave stock tips to. Reedy knew for a fact that Nolan had picked up some stock on a deal that Reedy had made a pile on, but he wasn't sure who exactly had passed the tip along. He said Fane made a habit of doing that, passing stuff to pols and judges. So that could be it. Nothing we could prove, though."

"And this Reedy is Mr. Clean?"

"I wouldn't go that far," said Karp. He ate some beef with oyster sauce and added, "But I can't help liking the guy. He's at least out-front that he's a sharpster. He's funny. And, I don't know, he's nice to me, at least. You know, weeks go by and nobody bureau chief and above gives me the time of day unless I wrench it out of them. Not to mention fucking Bloom and his gang. It gets old, you know?"

"Poor Butchie," said Marlene half-mockingly.

"Yeah, poor Butchie. You think I shouldn't hang out with him either, don't you?"

"Hey, I didn't say a word . . ."

"Yeah, but you gave me that look. Same as Guma. Karp's going white-shoe, the fucking sky is falling. Face it—what do you think I have to look forward to if I keep butting heads with the D.A.? Sooner or later he'll get me, and then where'll I be? Not to mention our little bundle of joy. Yeah, I admit it, sue me!

It'd be damn nice to have a little clout for a change."

"Nothing wrong with being ambitious, Butch," said Marlene quietly. "I'm not sure me or the baby has much to do with it, though. And as you said yourself, it's not exactly your league."

"Yeah?" Karp snapped. "Well, maybe it's time for a transfer. Is there any more fried rice?"

They ate in silence for a few minutes, and then Marlene spoke, pointedly changing the subject. "The worst thing about it is, Meissner's still out there. He's gonna start again too. He as much as said so."

Karp put down his carton. "He said so? When?"

"Oh, yeah, I didn't tell you. He called me after the hearing. He didn't actually say it was him, but it was him."

"What did he *actually* say?"

"Oh, the usual shit about how you can get away with anything if you're a superior type—"

"No, I mean exactly. What were his words?"

She looked at him. He was staring at her intently, his jaw tight. "You're thinking the same thing I thought," she said. "It's an angle."

"Yeah, it is. So what did he say?"

Marlene thought for a moment, recreating the brief conversation in her mind. Like most experienced trial lawyers, she had a good memory for what people said. She gave him an almost verbatim playback of the call and then said, "That's it. Not much there out front, but, like I said, there was something there. More the tone than anything else. This guy thinks his shit don't stink."

Karp said, "I agree he could hang himself if we can get him the rope. But that's the problem, isn't it?"

"We could watch him. And then, if he moves on another woman . . ."

She stopped because Karp was shaking his head vigorously. "No, that's what's been wrong with our thinking on this case. It's all based on common plan, pattern, or design. That's dead. Even if we caught him with a girl, and the panty hose and the whole deal there, we'd have nothing. A first-offense sexual assault. I want him for the knife job. The Wagner."

Marlene bristled. "You think I *don't*? And what do you mean 'wrong'? The pattern is our whole case. That's how we caught him, for Chrissake."

"That's how you caught him, sure, but that's not how you're gonna get him," said Karp. "You have to tie him . . . no, you have to get him to tie *himself* to the murder. And the only way to do that is . . ." He paused for several minutes, his eyes unfocused, his long index finger moving from side to side like a metronome, working out the play. At last he looked at her and said, "Shit, this could work!"

"What?"

He told her. She wrinkled her fine brow. "You think so? That he'll go for it?"

"It's worth a shot. I'd have to convince him that I'm as dumb as he thinks we are. Give me a couple of days to set it up, and we'll find out."

Later that evening, Karp called Fulton at home.

"I got a little problem you could help me with," Karp began.

"I got a problem too, Butch," Fulton replied. "I was just gonna call you. Amalfi tried to arrest me today. Did you know he was turned? Somebody's got him on a wire."

"Shit, no!" Karp said. "I don't know anything about that. Who was it?"

"Internal Affairs, the dirt-bags. But that's not the worst of it. You know how we were thinking that these shitheads were looking to set me up and lay all the killings on me? Well, it went down today. Manning sent me and Amalfi over to a hospital to kill Nicky Benning. I went in and faked it and then I figured Amalfi would be laying to take me out. I got the jump on him and I found this goddamn wire."

"Have you told the chief yet?" Karp asked.

"No, I wanted to talk to you first, see if you'd heard anything."

"Shit, that's a laugh! I'm the last to know and the first to get fucked," said Karp. "Look, the main thing is, this deal you had cooked up with Denton is out the window. We got to go to him together and rethink the strategy here. For starters, we got to at least sit down with whoever is running Amalfi. Our main job now is to nail down the case against Manning and Amalfi and pressure them to drop a dime on whoever is running this game. My thinking is, if it's presented as a massive high-level corruption thing, it'll take some of the sting out of cops being involved. That should bring Denton around to handling it like a real case."

"Yeah," said Fulton, "but I already know who's running it. Amalfi told me. It's Fane. And parties unknown."

"Oh, that's perfect! That's great! Bloom puts together a drug task force and half the people on it are in the dope business. Look, Clay, you have to get off the street. Things are gonna get crazy, starting tomorrow."

"Uh-uh," said Fulton, "we got nothing on Fane, except for Amalfi's say-so, which isn't worth shit. You're talking about a U.S. congressman here. We need a smoking gun."

"Clay, let *me* worry about constructing the fucking case, OK?" said Karp. "We got other ways of getting Fane. Meanwhile, when Manning finds out Benning's still breathing, he's gonna come after you."

Fulton chuckled. "Yeah, I thought of that. I had Benning moved to another hospital. I'll tell Manning he was gone when I got there."

"Fine, but what makes you so sure Amalfi is gonna be such a sweetheart? How do you know Manning doesn't know about the wire and you already?"

"Amalfi's shitting in his pants, Butch. He's got IAD on his ass, he's looking over his shoulder all the time. He won't do dick. Believe me, it's not gonna be a problem. Speaking of which, you said *you* had a problem."

It took Karp a few seconds to remember why he had called. "Oh, yeah. The reason I called, I need to borrow a murderer."

Fulton's rich laugh came over the line. "You came to the right place."

"What is this, some kind of joke?" said Alan Meissner, his voice angry across the phone line.

"It's no joke, Mr. Meissner," said Karp calmly. He had called Meissner shortly after he had finished his call with Fulton. Marlene was in bed and Karp was stretched out on the couch in the living area, relaxed and radiating sincerity into the mouthpiece.

"We really need your help on a police matter."

"Oh, really? What matter? And why me?"

"Well, let me be perfectly frank with you," Karp said. "The police are working on a series of multiple rape-murders. There's a pattern there, but they can't figure it out. I suggested that you would be ideal for helping them."

Meissner laughed. "You people must think

I'm simple. OK, I'll bite: tell me why you think I'm ideal."

"Because you know the bar scene in New York. Because you're extremely intelligent. And because you beat the rap."

"I beat the rap because I was innocent, Karp."

"Yeah, of course. But let's say for the sake of argument that you beat it because you're too smart for the police. OK, we accept that; we can't beat everybody. And just between you, me, and the lamppost, it was a shitty case. A bunch of women whining because they forgot how to say no, and then trying to tie it to a nasty slash murder. Real thin. And let me say this: I could care less if it *was* you with all those women. That's past.

"But the guy I'm talking about is a complete crazy. A razor artist. All we know about him is he's black. And real smart. In fact, if I had to guess, he'd be one of the only guys we've come across who was possibly smarter than you."

"I seriously doubt that, Karp."

"Well, give it a shot, then. Listen, I'm under a lot of pressure from the bleeding hearts around here to move on these rape charges. Not that we'd win, but it'd put you through a lot of trouble and embarrassment. If you help the police in this one, you'd look a lot better."

A long pause. Then Meissner asked, "What would I have to do?"

"Just look at the case files, talk to the cops, give them the benefit of your experience. It shouldn't take more than a couple of hours."

Meissner uttered a low chuckle. "OK, you talked me into it. But, Karp, if I get one hint that this is some kind of scheme to entrap me, I walk out, and I'll bring so much shit down on you you'll stink for the rest of your life."

"Hey, that's great," said Karp sincerely. "You got a right to be suspicious. But it's on the level. I'll send a driver around for you about ten tomorrow."

The next day was frustrating for Marlene: half a dozen court dates, racing from one courtroom to another, calling missing witnesses, fighting to focus on what she was doing, trying not to think only about what Karp was doing, up at the Twenty-eighth Precinct. Nothing started on time, of course, so her carefully constructed schedule was in tatters by eleven-thirty.

At the noon recess, she called Karp, but he was not yet back from the precinct, where he was supervising the first phase of their Meissner plan. Even Marlene agreed that she couldn't participate. Meissner might go for a complaisant Karp; having Marlene there would spook him out of his shoes. The afternoon passed in much the same manner. When she broke free at four-thirty, she raced to Karp's office, rushed through the crowded outer room, and flung open the private door without knocking.

"You should knock, Marlene," Karp said. "I could have been picking my nose."

She ignored this. *"What happened!"* she cried.

In answer, he grinned broadly and rolled his eyes like Groucho Marx and twirled an imaginary cigar.

"He bit? It *worked*?" she asked, bouncing on her toes with excitement.

"He ate it. He digested it," said Karp.

Marlene gave a long yelp of joy and, dashing around the desk, threw herself into Karp's lap. She kissed him hard enough to make his chair squeak.

"Brilliant man!" she exclaimed when the kissing stopped. "Tell all, omitting no detail!"

Karp shifted to settle her comfortably on his lap, kissed her again, and began.

"OK, the car drops him off at about a quarter to eleven. Me and Maus and Fulton spent about two hours before that cooking up a phony file: three murders, only one of which was real. It's really amazing what a good job they did because I don't think Clay has passed a cordial word with his guys since all this drug-lord horseshit started. Maybe they were glad about the distraction."

"What was it, the real one?" asked Marlene.

"Some pathetic slashing. The usual Saturday-night domestic. Anyway, we dolled the file up with clues. Cryptic notes. Purple ribbons. Wound patterns.

"So the bastard comes in, and right away you could see there's a battle going on. On the one hand, he's suspicious as hell. On the other hand, he's fucking *thrilled*. Real cops. Real grimy precinct house. The Two-eight, in fact—big-time Harlem crime: cops with shoulder holsters smoking cheap cigars, skells being dragged in and booked. It's better than TV.

"And Maus and Fulton—they're *deferring* to him, he's one of the real guys now. OK, he looks through the files, takes about half an hour. Nobody says anything. Finally he looks up with this superior smile and he says, 'Surely you've noticed that each of these women was killed on the second day of the month.'

"You should have seen the detectives. Maus slaps himself on the head. Fulton grabs the files. He checks to see if it's really true. He curses. *He* slaps himself on the head. Everybody's jaw is hanging down. Sherlock reveals the solution: he killed them for the welfare money. He's not *really* crazy. He *must have known the women*! Fulton is falling all over himself congratulating Meissner. Maus is licking his hand. Then Clay had a call and had to go out. We told Meissner thrilling cop stories for half an hour and then he left with the driver."

"And what's next?"

"They bring in the guy, the killer Maus and

Jeffers grabbed the other day. We plant a story in the *News*, make sure there's a photographer there when we book him, and make sure the story says the police acknowledge Meissner's invaluable help. I'll call him, thank him again, and set him up for the sting."

"Which is when?"

"A decent interval. Let him gloat a little. Say, the end of the week?"

"Can I watch it happen?" she asked.

"Of course. We're gonna sell tickets," said Karp. "Meanwhile, if you don't stop squirming on my lap, I'm going to have an embarrassing experience."

Instead of rising, she squirmed harder, leaned over, and stuck her sharp little tongue into his ear. "What sort of experience would that be?" she breathed. "Something disgraceful? Gouts of semen on your nice pinstripes? How about if I help it along?"

She shifted her weight and started to grope for his crotch, but Karp got his arm under her thighs and, cupping her hard round bottom, lifted her up off his lap and onto the edge of the desk. "If I don't finish this load of paperwork," he said hoarsely, "I won't be able to come home and nail you in the manner to which you have become accustomed."

She giggled. "Are you telling me that you are giving up the chance for a terrific impromptu orgasm in order to do legal business?"

"I am telling you that, counselor," said Karp,

"and if you want to know, it's making me sick."

Marlene stood up and rushed to the open window. "People of New York!" she yelled. "Sleep well! Karp is not getting his rocks off on company time. He labors on in your behalf."

The clatter of typewriters and the murmuring from the outer office stopped dead. A brief silence, then muffled laughter.

Karp raised an eyebrow in silent rebuke. "Are you completely finished or would you care to alert the networks?"

"Sorr-ee!" she said, grinning. "OK, I'll see you at home."

"I'll probably be late," said Karp. "I have a thing with Reedy. Drinks."

"Drinks? Very impressive—you're becoming quite the boulevardier. Don't forget to bring home one of those little folding parasols for my collection. Will there be call girls?"

"I hope so," said Karp.

"Well, I'll just have to get used to it now that my sweetie is mingling with the power elite. Meanwhile, Marlene'll be knitting booties and weeping softly to herself. Have a good time and don't bring home any diseases." She blew him a kiss and left.

Karp spent an hour on administrative paperwork, filling two wastebaskets with bureaucratic junk mail and dictating into a machine the responses that were absolutely required. Then he read through an eighteen-inch-high pile of cases that his ADA's intended for the four grand juries that ran nonstop in the New York courts, focusing on the homicides. He found two procedural errors, wrote notes telling the lawyers involved how to correct them, signed off on the ones that were ready to go, and distributed the case files among the wire baskets lined up on a side table.

The outer office had long since grown quiet. He checked his watch. Two hours gone, vanished into a black hole, which would take the same bite of his life the next day and the day after and the next, world without end. Karp had been amazed to discover, on becoming bureau chief, that he was a competent, even a talented bureaucrat. It was a talent he had neither expected to find in himself nor ever asked for, like a talent for farting tunes. Yet he had never ceased to resent the time spent at it and he had grown to hate those whose joy was the *production* of paperwork, with a strength of feeling that even he realized was slightly irrational.

He stuffed some journals he had not had a chance to read into his briefcase and slipped into his suit coat. Leaving the briefcase on his desk, he walked out of the office, his heels clicking on the tile and echoing through the dead halls.

On impulse, he got off the elevator on the fourth floor and stopped by the complaint room. He could not have explained what drew him there, to the grease trap of the criminal justice system; perhaps it was some desire to wash away the abstract fug of bureaucracy by a brief immersion in ripe legal grunge.

The waiting area of the complaint room was reasonably crowded for a weekday night. The cops, some in uniform, most in plain clothes, stood around in relaxed attitudes, joking, talking sports, and otherwise racking up overtime. There were not as many of them as there would be later in the year, around Christmas, when arrests and complaints would soar, not because of the increased activity of criminals but because cops needed extra overtime to buy presents.

Karp spoke briefly to a couple of cops he knew and entered the complaint room proper. There, in a warren of little cubicles, clerks sat by old typewriters; and the two ADA's on night duty circulated from desk to desk, interviewing cops and their witnesses, if any, and dictating the complaints in legal form to the clerks.

Roland Hrcany was on duty tonight. Karp spotted him through the doorway of a cubicle and waved. Hrcany gave him an odd look, as if he were surprised and mildly dismayed to see him there. After finishing with the case at hand, Hrcany came out of the cubicle and asked, "What's up, boss?"

Karp said, "Nothing much. I just dropped by to smell the Lysol. Having a nice night?"

Hrcany shrugged. "The usual shit. Domestics and muggings. Wives 'n' knives. The Nine is doing their semiannual cleanup of the faggot blowjob artist on the Williamsburg Bridge Plaza. It should get interesting later on. You gonna stay for a while?"

"No, I can't. I gotta meet some people for drinks midtown."

"Anybody I know?"

"Yeah, Rich Reedy from the drug thing wants me to meet a guy."

"Reedy, huh? You're moving in fast company, my man. Careful you don't lose your boyish charm."

The tone with which this was said lacked some of the lightness of Hrcany's usual banter. Karp met his eyes; there was something wiggling deep in the cold blue pools.

"I think I can handle the speed, Roland. It's nice of you to be concerned, though. As a matter of fact, all my near and dear seem unable to resist comment when Reedy's name comes up. Why is that?"

Hrcany saw from Karp's expression that the question was not merely rhetorical. He hung a grin on his mouth and said, "We got enough empty suits in this place. Reedy, white-shoe law firm, big money . . ."

"Karp sells out?" asked Karp.

"Something like that. Also there's a rumor going around you might be thinking about running for D.A."

"Does that bother you?" asked Karp. His antennae were picking up something from Hrcany that he didn't like. There were more male pheromones in the air than were called for by the conversation. He felt the belligerence rising in him.

"Why should it?" Hrcany answered, his voice bland. "It's just that you're always talking about how there's no place for politics in the D.A.'s office."

"There isn't. The law's the law, and . . . and, Roland, if you've got something on your mind, why don't you just spit it out? You think that my political ambitions, if any, are starting to color the way I run this bureau?"

Hrcany smiled and patted Karp on the arm. "Hey, don't start getting pissed off, Butch. Just shooting the shit. Your friends are just getting a little nervous, is all."

Karp took a long breath and let it out. He was getting touchy in his old age, although the expectations of others had always weighed heavily upon his spirit. He recalled the times when, as a basketball superstar in high school, friends had inquired solicitously about his health and humor before an important game; it had seemed to him *always* before a game, and never otherwise.

Karp waved his hands about to take in the complaint room, and by extension the system of which it was the lowest rootlet.

"Do you like this? Don't you think it could be run better?"

Hrcany snorted. "The Three Stooges could

run it better. The point is, though, even if it
was run well, it would still be fucked up. We're
trying to impose a system of jurisprudence designed for little English villages on this gigantic
city. *Fourteen* appearances to dispose of a felony? Come *on!*"

"We could still make a difference," Karp
said. "Look at the incompetence—things that
have to be done twice or three times because
nobody took the trouble to do them right the
first time. There's part of your fourteen-ap-
pearances problem. Look at the morale—half
our lives are spent training unprepared kids
because the senior attorneys burn out so fast.
That doesn't have to happen. That . . ."

He caught the expression in Hrcany's eyes
and stopped, suddenly embarrassed. You
weren't supposed to show interest or passion
about anything but sports. Just do the job,
make wisecracks, and put asses in jail. Karp
said, "It's late. I gotta go."

"Hey, give 'em hell, boss," said Hrcany.
"You got *my* vote."

There was still something in his voice that
Karp did not like, but whether it was just Roland's habitual faint mockery or something
darker, Karp could not determine.

It was still light, a dusty yellow summer twilight, when Karp left the building and was
lucky to find an empty cab on Centre Street.
Reedy had chosen a small dim place in the For-
ties off Madison, full of well-dressed men talk-

ing the ad game and television. Karp found Reedy at a table in the back, speaking into a phone. The older man smiled and motioned him to a seat. A waiter arrived and Karp ordered a beer, which was delivered in less than a minute.

Karp ate nuts and sipped at his beer while Reedy gave directions on an obscure legal or financial deal to some underling. Karp listened casually, the arcane language reminding him of the boredom he had felt sitting in long-ago classes in contracts and commercial law. Apparently someone called Telemax was about to transfer an enormous amount of money to someone else called Rotodyne, and Reedy was poised to run his fingers through the gold as it passed along, grabbing as much of it as he could during the few seconds it was between possessors.

Reedy at last hung up the phone and turned to Karp with a fierce grin. "Not a bad piece of work. I find it hard to sleep at night unless I've made a million during the working day, don't you?"

"I toss and turn for hours," said Karp pleasantly. "It must be nice being a lawyer."

"Pah! I don't make beans at law. I don't clear more than eight hundred K a year from the partnership. It's barely enough to pay off the house at Easthampton. The real money's in the market."

"So I've heard," said Karp.

"Do you have anything in it?"

"No," said Karp. "My mother always told me not to gamble."

"Good advice," replied Reedy. "I never gamble myself. Oh, I go to the track with clients and bet just to be sociable. And playing golf, of course. But the market isn't betting. Or at least it's not betting if you know who the winner is."

"And how do you know that?"

Reedy tugged at an ear. "I keep these open. You keep your ears open around the right people, you can make a lot of money."

"I guess," said Karp. "But even though I only made a C-plus in business law, I seem to recall that trading on inside information is illegal."

Reedy laughed sincerely. "Yes, of course it is. If I'm doing a merger and I go to you and say, 'Butch, ABC is buying XYZ and the shares are headed for the moon,' then it's go-to-jail time. But that's not the way it happens. Look, what would you say if I told you that you could turn a hundred K into half a million in a week, with just what you know now, if you'd kept your ears open?"

Karp was about to remark lightly, "I'd say I didn't have a hundred K," but seeing that Reedy's expression had grown serious, said, "You mean overhearing what you were talking about on the phone—Teledyne and Rotomax."

"Rotodyne," corrected Reedy. "It closed at fifteen and a quarter. It'll go to thirty before

. . . But that's actually all I'm allowed to say. In any case, you heard it. The stock will be in play. The law doesn't require you to expunge the information out of your head. Why should you? It's yours to use."

Karp nodded. "But in order for it to do me any good, I'd have to have a bundle to begin with, wouldn't I? Isn't that the way it works."

"Oh, that's not a problem," replied Reedy, smiling benevolently. "There's always loose money around for people who have a reputation for keeping their ears open. I'd write you a check for one hundred K right now, for that matter."

Karp felt a reflexive smile of disbelief stretch over his face. It faded when he saw that Reedy was serious. He opened his mouth to say something, but his mind was quite empty. Although he did not by any means wish to offend the older man, there was something in him that did not want to be beholden to Richard Reedy or anyone else for a sum equal to nearly three times the annual salary of an assistant district attorney. He was racking his brains for the form of a polite refusal when a jowly man of about thirty barged up to their table.

Reedy rose and shook the man's hand, and Karp pushed his chair back and stood to be introduced. Reedy said, "Frank Sergo, Butch Karp." Karp took the proffered hand, which was damp and cold, like a pack of hot dogs just out of the refrigerator. Sergo was nearly a full foot shorter than Karp, and fat, and the necessity of acknowledging this disparity, which no success in the marketplace could ever repair, seemed to annoy him. Karp had seen this before in short men, and he hoped it did not turn, as it often did, into active belligerence.

Reedy had briefed him on Sergo when he had set up the meeting—the newest of the boy wonders of Wall Street, nearly a billionaire at thirty, ruthless and proud of it. Karp had no trouble believing it. Immediately upon sitting down, Sergo literally snapped his fingers for the waiter, ordered a drink—a martini that had to be made with some exotic vodka and prepared according to directions so precise that they might have sufficed to assemble a nuclear warhead—and, ignoring Karp, began to talk to Reedy in a rasping monotone about money and about himself.

Karp had rarely met a man he liked less. It was not that Sergo was vulgar, or sloppy, or that every other word was an obscenity (all women in his conversation were *cunts;* all his business rivals were *cocksuckers*). Some of Karp's closest friends shared many of these traits, after all. Rather it was the hollowness that Karp detected within the shell of tough and brutal talk. Sergo's life was about nothing but the making and spending of large sums of money, together with complaints that the world failed to pay him the respect due his great wealth.

Sergo had launched a long and pointless

story about how badly he had been abused at that season's most elegant restaurant. To his satisfaction, Karp (to whom Sergo had still not addressed a word) observed that Reedy was as bored as he himself was.

"So they brought out the fucking caviar," Sergo said, his mouth working around a bolus of nuts and vodka, "and it was fucking *gray* caviar. So I called the schmuck headwaiter over and I told him I ordered *black* Molossal caviar, and if he thought I was gonna pay a hundred twenty bucks for gray caviar, he was out of his fucking mind, and if he didn't get the right caviar on the table in ten seconds I was gonna buy the fucking restaurant and fire every incompetent son-of-a-bitch in the place." He laughed, as if he had made a joke. "Fucking cheap caviar! I get *sick* from cheap caviar. You know?" He looked at Karp for the first time, as if to stimulate agreement. Without expression, Karp said, "It makes me puke."

Sergo accepted the remark at face value. "Yeah!" he said. "You might as well be getting fucking tuna fish."

Reedy took this as a convenient point of entry into the business of the evening. Sergo was, as Reedy said, looking for someone to back. He wanted to get into politics, and a D.A.'s race was one on which he could immediately achieve preeminence. As he put it, "I got everything else, I ought to have a politician, ha ha!"

Numbers were mentioned, shockingly high

numbers, to Karp, and as soon as what appeared to be an agreement was reached, Sergo rose heavily, without ceremony, shaking the little table and spilling his drink, waved to both men, and stalked out, waiters and busboys scurrying to remove themselves from his path.

Karp looked over at Reedy, his brows bunching dangerously and his jaw tight. Reedy grinned and shook his head. "Yeah, I know. It's disgusting, but there it is. The only beauty part is, the schmuck is a virgin. Besides the market, he knows from nothing and he won't know enough to meddle. He'll pay for practically the whole thing; you won't have to deal with a mob of people who think they've got some lock on you."

"Why the hell do we need that kind of money anyway?" asked Karp irritably. "I ran a campaign for Garrahy, his last campaign, with next to nothing and a bunch of volunteers."

Reedy gave him a pitying look. "Oh, yeah, Garrahy! All the hell Phil Garrahy needed at the end was his name printed on the ballot. Look, there are a million and a half voters in the county. How many of them know your name? Ten? That's what the money's for. To get your beautiful face on the tube, for Chrissake."

Karp fumed silently for a moment, knowing this was perfectly true and hating it. Then he said, "OK, we need money. What about the

asshole? What's *he* going to want?" asked Karp
sourly.

"I can deal with him," said Reedy confi-
dently.

Karp looked at him. "Oh?"

"Yeah, you know what we were talking
about? About inside information? You think
Sergo cares about what's legal and what isn't?
I could put him in jail in a minute."

"Then why don't you?" snapped Karp, suddenly tired and irritated beyond all endurance.

Reedy reached over and patted his hand.
"Because *you* will, after you're D.A. You're
going to go after your biggest political contribu-
tor and put him away for fraud. It'll be a gigantic public trial and after it you'll be so golden
in this corrupt town that you can run unop-
posed for the next thirty years."

Karp felt a grin moving uncontrollably
across his face. "You're quite a piece of work,
Mr. Reedy," he said. "Quite a fucking piece
of work. I'm glad you're on the side of truth
and justice. By the way, I hope you're not
thinking of defending Mr. Sergo when the
time comes."

Reedy looked startled for an almost invisible
instant; then his loud, frank laughter pealed
out, and after a moment Karp joined it. As he
laughed, the name of Marcus Fane popped un-
bidden into his mind, and he lost much of his
good humor. Fane and Reedy were business
and political associates. It was on the tip of his
tongue to broach the subject of what he had

learned from Fulton, to warn Reedy off the congressman, to protect his friend and sponsor. But, in fact, Karp was by nature a close-mouthed man; and a decade of keeping criminal investigations confidential had not made him any more liberal with his words. The moment passed, yet Karp was surprised to feel a pang of regret.

SIXTEEN

A ringing phone dragged Sid Amalfi up out of a drugged sleep. He checked the bedside clock—three-fifteen in the morning, the pit of the night. He fumbled for the phone, knocking over the bottle of sleeping pills on the nightstand. His heart was pounding even before he answered.

"Sid? Dick. We got troubles, man. You gotta meet me now."

Amalfi struggled into a sitting position. "Now? For Chrissake, Dick, it's the middle of the night. What the fuck is going on?"

"I can't talk on the phone," said Manning, his voice tense. "You got to get over here right now."

Amalfi rubbed his face vigorously, trying to push away the urgent need for sleep, trying to straighten out the web of stories that he had told in the past few days, trying to stay alive.

"Ah . . . Dick, you want to give me a clue about what this is all about?"

"Fulton," said Manning. That was it, then. Amalfi had told Manning that Fulton had simply skipped at the hospital; there had been no opportunity to commit the murder they had planned. Now Manning had either found out that Fulton was not crooked or had discovered another way to get at him. In either case, it was essential for Amalfi to cover himself. Fulton knew all about him; Hrcany and IAD had the tape, so they knew everything too. His only out was to lay everything off on Manning. Then maybe . . . A plan started to jell in his sleep-addled mind. He said, "OK. Where?"

Manning gave him an address in an industrial area near Kennedy Airport. When Amalfi pulled up in his car thirty minutes later, Manning stepped out of the doorway to a welding shop and got into the passenger side.

"Jesus, I'm glad to see you!" Manning said.

Amalfi yawned hugely. "I'm falling out here. Wanna go get coffee? I can't keep my eyes open."

"No, we don't have time," said Manning. He looked down the street and checked the rear mirror.

"You gonna tell me what this is all about?" Amalfi asked. He yawned again. The sleeping pills were still dragging him down and he fought against their pull.

"Yeah," said Manning. "It's Fulton. He's working undercover."

Amalfi feigned vast surprise. "Jesus! That cocksucker! What're we gonna do?"

"He doesn't know that I know. I got him to come here. He should be here in half an hour.

Look, when he gets here, you got to take him out."

"*I* got to take him out? Why me?"

"Because I found out where he's got that fucking tape stashed. The one Tecumseh made."

"How the fuck did you find *that* out?" asked Amalfi suspiciously.

Manning grinned. "I got friends in high places, man. Anyway, I got to pick it up before anybody finds he's dead. That's why you got to do the job and I got to travel fast. Are you cool?"

Amalfi yawned again and nodded. This was moving a shade too quickly, but he thought he was still ahead. It might even work out better. When Fulton arrived, he'd tell him about Manning and they could pick him up with the tape in hand. Good.

Manning nudged him. Amalfi looked over and saw that he was holding out to him a .38 revolver wrapped in a handkerchief. "It's clean," Manning said. "One in the ear and it's all over. After I have the tape, with him gone they got horseshit on us."

Amalfi took the gun and put it in his jacket pocket.

"OK, give me your gun," said Manning.

Amalfi stifled a yawn and looked at Manning in surprise.

"Why the hell do you want my gun?"

"Because I don't have one. Shit, Sid, I'm so fucked up behind all this, I slipped the clean one into my holster and I was halfway here before I remembered. What's the difference? You got the clean one and I'll have yours. You can dump it on your way home. But I'm damned if I'm gonna do what I have to do bone-naked."

Amalfi shrugged and handed him his own .38 Chief's Special.

"When did you say Fulton was gonna get here?"

Manning looked at his watch. "Around twenty minutes. I'll be going now, OK?"

"Sure, Dick," said Amalfi. He settled himself into his seat and leaned back against the headrest. He felt a yawn coming on again, and this time he didn't stifle it.

Manning waited until Amalfi's mouth was all the way open and his eyes were squeezed tightly shut. Then he reached over and stuck the muzzle of Amalfi's gun into its owner's mouth and pulled the trigger.

Manning waited until the corpse of his former partner had stopped twitching, a surprisingly long time. Then he carefully searched the body and the car for recording devices. Finding none, he removed the clean .38 he had given Amalfi, pressed it into the corpse's right hand, and fired a shot out the open window into the blackness of a large junkyard across the street. Having ensured that Amalfi's hand would bear the microscopic chemical evidence produced by firing a revolver, he removed the clean gun, put it in his pocket, thoroughly wiped Amalfi's own .38, and placed it in the body's limp hand.

Manning left the car and stood in the darkened doorway of the welding shop. Ten minutes passed, then a car Manning recognized came slowly down the street. It parked behind Amalfi's car and Clay Fulton got out. Manning stepped out of the doorway and waved to him.

Clay Fulton saw Manning wave and pulled over to the curb. Fulton was tense and excited, but confident that this meeting was going to break the case open. During the call from Manning that had brought him here, Manning had cast broad hints about introducing him to his main man. He had also complained about Amalfi, that he was acting funny—nervous and distracted.

As well he should be, with a wire on him and hanging around with a cold-blooded shithead like Dick Manning. Fulton reflected that this would probably be his last night under cover. Whatever happened, he was going to go to Denton in the morning, pull in the IAD team, and see where they stood. Now that IAD was involved, his own role was less necessary, but he felt that the possibility of uncovering Manning's backer was worth hanging on a little longer.

He stepped out of his car and looked around. A good neighborhood for something bad to happen. For the first time he felt a twinge of regret at having come alone. But, of course, that had been the whole point from the start.

It was the most plausible thing about him undercover: he really was on his own.

And there was no way Manning could know he was undercover, at least not with enough certainty to act. The only people who could betray him were Denton and Karp. No problem there. And Amalfi. But Amalfi was hooked by IAD. And IAD guys didn't even talk to priests about what they did. So while there could be some additional risk from out of left field, it was a calculated risk that Fulton felt that he had to take.

"What's up?" said Fulton as Manning came toward him.

"What's up is, Sid ate his gun," said Manning, pointing to Amalfi's car. Fulton walked over to the driver's side and bent over to look in the window. It was obvious what had happened, but Fulton instinctively reached out to assure himself that there was no pulse in the man's neck. As he did so, Manning came up silently behind him and hit him as hard as he could on the back of the head with the clean pistol.

Karp put the phone down hard, a mixture of annoyance and vague fear roiling his early-morning stomach. He drank some lukewarm coffee and chewed off a chunk of cold toasted bagel, which helped not a whit. Fulton was not to be found: not at the precinct, not at home, not at the various bars and restaurants that Karp knew about. OK, he was undercover, he had dropped from sight before this, but Karp knew that this time he was dangerously exposed.

Karp raised the phone again and dialed Bill Denton's private number, but put it down after the second ring. He was loath to call the chief of detectives, to tell him that the whole elaborate scheme to protect the police was blowing apart, until he had everything nailed down, and he could not do that without Fulton. On the other hand, Fulton might be in there with Denton right now, working on damage control, excluding Karp himself. Karp tried to turn those thoughts aside. Everybody was OK, nobody was screwing anybody, they'd get the bad guys in the end. Period. He decided to give it another day.

But he had to move; he was strangling at this desk, engulfed by the paper shadows of old crimes. He got up and stalked out of his office. Three people, including his secretary, tried to get his attention in the outer office, but he rushed past them, mumbling evasions.

His steps brought him, almost without thought, to the office of V. T. Newbury. This was a small boxlike affair, with a dusty window, tucked away in an obscure corridor of the sixth floor. Newbury was in, as he usually was. A specialist in fraud, and money laundering, and the sequestering of ill-gotten gains, he normally had little contact with the grungy realities of the Criminal Courts Bureau.

When Karp walked in, Newbury was at his

desk, half-glasses perched on his chiseled nose, running lengths of the green-and-white-striped computer printout known as elephant toilet paper through his hands, and muttering to himself.

He looked up when he saw Karp, and flashed his perfect smile, then returned to making marks on the printout. Karp sank down in the rocking chair V. T. had provided for his visitors. Newbury had largely furnished his own office: battered wood-and-leather furniture, a worn Turkish rug on the floor, good small framed prints and watercolors on the walls, so that it looked more like the den of a not-very-successful country lawyer than the official seat of a New York assistant D.A. Karp often came here. V.T. was the only person in the building who neither wanted anything from him nor wanted to do anything to him.

"How's the war against crime going?" Newbury inquired, continuing his notations. "Not well, by the way you look."

"The usual shit," said Karp. "What're you doing?"

Newbury wrote down some figures and looked up. "Actually, I'm finishing up that thing you asked me to look into."

"What thing?"

"Oh, terrific! I'm ruining my eyes, not to mention having to entertain Horton for the weekend, and he's forgotten all about it."

"What are you talking about, V.T.? Who's Horton?"

"My cousin Horton. In order to get a look at this material, I've had to let him inveigle himself into a weekend at our place in Oyster Bay. A golf ball for a brain, which means I'm going to have to spend a weekend listening to how he birdied the bogey on the fourteenth hole. He married Amelia Preston, for whom at one time I myself had a moderate sneaker. I can't see how she puts up with it, although perhaps we can polish our relationship while he's out bogeying."

"You lost me, V.T. What does . . . ?"

"Fane," said V.T. "The congressman and the dope murders? Hello . . . ?"

"Oh, shit! Yeah. So what, did you get anything?"

"Yes, I did, although I don't know how useful it'll be to you. First of all, do you know what a leveraged buy-out is?"

Karp did not, and V.T. said, "It's simple in principle, complex in operation. Basically, a group of investors buy up enough of the public stock of a company to give them a controlling interest. They do that because they either think the company can be run better than current management is doing, or, more usually, they see a company that's undervalued on the market. They buy it, and then they sell it for a profit, sometimes a huge one. With me so far?

"The leverage part comes from the way they get the money to buy the stock. Essentially, they borrow it against the assets of the firm they're buying, and pay back the loans from the sale of the firm itself. Or, what they're starting to do, is go on the bond market with high-yield unclassified offerings, but—"

"So Fane has been doing this?" Karp interrupted.

"In a way, in a way. You understand that when a deal like this is going down, when the stock is in play, as they say, its price can go ballistic. And of course if the buyers tender for the stock above market value, you can make a fortune. Fane has been into some very good things. As has our friend Judge Nolan. In fact, in recent months three of the very same deals: Revere Semiconductor, Grant Foods, and Adams-Lycoming."

"That's not illegal, though, is it?"

"Who knows? It depends where they got their information, because they must have had it from somewhere. Insider trading: that's when someone who has advance—"

"I know what insider trading is," said Karp, thinking about Reedy and his lecture. But this thought brought another, and he said, "What about Agromont?"

Newbury cocked his head and regarded Karp narrowly. "Agromont. Well, well. You *have* been doing your homework." He tossed the printout onto the desk. "You don't need old V.T. anymore, if you're that well-connected."

"All I know is the name. I was at a party when Fane told Reedy that Agromont was a done deal."

"That's also very interesting. OK, the story is

this. Agromont is a medium-size conglomerate. They're in food, machine tools, cosmetics, and at the time they also owned a good deal of New York real estate, mostly on the West Side. They had the old American Line pier. In any case, someone made a run on the stock last year— bid it up like crazy—but the company fought them off. Sold off some assets at fire-sale prices. A lot of people were left holding the bag."

"How so?" asked Karp.

"Well, if you've tied up a lot of capital in a big block of stock and you fail to get control of the company, then you can't realize your profits. Some people made a bundle by riding the play and getting out before the showdown. But the main people were left holding a big chunk of overvalued stock. Which has sunk since.

"So they can either take their loss or try again. And Cousin Horton is very much convinced that they are going to try again. Someone has been nibbling at their stock. Little bites from a dozen different buyers: not enough to put it in play, but more than it usually moves. That could have been the origin of your cryptic comment from Fane. Telling a friend that the stock was shortly to go into play and that he should get in long on it."

"So is Fane buying?"

"He's starting to, it appears. But most of his purchases will probably be through someone else. Would you like me to look into it?"

"No, what do I care what stocks he buys?

I'm not the SEC. But . . ." Karp rocked and looked out V.T.'s window at the little park behind the courts building and the low tenements of Chinatown beyond it.

"Yes?" asked V.T.

"But what I'd really like to know is, could someone use this kind of stock manipulation to launder money, maybe dirty money?"

V.T. thought for a moment, sounding the tuneless hum he favored when in deep contemplation of chicanery. He said, "Well, what I'd do is, I'd take the dirty money in cash to an offshore bank in the islands, a bank I controlled. Then I'd lend the money to people who were in a position to rig the market, and who needed liquidity to do it, and were willing to trade information on deals at a very early stage. Having got that information, I would use whatever honest dollars I had to make a killing."

"Very neat, V.T.," said Karp, who could barely balance his checkbook, with sincere admiration. "Would it really work?"

"I don't see why not. Our fictive man is insulated from the dirty money entirely. The offshore bank made the loan. It's not required to tell anyone where its capital came from, which is the true charm of the islands. There'd be a dummy holding the passbook for the actual account, which, of course, would never be tapped directly. And the profits on the market are honest gain, the result of sophisticated analysis of trends guided by vast experience—or so my cousin is always telling me. Our man pays taxes on it too—he's no mobster.

"So he's as safe as the Morgan Bank. And, of course, since he's not paying a premium for the money, he can buy a lot more stock than his competitors in a bidding contest. The people he was backing would be murderous traders.

"The only possible hitch is if someone traces a cash deposit back to him—unlikely—or if whoever gives him his info rats him out as an inside trader to the feds or the Stock Exchange—slightly more likely."

"Uh-huh," said Karp. "Does Fane control an offshore bank?"

"Doesn't everyone? But, if so, it's improbable that the connection is direct. Let me check it out, though." He made a note in his diary with a silver pencil. "Anything else?"

"No, thanks a lot, V.T., this is great," said Karp. He stood up and made to leave, then paused. "Oh, yeah—who was it that tried to buy Agromont?" he asked.

"The main player was a slightly greasy and very wealthy little arb named Sergo. He also bought their West Side property and the pier." He saw the change in Karp's expression and asked, "A friend of yours?"

Karp said glumly, "We've met," waved good-bye, and stalked out. The implications of what he had learned from V.T. were still whirling around his brain when he entered his office again, to find Roland Hrcany waiting with an odd smile on his face. He was sitting at Karp's conference table and he had a cassette recorder placed in front of him.

Karp gestured at the recorder and said, "Is it time for our dance lesson? What're you up to, Roland?"

"It's a little surprise," said Hrcany. "See if you can recognize the lyrics." He pressed the play button and the conversation between Amalfi and Fulton on the fire stairs at Roosevelt Hospital filled the room, their speech hollow and echoing, like the voices of ghosts on old radio shows.

When it was done, Karp asked, "That's definitely top-forty, Roland. You mind telling me where you got it?"

"I got with IAD and wired Amalfi," said Hrcany.

Karp looked out the window and rubbed his face. "Why did you do that, Roland?" he asked in a tired voice.

"I got a tip from an informant that Amalfi and Fulton were both involved in these drug-lord hits," said Hrcany.

"And you didn't tell me about it."

"No," said Hrcany, beginning to feel uneasy. Karp was taking this altogether too calmly. "I thought, you know, you and Fulton . . ."

"Uh-huh. You thought that I was protecting Clay," said Karp. "That I was, ah, conspiring to cover up a bunch of homicides to protect a friend. No, it's OK," he added when Hrcany protested, "as a matter of fact I guess I *was* involved in something not too far from that.

Good investigative zeal, Roland. I guess you were relieved to find that Clay was working undercover too. You've kept this pretty close, I guess?"

Hrcany nodded. "Just Waldbaum of IAD knows about it." He paused. "And the D.A."

Karp spun around and faced Hrcany, his eyes shooting sparks.

"You told *Bloom*! Why the *fuck* did you tell Bloom?"

"Shit, Butch! What was I supposed to do? I thought you were in the bag with Fulton. You said yourself, there's all kinds of serious players involved in this, and . . ." His eyes widened in horror. "You think *the* D.A. is . . . ?"

"Great!" said Karp. "The penny drops. As a matter of fact, I don't think Mr. Bloom is working for a bunch of killers. But some of his friends might be, and Sanford Bloom never kept a secret for more than ten minutes in his whole life. He's a mouth on legs."

Karp rose and paced nervously back and forth. "Roland, didn't you *think*? Clay's out there exposed . . . Christ! When was this? When did you tell Bloom?"

"At the staff meeting—yesterday morning, about ten."

Karp sat down again and blew out his breath through puffed cheeks. "Then it's too late," he said. "I can't find him anywhere. They've got him."

He sat there for a while, looking out the window, unable to think of any constructive activity. He barely heard Hrcany's embarrassed leave-taking. After some indeterminate time he was roused by a tapping on his door. It was Doug Brenner, his driver. Karp remembered that he had made an appointment to meet Brenner and Marlene outside the building fifteen minutes ago, to run up to the Twenty-eighth Precinct for the sting on Meissner. He made some noises of acknowledgment, put on his jacket, and allowed Brenner to lead him away.

In the car Brenner said, "We'll never make it up to Harlem in time."

"Yes, we will," replied Marlene. "Use the siren."

Which they did, and did arrive at ten past noon, not too far off the appointed moment. Marlene secreted herself in an interrogation room while the two men went to the homicide squad room, to find Alan Meissner being one of the boys with the King Cole Trio.

Karp smiled all around. Maus finished a cop anecdote and everyone laughed. Then Karp said, "Well, we've invited Mr. Meissner here to help us out again. Art, you want to review this case?"

Dugman stood up and began, in a professorial tone quite removed from his usual cynical profanity, to outline a serial murder case. The case was wholly fictitious, having been adapted from a B movie Maus had seen on late TV recently, and cheerfully embellished by the detectives of the Two-eight.

When he had finished, Karp said, "Look,

Alan, guys, this is going to take at least an hour—why don't we have lunch? We can order in sandwiches and drinks from that good deli on Amsterdam, my treat."

General agreement: Karp wrote the orders down on a slip of paper—pastrami on rye, corned beef, Cokes, Dr. Brown's. The detectives made themselves appear busy, thumbing through, stacking, and arranging piles of folders. Lanny Maus turned on a small cassette tape recorder, coughed into its microphone, said, "Testing, testing," and sang two bars of "She's So Fine" in a good falsetto. Laughter. He tossed the mike aside, but did not turn off the recorder.

Karp put an apologetic expression on his face and offered the lunch-order slip to Meissner, saying, "Would you mind calling these in, Alan? It'd save some time. The number's up on the wall by that phone."

Meissner was glad to help. He sat on the edge of the desk and dialed the number penciled on the wall. The phone rang twice and was picked up. A man's voice said, "Hello." Meissner thought it sounded vaguely familiar. Meissner said, "Is this the Amsterdam Deli?" The voice said, "Hello, can I help you?"

Meissner slammed the phone down with a bang. The detectives and Karp looked over at him mildly. His face was turning bright red.

"Something wrong, Alan?" asked Karp.

"You   fucking   son-of-a-bitch!" Meissner yelled. "You tried to trick me."

"I'm sorry?" said Karp. "What's the matter, don't they have any pastrami?"

"That wasn't the delicatessen, you phony bastard! That was him on the phone, the boyfriend. You set me up, you fucker!"

"Boyfriend? What boyfriend, Alan?" asked Karp.

"You know goddamn good and well what boyfriend!" screamed Meissner. He was standing less than a foot from Karp now, and little flecks of foam were jumping from his mouth onto Karp's suit coat. Karp flicked them off with his handkerchief and said, "Yes, *I* know what boyfriend, Alan, but I wonder how *you* know. Did you recognize his voice on the phone? From when he called, just before you murdered Ellen Wagner?"

Meissner uttered a strangled cry and leapt for Karp's throat. Karp batted his hands away, and in an instant Jeffers, moving faster than anything that large had a right to move, had Meissner locked in a chokehold with his feet dangling six inches off the floor.

Meissner was struggling wildly, kicking out at everything within reach, like a four-year-old in a tantrum. Jeffers grunted as a heel connected with his shin; he tightened his grip. Dugman moved in, and Karp saw that he had a leather sap in his hands.

"No, don't hurt him," Karp yelled. Dugman grimaced, but put the sap away and brought out cuffs. Working together, the three cops were finally able to get Meissner cuffed and forced down into a chair.

"He feisty, all right," said Jeffers, adjusting his rumpled suit. "Raping all them women must be good training."

Meissner stared up at Karp, his face flushed with exertion and contorted with impotent rage. "You can't do this," he shouted. "This is entrapment."

"No it's not, Alan," said Karp calmly. "It's called a spontaneous expression showing consciousness of guilt. You need to check your law books again. Art?"

Dugman formally rearrested Meissner for the Wagner homicide and read him his rights. Meissner did not take his eyes off Karp's face; the force of his silent hatred at last made Karp uncomfortable and he turned away, to see Marlene come running in.

Marlene looked at Meissner, waved gaily, and called out, "Hi, smarty-pants. Gotcha!"

At this, Meissner began shouting vile obscenities and threats. He continued to do so as two uniformed officers dragged him down to the precinct cells.

"My, he was upset," said Marlene. "And he seemed like such a calm, sophisticated type on the phone. Intelligent too. So, my hero, have we really got him?"

"Yeah, I have a good feeling about it," said Karp. "It's a solid consciousness-of-guilt case now. He just ran on spontaneously, which will be obvious from the tape we made. It's going to be real hard for anyone to defend against, and it'll stand up legally too. If I was his lawyer, I'd advise a cop-out."

"Which we won't accept," said Marlene firmly.

"Uh-uh. We hang tough on the top count. You earned it. Who're you calling?"

Marlene said, "JoAnne Caputo. And the others. They could use a laugh."

While Marlene made her calls, Karp sought out Art Dugman in his tiny cell of an office. Neat, was his first impression, and reminiscent of a former age. Awards on the wall, pictures of PAL teams, photographs of young black patrolmen in the fifties, unsmiling and austere. Pride of place on the wall went to a framed exhibit of four deformed bullets: neatly typed legends beneath them set out the circumstances in which they had been, on separate occasions, shot into and yanked out of the body of Art Dugman.

On the uncluttered desk stood a dozen or so photographs of family members, most of which showed children in graduation gowns representing successive levels of education. Karp had not thought of Dugman as a family man: he seemed rather to have been exuded from the streets, living entirely on the underlife of Harlem, like some beneficent parasite.

After an interlude of stiff conversation about the Meissner case, about the job, and about sports, Karp turned to the subject of his visit, asking, with no great emphasis, whether Clay Fulton's whereabouts were known.

Dugman's deep yellowish eyes narrowed. "Shit, I don't know where the fuck he is. It ain't my turn to watch him. Maybe the Bahamas. Brazil."

Karp took a deep breath, stared briefly into the abyss, and told Dugman the whole story: Fulton's odd behavior, the searing interview with the chief of detectives, the swearing to secrecy, the revelations of Tecumseh, the discoveries about Manning and Amalfi and the suspicions about Fane.

Dugman's face was as impassive as a cypress tree for the duration of the narrative. Then he began to make a peculiar sound deep in his gullet, a rhythmic buzzing that Karp ultimately deciphered as a chuckle, a sound that at last broke out into frank laughter.

He laughed until tears streamed from his eyes, interspersing the roars with exclamations such as "He got over me, that boy," and "Son-of-a-bitch tricky damn mother-fucker," laughed until Karp was made uneasy and said, "I don't see what's so funny, Art. We're in deep shit, here."

Dugman subsided and wiped his eyes with a pearly silk handkerchief. "Yeah, well, whatever, it's better than what I thought it was. God damn!"

"I'm glad you're glad," said Karp, not without asperity, "but Clay's still missing, and I'm getting worried."

"Ah, shit, Karp, don't worry about the Loo," said Dugman. "Man can take care of himself.

He's probably cooping it in some damn museum. He done it before. He'll turn up."

Karp shook his head. "He's not cooping. I'm almost certain somebody tipped the bad guys he was working for the chief. He didn't turn up at home last night. Or call in. Martha's real worried."

Dugman's face clouded. "You think somebody snatched an NYPD detective lieutenant?"

"It could happen, with these shitheads. They think they can do what the fuck they want. Let me say this: I hope to God he's just kidnapped."

Dugman snatched up his phone, punched in the familiar number of the Thirty-second Precinct, and asked to speak to Detective Amalfi. He listened for a minute in silence. "When?" he said. Then, "Is Manning around? Uh-hunh. No, no message."

He hung up and when he looked at Karp his jaw was tight and twitching. "Amalfi bit his gun last night. Manning's got a regular day off, but he ain't at home."

"Manning's got him, then," said Karp.

"Not for long, the motherfucker!" said Dugman ferociously. "We gonna turn this whole city upside down."

"I don't think so, Art," said Karp. "I think we're gonna have to do this ourselves, real quiet, and I think Clay would agree."

"You saying what I think you're saying? That the chief'd let a lieutenant go down? Someone like Clay Fulton?"

"I think he'd let a bus full of lieutenants go down on this one, Art. I don't think he's thinking all that straight, if you want to know. Sure, he wants the killings stopped, but after that his first priority is to protect the department. That's why this whole cockamamie business with Clay going under started in the first place."

Dugman took a cigar from his breast pocket, stripped off the cellophane, and lit it. He sat contemplating his blue smoke for a while. Then he said, "OK, let's start that way. Manning's place. Club Mecca. Choo Willis. His boys. We can do that much, just the three of us. But if that draws a blank . . ."

"If it does, then we'll worry," said Karp. "And, Art, call me anytime you get anything."

There was a message from V. T. Newbury waiting for Karp when he got back from Harlem. He went to V.T.'s office and found him virtually unmoved from where he had been that morning, although looking rather more tired.

"I think I have your answer," he announced when Karp had seated himself in the rocking chair.

"That was fast," said Karp. "What's the answer?"

"What's the question?" V.T. shot back with a wan smile. "But really, what you said about Agromont was the key. So I thought of Poppie Foote."

"Poopie what?"

"Poppie Foote. We were at school together.

He married my sister Emily's best friend, Anne Kring. Surely I've mentioned Poppie?"

"Not recently, V.T.," said Karp. "But you were saying . . ."

"Yes, I recalled that he'd touted the stock last year when it was in play. He's a specialist at Bache and he handles Agromont. In any case, here's the story. As I said before, when the takeover bid went sour last year, half a dozen people were left holding the bag in a big way, including Mr. Sergo and your congressman, but it was a lot worse than I thought. Essentially, they had leveraged everything they owned; the notes were coming due, the market was down generally, so even if they sold out, they couldn't get clear. The Street was talking about Sergo going belly-up, in fact.

"But starting about ten months ago, Sergo got cured in a big way. He was flush with liquidity and back in action. I don't have the details on Fane, but my sense is, the same thing happened to him. So the question is, where did the money come from?"

"Where indeed?"

"It came from offshore, as I surmised earlier. A brass-plate operation in the Caymans called Burlingame Imperial, Ltd. The rumors are that it's a way for people in the U.K. to play the American market without their tax people knowing about it. Everyone thought Sergo was very clever for tapping this loot."

"And is it British money?"

"One doubts it. The major British players

don't seem to be involved. But it could be the royal family for all I know. The darker streams of international finance flow very deep. Or maybe Sergo started the rumor. Oh, and this too: the place didn't exist a year ago. Poppie knows that for a fact."

Karp nodded. "And who owns this ghost bank?"

"Oh, it doesn't matter who owns it. These places are always owned on paper by secretaries and maiden aunts in nursing homes. The issue is who controls it, and that's terribly hard to discover. That's why they're located offshore. But I can tell you who did the legal work involved in chartering it."

"Who was that?" Karp asked, almost knowing.

"Your new friend Mr. Richard Reedy."

SEVENTEEN

"You're moping again," said Marlene at breakfast the next morning. "Why are you moping?
God's in his heaven and Meissner's in jail. You
have a sexy pregnant girlfriend, a good job, in-
door work with no heavy lifting—what's to
mope?"

"I'm not moping," said Karp, aggressively
snapping the sports section of yesterday's *Post*.

"Yes, you are," Marlene insisted. "And how
I know is, you positively rejected my patent
sexual availability last night, conveyed by many
a squirm and sigh, preferring to sink into sod-
den sleep."

Karp looked up from the paper. "I'm sorry,"
he said.

"Oh, not to worry," said Marlene. "I'll stop
off and pick up some new batteries for the vi-
brator." She drank some coffee. No reaction
from Karp. She continued, "But, really, I'm
concerned. And I'm also starting to get mildly
pissed. You can't keep dragging these black
clouds into the house and expect me to cohabit
around you like everything was just fine. It

makes me think that maybe it's me, but I know I haven't done anything, and it drives me crazy. I'm not going to put up with it anymore."

"I'm sorry," said Karp again.

"Saying 'sorry' liked a whipped dog doesn't cut it either. Come on, Karp! This is good marriage practice. Share your inmost thoughts with your near and dear."

Karp shrugged and rubbed his knuckles over his mouth. "It's embarrassing," he began.

"What, you wet your pants before you go in front of a jury? Shit, everybody knows that. You're famous for it and nobody holds it against you."

Karp laughed out loud in spite of himself. "No, it's this fucking drug thing. I've been an asshole and I don't like it. I've been ignoring my instincts for months now and I've made a complete fuck-up of it."

"Welcome to the club," said Marlene. "Everybody blows one occasionally. So what's the story?"

"No, it's not just blowing a case. I just got myself involved in . . . sliminess. Politics. I didn't look where I should've looked because I didn't want to see. I wasn't on top of the investigation itself because I was playing games. I was playing games with Chief Denton. I was playing different games with Reedy and Fane. And then, of course, Roland started playing his own games. Why not? The fucking *boss* is doing it, right?"

And then he did tell her the whole story, from the conversation in his office with Clay Fulton about the drug-lord murders, to the scarifying interview with Bill Denton, to the revelations about Amalfi and Manning and Fane brought out by Tecumseh's confession and the further investigation by Clay. Reluctantly he also described his own involvement with Fane and Sergo and Reedy.

"And so there we have it," he concluded, "the whole investigation down the drain and me standing there like an idiot faked out of my jock. And there's Clay."

"Yeah, there's Clay," said Marlene, patting Karp's hand. "Do you think they, Manning, would actually kill him?"

"In a minute," said Karp. "All they need is Tecumseh's tape recording, and pow! pow! he's dead. Amalfi's gone, so the tape he made with Clay is pretty much useless, and the Tecumseh tape is all there is to connect Manning and Amalfi and Choo Willis to the killings. I'm on the tape and I can vouch for it, which makes it significant as evidence. So Manning has to have it.

"I don't even want to think about what the fucker is doing to Clay right now to get him to tell him where it is. If he gets it, and gets rid of Clay, we can't touch him. With the money they have, they can buy every snitch in Harlem. Oh, yeah, they can kick him off the force, but I doubt he's depending on his pension. Basically, we have no serious legal case. And, of course, Manning is the only connection we have with Fane, Sergo, and Reedy."

"I don't understand," said Marlene. "These stock guys all of a sudden decided to be dope dealers?"

"No, it probably went in stages. Fane owns the Club Mecca, where Choo Willis hangs out. So he had to know that Willis was a big-time dealer. Maybe they were even partners. Fane is in stocks with Reedy and later with Sergo. They're doing OK, but then Sergo comes up with this Agromont deal. Now they can get *really* rich.

"Maybe Fane approaches Willis with the idea about using drug money to buy stock. It's a perfect laundry when you add the off-shore bank. Drug money goes out—loans to buy stock come back in. The profits from these LBOs are so huge that the dirty money is swamped when the deals come off."

"But the Agromont deal didn't come off, you said," Marlene objected.

"Yes, that's what started this mess. They, the stock guys, were going to lose everything, including the cash they had got from Willis. They were running millions through their bank, but now they needed hundreds of millions."

"There's that much in dope?"

"In coke there is," said Karp. "And, of course, the more you buy, the better the deal from the suppliers and the bigger the profits. But the only way they could get as big as they had to get as fast as they needed to was to take over other big dealers. Which meant they had to have a foolproof way of knocking them out. That's where Manning and Amalfi came in. Manning was dirty already; he knew Willis. And the rest is history."

Marlene shook her head. "It still seems incredible. Guys like that . . ."

"I met Sergo," said Karp. "It's not that incredible."

"Are you positive Reedy's involved?" Marlene asked.

"I'm not positive about anything anymore," Karp replied grimly. "I'm pretty sure he's involved with the stock deals. He set up the offshore bank. He must have known what it was being used for. He's tight with Fane and Sergo. But whether he had actual guilty knowledge of the murders? That I can't say for sure."

"You sound like you'd be sorry if he was really deep in on it."

Karp nodded. "Yeah. I guess. I have to admit he got to me. That's really what makes me writhe inside. He read me like a book and got to me." He laughed. "I guess I'm queer for elderly Irish lawyers. Garrahy really meant something to me. I felt . . . I wanted that slot filled again, and he saw that and moved right in.

"And the chance to be D.A. That was the corker." He waved his hand to indicate the loft. "I mean, look at this! We're going to have a baby, for Chrissake! Is this a place for a kid? Five flights walking up and a floor full of splinters and God knows what kind of shit lying around. And you're going to have to stop work, at least for a little bit—"

"I'm not."

"OK, great, you're not. You're going to squat down in front of Part 30, say, 'Excuse me, your Honor,' pop the kid out, hand it to the stenographer, and continue the case. I wanted . . . I don't know, something more solid, a little comfort, a house maybe. Shit, Marlene, I'm thirty-three years old, and what do I own? Three suits, a first baseman's mitt, and a pair of sneakers."

"You have a rowing machine," said Marlene.

"Thank you! I rest my case. But you catch my drift. This can't go on. Running the bureau, dancing little circles around Bloom, waiting for a knife in the back. So when I saw a possible out . . . And now it's all shit, and Clay is fucked, and I don't know how to crawl out of it. So . . . am I moping? I'd like to change my plea on that. First-degree mopery. Yes, I'm moping. I have moped. And I plan to mope some more."

The King Cole Trio sat in their dusty black van in the street outside the Club Mecca. This was a four-story building with apartments on the top two floors, offices on the next one down, and the nightclub itself occupying the rest. It had a gaudy tan stucco Moorish facade on its street side and a large green marquee that carried the club's name in neon letters shaped like Arabic script and an expanse of lettering that advertised the club's show.

The men did not talk as they worked, the only sound in the van being the snick-clunk of reloading weapons. The club had closed its doors to the public at three A.M., but the Trio knew that for a good number of its habitués this merely signaled the start of the evening.

The detectives left the van and marched abreast to the front door. All three carried Ithaca twelve-gauge pump guns. The door was covered by a steel gate pierced with fanciful Moorish designs and secured by a Yale lock. Maus knelt and brought out a ring of keys. "We don't need no stinkin warrant," he muttered, and after several tries found a passkey that worked.

They entered the darkened lobby of the club and walked softly down the carpeted hallway to where a strong light shone from under a door. The door, a cheap interior wood-core model, was locked. Jeffers backed up a few yards, braced, propelled himself into violent motion, and crashed through the barrier with no more apparent effort than an ordinary man would use to pass a beaded curtain.

The nightclub they entered had two levels: an upper horseshoe filled with tables, on which the three detectives now stood, and a lower level consisting of a deck of tables grouped around a large dance floor. Both faced a full stage decked with a heavy red-and-gold curtain. There were a dozen or so people on the lower level: showgirls, demiwhores, and a group of Choo Willis' hard boys. Five of the men were playing cards at one of the tables.

The scene was brightly lit by the overhead cleaning lights.

Art Dugman went to the wrought-iron railing that rimmed the upper level and fired a round from his shotgun into the ceiling. Shrieks from the women, curses from the men. Plaster floated down on the card table and the men around it, dusting their clothes and the cards and piles of paper money on the table like light snow.

Dugman marched down to the lower level in silence. No one moved. All the players sat frozen like mannequins in a store window. They had all recognized the King Cole Trio, and no one wished to make any inadvertent twitch that might be construed as an attempt to extract a weapon.

As Dugman approached the card table, one of Choo Willis' lieutenants, a large shaven-headed man known as Buster, spoke up. "What the fuck is this, Dugman? Ain't you got no other shit to do?"

In one swift movement Dugman pumped a shell into the chamber of his shotgun and placed its muzzle against Buster's upper lip. "Are you addressing me?" asked Dugman mildly. "I don't believe I solicited a comment." He continued to push on the shotgun. Buster's head arched backward. His chair tipped. Dugman kept the man artfully balanced with just the pressure of the shotgun's muzzle on the man's lip. A thin trickle of blood and saliva started down Buster's chin.

"I'm looking for Choo-choo," Dugman said. "Where is he?"

Buster's eyes bulged and he mumbled something.

Dugman cocked his head. "What's that, Buster? I can't make out what you said."

The muzzle of the shotgun, greased by Buster's copious sweat, had worked its way up until it was now lodged under the man's cheekbone.

"He ain't here. I swear to Jesus, he ain't here."

"Where is he, then?"

"I dunno. He din tell me nothin."

"Was he here tonight?"

"Yeah, early. He was in his office, upstairs. Then he call an say he going out and won be back. An he lef. Hey, man, my face hurt."

Dugman ignored this comment. He asked, "He see anybody?"

"The fuck I know, man? He in there with the door locked. He call down for some drinks and food bout eleven. Thas all I know, man."

Dugman looked at Buster and saw that he was not lying. Gently he shoved on the shotgun and Buster went over with a crash. Dugman swept the barrel of the shotgun across the table, knocking glasses and ashtrays to the floor, and then gathered up the tablecloth as a sack, with the money and the cards inside.

"Thank all you gentlemen. And ladies. And thanks for having your contributions to the Police Athletic League ready on the table when I arrived. That is most considerate."

He walked back up the stairs to the second level and, leaving the crowd to sit under the guns of Maus and Jeffers, went to check out the office of Choo Willis.

Clay Fulton was tied into a heavy chair with electrical wire. He was in darkness, blindfolded, in a small room. Although he could see nothing, he could still smell, even though they had broken his nose. He could smell damp, and salt, and his own filth. He thought, from the smell and the sounds, that he was near water, the sea, or the tidal rivers. He was naked and cold. He heard a door open, a scrape, and then someone emptied a bucket of cold stinking water over his head.

He gasped involuntarily. Another scrape of furniture. They were arranging themselves. Someone—he thought it was Manning—said, "Where's the tape, Fulton?"

He didn't answer. He figured he could hold out another twelve hours. Counting one lie. He could buy maybe two, three hours with a lie. Then there would be nothing left. If somebody didn't find him before then, they would have drained everything out of him. There would be nobody home to resist. He would tell them and they would get the tape and they would kill him. He wished the lie he had told about lots of copies was true. In fact there was only one tape. He wished he could see his wife.

He felt the cold pinch as they attached the electrodes. Manning had been in Nam, he recalled. He had learned what there was to learn about making people hurt. They were going to send him a message again, as the saying went. They cranked the generator. Fulton heard himself scream, but as from a long distance away.

"There was nothing in the office at all?" Karp asked.

"Nothing," said Dugman. "And nothing in Manning's apartment, or Willis' place either." Dugman had been up all the previous night, breaking and entering in a good cause, and he was tired and red-eyed. They were in Karp's office late the next day, and Clay Fulton had been missing for over forty-eight hours.

"You tried everyplace? Willis' associates, Manning's—"

"We didn't hit Fane," said Dugman.

"No, he's not anywhere near Fane," said Karp, instinctively sure of it. He felt as bad as Dugman looked, oppressed with the futility of going forward with what in any case had been a thin hope. Three cops could not expect to find someone hidden in one of the hundreds of thousands of buildings in the city. And Fulton might have been taken out of town.

"We gonna have to open this up, my friend. Splash it all around the world," said Dugman.

"I guess," said Karp listlessly. He toyed with a pencil. "Just . . . You said that Willis was in his office last night. And he was alone. He must have made some calls. Would it be possible to—?

"No, wait a sec, there," said Dugman. "I didn't say nothing about him being alone. He had at least two people in there. What I said was nobody *saw* him with anybody. But there was two people in there."

"How do you know that?"

"The food cart," said Dugman, yawning and rubbing his rubbery face. "They cleaned up after serving, and it was a service for three. Two beer glasses. A soda. Look like some kind of cocktail. Three plates—crumbs and chicken bones. And three coffee cups. No, two coffee. One had tea."

"Nothing else? Nothing written on the napkins?"

Dugman gave him a deadpan stare. "You been watchin too much TV, my man. No writing on the napkins, no poison darts, no matchbooks with the name of the place he at. None of that shit. Two glasses, two beer bottles, one soda glass, one soda can, three plates, three napkins, knives, forks, spoons, cream and sugar, and a coffeepot. That's all."

The detective rose to his feet and stretched. "I got to go get the real search going. Maybe we'll check, see if we can trace any of the calls they made—that's a good idea, anyway."

"No teapot?" Karp asked abruptly. He desperately did not want Dugman to leave, to start a chain of actions that would make the entire miserable affair public and out of control.

Dugman snorted. "Huh! You persistent, I give you that. No, matter of fact, there wasn't no teapot." He thought for a moment. "No tea bag neither."

"Then why did you say one of them had tea?"

"Because of the lemon. There was a squeezed lemon on the saucer of one of the cups. Nobody drinks their coffee with lemon, do they?"

Karp felt a flood of excitement and satisfaction wash through him, a feeling a rightness and release. He reflected that it was exactly like that feeling he used to get when he launched a three-point shot from twenty-five feet out and knew deep in his body, in a way that defied the telling, that it was going to float into the basket without touching the rim.

He said, "No, not many people do," in such a strange tone of voice that Dugman stopped and stared at him. Then he said, "Art, did you ever just know something? Like about a crime. When you all of a sudden knew who did it, or how he did it?"

Dugman said, "You mean like a hunch?"

"Yeah," said Karp, "but more than that. Like a certainty. I know where they have Fulton."

"This is a fucking fort," said Maus. "How the hell are we gonna get in?" The King Cole Trio were standing outside their van in the trash-strewn shadows of the West Side Highway looking across Eleventh Avenue at the immense front of Pier 87, the old American Line property. The main entrance, through which trucks and cars had once unloaded and provisioned transatlantic liners, was sealed with corrugated steel. There were several smaller doors on either side of the main entrance, and these were barred with heavy steel grids.

"Well?" Maus spoke again irritably. "How are we?"

Art Dugman looked up from the building plans he was studying. He had reading glasses on, which made him look disconcertingly professorial. "When I figure it, you be the first to know," he said. He resumed his study. The plans showed that the building had three working floors. The ground floor was essentially a huge open bay, largely devoted to vehicular traffic and the reception and handling of baggage and cargo. The rear of this area had been assigned to customs. The second floor was a reception area for passengers; first class, second class, third class all had their separate entranceways, lounges, bars. The top floor was offices.

That was the plan. What the interior of the building looked like now, fifteen years after the last liner had docked, was anyone's guess. If this had been a normal police operation, Dugman would have covered all the doors and sent a squad down through the roof, clearing the building from above, by the book. Going into a monster like this was an impossible task for three men, especially on no better information than Karp's hunch. Dugman folded the plans neatly and climbed back into the van. He looked into the ice chest and found a soda and half a roast-beef sandwich that Maus had bought the previous day.

He drank some soda against the oppressive heat and took a bite of the sandwich. It was dry and gristly. He thought of searching for one of the plastic sacks of catsup or mayo that were usually to be found scattered on the floor of the van, but decided not to bother. He put the rest of the sandwich into his coat pocket and closed his burning eyes.

Jeffers was stretched out full length on the carpet covering the rear, a *Post* draped over his face. Gentle snores came from beneath the paper, fluttering it. Dugman turned around and looked at him with irritation. He said in an unnecessarily loud voice, "Hey, Jeffers! You on the job? You protecting the public?"

Jeffers grunted and said sleepily, "I'm thinkin about it. I'm getting my courage up to face them miserable mean streets once again. Anything goin on?"

"Yeah, we sittin with our knittin out on the street. I can't think of a way to get into that damn pier without a fuckin strike team."

"We could just go up to the door and say, 'Open up! This the *po*-lice.' It work for me."

"Yeah, and they'll cut the Loo's throat between the *po* and the -lice."

"So what're we doing here?"

"We waiting, son," said Dugman. "Either for a inspiration from the Lord or for that radio to light up and tell us that they found the Loo.

Or for something. We might as well wait here as anywhere."

"Fine with me," answered Jeffers, readjusting the paper over his face. "Wake me up if something happen."

The sun moved across Manhattan and began its slow descent toward its home in New Jersey. The front of the pier was thrown into ocher shadow. Dugman sat in the passenger seat of the van listening to the irrelevant crackle of the police radio, dozing fitfully. Maus lurked behind a highway pillar watching the pier building, whistling "I Heard It Through the Grapevine." In the back of the van Jeffers snored more deeply.

Dugman was just thinking about walking down 47th Street to hustle a takeout dinner when he heard the sound of quick footsteps.

"Hey!" said Maus when he reached the van. "There's somebody coming out of the pier."

Dugman slipped out of the van and went to look. One of the small doors on the side of the pier had opened and a slender black man had emerged from its shadows. He locked the door from the outside, walked toward a black late-model Chevrolet parked in front of the pier, opened its door, and started the engine.

He stood outside for a minute, allowing the air conditioning to blow the day's heat out of the interior, then entered the car and drove off.

"Let's go get him," Dugman snapped, dashing around to the passenger side.

Maus jumped into the driver's seat, gunned

the van's engine, and took off south on Twelfth Avenue. He kept the van half a block behind the Chevy for several streets. There were no other cars moving on the avenue, which was lined on both sides with idle semi-trailers.

Maus moved the van up to within two car lengths of the Chevy, then trod heavily on the gas. The van leapt forward, ran up alongside the car, and swerved in front of it. Dugman had a glimpse of the driver's panicked face before the van drove the Chevy into the side of a parked semi with a screech of metal and brakes.

It was a perfect pinch. The rear of the van pinned the driver's door shut and the other door was crushed against the side of the trailer. The driver was trapped. Dugman got out and stood in front of the Chevy with his arms crossed, wreathed by escaping steam from the car's broken radiator. Jeffers grabbed his shotgun and went around to the rear of the trapped car. When he was in position, he whistled, and Maus rolled the van ahead enough to free the driver's door.

Jeffers popped it open and yanked the shaken man out. He spun him around, placed the muzzle of the twelve-gauge against the base of his skull, braced him against his own car, hands on the hood, and patted him down one-handed, coming up with a 9mm automatic pistol and a four-inch butterfly knife. He pulled the man's hands behind him and snapped on handcuffs.

Dugman approached and looked the man in

the face. He was a young man, not more than twenty, and Dugman did not recognize him—one more of the street's unlimited supply of apprentices to the drug trade.

"You got a license for this gun, son?" Dugman asked politely, holding up the weapon.

"Fuck you, asshole!" the kid yelled. "I din do shit, an you fucked up my car. Who gonna pay for it, nigger?"

Jeffers said, "He must not be local, talkin' like that."

Dugman shoved the pistol into his belt and nodded. "I don't guess. Where you from, son? Brooklyn?"

"What the fuck you care? You gonna bust me, go ahead!"

"Take him around behind the trailer," said Dugman.

Jeffers grabbed the kid's arm and started to lead him away. The kid did not expect this. He looked around wildly, took a deep breath, and started to shout, "Hey! Help! Police brutality! Hey!" It was the kind of thing that often worked to advantage on the crowded streets of Bed-Stuy.

Not pausing in his stride, Jeffers tossed up his shotgun, grabbed it five inches from the end of the barrel, and jammed its front end neatly into the kid's open mouth. He jammed it upward until most of the kid's weight was hanging from his soft palate. A high whistle of agony came from the kid's throat.

Behind the trailer, Jeffers kicked the kid's feet

out from under him and threw him facedown on the pavement. Then he sat down heavily on the kid's back.

Dugman squatted on his haunches near the kid's face. He said in a conversational tone, "Now, you ain't from around here, so we got to make some allowances. Up in Harlem we let a lot of shit go by, but one thing we don't let go by is snatching no New York City Police Department detective lieutenants. You think you been in trouble before. You been to Youth Hall. You maybe been to Rikers a time or two. But now you're in Harlem trouble, son. It's another world. What we got here is way, way beyond police brutality. Am I getting through to you?"

"Breathe . . ." the kid gasped.

Dugman motioned to Jeffers, who leaned forward and took some of his weight onto his feet. Air sucked into the kid's lungs in a rush. A trickle of blood leaked from his mouth and spotted the pavement.

"Now," Dugman continued, "you could be a big help to us. We need to know exactly where they got the lieutenant, and where Manning is, and how many guys are in there, and where they are. And the layout inside. Can you do that?"

The kid gasped, "Fuck you, cop!"

"We don't have time for this shit," said Dugman. He leaned forward until his face was only a few inches from the kid's staring eye. "You ever eat your own flesh, kid?" he asked softly.

The eye just stared. The kid had no ready answer.

Dugman said to Jeffers, "Cut off his ear!"

Jeffers took out the butterfly knife, snapped it open, grabbed the kid's right ear roughly and began to saw away. Blood rolled down the kid's face into his eye. The kid howled and heaved, but Jeffers might have been the Chrysler Building for all it mattered.

Dugman leaned over and pinched the kid's nostrils shut, and when his mouth popped open he shoved a bloody mass into the kid's mouth. The kid immediately spit it out, gagging and retching. He was sobbing now, and his nose was running.

"He doesn't like ear," said Dugman. "Too bad."

"Want to try some nose?" suggested Jeffers.

"Nobody like nose," said Dugman. "Besides, his all running with snot. It's disgusting. No, whyn't you roll him over. *Everybody* like pecker."

They left the kid, crying and cursing, manacled to the bumper of his car, and drove back to the pier. After a block or so, Dugman remarked to Jeffers, "You were real sloppy cutting off that ear. I tell you to cut off some mutt's ear, I expect it to *fly* off his head."

Maus said, "Oh, right! I got to drive, and you guys get all the fun part. How come I never get to torture suspects? This sucks, guys, I mean it. I'm sorry I joined the cops now."

Jeffers ignored this and said to Dugman,

"Sorry about that, boss, I guess I didn't get enough sleep."

"You was using the wrong side of the blade, fool! You suppose to use the sharp side, cut off a man's ear."

"No kidding?" said Jeffers, opening his eyes wide. "Shit, I better write that down. And while we at it, what *did* you shove in that kid's mouth?"

"Piece of Maus's roast beef. I slopped it in some of his blood."

"You fed him Maus's roast-beef sandwich!" Jeffers exclaimed. "Hey, Sarge, I got to tell you that's over the line. I might have to write you up for that. No wonder he puked."

Maus said, "When you guys stop fuckin around, you want to tell me what he said?"

Dugman said, "Yeah, he was real cooperative after we unzipped his fly. There's five guys in the place besides him. Willis, Manning, and three others. One guy's at the entrance, sits in a little guard office by the door. The rest of them are on the second floor. Water and power's cut off. They use electric lanterns. They got the Loo in a storage closet on the second floor."

"Is he OK?" asked Maus.

"He still screaming, the kid said. The kid said he was going to get some tape that the Loo had. That's why they were beatin on him. He finally broke down and told them where it was. I figure they won't do him before they got the tape in hand; he could just be buying time. So he's still alive, but he ain't gonna stay alive unless we do this right."

Maus parked the van under the expressway and Dugman told the other two men what he expected them to do. He racked a round into the chamber of the Spanish 9mm he had taken off the kid and checked his own big .357 revolver. Maus and Jeffers also checked their 9mm automatics, huge weapons that sat uncomfortably heavy in their shoulder holsters, and Maus picked up his shotgun and a roll of gaffer's tape.

They walked across the deserted avenue to the pier. It was twilight, but the concrete still held the day's heat. As they walked, they each glanced up nervously at the windows of the building, now in deep shadow, like the embrasures of a fortress.

Dugman opened the door with the key he had taken off the kid. They slipped silently into echoing moist darkness, dappled with shafts of light from glassless openings on the river side of the structure. A paler light also came from a small guard post built out of the right inside wall of the building.

As they approached, a voice called out, "Hey, Sloopy, you back already?"

Jeffers accelerated like the linebacker he once was, smashed through the flimsy wooden door of the office, and smashed the man to the ground with a blow of his pistol. The man collapsed and was quickly trussed and gagged with gaffer's tape.

Dugman and Jeffers started up the enclosed concrete main stairway. Maus ran across to the other side of the loading bay to a doorway, went through, and started climbing the outside fire stairs.

At the second-floor landing Dugman opened the door a crack and peered through.

"You see anything?" Jeffers asked in a whisper.

"Yeah," whispered Dugman. Through the crack he could see most of a large and partially ruined room, a passenger lounge of some kind, with a long bar along one wall with a large cracked mirror behind it. Part of the ceiling had sagged, exposing pipes and beams, and the pastel murals depicting luxury ocean travel were buckled and stained. A few pieces of broken furniture lay scattered around and there was a pile of the padded cloths movers use abandoned against one wall.

"Two guys sitting at a table," he said. "A guy lying on a couch. I don't see Willis or Manning."

"What do we do?" said Jeffers.

"I'll go right, you go left. Watch the—"

There was a distant sharp report. And another. Then two louder explosions. Dugman saw the two men at the table spring to their feet and draw pistols from their clothes. The man on the couch sat up, shook his head, reached down to the floor, and came up with a MAC-10 machine pistol. A door slammed somewhere and someone shouted, "What the fuck . . . !"

The men looked away at the source of the shots, and Dugman sprang into the room with his revolver in both hands. Without warning, he began firing into the man with the MAC-10. Hit three times, the man fell back on the couch, and as he fell his hand tightened convulsively on the trigger of the little automatic weapon, spraying fire at his two companions. One of them was struck by the full force of the burst and went down screaming.

The other one got off a shot at Dugman, which pierced his suit coat. He felt the tug of the cloth and thought briefly that he had been hit. He was swinging his gun around to the new target when he heard the rapid fire of Jeffers' pistol from somewhere behind him and the third man cried out and disappeared behind the table.

Dugman rose creakily from the crouch he had assumed and snapped a Speed-loader into his revolver. They heard running footsteps and the slam of a door. Jeffers started to move in the direction of the sounds, but Dugman placed a restraining hand on his arm.

"No," he said, "drop on down to the entrance. There ain't but one way out, unless he's got a boat. Maus has the top covered."

"What about Willis?"

"He'll keep. Just go. I got to find the Loo."

Jeffers ran off down the stairs. When he was gone, Dugman glanced briefly at the three men they had shot, enough to make sure all of them were dead. One was still rasping out breath, but Dugman saw that his belly and chest had been blown apart by the automatic fire at close range. He stepped over the man and walked toward the storeroom where the kid had said Fulton was being held. A smell like that of an ill-kept monkey house reached his nose before he had the door open. His stomach turned over as he stepped into blackness.   .

EIGHTEEN

It was dark in the little room and the floors were slippery. Gun in one hand, reaching out with the other, Dugman advanced into the room. After four steps his foot struck something and he heard a groan.

With his hands he determined what it was he had found. He holstered his gun. Then he dragged Clay Fulton, still bound to his chair, out into the fading light of the lounge.

Dugman tore off the wires that held him to the chair. In a small alcove under a window he quickly made a pallet of the mover's pads, heaved Fulton over to it, and covered him with several more.

He felt Fulton's pulse and was gratified to find it reasonably strong. Fulton opened his eyes, or rather one eye, as the other was closed by a massive bruise. "That you, Dugman?"

"Yeah, it is. You look like shit warmed over, Lieutenant."

"What the fuck took you so long?"

"I took some leave, went to the islands. Cheap fares this time of year."

From the battered face came something that could have been a chuckle. They were both silent for a minute, and Dugman said, "For a while there, I thought you were in the islands."

"Yeah," said Fulton. "Sorry about that. Somebody explained?"

"Yeah, Karp gave me the whole story—what I needed, anyway. He figured out you were here, by the way."

"He's a smart motherfucker," said Fulton. "I don't even know where I am." And then he reached out and grasped Dugman's wrist with remarkable strength. "Manning," he said. "Did you get him yet?"

"Not yet. He's in the building, though. He can't get out, unless he can get past Mack. It never been done."

Fulton did not relax his grasp. "No. Listen. You heard the story. Look. He has an ankle gun."

Dugman said, "Sure, Loo. We gonna pat him down real good."

Fulton shook his head from side to side. He fixed Dugman with his one good eye, staring across to him the meaning his mouth could not express. "No. That's not what I mean. He could draw on you. When you're not looking. You understand?"

Dugman nodded. He understood. Fulton's grasp slipped away and he fell into an exhausted unconsciousness. Dugman got up and yelled at the top of his voice, "Hey, Maus!"

An answering shout came from above. Dugman walked over to a glassless window and stuck his head out. "Maus," he shouted. "Window, north side."

In the gathering dusk, Dugman could just make out Maus's white face sticking out of a window on the third floor. "You see anybody up there?" he called.

"No. Willis passed through a while back. He came up to take a piss. They been using the top floor as a latrine. It's pretty disgusting, but what the fuck, they're criminals, right?"

"What happened to him?"

"I braced him and he took some shots. I shot him back a couple."

"He dead?"

"Well, I can't say, since I'm not a licensed physician. But he took a full pattern high and low. There's hair on the ceiling. Do you want me to try mouth-to-mouth?"

"I want you to clear the building. We got to get a bus for the Loo real fast. Mack carried him down. Manning must've skipped."

"OK, I'm coming down," called Maus. Dugman heard the sound of steps and a slamming door, and then the pounding of feet on iron treads.

He turned and walked heavily toward the stairway. He opened the door and let it slam shut. The sound reverberated through the empty building. Dugman walked silently back into the room, carefully avoiding the crunchy fragments of plaster that littered the floor. He crouched down behind the bar and waited.

After about five minutes he heard furtive steps, and Manning appeared in the dusty glass of the mirror, moving cautiously in short rushes, bent nearly double, with a pistol held out two-handed in front of him. Dugman waited until Manning's back showed in the mirror and then he rose smoothly to his feet and said, "Drop the gun, Manning."

Manning dropped the gun immediately and turned slowly around to face Dugman, who held the Spanish automatic on him steadily.

Manning smiled and said, "Tricky, ain't you? I must be losing my touch."

"I'd say so," said Dugman. "OK, turn around and hands on the wall. You know the drill."

Manning faced the wall with his hands against it and his legs spread wide apart. Dugman gave him a perfunctory pat-down, relieving him of his handcuffs. He backed away and Manning turned around.

Manning said, "You was always pretty smart, Dugman. I heard you was quite the man in the old days. Lots of sugar around in Harlem for a cop in the old days."

"Do tell," said Dugman.

"But let me tell you, my man, it ain't nothing to what they got now. I'm talking millions. Millions of dollars. Would you like to have a million dollars?" Manning was speaking rapidly, and Dugman could see a film of sweat speckled with gray plaster dust across his forehead.

"I sure would," said Dugman.

"It could be arranged," said Manning.

"I'd have to take care of my people."

"That's no problem," said Manning. "I got people who owe me. Millions ain't zip to them. You got no idea how much is involved. I'm not talking buying a hat, chickenshit police pads. This is serious money. Money for life. And it's clean. It's in accounts in the islands, man. You go down there and live like a fuckin king, and nobody can touch you."

"Keep on talking," said Dugman. "You starting to get my attention." His eye fell on Manning's pistol where it had been dropped. Casually he turned away from Manning and walked slowly over to pick it up.

As he expected, he heard the sudden movement, the snapping sound of metal leaving leather.

He stood and turned, his pistol, already cocked, pointing straight out from his body. Manning's ankle gun had cleared its holster and was rising, a blur of motion. Dugman shot him through the chest with the Spanish automatic. Manning fell backward into a sitting position and the little ankle gun went flying. His face had the stupid expression worn by the recently shot. Dugman took more careful aim and shot Manning twice more in the center of his chest.

* * *

Karp arrived at the pier building just as the ambulances were taking away the last of the corpses. He picked out Dugman standing with a group of police officers and caught his eye. It was quite dark by now, and the night was lighted by the glow from the city, and from the Jersey shore, and by the white glare from a local TV crew, all of it laced with the colored scintillations from the various police and emergency vehicles.

"How's Clay?" was Karp's first question.

Dugman said, "He been chewed up some, but I guess he'll live. He's a tough son-of-a-bitch for a college boy. He's in Bellevue."

"Who do we have?"

"Nobody much," answered Dugman. He pulled the stump of a cigar from his coat pocket and lit it. "Choo wasn't using his regular people for this particular job. The two survivors were just a couple of mutts from Brooklyn. We questioned them but they don't know shit. They didn't even know Clay was a cop."

"I heard something about that questioning," said Karp sourly. "I heard you cut off some kid's prick, as a matter of fact."

Dugman laughed and coughed on the cigar smoke. "Yeah, we did. We threw it in the jar with the others. Want to see?"

"I don't want to *know* about it, Dugman. Willis got shot, I understand."

"Dead."

"Uh-huh. And Manning?"

Dugman looked off toward the river and blew a long plume of Macanudo eastward. "Well . . . about that. I was on the line with the chief. Have you talked to him yet? No? Be a good idea. The thing of it is, Manning is on his way to the morgue with a John Doe tag—"

"Christ! You killed Manning too?"

"Well, let's say he took a round in the lung and two more right through the pump from a big old nine belonged to one of the mutts. The circumstances are still under investigation and so on and so forth."

"Meaning you're still working on your cock-and-bull story," Karp snapped back. He gestured to the TV crew. "The press?"

"Yeah," said Dugman. "The police stumbled on a nest of felons while looking for fugitives. They opened fire, we returned. Four dead. Page twelve."

"You don't think you can bury this completely?"

"I try not to think at all," said Dugman, "when the Chief of D. has got his nose up my crack. You got a problem with any of this, you need to talk to him."

"Yeah, I got a problem," said Karp bitterly. "The problem is, the guy who engineered this whole fucking scene is gonna walk away from it smelling like a rose."

"You mean Mr. Lemon Coffee?"

"That's him," said Karp. "And Fane. And Sergo. Although I have a feeling that Fane and

Sergo are going to be harder to connect with the actual murders. Reedy's the key player. He was there at the club. He must have tipped Manning about Clay being undercover as soon as he got it from . . . whoever he got it from. By the way, you did secure the plates and cups from the club?''

"Yeah, after we talked, I sent some people over to collect the whole tray. You think it'll be enough?''

"Not nearly.''

"So how you gonna bust him?''

"I don't know yet. I'll think of something.''

Dugman smiled crookedly. "Well. You might at that. If you do, and it's OK with the chief, let me know. I'd like to bust a rich white dude one time. Make a nice change.''

Two hours later, Karp, although he still hadn't thought of something, was feeling considerably better. He was stretched out naked, facedown, on a throw rug, while Marlene walked up and down his spine, wiggling her toes. Marlene was wearing a T-shirt with a picture of Albert Schweitzer on it, and nothing else.

"Mm, that's getting there,'' said Marlene as she trudged. "You felt like Grand Street asphalt when I started. How do you feel?''

"More,'' said Karp with a deep sigh.

Marlene knelt astride his back and began kneading his shoulder muscles. "God, you're tense!'' she exclaimed. "I'm surprised. You should be positively laid-back now that this drug-killing is solved."

"Not finished," mumbled Karp into the rug.

"It's not? You got Clay back, didn't you? By the way, I ran into Martha at the hospital. She was shaking with relief. I didn't think Clay looked all that bad, though. I mean, considering he's been tortured. So what's the problem, anyway? If you have Manning . . . you do have Manning, right?"

"Dead," said Karp.

"Oh, I see. That's the problem."

She massaged him in silence for a few more minutes, then said, "It's Reedy. You can't get Reedy."

"Mmm-hm," said Karp. He was trying not to think about Reedy, trying, in fact, not to think about anything but Marlene's hands on his back and the thin bar of intense heat that was pressing against the small of his back where her groin touched it. He was also thinking about spinning around and pulling her down on him for a sweaty clinch on the floor, balancing this possibility against the delights of the continuing back rub.

But Marlene abruptly stopped her rubbing, stood up, and sat on the bed. She pulled a Marlboro from a pack and lit it. Karp looked up at her. "Something wrong?" he asked.

"No, except I'm starting to get tense myself. The fucking job."

"Leave it at the office," said Karp.

"Oh, yeah, look who's talking! That's *my*

line. The problem is, I got one trial pending, which is Meissner, and about a hundred other cases, mostly rapes, which I should be preparing seriously, because with the new law we could win some of them, or at least muscle some good pleas, but I can't because as soon as Meissner is finished I have to leave.

"Also, there's only a couple of other people in the bureau who know how to handle the new law, who understand how to develop cases. It's a completely different situation. Ideally we should set up a structure, train new ADA's, run programs to get the cops up to speed, contact the E-wards and the crisis centers—to pull it all together. Like you always say, the D.A. is the captain of the team. But in this case, there's no captain, no team."

"What do you want me to do?" Karp asked. "I could talk to some of the zone commanders—"

"No!" said Marlene vehemently. "That's another thing that's wrong. Look, don't take this personally, because you've actually really been terrific all these years, and all, but . . ." She took a deep drag and let it out. "I can't work for you anymore. The rules are right. I thought it through after we nailed Meissner. There's enough tension in my life without adding the craziness of working for my husband."

She grinned at him. "Especially considering I'm a nervous wreck to begin with. Look at that fight we had about Meissner, all the nasty things I said about you and about the baby."

"You didn't mean all that?"

"Of course I didn't mean all that. Look, it's one thing to take me seriously; it's another thing to take me seriously when I don't want to be taken seriously. But that's an example, and it comes from working for you. It would just screw up my working life *and* my personal life, not to mention the Little Stranger to be. So that's it."

Karp felt a mix of satisfaction and disappointment; the disappointment was odd because he had wanted Marlene to quit, but he found that he did not like the thought of Marlene being whipped by anything. He said, "You could transfer to another bureau."

"Which one? Felony is Sullivan, one of Bloom's empty suits. Can you see me working for Charlie Sullivan? I'd last three days. Rackets? Fraud? Narco? Possible, but they don't sing to me. I want to do rape; rape needs doing, but I can't figure out how to make it happen." She laughed ruefully. "All those damn cases; it's a shame we can't work a Meissner on all of them. Your basic rapist doesn't take calls when he's on the job."

She put out her cigarette and crawled into bed and Karp followed her, and they had a close-knit and vaguely sad little bang, which blended imperceptibly into a deep and merciful unconsciousness.

From which Karp awoke with the solution to all his problems glowing in his mind with crystalline perfection. He had come floating up out of an unremembered dream and there it was—perfect, legal, nasty, and decisive—tying up a hairy mass of loose ends. Oddly, his mind buzzed with the notion of reversible error. A legal concept, one of the pillars of the system: judges made mistakes, which were reversed by other judges. In the trial of life, the judge that banged his gavel irritably and without recess in a corner of Karp's soul had found him guilty. He had misjudged Clay; he had misjudged Reedy. Your Honor, if it please the court, this particular set of errors is indeed reversible. Is it? You can remove the shame? The self-contempt? No, sir, but I can nail the bad guys. That was something.

And he could. All that was required was the cooperation of the guilty.

Karp's first call that morning, once he was settled (and his staff commenting on how uncommonly cheerful he was looking) was to Denton. Denton was in a meeting of chiefs and commissioners and could not be disturbed. Karp said to the secretary, "Would you take a note in to him? It's urgent. Say, 'Butch says that if you want him to stay on the reservation on the Pier 87 thing, I need ten minutes of his time right away.' "

The secretary was impressed and agreed to take the note in, promising to call back when she had an answer. Karp rang off and called the district attorney and made an appointment to see Bloom for five minutes one hour

from now. The police-department secretary
rang him back. "Denton says be here in fifteen minutes."

This was just enough time for Karp to walk
at a quick pace out of the Criminal Courts
Building, south on Baxter to One Police Plaza,
check through security, and ride the elevator
up to the fourteenth floor, where the departmen-
tal superchiefs had their offices. He announced
himself to the receptionist, and shortly thereafter Denton walked into the room, in shirt-
sleeves, looking irritated. He jerked his head at
Karp and led him into a small and unoccupied
private office.

"What is this, Butch? I'm up to my neck in
budget."

"Sorry," said Karp. "This won't take long. I
need your blessing, apparently, to go ahead
with the prosecution of the ringleaders on the
drug-lord killings."

"I thought we had an understanding on
that," said Denton, glowering.

"We did, but obviously the situation has
changed. Sweeping up some sick cop is one
thing; covering up a massive conspiracy to use
drug money to finance stock manipulation is
something else entirely."

"What are you talking about?"

"Manning and Amalfi were hired by Richard Reedy and Marcus Fane to wipe out the
competition in the Harlem drug trade, to pro-
duce the cash they and some other people
needed to get them out of a hole they were

in on some stock deal. They also arranged for the kidnapping and torture of Clay Fulton. Fulton has a tape that ties Manning to the killings and he has a taped confirmation from Amalfi of the connection between Marcus Fane and the killings Amalfi and Manning did. We also have circumstantial evidence linking the flow of money from an offshore bank to a series of stock deals on the one side, and to drug money on the other. Reedy set up the bank. He was there in the Club Mecca the night after Clay got lifted, probably talking to Willis and Manning."

Denton listened to this impassively. "And what do you want from me?"

"I think I've figured a way to tie Reedy to the dirty cops, but Manning and Amalfi's part in the killings can't be concealed."

"No way," said Denton. "They're dead. It's finished."

"It's *not* finished," said Karp. "A bunch of Wall Street and political scumbags have raped the NYPD. They've corrupted officers; they've killed with total impunity; they've kidnapped and tortured a police lieutenant—"

Denton was still shaking his head. "There's a cap on it now. If we go forward—"

"Bullshit, a cap!" cried Karp. "There's no way you can keep this quiet now. Too many people know about it, from Willis' people, to the cops who hauled the bodies away from the pier, to the docs taking care of Clay. You think they don't know what torture looks like? What's the cover story on that? Hey, Doc, I was on the job and I just happened to catch my prick and my nipples in an electrical outlet?

"Not to mention the bad guys, all of them in businesses where every secret has a price tag. And the press is already starting to nose around. You're figuring you can lay the drug-lord killings off on Willis, maybe Manning was working undercover too, got shot, poor bastard. Excuse me, but I still can't believe that you and Clay Fulton were going to stand up and salute at an inspector's funeral for Dick Manning.

"Bill, what can I say? If I really thought you were a run-for-cover type of person, I wouldn't even be here. I was willing to hang out there for you when this started, but . . ."

Karp took a long slow breath and let it out. "I'm telling you, the time for that is way past. Nobody will believe the story, and to be absolutely frank, you're too damn honest to be a credible liar under the kind of pressure you're gonna have to face. Your only choice is how you want the story to come out.

"And what's the story? The business we discussed a while ago, the crazy-cop angle—that's ancient history. It never happened. The truth that'll come out is that the NYPD had a worm and they assigned the best they had to go after it, and it worked. The bad guys are dead. And look who's really responsible for the mess—not cops: some greedy Wall Street and political sharks. When those names hit the papers, the cop connection will be four inches in the second section."

Denton looked straight at Karp for a long time, until Karp's eyes ached with the effort of keeping his gaze focused on the other man's steel-blue eyes. Then Denton turned away abruptly and moved several paces away, as if to physically distance himself from the decision he had now to make.

At last he said, "What you've got on Reedy seems pretty light. How do you plan to get him?"

Karp told him, and an almost-smile moved across Denton's thin mouth. "That's a long shot, isn't it?"

"It's worked before," said Karp. Relief began to spread through his body; Denton was going to buy it.

Denton said, "OK, go for it. If it works, we'll play it your way. If not . . ." He shrugged, shot Karp a dark look, and went out of the door.

Karp went back to his office at a trot, made a few calls, and then it was time for his meeting with Bloom. Karp had to push through a crowd of TV people, with their equipment, waiting for a statement from the D.A. on a particularly exciting East Side killing.

The district attorney was not glad to see him, nor was he happy at having his elaborate schedule interrupted.

When Karp came in, Bloom asked abruptly,

"Is it about this business on East 63rd? My sister lives in the next building. Everyone's terrified, she says. Can't I do something, she says. It's a good building, how can they get at you in a good building?"

"No, I'm sorry, it's not," said Karp. "This is about the wrap-up on the drug-lord killings."

"Wrap-up, huh?" said Bloom with distaste. "It certainly took us long enough to figure out that it was another dope dealer. What was his name—Williams?"

"Willis," said Karp. "But he wasn't doing the killings. The actual hit men were two police officers named Manning and Amalfi."

Bloom began to smile, and then saw that Karp was not making a joke. "Oh, my God!" he said. "Not the ones who were on my . . . ? Oh, that's all I need!"

"Didn't you know?" asked Karp. "I thought Roland told you the whole story."

"No, I didn't. He just told me this Fulton was really undercover and not the real killer. I had no idea . . ." He got up from behind his desk and paced briefly, running his fingers through his beautiful gray-blond hair. When he looked at Karp, it was clear that he had been thinking clever thoughts. "They've been arrested, have they?" Bloom asked.

"No, Amalfi's dead. Killed himself. Manning's at large, but he doesn't suspect that we know. We wanted him loose because we thought he might lead us to the people he was really working for."

A puzzled frown creased the TV makeup on the D.A.'s brow. "Working for? Surely it was Williams who hired them—"

"Willis. No, apparently the additional drug money produced by the scheme was being funneled into a laundry operation run by some Wall Street types. I'm getting a report on the whole thing together for you. It's fairly complex." The D.A. had no comment on this. He just looked blankly at Karp, working his clenched jaw.

As Karp got up to go, he added, "But I just stopped by on my way out—we're going to pick up Manning right now. I wanted you to be fully informed, because it's going to be a huge scandal."

Bloom fixed his usual hearty false smile on his face and thanked Karp for coming by. As Karp went out the door, he said, "Umm, I don't have to tell you the importance of keeping this whole thing entirely quiet until we get Manning and we have a statement from him."

"Oh, of course," said the district attorney. "Mum's the word."

"I'm glad you're here," said Art Dugman as he opened the door. "The phone already rang once."

"You didn't answer it, did you?" asked Karp.

"No, but the tape's set up on the extension in the bedroom. You can listen in there. He'll probably call again."

Karp strolled through Manning's apartment and looked around. "Pretty nice," he said. "You detective sergeants do OK."

"It's the fringe benefits," said Dugman. Then the phone rang. Karp hurried into the bedroom, sat on the bed, hit the record button on the tape machine plugged into the phone receiver, and nodded to Dugman, who could see him by way of the bedroom mirror, and who was poised at the phone in the living room. They lifted the two phones simultaneously.

"Manning?" said the voice on the phone.

"Uh-huh," said Dugman.

"Jesus, Dick! Do you know what's happening? They raided the pier. Willis is dead. I can't get hold of Marcus Fane—they say he's out of town. Christ, the whole thing is going up in smoke."

The voice was wavering just on the edge of control. Dugman said, "Calm down."

The voice snapped back, "I'll calm down when you're out of the country, goddammit! They're coming to arrest you right now, and your place is being watched. Now, look, there's a private jet fueled and ready to go at La Guardia, the general aviation terminal, gate four. They're expecting you. They'll fly you direct to Grand Cayman, and after that it's the way we planned it."

Dugman cleared his throat heavily and looked over at Karp, who nodded. "Sorry, I just woke up. Why do I have to leave the country?"

"Why? For shit's sake, Manning! They have the tapes. Booth and Amalfi, they both name you, and Amalfi fingered Marcus. Fulton's free, and that sheeny bastard has the whole damn story. But he can't do anything without—"

"Amalfi's dead," said Dugman.

"I know he's dead. For God's sake, Manning, what's wrong with you? They think it's suicide now, but God knows what they'll turn up if they really start to dig into it. And now that they know who they're looking for, they can build cases on the other jobs you did. Do you want to go to jail for the rest of your life? I can't protect you anymore, don't you understand that? Now, get out of there!"

The voice rose nearly to a scream. Then, when there was no response, the voice said tentatively, "Dick! Dick? Are you there?"

Karp said, "No, Mr. Reedy, Dick can't come to the phone."

"What! Who is this?"

"This is the sheeny bastard, Mr. Reedy," said Karp. "I guess you don't want me to be D.A. anymore."

"So," said Marlene after Karp had related the story of what had happened in Manning's apartment, "I guess he hung up pretty fast when you said that."

"Yes," said Karp, "he didn't stay to chat.

Odd, because previously he was always so sociable."

"And the bad guys are in irons?"

"Surprisingly, yes. Maus and Jeffers grabbed Reedy moving out at a dead run, with his passport, a second, phony, passport, five grand in traveler's checks, and twenty grand in Krugerrands in his briefcase. We made the point to the judge that Mr. Reedy was not a good risk to stay for trial."

They were in Marlene's little office. Karp's office had become the focus of enormous attention from the press as news of the scandal leaked out, and nearly uninhabitable. "Yes," Karp continued, "I said that if Mr. Reedy was not sent to Rikers Island he would turn up in some other island beyond the reach of justice. I thought that was pretty good, myself."

"And so it was, my jewel," said Marlene, "and it deserves a long, soul-shattering kiss."

Somewhat later Marlene said, "Do you think you really have him?"

"Reedy? Yeah, I think we can make at least the accessory charge stick. That's quite apart from the fraud stuff V.T. is working on, not to mention the feds taking a couple of whacks at him. And obstruction of justice, of course. He certainly demonstrated guilty knowledge of the crimes on the phone. I owe you one for that, incidentally."

"Be still, my heart," said Marlene. "What, you mean the way we did Meissner? But that was your idea, originally."

"Yeah, but you brought it up last night. You mentioned something about using the scam in the other rape cases, and it must have stuck in my mind. It bubbled up out of my subconscious and it was all laid out when I got up this morning. Magic."

"Not to mention that, until you met me, you didn't know you *had* a subconscious. Or a conscious. But to continue—what about the murder charges?"

"Well, we'll go for them, sure. But I don't know . . . convincing a jury that a distinguished Wall Street lawyer hired two cops to murder dope pushers? Hard to believe. Hard for *me* to believe. And we don't have any direct witnesses."

"Except Fane," said Marlene.

"Except Fane. Of course, if we could get one of them to rat the other one out, that's a different story. It's the prisoner's dilemma: if one rats and the other holds his mud, the rat walks and the stand-up guy goes over for a long one. If they both rat, both have to do time. If neither rats, they still do time, but less of it. Both our guys are pretty hard-boiled, they've got good counsel, and they won't go for the usual tricks.

"But we've got the better case on Reedy," Karp added after a pause, "and he's definitely looking at serious upstate time. I'm betting he won't be able to sit in jail and watch Fane walking around free. But we shall see."

"So we shall," said Marlene. "And by the

way, how did our fearless leader receive the news?"

"Like the great American he is," said Karp. "I told him we had Reedy and what had gone down. And then there was a pregnant pause and I said, 'I guess we know how he knew that we were on the way to arrest Manning.' And he didn't say anything, just had on that shit-eating smile. And he was sweating."

"My God!" said Marlene. "Do you think he was *in* on it—like Fane and Reedy?"

"No, he's not that kind of crook, to give him credit. He's just a schmuck. He just likes giving tidbits of information to influential people. Reedy probably prompted him by saying he was *very* interested in the case and wanted to follow it as closely as possible.

"Anyway, then I said it would have to come out in trial, that we hoped that Reedy would call his accomplice, not knowing Manning had been killed, and people would want to know who tipped him off. Not to mention how Reedy learned that Clay was undercover."

"Did he wet his pants?" Marlene asked.

"I couldn't tell. He was sitting down," said Karp. "So then I said something like, 'I guess we could establish that you were part of the plan from the very beginning and that the reason you were feeding Reedy information all through this case was so that he wouldn't get suspicious that we were on to him. Fulton being nabbed was a simple unpredictable glitch.' And so on."

"He must have liked that," said Marlene.

"He was fumbling at my fly," said Karp. "In fact, his gratitude was so embarrassing that I felt it necessary to change the subject."

"Oh? What to?"

"Well, I mentioned that I had a bright and experienced attorney whose services we were about to lose because of the nepotism rules. Which I heartily supported, of course."

"Of course," Marlene agreed.

"And also that because of the change in the rape law we had a good opportunity to increase our success rate in these cases, provided we had someone in charge who was experienced in same, and that, given all this feminist agitation, har-har, it might be seen as a shrewd political move to, ah, set up a rape bureau, with the right person in charge, of course."

"Of course," said Marlene. "And did he solicit any recommendations for such a post?"

"Indeed, he did," said Karp. "And I took the liberty of putting your name forward. Which was accepted, on the spot. How do you like that? The last little spurt of nepotism."

"Yippeee!" Marlene shouted, jumping to her feet. "Let's hear it for corruption! Karp, you are quite a piece of work!" She kissed him soundly and looked at him, beaming the celestial smile that she was capable of when—and these occasions had been few in recent months—she was completely at peace.

Karp grinned back at her and said, "I guess you still want to marry me, then."

"Yes, naturally, we've already ordered the cake."

"Yeah—God!—it's only ten days away."

"Actually, it's nine," said Marlene, frowning. "You should write it in your little book. Which reminds me—all is prepared except for two small details."

"Which are?"

In answer she waggled her left hand in front of his face.

"Oh, shit!" said Karp.

"Yes, a ring is traditional," said Marlene. "Fortunately, to save you a trip to the K-Mart, I should tell you that your Aunt Sophie has volunteered one. It belonged to your mom."

With feeling Karp said, "Good old Aunt Sophie! How do you feel about that?"

"I'm honored, actually," said Marlene. "Although it's gonna blow them away at St. Joseph's. As you may recall, it weighs about four pounds and has little Jewish stars and Hebrew letters all around it."

"Yes, they spell out, 'Guaranteed: not a shiksa,'" said Karp. "What was the other thing?"

"Guma. He's coming, of course. But somehow, in his usual expansive way, he invited Sylvia Kamas to be his date. I thought you should know beforehand."

"I see," said Karp, starting to giggle. "He's going to pretend to be John Ciampi in the middle of a hive of Ciampis, including the real John Ciampi. How are you going to handle that?''

"Don't worry, my prince," said Marlene. "I'll think of something.''

We invite you to preview the forthcoming Butch Karp novel, *Material Witness*, available now from Dutton.

The dying man in the white Cadillac moaned and said a name that the driver didn't catch. He was not in any case interested, although he was mildly surprised that the man was still alive. The driver peered through the swishing wipers, looking for a good place, trying to control his irritability. He thought he was too old to be driving around with corpses; it was something he had done a good deal of in his youth, and he believed that he had more or less put away childish things.

The driver had planned at first to dump the car and the body in a parking lot at Kennedy, or alternatively, to drive down some mean street in south Jamaica and leave it. The problem was that the guy wouldn't die, and the driver had a long-standing objection to shooting people where there was even the slightest chance of a witness. In this way he had survived nearly all of his contemporaries. He was fifty-four, in good shape, and at the top of his profession.

When he saw the small, darkened shopping center looming through the light rain, he made a quick decision, pulling off Jamaica Avenue into the parking lot, signaling carefully as he did so. A second car, an anonymous blue Chevrolet sedan, entered the lot behind him. The Cadillac led the Chevrolet around to the back of the long commercial building. Both cars shut off their engines and their lights.

The driver of the Cadillac switched off the dome light and left the vehicle. He was a medium-sized, stocky man of vaguely Mediterranean appearance, a look accentuated by his deep tan. His most remarkable feature was his mouth, which was large, floppy and bent down, like that of a flounder. In this mouth was clenched the stump of a thick cigar. He wore horn-rimmed glasses and his pepper-and-salt hair was conventionally cut. Against the chill rain he had put on an unfashionable little waterproof tan cap, and as he stood waiting for the other driver to emerge, he hugged a tan raincoat around his body. It was not really adequate for the weather, but he owned no winter clothes anymore. Although he had been raised in New York, all his business interests were now in warm climates, and he intended to keep it that way. He wore old, thin pigskin gloves, as he always did when working, even in a warm climate.

The other man was younger—in his mid-twenties—and shorter, despite the lifts in his small, pointed tan loafers. He wore black gloves and was dressed more suitably than his partner in a thigh-length leather coat. Despite the November cold, however, he had the top two buttons of his coat open, revealing a sprout of dense hair at the V of his patterned silk shirt, amid which nestled a set of heavy gold links. Visible among these were a cross, a St. Christopher medal and a charm in the shape of a hand making a rude gesture with the middle finger, all in gold.

Above this mass of metal was a jowly dark face that bore a thin, down-hooking nose and a sensual, petulant mouth. The eyebrows were heavy and touching each other, and the eyes were small and too close together. It was a face made to sneer.

The younger man approached the Cadillac. "So, Carmine—what're we doin'? Where the fuck is this place?"

The older man said, "He gets off here." He pointed over at the end of the lot, where a big semi-tractor, a red Toyota and an old panel truck were parked, and added, "Go over and make sure nobody's in those."

"What the fuck, Carmine! They're empty. It's fuckin' one in the morning. You think they're making deliveries?"

The older man suppressed a sigh. "Just do it, Joey, huh? Just once, *do* something I ask you to do, without a song and dance, OK?"

Joey muttered something and stalked off across the gleaming asphalt. He glanced cursorily through the front windows of all three vehicles— he had to climb the step on the semi to do so— and then trudged back to the car.

"Like I said, nothin'."

Carmine nodded. "You thought, but now you know." He gave a last look around the full circle of his vision. It was a good spot picked at random. The back of the shopping center gave onto a straggling high hedge shielding a cyclone fence, beyond which was the blank rear concrete block wall of a tire store. There was no view of the streets on either side.

"OK, let's move him to the driver's side," said Carmine.

Joey was about to complain about this too, but stifled his remark. Guy wanted to be an old lady, let him. The two of them dragged the dying man out of the passenger seat and wrestled him behind the wheel.

Joey was panting from the exertion. "Now can I do him, Carmine?" he asked irritably.

"Yeah, go ahead—no, from the passenger side, not through the window."

Joey grunted, pulled a large automatic pistol out of his waistband and stomped around the front of the Cadillac. He leaned in through the open door and fired two shots into the temple of the man in the driver's seat. The sound echoed off the concrete walls, and the interior of the car lit up like a little stage. Joey put the gun away and slammed the car door.

"I do that right, Carmine? You got any comments on that?"

Carmine looked at his cigar, which had gone out in the light, misty rain, and without further comment entered the Chevrolet. Joey got in and they drove back to Jamaica Avenue and several streets east on it in silence. Then Carmine pulled the car over under a street lamp.

"What now?" asked Joey.

"Map. I want to see what's the quickest way to La Guardia."

He studied the map for a moment, then folded it neatly and put it away in the glove. But as he made his instinctive glance at the rearview mirror, he checked and cursed.

"What?" said Joey.

"Look out the back, Joey. What do you see?"

Joey looked, and saw a semi-tractor pulling out of the parking lot they had just left. "What the fuck! Carmine, I swear to God I looked in the fuckin' truck—it was empty."

"It wasn't empty enough. They got a place behind the cab where the guy sleeps. Did you check that? No, what am I, crazy? Why am I asking?" He gunned the car into a wide U-turn and shot off west in pursuit of the tractor.

"Maybe . . . shit, maybe he didn't see nothin'," said Joey.

Carmine did not consider this comment worthy of reply.

Patrolman William Winofski, of the 105th precinct, cruising his radio motor patrol car down Braddock Road in Queens Village in the calm center of the graveyard shift, was entirely justified in expecting that nothing would trouble his working life. Cops love Queens. The City's largest borough sprawls toward the rising sun from the broken and troubled lands of Brooklyn, a boundless inhabited steppe, until it merges with the uttermost and mysterious East, Long Island. Cops love Queens because it is calm: in its vastness occur each month fewer crimes of violence than take place in a single Harlem or Bedford-Stuyvesant precinct. Cops love Queens so much that they park their families there; more NYPD officers live in Queens than in any other borough. Easy living and easy policing—on the leafy streets of Queens the only gunshot to be heard from one year to the next is from a cop committing discrete suicide in his finished basement. It was, additionally, a Tuesday night, just after Thanksgiving, chilly and raining: good cop weather. Even over south in the 103rd, in Jamaica, Queens' own excuse for a high-crime area, things would be quiet.

That was fine with Winofski. He realized how good he had it compared to others on the job.

The 105th was one of the City's quietest, a long, narrow strip making up most of the border with Nassau County, so far east that nomadic Mongols could often be glimpsed on the horizon. His major worry in life came not from the guns of malefactors but from the current plight of the City itself. It was 197—, and the town was broke. Winofski had only three years in; he would be one of the first to go if the promised cutbacks actually hit the NYPD. He had already glanced at a post office recruiting bulletin. The benefits were better, and carrying mail would be exciting compared to patrolling the 105th in the wee hours.

Winofski looked at his watch: nearly 4:00 and halfway through his shift. He would cruise through the little shopping mall at Jamaica Avenue near Springfield Boulevard, check the back to insure that nobody was doing any unauthorized Christmas shopping, and then run west on Jamaica to one of the few all-night restaurants supported by the quiet, early-to-bed neighborhoods of the 105th precinct.

The parking lot of the mall was black and shiny and empty of cars. He swung the RMP around the stores to the service area and drove slowly down the narrow alley. As expected, the corrugated iron delivery doors were shut and intact, and the back doors to the buildings were at least closed. Everything was as it should be, except for the white Cadillac Coupe de Ville parked in the middle of the service alley. The car registered but dimly on Winofski's mind. He was not anxious to get out in the rain to check it.

But when he came around the other side of the mall, instead of pulling out onto the avenue, he swung around for another pass, one that brought him closer to the white Caddy. The car was new and clean, glistening in the rain, its windows giving back the gleam of the alley's fire lights. As he passed it, he slowed. Winofski was raw and lazy, but he was still enough of a cop to sense in the fact of a luxury car parked in the back of a deserted parking lot, glowing like a beached whale, that air of indefinable wrongness that the police learn to associate with crime.

He backed up and studied the car for a minute. The interior was invisible because of the reflections. He took down the license and called it in for a stolen-car check. The car looked intact and undamaged—still, joy-riding teens were the likely cause, at least in this precinct.

The check came back negative. The car was registered to a M. C. Simmons, at a Forest Hills address. Winofski figured some housewife had lost her keys just before the mall closed and hadn't wanted to pay a locksmith overtime. Her car would keep until tomorrow, and if anything went wrong, she had zero deductible.

The rain was heavier now and very cold. Winofski cursed softly and pulled the collar of his black slicker up as he scuttled over to the driver's side of the Cadillac. He snapped on his six-cell flashlight.

The left rear window was punctured and crazed and stained red. There was a human face pressed against the glass of the driver's window. The face was dark, sucking up the beam of the flash, but the single eye that was showing bulged hideously and gleamed like a cue ball in a spotlight. Winofski's heart jumped; he touched his gun and looked inanely about, although there was no one awake within a half mile of him. He then peered more closely at the window, moving the flash around to illuminate different planes of the man's face. Winofski's experience with violence was limited, but he knew what a bullet hole looked like and that a man who had two of them in his head was likely to be a victim of homicide.

Winfoski was not a particularly ambitious policeman, nor did he consider himself clever. As a result, he did not touch the car, or drag the body out, to see if it was really dead, or go through its pockets, or investigate the glove compartment or the trunk. He did, in fact, none of the things that patrolmen occasionally do when they find dead bodies in cars, but instead—now in a mild daze—fell back upon his excellent police academy training and did it by the book. He (1) secured the crime scene. No problem there. And (2) he called it in. And (3) he waited for the arrival of a sergeant and a homicide detective.

The sergeant was there in eight minutes. The ambulance from the New York Medical Examiner and the man from Queens Homicide both arrived about five minutes later. The sergeant was grumpy and appeared to blame Winofski for getting him out on a night like this. The man from the ME was quick, casual, and exhibited the cheerful and vocal cynicism of his kind. The homicide detective was old, tired and quiet, dressed in a gray plastic raincoat buttoned up to the neck and a shabby tan canvas rain hat. His name was Harry Bello. Winofski thought he was the oldest serving officer he had ever seen; he looked like Winofski's grandfather, who was seventy-five. In fact, Bello was fifty-six, but with a lot of hard miles.

Unlike Winofski, of course, Harry Bello had

seen a lot of bodies, most of them killed violently. He looked at the dead face pressed against the window, then at Winofski, with eyes that seemed to the young patrolman to be only slightly more lively than those of the victim.

"You touch anything?" he asked.

Winofski said he hadn't. The sergeant agreed. Then Bello asked what time he had found the car.

"A little before four," answered Winofski. Bello grunted and turned away. The van for the Crime Scene Unit arrived, and the crime-scene detectives rolled out and began taking photos, stringing yellow plastic tape and looking for clues. One of them was singing "It's Beginning to Look a Lot Like Christmas."

After checking with the CSUs, the M.E. opened the door of the car, and the man's head and upper body slumped out of the car. The two holes in the man's left temple showed matt black against the shiny brown of the skin, and the exit wound showed the usual souffle of hair, bone, blood and brain tissue bulging out of the skull like a mushroom. With the head down, this began to ooze and elongate in a manner that brought sour gases into Winofski's young throat.

The M.E. said, "I'm gonna take a chance and pronounce this guy dead at the scene." Then he and his assistant rolled up a gurney with a body bag lying open on it, and began to heave the corpse out of the car. It took a while.

When the body was lying flat on the gurney, Bello stepped forward slowly and looked at it. The man was dressed in a loose suede car coat over a turtleneck jersey that had once been bright yellow, but which was now thick with dark blood. He had dark slacks on and suede loafers. The belt of the car coat hung down almost to the ground. Bello picked it up and tossed it onto the body. It had a dark, oily stain at its end. Bello reached into the corpse's back pocket and drew out a wallet.

"Jesus, he's a big motherfucker," said the M.E.'s assistant. The man was so tall that the body bag would not zip up all the way.

"You think he's with the pros?" the M.E. asked. The others all looked thoughtful. The equation was simple: black man, height of a giant, expensive car.

There was no money in the wallet. It contained, however, several credit cards and a driver's license in the name of Marion Simmons.

"It's Marion Simmons," said Bello in a flat voice.

"No shit!" said the M.E.

"Ay-ay-ay!" said the ambulance assistant.

"Marion Simmons?" said one crime-lab guy, a Lebanese who didn't follow pro basketball.

Winofski, who did, simply gaped at the enormity of it all, and mentally kicked himself for not having recognized the name when he made the stolen-car check.

The other crime-lab guy didn't respond at all, since he was buried in the well of the backseat, where he had just found another ejected case of a 9mm pistol cartridge. There was one on the front seat too. He placed it in a plastic bag and crawled backward out of the car.

When he stood up, the M.E. called out, "Hey, Ernie! You know who this is? It's Marion Simmons."

Ernie said, "Who, the stiff? Jesus!"

All the men paused for a moment in silence, watching the rain bead up on the body bag. With the exception of the Lebanese immigrant crime-scene tech, each had seen Simmons alive, and not just alive, but radiating the fierce energy of the professional athlete in the first flush of youthful prowess. That he was now mere meat shocked even these professionally unshockable men.

Then Bello coughed heavily and asked Ernie for a plastic bag to put the wallet in, and Ernie showed Bello the 9mm cases, and the Lebanese began to dust the interior of the car for prints, and Winofski remembered that he was supposed to call for a tow from the police pound for the Cadillac and walked back to his RMP, and the M.E. said, "Shit, I'm freezing out here. Let's get this thing on ice, Julio."

Bello went back and sat in his car with the door open and lit another cigarette from the butt of the one in his mouth. He was trying for cancer, but no luck yet. He thought about taking a hit from the flat pint of CC he kept in the plastic briefcase lying on the seat. But no, he hadn't actually ever drunk at a crime scene yet: before, yes; after, God, yes; but not actually at. That was one rule. Another was, he was not going to bite his gun. He was not going to end up in a body bag with the M.E. cracking jokes by way of a send-off.

Stupid, but there it was. The rules and habits formed over twenty-five years on the Job were rooted deeper than even his despair.

"Hey, Harry, check this out."

It was the crime-scene tech, Ernie, and he was holding up a large plastic bag containing another plastic bag full of white powder.

"It was in the glove," said Ernie. "Must be eight hundred grams."

"Toot?"

"You betcha. Good shit too. Commercial grade. My tongue is still numb. Now we know how he could jump like that. Coupla hits of this and *I* could get fuckin' rebounds off of Kareem. Jesus, what a thing, though! Kid was averaging, what? twenty-five, twenty-seven points a game the last six games, getting triple doubles too. The Hustlers are fucked." Bello was unresponsive; Ernie paused and said, "You a fan?"

Bello shook his head. In fact, he watched a good deal of basketball. It was basketball season, the City was a basketball town, and Bello spent most of his off-duty hours staring at whatever the TV threw up at him, and drinking, until either the station signed off or he did. Necessarily, some of what he watched was New York Hustlers games, so he had seen the thing on the gurney leaping through the air and doing the other skillful contortions characteristic of NBA stars. But he had not envied Simmons his skill as he now envied the athlete's current state.

Ernie saw that he was not going to generate a conversation about the Hustlers' prospects without their star power forward and drifted back to his van. Bello stared out the window for a few minutes. There were half a dozen things he should be doing now; minutely inspecting the car, getting the feel of the scene, making sure the crime-scene guys hadn't missed anything, scanning the neighborhood, insuring the integrity of the chain of evidence. He should have found the shells and the dope. He should be on the horn now, trying to establish what Simmons had been doing during the last evening of his life.

Homicide—at least the kind that cops called a mystery, like this one here—was like an hour-glass: the sand started running at the victim's last heartbeat, and after that you had twenty-four hours to figure out whodunit. After that the odds that you would ever find the killer went down precipitously. Bello wasn't jumping on this case because his jumping days were over and because he was fairly sure that it was not going to be his case. Not once the brass found out who the victim was.

He looked up. Winofski was standing there, dripping and looking ill at ease. He said, "Um, they said to hold everything just like it is." Winofski had never been the first officer on a homicide before, and since he had learned about Simmons he had been filled with both apprehension and excitement. People would be buying him beers for the rest of his life on this one. He was worried about Bello, though. The homicide DT was supposed to own the crime scene after the first officer, but this guy didn't look like he owned his raincoat.

"Do you need, like, any help?" Winofski offered.

Bello looked at him. His eyes were like lumps of burnt coal. He shook his head.

Sirens sounded in the distance. Winofski looked startled and became even more nervous when, after a few minutes, they could see flashing red and blue lights as what appeared to be a motorcade swung into the alley. Shortly thereafter, there were three more cars parked at different angles around the crime scene with a large white van from one of the TV stations disgorging cameras and mike booms and a blow-dried reporter.

The suits were out in some force, looking remarkably spiffy for men who had been dragged from bed in the deep of the night to observe the

loading of a body bag into a M.E. bus. There were
five of them: a preppy blonde from the Deputy
Police Commissioner for Public Affairs; the Chief
of Patrol, Queens, in full uniform; the Chief Inspector in charge of Queens Homicide; a man
from the Queens D.A. named Thelmann, and Detective Lieutenant Brian McKelway, who was
Harry Bello's watch commander.

These, with their associated drivers and the TV
crew, made a considerable crowd as they wan-
dered around shaking hands with one another
and observing the scene, so that the citizens of
the City might know, when they saw this scene
for eight seconds on the news, that justice was
being served, and that the murder of one of the
most famous people in the City was not being
casually ignored.

They were also there to begin an operation
known to members of the NYPD as a slick. In the
Vietnam War, a slick was a medical evacuation by
helicopter—a rescue. In the NYPD the term had
come to mean a gathering of suits at the scene of
a politically important crime in order to pre-estab-
lish credit and protect against blame. If the murder of Marion Simmons resulted in an arrest and
conviction, they would share in the credit. Were
they not there at the very beginning, expressing
confidence and professionalism before the cold
white glare? Exerting leadership right on TV? If
the result was failure, surely it was the fault of
incompetence in the lower ranks, and one of the
main functions of a slick was to choose a fall guy.

As the brass milled around, getting wet and
waiting for the TV to set up, Lieutenant McKelway wisely headed straight for Harry Bello, as
being the only person likely to know anything.

Bello had been only six months on McKelway's watch, and the lieutenant was not pleased that this particular case had fallen, in the luck of the draw, to the man he considered least likely to succeed in solving it.

He led Bello by an arm away from the crowd and the lights.

"What you got, Harry?"

Bello looked at his lieutenant blankly. McKelway was a medium-sized, scowling man with short red hair and freckles. Bello didn't know whether he was impatient and irritable with everyone or just with him, nor did he much care.

"I got a dead basketball player," he responded in a dull voice. "Took two in the head at close range. A nine. We got the casings. And the car's full of dope."

"Dope! Oh, Christ!" said McKelway. He glanced nervously over to where the suits were conversing. McKelway was a hard-charger, twenty-three years younger than Bello, bound and determined to make captain by fifty, and pinched by the fate that had placed him in one of the relatively unmurderous precincts of Queens. This Simmons thing was a case that could get him to Manhattan, where juicy cases dropped from the trees every day, or to Brooklyn. Brooklyn was where Bello had made his own spectacular reputation.

He turned back to the older man, and wondered yet again whether this feeble boozer was really the legendary Bello of Bed-Stuy. McKelway realized that they had parked Bello with him as at a rest home, but he had also thought that the magic of the name might have added some luster to his group. But in this he had been disappointed. Bello did not tell cop stories; he was not free with tricks of the trade; he did not respond to the good-natured jibes that passed for social interaction in the squad room. He was quiet and punctual, but passive as a rib roast and about as useful in a homicide investigation.

Nevertheless, he was the responding officer of record on this mess, and would have to be handled, forthwith.

"Ah, Harry—this case—you're gonna need some help with it, right?"

Bello looked at him noncommittally. He might have been watching a late movie.

"So I thought I'd call in Fence and Morgan to, ah, do the field work and just support the case. We'll get together tomorrow when we're all fresh and decide how to play it, OK?"

Bello nodded.

"OK, good. Now on this mess here—me and the chief inspector'll handle the questions. You just stand by in case we need you. And for chrissake, don't say anything to anybody, especially about the dope."

McKelway walked back to his lords and masters. Bello stood at the edge of the crowd, the rain dripping down his hat, trying to fix in his mind why he didn't just hand in his shield. He remembered. It was to avoid having to spend seven, rather than just two, days a week sitting in front of the TV getting drunk. On nice days he sat in Doris's garden, out back, watching the weeds take over. He wasn't sure he could take it full-time, not with a gun in the house.

Two more TV vans had arrived, and another couple of cars containing police officers. Bello saw Darryl Fence and his partner, Chick Morgan, get out of their unmarked and confer briefly with

McKelway. Fence and Morgan were hot this year. Bello didn't blame McKelway for steering Simmons to them. He had been a hot detective too, once, him and Sturdivant. He shook his head violently. A silly thing, but he always did it when the image from the hallway on Lewis Avenue came into his mind.

It was down to a couple of times a week now. It would pop into his head, a scene lasting little over a minute that turned his whole life into shit. The booze helped. Maybe it would kill enough brain cells after a while, maybe the very cells that stored the memory: he didn't know, but he was willing to try.

A sudden actinic glare told that the suits were on TV. They spoke into the mike booms, poking at their faces like the greedy mouths of nestling birds. Nobody asked Bello's opinion. He spoke briefly with the crime-scene people, collected his evidence, got back into his car and drove away.

The next day was a regular day off. He stayed drunk most of the morning. In the late afternoon he made himself a ham sandwich and staggered out into the backyard. Wet leaves from the big sycamore lay in dark piles on what used to be flower beds. In the yard next to his, he could see through the low chain-link fence that his neighbor was out wrapping his fig trees in burlap. All over the City, men of Italian extraction were doing, or had done, this homely task so that they could cheat nature and grow figs in a climate hostile to their cultivation. Bello had a fig tree too, but it wasn't wrapped.

His neighbor waved to him, and Bello waved weakly back and then got up and went into the house. The neighbor was the kind of man who like to chat across the fence, and today he didn't want to talk to the guy. The neighbor was a retired cop, shot in the line of duty. He had his three-quarter pension, a wife, a large and noisy family, his fucking fig trees, and . . . What else?

His . . . Bello's mind couldn't formalize the concept of honor, but the loss of it had strangled his heart. He could think only that his neighbor hadn't let a partner of twenty years get killed in a stinking hallway in Bed-Stuy. Bello sat in front of the TV and watched nothing in particular until he fell asleep.

His next shift was a swing, and he arrived promptly at four at the homicide squad room in the 105th, a building on Hillside Avenue, not far from the Queens County courthouse. There was a note on his desk that McKelway wanted to see him. He knew what it was about. He took out his notebook and sat down at the old Royal and carefully typed out his notes from the Simmons killing. He put them, together with the DD5 situation report, in a case jacket. Bello was a rapid and accurate typist. He could even type drunk. He had typed up all the reports when he and Jimmy Sturdivant . . . he shook his head from side to side like a housewife trying to shake a spider from a rag mop. Then he picked up the large manila envelope that held the evidence bags from the cirme scene and went to see McKelway.

He knocked on the door and went in and mutely placed the stuff on the lieutenant's desk. He said, "This is all of it. I don't have the autopsy yet."

McKelway looked surprised. "What's all this?" he asked.

"The stuff on Simmons. I figured you wanted it for Fence and Morgan."

McKelway leaned back in his swivel chair and gave Bello a look that even in his fogged state struck him as very peculiar—appraising, contemptuous, but with a tinge of something close to fear.

"No, Harry," said McKelway slowly. "What I wanted to say was that it's your case. All yours."

Make Room For Great Escapes At Hilton International Hotels

Save the coupons in the backs of these ⚊ Signet and ⚊ Onyx books and redeem them for special Hilton International Hotels discounts and services.

June
REVERSIBLE ERROR
Robert K. Tanenbaum

RELATIVE SINS
Cynthia Victor

August
MARILYN: *The Last Take*
Peter Harry Brown &
Patte B. Barham

JUST KILLING TIME
Derek Van Arman

July
GRACE POINT
Anne D. LeClaire

FOREVER
Judith Gould

September
DANGEROUS PRACTICES
Francis Roe

SILENT WITNESS:
*The Karla Brown
Murder Case*
Don W. Weber &
Charles Bosworth, Jr.

2 coupons: Save 25% off regular rates at Hilton International Hotels
4 coupons: Save 25% off regular rates, <u>plus</u> upgrade to Executive Floor
6 coupons: All the above, <u>plus</u> complimentary Fruit Basket
8 coupons: All the above, <u>plus</u> a free bottle of wine

(Check *People* Magazine and Signet and Onyx spring titles for Bonus coupons to be used when redeeming three or more coupons)

Disclaimers: Advance reservations and notification of the offer required. May not be used in conjunction with any other offer. Discount applies to regular rates only. Subject to availability and black out dates. Offer may not be used in conjunction with convention, group or any other special offer. Employees and family members of Penguin USA and Hilton International are not eligible to participate in GREAT ESCAPES.
